1

OF THE "PHOENIX CHILD" SERIES

PHOENIX CHILD

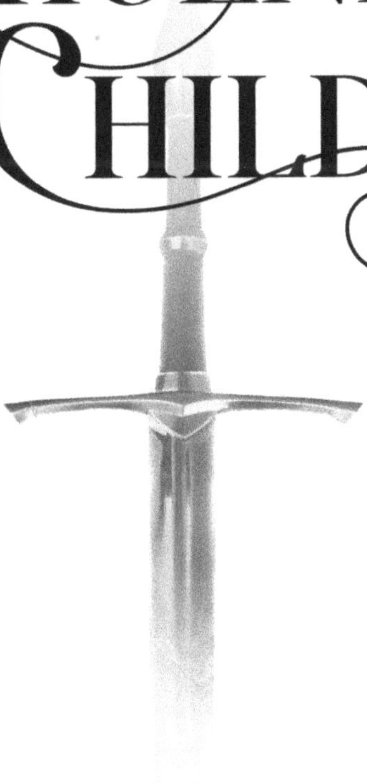

S.P. STAVROS

Copyright © 2024 by S.P. Stavros

All rights reserved.

No part of this publication may be reproduced, distributed, or transmitted in any form or by any means, including photocopying, recording, or other electronic or mechanical methods, without the prior written permission of the publisher, except as permitted by Canada copyright law. For permission requests, contact spstavrosauthor@gmail.com.

The story, all names, characters, and incidents portrayed in this production are fictitious. No identification with actual persons (living or deceased), places, buildings, and products is intended or should be inferred.

Book Cover by Miblart

Edited by Emily Michel

For my Family The author expresses gratitude towards individuals who have helped in her writing journey.

She thanks Shelley for being a great role model, Nick for being an inspiring alpha reader, critique partners for providing feedback, social media author family for their support, and A.K. Wilson for hosting a Twitter space that gave the author confidence.
The author also thanks her sister for the idea to kill off a character in their book.

Warning:

WARNING:

This content contains sensitive material that may trigger emotional distress or discomfort. Reader discretion is advised. The author and publisher are not liable for any adverse reactions or consequences resulting form exposure to these topics.

The topics described as followed:

Implications of rape, Implications of murder, Implications of sexual assault, Implications of human trafficking, Loss of a loved one , Violence, Foul language, Kidnapping, Mental Illness, Emotional Abuse, Physical Abuse

For Pronunciation

Names:
Calida (Cah- Lee- Dah)
Evaine (Ee-Vi-Nuh)

Old Norse Words:
(translation may vary)
Skreyja – incompetent
Daufi – deaf-mute/stupid
Bacraut – asshole
Skitr- shit
Burlufotr-clumsy footed
Beiskaldi-gripe/bitch
Oflati-gaudy person
Alicarl-obese person

Medieval Words:
Bedswerver-someone unfaithful
Dorbel- a petty, nitpicking teacher/nincompoop
Leasing-monger- a liar

Zoilist- a belittling, critical person
Raggabrash-unorganized, messy person

FRUINIA
SYNIEL
FLUCCATIA
BAEKKIORON
AQURI
QUEEN'S PALACE
ELEARI
PORAMUN CREEK
WEOMMADRAN

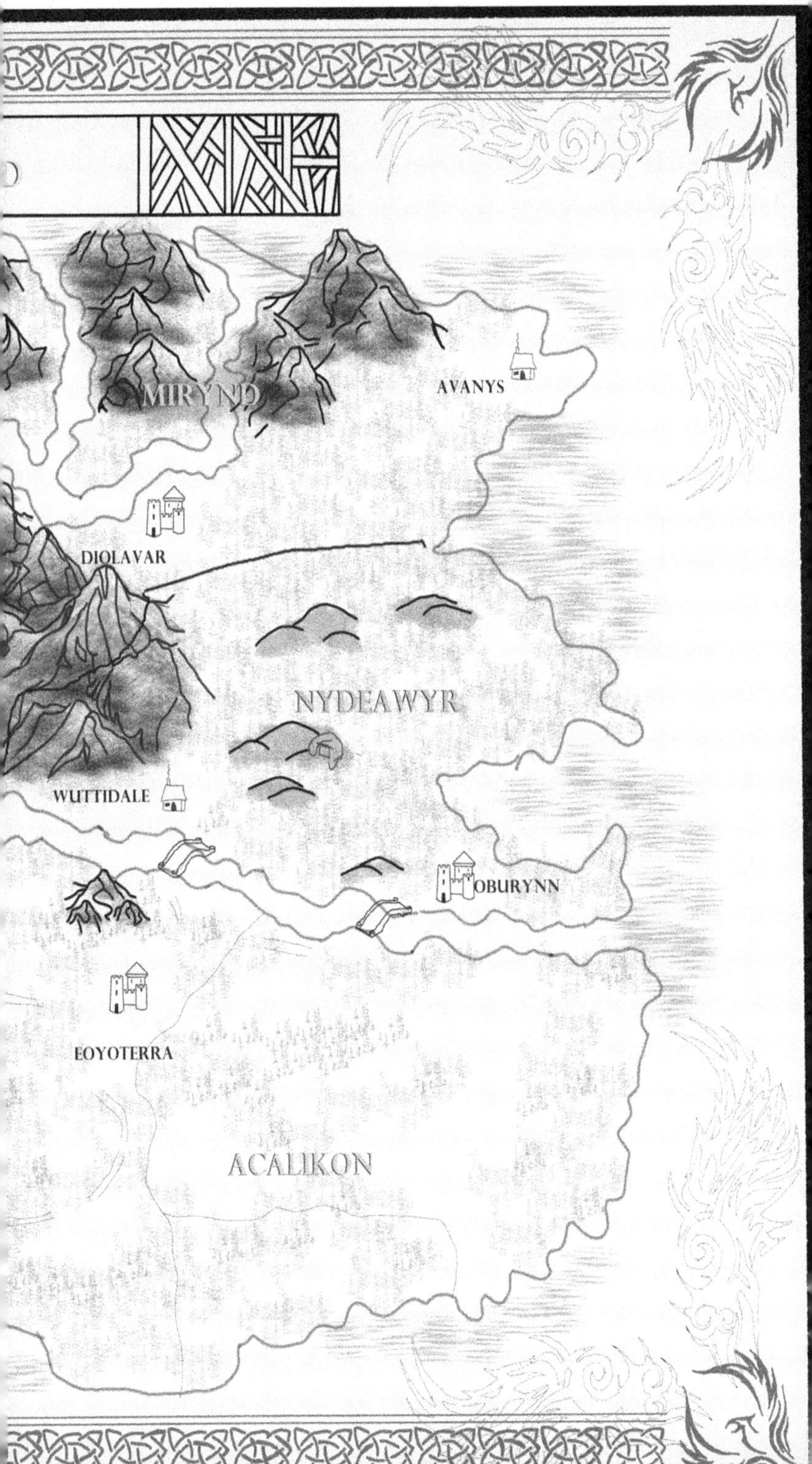

MIRYND
AVANYS
DIOLAVAR
NYDEAWYR
WUTTIDALE
OBURYNN
EOYOTERRA
ACALIKON

Prologue

All the events flooded her head like crashing waves drummed up in a freak storm. Images of her mother's icy glare pierced her. The absence of her and her father from the home. The late hour they had returned. Their lateness allowing the intruder enough time to strike.

Flashes of dirty grey and pink material and blood-soaked sheets. Her mother's broken body and Rayner weeping. The destruction on the other side of her bedroom door. Destruction similar to the creatures she heard in the stories from the older people in town. Like a beast from the old legends told to frighten children into good behaviour had torn through the roost. Huge, horrendous monsters that indulged on the innocent and weak, merciless and evil by reputation with good reason. They were the embodiment of all things awful in her land. The reminder of those creatures spread heat into her scalp. Feeling hot enough to melt, the flames moved her hair without her knowledge and pulled the energy out of her body.

Cressida's gaze had changed to a glare.

"This is all on you. You are to blame." A harsh whisper escaped her throat.

Then with a grimace, she turned away from her daughter, effectively shutting Calida out.

What would happen to her now? Would Momma live? All the blood... So much blood...

Calida's body filled with an emptiness that matched the look cursed upon her mother. The woman who sat in her parents' bedroom right now was a stranger to her own daughter. Fear and torment swirled around in her mind. Dread ate at her stomach and became a beast crawling up her throat, threatening to spew out like vomit. Limbs as heavy as bricks, they lay useless at her sides. Her mind was consumed by a monster raging through the door to take her away. Like whoever harmed her mother and left her to ... die.

Why did that intruder do that to her mother?

"My mama is gone." Her voice shook.

A fire in her hair spread until it engulfed her head, replacing her flaming locks. But as quickly as it came upon her, it disappeared. Along with it, her memories of the traumatic events vanished. With a moment of peace, the darkness crept up on Calida's vision and consumed her until there was nothing. The void filled with memories of earlier in the day, before any of it happened.

Her foot edged the bush as she hid. The wild, unruly hair resembling flames fell into her eyes. With an absent blow to the stray strands, she focused her attention on the deer that plodded by her hiding spot. Her breath froze as she feared to make any movement. Clenching a fist, she sprang from the brush. With a spring to her step, she ran after her prey. Arms outstretched, she lunged forward and tussled to keep a grip on the startled deer's neck. It bucked her to the ground and reared to take off when a whistle of wind darted past her.

Whipping her head around, she realized there was an arrow in its flank. Coming down the path was her father, a man of stocky build and tanned skin. Rayner's dark eyes met her amber ones. As frustration bubbled up, her cheeks flushed.

"I almost had it, Papa," seven-year-old Calida pouted.

He snickered as he stowed the bow he had used a moment earlier and then crouched to her level.

"I'm sure you did. I just beat you to it."

Rayner offered a hand up and she went to straighten her shirt and find the bush where she had left her dagger.

"Remember, darling, we must put the creature out of its suffering first," he said.

She gazed at her father over her shoulder "Yes, I didn't forget, Papa. Like you always say."

Her father smiled at her and nodded before he went to the deer and pulled out the dagger he kept on hand for the finishing blow to their prey.

It only took a moment to retrieve her blade before she was back at her father's side, where he set out all the tools to peel the hide and carve out the inside parts. Much of the meat would fetch a pretty coin on the market. The nobles loved venison like it was living water.

Father would hide some belly and leg meat for her mother to cook, but he sold most of it to the nobles. Rayner broke the silence. "May we be prosperous as you were, kind creature."

The air settled just before the dim light of the forest was broken by a ray of sun through the leaves above.

"We give our thanks to the use for our health. May your body rest in this forest and provide further to all," Rayner said.

One swift slice ended the deer's life, then it was up to her.

"May you be p-propserous." She cringed as her inexperienced lips fumbled the last word. It was always the last one in her greeting she messed up.

Prosperous. Prosperous.

Calida pulled her small skinning knife out of her pocket and unsheathed it. A mess of blood stained her hands as she worked at removing the flesh off the animal.

The forest stood silent as father and daughter efficiently butchered the carcass. The wind brushed around in the leaves overhead, a subtle ambience to their routine actions. Suddenly, a gust smacked a handful of stray grass into her mouth. Calida stumbled over, spitting out her red hair and the taste of dirt.

"Papa! Gross!" Calida wiped her face and scowled at her father. It was just like him to use the wind to play a prank on her.

In the forest, he would carry her on his shoulders like she was light as a feather. When she turned seven, his ability to tower over her never changed. All she could imagine was her strong and constant papa who would stay by her side always.

Rayner dug into the soil at the base of the tree next to them. It was only right to return the deer they had shot down back where it came from. Calida helped make the hole until it was large enough to fit the leftovers of the deer. The bones weren't something her father could carry home alone, as she was still too small. He had promised when she grew tall enough Calida could help carry them back for bone soup. A smile quirked on her face as the brush rustled around her, reminding her of all the times she had come to the woods with her father. Never was a single time a dull moment.

He packed the meat in the deer's hide and slung it over his shoulder. Calida flashed him a brilliant smile. With a large hand grasping her small one, the two made their way back to town. The breeze tickled her cheek, and Calida giggled.

"Papa, don't tickle..."

"I don't know what you mean, darling." He chuckled.

With a scrunched-up face, she tried to glare at her father, but her attempts were met by strands of red poking her eyes and mouth. As she spat out the wily mane, she laughed.

"Papa!"

If only she had gotten her magic already, she could get him back for all his pranks and maybe finally have an upper hand. Most days she tried to hold out her hands like Papa did in hopes of summoning her powers, but it was useless. Not even a single tingle. There was at least one child in the next town over that had gotten their magic at her age. Papa had told Calida it would come when it was supposed to, but she wished it would come now. Mama and Papa had theirs to use, but she wanted to show off. Maybe even prank the local boys who liked to pull on the pigtails of girls in town. According to her father, it first presented itself in the hands. They were commonly used and too close to our heart. But Calida could strain and stress for days and not encounter anything.

The seven-year-old could still remember the last time she complained about having no magic. They had been in their special field of flowers when he lectured her again that there was no need to worry. How could she not get her magic with two parents attuned?

It did nothing to convince her. Calida had always been a stubborn child and this case was no different. For all she knew, her parent's powers canceled each other because of their differing types. While Papa could control the wind, Mama could manipulate metal. Maybe there was no way to give her either of them. What if by some accident she was switched at birth, and she didn't even have powers? She didn't know what to do. The desperate need to get the ability to use wind or metal made her want to stomp on the ground until she was in a full childish tantrum.

As the trees thinned and Rayner and Calida broke

through the edge of the forest, they found their special meadow. The wildflowers were at the mercy of the wind around them. A large grin spread as she jumped in excitement at seeing her meadow. She ran into the field and spun endlessly, giggling at the warm light and chirping birds.

She stopped and crouched beside the brush of prickly flowers.

She held a hand to her mouth as she schemed. Jumping into action, Calida darted into the brush around the clearing. Every now and then, she peeked out from her hidden spot to watch her father stroll into the flower field.

She giggled as Rayner bent over to sniff one.

"Oh, I wonder where could my daughter have gone?"

He continued to stroll at a lazy pace, like he hadn't a care in the world.

Calida faded into the flowers like a cat hunting her prey. When she was close enough and his back turned to her, the girl pounced, knocking them over. Sweet smells and buzzing bees exploded around them. Their laughter joined the joyful birdsong overhead. The swish of Rayner's outstretched hand stirred the pollen around her, and she screeched with happiness.

Cuddled up, she rested her head on her father's chest. Nothing could disturb her now.

"If you feel unhappy, remember... My silly face!" Calida looked over and laughed at Rayner's tongue sticking out and skewed eyes.

"Whatever you say, Papa!" She rolled her eyes. A long sigh left Rayner's chest, and she glanced up. "My dear Eesa, what has you so exhausted?" Damn it all, she did it again. Exhausted. Exhausted.

"That's a big word for such a little lady. Exhausted. Hopefully, you'll remember that word later on."

"I mean, I remember the flowers and the nice smell around

me. I did like the look of the leaves I saw. Maybe when I'm older, I'll be a flower." Calida shared more and more about people turning into flowers and their feet becoming squirrels. If she could be a flower, then she would be fun. With the bees and beetles as friends, what could go wrong?

A soft chuckle left his mouth. "How are words and flowers related?"

Calida tilted her head to the side and scrunched her eyebrows. Flowers were pretty and had lots of friends. They made her think of her favorite fruit soup. Sweet, colorful, and perfect on her cloth doll.

"Flowers taste like wordy fruit!" An innocent smile spread across her face.

Her father stared at her in bewilderment.

They lounged outside, enjoying the sunlight as they recounted the events of the last few weeks. Things they learned or shared. Calida told her father about the girl she had met in the market one day. In a moment, Calida had snuck away to give her a piece of cheap fruit, but Calida wished she had a pretty dress for the girl. It wasn't fair she could have a doll and a dress without a stain, but someone else went without.

Her father talked about his brothers in his faction and the friendliness he had when play fighting. He told her about the daughter of his friend, Sir Vaughan, who was her age.

She sat in his lap and stared up at him.

"You would like her, darling. Her father spoke fondly of her lively nature."

Before long, the sun started to set, and they were forced to return home. Rayner pulled his daughter to her feet. Hand in hand, they strode home. Calida decided to skip halfway through until she grew tired of it. Her father whistled a tune that Calida bobbed her head to. Soon, they were entering town and walking down the path to their home.

The wind messed up Calida's hair while she skipped, tick-ling another giggle out of her.

"Papa!"

That was the last good day of her childhood she could remember.

One

Calida staggered through the door. The eighteen-year-old had found a large bag of potatoes for only one silver galatos. Her entire way home, she expected someone to realize the prize she had gotten away with in the market.

"What took you so long?"

Calida slumped the bag onto the ground with a grunt. She had bought enough to feed an army. She shouldn't need to go to the market for another week with all of this.

As she silently pulled the bag along the ground, unable to speak and drag the heavy weight, her mother tapped her foot impatiently. Then, when she took too long to stop and answer, the clanging of pans and metal scraping on metal pounded against her eardrums.

"Answer me, you impudent child!"

After more dragging, she was beside the kitchen's washing basin and Calida propped up the bag, opening it for easy access. Last time she didn't, her mother grew angry that it wasn't already open and insisted Calida stop what she had been doing to open it.

Cressida muttered complaints as she scrubbed Calida's father's cup on the table. It was the only dish she insisted on cleaning, but if her daughter didn't help, she became more upset.

Calida trudged back to the door and picked up the purse holding the vegetables she bought, vegetables she needed to dry or else the bugs would come for them. She laid them on the table beside the washing basin and turned around to get the salt, but a sack of laundry came sailing at her unexpectedly. She stumbled as she took the brunt of the impact.

"Be more on top of the chores this time."

Calida gritted her teeth. She would be more on top of it if it wasn't all left to her.

It was useless to shout at her mother. Cressida didn't understand Calida's perspective. It was better to be silent than to defend herself.

"Of course, why would you speak to your mother? Should I even expect love from you?" Even with all her criticism, she still loved her mother. Calida's chest tightened and weighed her down. If someone could suffocate from *wrongdoings* and criticisms, then it was a miracle she was still alive.

"I will take care of the laundry after I salt the vegetables."

"No. Do the laundry now. I will do the salting later. Last time you did it, we had a swarm outside our door."

Calida barely held back an eye twitch. Last time she salted *like all the other times,* she had salted the vegetables well. Cressida had been shouting anxiously the entire time she salted about the swarm growing outside their house eating the food. The pests had been attracted by a dead rabbit nearby. Calida saw it when she had gone out for the dried meat she had hung up. The bugs were completely unrelated. Not that it stopped her mother from complaining.

"Yes, mother." She sighed.

Calida shouldered the laundry sack and walked to her room to get her laundry beating stick.

"Where are you going?!"

From her bedroom, she controlled her breathing. If she lashed out at her mother, they would only fight, and it would resolve nothing. Calida would end up apologizing later for being a young, foolish girl. She snatched the stick and urn of wood ash from beside her bed and marched back into the living area.

"I just needed to fetch my laundry stick, *Mother.*"

Cressida stood up from the table and shouted. "Is that attitude I hear, Calida?"

Calida bit her lip to keep from yelling back. Her mother heard attitude and verbal attacks in her words no matter what she said in protest.

"No, Mother. I was only making a statement." *Because you asked*. Calida left the last part out; it would only get her mother upset.

"You have to answer me properly. You will not accomplish anything, anywhere, if you give me such an attitude."

Calida stared at the ground as the hurt swirled into numbness. Her heart stabbed her chest, and the pins and needle prickled her fingers until it covered her body and mind. Without a word, she trudged out the door with the bag of laundry and her stick.

The door swung closed behind her, and with it, the breath she held. In the outside air, Calida inhaled deeply. Her mind drifted to the memory of what she saw in the market that morning. Someone new had come with a skit to bring buyers to his stall. He was an object magic caster. The man had called the attention of those around them and then showed something like a "magic" show. He had a necklace in his hand and explained to the crowd what he was about to do. The man wore a mysterious cloak that covered his face. He held up the necklace and then it vanished in his hands, only for it to suddenly appear on a wealthy lady wearing a rich blue dress in the front of the crowd.

Like the rest of the crowd, Calida was absorbed by the man's display. He invited the woman to the front to play his assistant, then he performed one more trick. He told the woman she could keep the necklace if she were able to use the ring he held in his other hand to turn invisible. He plopped the ring in her hand. She clutched it tight and closed her eyes as she wished herself invisible.

The crowd gasped out when, before their eyes, the woman disappeared.

Calida had been enthralled by it, but thanks to that nagging little impression in her mind, she was thrown off by a wandering worry if it was rigged from the start, and if an innocent woman had just been taken. Objects that could make you invisible were rare because of how long it took to make them. The lady had been wearing the enchanted necklace that no doubt could transport anything. Calida could only wonder if she had been taken by the seller for nefarious reasons. She had stayed silent, though. What could she do? What if she was wrong? She didn't know what she would do if she were to blame for yet another incident and nothing was wrong. She could hear her mother's voice in her head.

It's your fault...It was only a little skit for the audience. Why must you make more out of than there was? What a paranoid, petulant child.

Calida had diligently kept her mouth shut, just like her mother had said. A loudmouth led to folly. The lovely event twisted to something upsetting in her mind.

As she walked down the path carrying the soiled laundry her mother had left outside the home, she was no longer excited about being outside. In her peripheral, her friend tied up her horse and approached.

Jetta Arundel walked beside her, and Calida stayed silent, not looking for conversation as she hoped to finish the laundry without incident.

"When will you come live with me at the Crescent League base?"

"I am needed here."

Her friend grabbed her arm and stopped them. "You are only needed because your mother refuses to lift a finger."

Calida shrugged off Jetta's arm, and the two set off into the forest behind the house. The leaves were almost the same color as Calida's red hair. The same red bubbled inside her from bottling up her emotions for so long. They strolled down the path.

Her skin crawled with the need to do something, say something, just to fill the silence. But she did not want to say something while she was in such a vulnerable state. Why would she need to share anything, anyway?

Stop that yelling this instant! Why must you yell at me when I have not done such things to you? How peevish.

Calida flinched at the memory of her mother's sharp words. The *dear daughter* of a Faction Knight argumentative. Nonsense. No explanation, just the statement. So, when her friend, the lackey of the esteemed Crescent League faction, made a statement about her mother, something triggered inside her. The hurt under the numbness blossomed like a stab wound.

"She is getting older. I am her dutiful daughter, so it falls onto me."

Calida was someone who stood above commoners and gained preferential treatment. Calida was fortunate to have what she did. Unlike Jetta, who grew up on the streets.

"Friends are there long enough to use and then they leave. You must love your family forever, child."

"Calida, don't tell me you believe that."

She didn't tell her. Her mother was getting older and couldn't do the same things other older woman could do without complaint. She took care of her mother and the house. Cressida had no interest in the emotional health of her daughter, including the jealousy over the looks of Calida's dearest friend.

Jetta's black hair was always kept in a knot on her head. The strands fell out constantly, but she would hurriedly fix them to keep her esteemed faction standards. Sometimes, Calida wished she could have Jetta's hair. Any hair but her own. The fiery locks upon her head were akin to an animal's mane. Wild, tangled, and large in volume. Frequently, she wished to have Jetta's appearance entirely. Her pale skin and eyes that were almond in shape and colour. And on her head, Jetta wore the Crescent League headpiece. The accessory represented the remarkable guild, and meant they held their members to a higher standard.

The trees thinned out, and the burble of water lazily moving down the river greeted her ears.

She reached the edge of the nearby stream and made a pool of water in the stream's mud. Scrubbing the laundry against the stones, she removed the filth before she churned the clothing with her laundry stick.

"Let me help you." Jetta tried to pull some of the laundry away.

"No!" It was her responsibility. Hers alone.

Jetta huffed before she crouched by the closest tree, staring intensely at Calida.

Tears pricked Calida's eyes. Her vision clouded as she tried furiously to hide her emotional fault. She churned even harder. Her mouth tightened as she fought off the sadness welling up. After so long feeling this sense of black and white, her chest hurt in protest.

It had been so long since her mother smiled her way or

lovingly said, "my beautiful daughter." Not that she was convinced that Cressida was her mother, nor Rayner her father. She didn't think they truly considered her their daughter, either. Why would they? She was so vastly different from her parents. Her fire-red hair was unruly and wild and stood out compared to her father's brown and her mother's blonde.

Calida's complexion was similar to her mother, but there were noticeable differences, like an upward tilt of the nose or higher cheekbones. Calida stared into the muddy water as she shook off the spiralling thoughts. Who in their right mind would think there was even a chance for a girl from the backwaters of Eokiaroth to have such an adventurous life? For all she knew, her father's great-grandfather was a redhead, and she was granted his hair.

What a selfish girl she was.

The image of her furious parents dragged her further into her emotional maelstrom Their imaginary gazes pierced her sluggish work pace until she got on her knees and vigorously scrubbed the cloth clean.

Do you think your looks are all important now, child?

She was not good at making friends, limited by her responsibilities. What else could she do but try to gain her parent's approval? Nothing.

Her father had grown distant since *that incident*. When he was at home, he would side more often with her mother. Even if she said something that was not right and he should do something, anything, Rayner would stay silent as if it weren't his problem.

As if *Calida* was not his problem.

Her hands slowed again as her mind wandered. She aimlessly scooped wood ash onto the dirty clothing closer to her, smearing it into the stains.

"Have you made any new paintings lately?" Jetta asked.

Calida stared at her rippling expression in the river. The

water distorted the image of her pale skin and auburn hair. Emotions bubbled up and suffocated her throat until all that remained was a wall of hurt, and the forest was suddenly too small.

Who could have time to create paintings when she should be working hard to please her mother?

Her friend knew her own mind, and she knew what Calida's mother was like. Jetta grew up an orphan, abandoned before she could remember her parents' faces. Yet she still knew Calida's mother wasn't any mother at all. Children from all over the continent worked or were enslaved. They were condemned to living in the slums. Calida wished to have the same ambition and confidence her closest friend had. It was her distant dream to sell paintings in a market.

"No, I haven't had the time."

Nothing she made was good enough, anyway.

Just like her attempts to keep up with the chores and household duties. Her mother could keep living life free from the "child-rearing burdens" as Calida lived in the background, staying quiet.

Her chest felt hot, like a flame was building up inside her, but she had it caged. She refused to let out whatever was inside her. Letting it out could be dangerous, with side effects that could be dire.

Her friend stood up and placed a hand on Calida's shoulder, only to pull it away quickly as if she burned herself, shaking it to quell the sting.

"Maybe your mother loves you in her own way."

Calida strained a laugh as she stood up. She churned the clothing again as the last step before returning with the wet laundry to be hung to dry.

"Soon enough, maybe I can sell my paintings, too," Calida said.

She closed her eyes and breathed through the guilt in the

back of her mind. If only Jetta would shut up. Calida's hands pumped the stick in and out of the water as she pushed back the dying rage, guilt slowly eating away at her. Jetta was her only friend and she hadn't done anything wrong. She didn't deserve that.

Her friend stood quietly beside her as she churned the laundry. After a while, the water cleared, and the two women could load up the laundry to take back for hanging.

Jetta grabbed laundry from the pile and shoved it into the sack Calida brought with her.

"What about your father? Could you manage being completely detached? Eventually, you might end up being alone for the rest of your life."

Calida clenched her teeth. *You mean alone like you?*

Neither said anything for a moment. Calida's head swirled as regret floated to the surface.

Her throat closed and tears prickled her eyes at the idea of the one person she considered a sister leaving her.

"That was out of line." Jetta said.

She had said it out loud. What was worse than thoughts when they betray you?

Calida curled in on herself and then collapsed onto the ground. Her body shook and tears obscured her sight. *How could I be so awful to Jetta like that?*

"It was true, though." Her friend pursed her lips in thought.

Calida shook her head hard and glanced up tearfully at Jetta's nonchalant gaze.

"Doesn't matter. Angry or not, sisters do not say that to one another."

Jetta's face softened, then she knelt on the ground and cradled Calida's head on her lap. The wetness from her eyes dampened her dark pants. Her hand softly petted Calida's hair.

After a moment in silence, the two got up, covered in dirt and mud. They carried the bag of wet laundry to Calida's house together.

Her raw throat and dried eyes were the only evidence left of her meltdown at the river.

They walked to the back of the house where the small garden lay to hang up the clothing. However, the last clothesline she hung up had been cut.

Cursing in frustration, Calida searched for the end and started to tie it once more. It was too high, and no matter how hard she tried, Calida couldn't reach.

"Let me." Jetta pushed aside her hands.

Suddenly drained of energy, Calida let her take over without protest. Jetta pulled out her throwing knives and tied the string around two of them. Calida sat down as she observed her friend hover her hand and close her eyes for a moment, but she swung the knives up and around the tree high up. Her hand moved as she manipulated them, and she tied the line on one end, then did the same on the opposite side.

Calida stood up once more before Jetta gestured for her to sit down.

"You did the cleaning. I will do the hanging."

Calida sighed and nodded, giving up resisting her stubborn friend.

Jetta pulled out a tunic from the laundry bag and hung it up. As she pulled to straighten the material, the clothing glowed green. The natural energy, provided by who had worn it and the river it was washed in, poured from it. This continued until everything was hung up and all the energy was on the surface of the material. If Jetta wanted, she could take that energy and use it to fuel her metal magic. Someone else with an affinity for natural magic could use the energy from the material to accelerate the drying process.

In no time at all, the clothing was hung up, and all Calida had left to do was salt the vegetables.

Her hands smoothed out her best dress as Cressida braided a ribbon of fabric into her hair. Calida had on a stain-free dress and a clean face. It was strange that her mother insisted she was spotless from head to toe. She looked up and met her mother's gaze as she walked around to the front of her hair. Cressida clicked her tongue as she assessed Calida's appearance.

"I doubt you could accomplish any better."

Calida looked at her lap as her hands wrung the fabric of her dress.

Her father walked in as her mother stood behind Calida, appearing like she had finished the tie in Calida's braid. Rayner shifted from foot to foot as he waited for the women to leave Calida's room. Tonight, they were attending a celebration of the marquess's wedding.

When Calida was a child, they would leave her with a local woman. It's rare that they gave an invitation to her father to a celebration or social gathering. As a knight, nobility would rather he guard them. Well, in the case of those appointed as knight through a faction, he would be given the grunt jobs of the average guard. Many of them wouldn't dare invite a commoner to their parties, knight or not. A frown appeared at the reminder of the haughty nobles who loved to step on the toes of those below them. Her mind suddenly swam with the visits to her father's faction and watching noble after noble treat her father and his brothers in arms like they were dogs.

Calida stiffened as Cressida gave her a slicing look when Rayner fidgeted restlessly. Her arms scratched along the chaffing fabric of her green dress as she scrunched it up and then smoothed it out once more.

Cressida stepped away as she vainly finished messing with

the ribbons in Calida's hair. She stood up and quietly waited for her mother to tell her what to do next.

"Don't my girls look beautiful?" Rayner said.

"We are, aren't we?" Cressida grabbed onto Calida's arm as her daughter forced a smile.

If only she could stay back and paint.

"I know you aren't excited about this, Calida. But I am sure your mother has explained how important it is that you attend."

She had not explained anything. Her mother gripped either side of her shoulders and squeezed hard. It was stealthy enough that her father did not see it, as always.

"Of course, Father. It is only natural that the daughter of a faction knight attends." Calida said.

A small smile peeked on Rayner's face and then fell at the formality. His eyes filled with hurt before he scratched his head, looking away, but then when he turned back to her, the hurt was gone.

Cressida interjected. "We still need to add a sprig of lavender to your braid. Then you will be perfect. After that, we will be ready to go."

Just never perfect enough.

Grabbing Calida's hand, she dragged her out of the bedroom and into the main living area. Her mother sat Calida down and then she wove a sprig of lavender between the weaves of the braid.

Hands softly floated down Calida's hair until her mother gently grasped her hands and gave her a sad smile while her father looked at the two women. He walked to the door and gathered their capes for the evening. Cressida, with her hands still on Calida's, squeezed tight and glared at her in warning. *"You are too argumentative. Why must you attack me so?"*

Rayner turned around and brought over the capes.

"Calida, you look so beautiful. The flower was the perfect touch," she breathed, the smile not reaching her eyes.

Her heart ached from the compliment. How could the woman responsible for the cause of her mother's pain and suffering be anything like that word, "*beautiful*"?

"*It's your fault.*"

"I noticed you made a pound cake this morning. Is there a special occasion?" Calida said.

Her father held out the cape to her mother, who grasped it and put it on. Cressida smiled softly. Any other time she would nitpick Calida's lack of proper manners about when it's appropriate to ask a question, but today her father was home. She was different around him, even though her father was so mellow that he was basically an extension of his wife. He was completely unaware of her mother's behavior. Rayner's work was his escape from the pain caused by *that incident*.

"Yes, there is."

Calida waited for her to explain.

"What's the occasion?" she asked when her mother didn't. She stood up and put on the other cape held out to her.

Cressida paused and thought about it.

"It's a good day to be alive, is all. There need not be any other reason. Right, *my dear daughter*?"

Maybe she needed more of a reason. Calida kept her thoughts to herself.

She was compliantly coming to the wedding with her parents because her mother pressured on her how important it was.

"*This is a very important night for our family. You are to attend and be polite.*"

When she was younger, there had been a time she would speak for herself, loud and free. As a young girl, she had been learning just what was up to her to achieve. Not long after the *incident,* it fell on her to look after the home and Cressida. It wasn't overnight, though. It started small.

"Calida, be a dear and mend the garden."

Then it became more. "Be a dear and go into town for groceries."

Until she was taking care of the house. "Be a dear and pay the taxes to the beady-eyed nobleman."

She paraphrased the last one, but it changed nothing at all. The nobleman who would visit in town was a cockroach of a man. It was out of line to call him such in public, but it did not stop her from saying it in her mind.

Her father entered his bedroom, leaving Calida alone with her mother.

Cressida stared her daughter in the eyes.

"You will be silent, and you will be polite. They are uncaring people who would have nothing against sending you away from us."

Calida met her mother's eyes steadily and nodded. All her life, she had heard the same spiel. Be well mannered or you will never see your family again. The people around us have nothing against sending you to a nunnery or to an asylum funded by the nobles.

Rayner sauntered into the living area from her parent's room dressed in his formal uniform befitting a knight such as him.

"Don't forget to have some fun, Calida. Make some friends and socialize. It's a party after all," Rayner said.

Cressida walked over to her husband and laid a hand on his chest. "Maybe she will find a man to look after her."

Her mother looked back at Calida and gave her appearance one last inspection. Then they exited their small home, all dressed in the fanciest outfits they could muster from their station, mounted their horses, and headed out to the event she would have to endure for the rest of the evening.

alida resisted the urge to scowl. If the door was close to where she was, then her escape would be eminent. Hordes of noblewomen strolled by her, snickering at her simple dress. If it wasn't enough, her parents had mysteriously disappeared as soon as they had passed the banquet table in the middle of the room. She had only taken one peek at the lush bread. On the inside, she was yelling out in frustration and desiring to crawl into a corner.

" *Do not take a single step out of line, Calida.*"

While being in the same room as these judgemental nobles was tiresome, the idea of her mother's nagging later was far worse.

I can't go wrong with food, right?

Calida bit her lip as she glanced at the lavish food available. "Maybe just a small bite."

Each decadent dish was designed for danger. Something she wanted to experience for the first time. A spark of excitement ignited in her.

She explored the golden crusted pies and flaky rolls. There was a soft and airy bun that had a bittersweet coating on it was like nothing she had ever tasted before. A whole roast of chickens and pigs which had a smell that could bring a dog to heel. Her eyes closed in bliss, unable to stop the look of content on her face. The savory scent of the glazed meat. She picked up a miniature pie, and then bit into a sweet cloud that melted in her mouth. If this was happiness, she wished it would never end.

Calida's anxiety washed away. All it took was one bite of food to forget that she was alone at a party, abandoned by her parents at the banquet table. Surrounded by socialites who flittered from group to group. The white noise of chatter, gossip, and political bickering. Slowly the sound blurred out and silence sat around her for the first time in a long time.

She closed her eyes for a moment until excitement sparked in her.

With renewed vigour, she scoured the table to find something new to try. Her lips quirked into a tiny smile and her eyes glittered. She almost danced around in glee but held back. In the back of her mind, she remembered it was unmannerly, even if she wished to do so.

"Good evening, my lady." A deep voice spoke directly behind her as she tried the chicken. It was so sudden she startled, and the chicken she had been holding combusted into flame and then ash. *Damn it to hell.*

She frowned at the ashes in her hand and then wiped them on a nearby napkin. The first thing that troubled her was the sudden combustion. It hadn't happened in at least a fortnight. Whatever it was, it was rather odd. She hadn't ever seen flame-producing magic anywhere in her town, but she was heavily sheltered.

The next thing that troubled her was the man behind her. *"My lady."*

She was no lady of the court. There was no doubt the man was trying to gain the attention of someone else, although it scared the raggabrash out of her. The man's voice was startlingly deep. The type of depth that made her uncomfortable. She liked the sound too much.

Continuing to peruse the banquet table filled with a bountiful of food, Calida examined the dessert on the table that looked like another miniature pie. This one had a creamy filling and a golden crust. She picked it up and bit in. The aroma wafting from it was rich, fragrant spices. There was also a delicate taste that she could only assume was vanilla. She had never tried vanilla before. Often it was in the bakeries, but it was something much more popular with the nobility. Many of the commoners near her couldn't afford such luxurious treats. With gusto, she ate the remaining dessert and smiled in delight at the creamy texture of the filling. It was light, but the crust was flaky and melted in her mouth.

If only there was a pillow made of this, I would live forever in its bliss. Holding back a squeal, she licked a crumb off the corner of her mouth.

With the bite of food in her mouth, a man cleared his throat and gently touched her arm. She jumped away.

Turning around, Calida took in a sharp breath as she gazed upon a man who was someone to gawk at. He was most definitely attractive; no amount of time would prepare her for what she saw. His short hair was militant and neat, the sharp jaw line on his face complimented his broad shoulders. He towered over her, but his face held a gentle familiarity to it. She felt like she had seen him before, but she couldn't put her finger on it. Her heart pattered and the desire to fling herself into his arms almost overwhelmed her.

I don't even know him.

Suddenly, the food that had been in her mouth was in her throat. Her face turned a deep red as she tried to cough to clear the blockage. She struggled to address the man who spoke. He gazed at her, bemused. Maybe even a bit intrigued by her strange expression before she started coughing. Then his expression cleared as he realized she was choking. *Dear Eesa, I would have choked and gone to meet my maker before he noticed.*

He swiftly called for a servant to fetch him a glass of water while he patted her back and waited. The coughing dissipated, leaving her throat unobstructed. Just as the servant arrived with the water, Calida was shrugging off his arm and stepping a short distance away.

"I have no need for the water."

She resisted the urge to lose herself in his gaze.

The man had captivatingly blue eyes that could hold a woman's soul still. Most definitely nobility because intricately woven thread made up the jacket he wore. That garment could never be owned by someone even remotely close to her station. What really grabbed Calida's attention was his hair. The colour looked like clean hay put down in a horse's stall. It was like a young stalk of wheat that has its flexibility and strength. *If only I could touch it.*

"Who said the water was for you?"

He gracefully took the water from the servant, then he turned towards her and drank it. A sneaky smirk appeared on his mouth, hypnotically capturing her attention.

"Mannerly women are innocent in mind and action."

Calida paused a moment. What was she thinking? This man was a stranger, and she was too likely to become emotionally attached, all because of her tendency to cling to even the smallest amount of interest.

"Just because he likes you doesn't mean he's trustworthy. This is for your own good."

"Greetings. The Earl of Weommadran, Dominic Goldwyn, presents himself to you, fair maiden, Lady of the Plain of Eleari, Calida Rhodes." Dominic bowed formally and presented a hand for her, his eyes gazing straight into hers before he gave a wink.

Calida was speechless. She was not a *lady*. It had to be a joke, and a poor one at that. The Rhodes family was not of any noble status. Her father was an Elite Dominion knight, they did not get a noble title. In fact, nobles would often mock them. While nobility could join the guard, they preferred to live in the lap of luxury, spending their time eating delectable dishes and flittering about, spreading gossip. How could he know her name and then made a joke out of her status? It was outright arrogant and rude.

Her hands warmed as her anger spiked at the audacity of

this man, twitching with the urge to just wrap him up in a ball of flames. *Where had that thought come from?* A frown formed on her face.

"I beg your pardon?"

He stood up tall and smoothly took back his hand like he had never offered it. Then he smiled and said, "When your father spoke of you, I underestimated just how beautiful you would be. My lady, you are not like any other. Your complexion shimmers more than the sun shines on us all. In all my days, you have blossomed over the years since we parted."

Calida blinked. And blinked once more. What kind of man says such a statement like that?

"I...ummm... what?"

Two

The earl was obviously in need of a good bloodletting. His mind was bogged down by a demonic possession, surely. She couldn't conjure up any other reason for his behaviour. Calida stepped back and tried to make her escape. However, Lord Dominic's hand wrapped around her arm and kept her from running out the door and all the way home. Her lips tightened in a forced smile.

There were an endless number of things she would love to say to this dorbel of a man.

"It would please me greatly if you would accompany me as I mingle with the guests," Lord Dominic said.

"Milord, I do protest. I don't think you thought this through. Someone of my status shouldn't be on the arm of one of our kingdom's more eligible young nobles." A frown deepened on her face.

If he wants my presence, maybe I should just graciously accept? He was obviously not of sound mind, which was concerning. Maybe somehow having a dutiful person nearby would save his soul from being consumed. *Not that I can truly save him if he is already so far gone.*

Dominic peered down at Calida with a brilliant smile, amused by something unseen by her. She couldn't help considering he was likely a narcissist and loved to be in the company of those he viewed as less intelligent.

"Just stay quiet and be polite, you ungrateful child."

Calida inhaled to will away her mother's voice in her head.

"Oh nonsense, anyone who has something to say is obviously not worth our time," Dominic said.

Why does he insist on entertaining the idea of associating with me, a common maiden?

With that, he dragged her along as he went to chat with the nobles about nonsensical topics. There were various topics from the benefits and side effects of blood leeching to others how many sugars in your tea were the best for full effectiveness of the flavour. She tried to add her input at certain moments, but she was either ignored or laughed at. Her feeling of being an outsider built up the more she socialized. *How do they never feel this ostracizing mockery?*

The earl migrated to another group soon after finishing the last conversation about show horses. The next group was two older noble women. Each had on jewels and fabrics that said everything about their higher status and fashion sensibilities. Lord Dominic introduced Calida to Lady Meredith and Lady Karin. Lady Meredith was apparently a very distant relative of the Queen's nephew, and Lady Karin had just recently moved from Mirynd.

"I cannot believe they haven't gotten rid of those pests yet." Lady Meredith continued her earlier conversation with Lady Karin, her chin tilted up, showing the disdain on her face.

"Pests? What are you talking about, Lady Meredith?" Dominic said.

"A swarm of pixies upturned the Dale's carriage," Lady Karin said.

The old women shook their heads in disappointment and their faces were frowning in disgust. Neither were happy, but not surprised by the news. Lady Meredith's face crinkled into a sneer.

"Isn't it just like pixies to take a simple affair too far?"

Isn't it like nobles to blame a simple creature? Unfortunately, pixies *were* typically troublesome creatures. They would swarm a person and cause so much trouble that they leave the encounter with nothing but their undergarments. Not to mention their pixie circles... Most people avoided their swarms, not that the trouble was the pixie's fault.

When Acalikon was still mostly undiscovered, settlers were adventurous and found the heart of the pixies' domain to be the perfect place to settle down, pushing them out of their normal life. No longer could they have whatever they wanted to eat or play cute pranks on their friends. The pixies had been forced to share their food supply with settlers, and the pranks the pixies played only made the settlers upset with them.

Lady Karin rolled her eyes. "Lady Meredith, we both know that we can't truly blame the pixies. They are simple creatures. They repaid the Dale household for their actions. Acting nothing like a noble family should. They adopted that filthy sewer rat." She fanned her face aggressively. "I cannot even speak that abhorrent boy's name. He has muddled the Dale's family lineage ever since."

Calida inhaled sharply. *Someone needs to put these women in their place. This is completely unacceptable of Lady Karin. Do they seriously think that it is alright to gossip openly like this? The Dales have raised a respectable young man.*

Calida hated those who would gossip about others without the person being present to defend themselves. It wasn't right to judge someone harshly without even talking to them first.

"I beg your pardon, but shouldn't a lady of the court

converse with the guilty before falling victim to prejudice? I hardly think the Dales deserve such spite," Calida said.

Her anger grew, her eyes burned, and her lips tightened. As the heat wave radiated off her skin, her body shuddered and her palms warmed until flames sparked in Calida's veins. But as fast as it appeared, it disappeared.

The group blinked at her like they didn't even realize she was there. Dominic's eyebrows rose in surprise, none of them expecting her reaction. They took a pregnant pause before Lady Meredith suddenly changed the subject. Calida stepped back, disgusted by their nonchalance.

Did they feel so entitled that if they are called out, the noblewomen would rather ignore her than face the truth? What made them think they could say whatever they want without defending their comments?

Absorbed in their new topic, the two women walked away. They did not utter another word on the subject about the Dales. Calida did not get to defend them in their stead. She knew the Dales personally. Jetta was the sister of their adopted son. Her friend barely talked about that time in her life, but from what Calida knew, the lord and lady adopted her older brother but had left her behind. The Dales were generous and kind folk, unlike other nobles. Lord and Lady Dale did not deserve the insults of two busybodies.

Jetta had explained to her once when they were younger that the orphanage rarely adopted out the girls under their roof. Lord Sullivan funded the orphanage, so it made perfect sense that the Dales had no way of adopting the pair. It was rumored that he kept the girls behind to be his "wards" at his personal home, women who were sheltered in his home "out of the goodness of his heart." She had never met her friend's brother, but Calida had many interactions with his adoptive parents because of Jetta.

Calida sighed in resignation. It would do no good to chase down those noblewomen and set them right.

"That is rather interesting," Lord Dominic said.

Calida whipped around and glared at him.

"Rather interesting? They just blatantly insulted a noble couple! In Poramun Creek, you would get slashings for doing that!" Her cheeks warmed with a fiery temper. He did not even try to defend the Dales. *What an arrogant oflati!*

"Milady, this isn't Poramun Creek. I am the earl from the shire Weommadran, Calida Rhodes. The court is all about knowing other's perception and political leanings and how to use it to your advantage."

Calida studied Lord Dominic, seeing him for the first time. He crossed his arms over his chest and relaxed his strong shoulders. She hoped to find at least one more noble, like the lord and lady who could be kind. Yet again, she was disappointed. Her hidden hopeless romantic side hoped he would have been sweet and cared at least more than other nobles she had met. It wouldn't be the first time Calida was wrong.

"Milord, it's wrong to gossip without giving the person a chance to defend themselves! Do you even have a selfless bone in your body?" Calida said. She clenched her teeth at the snobbery of Lord Dominic Goldwyn. Not that she should be surprised. Calida had not encountered many selfless nobles.

"You will find that people here are not the type to care about sympathizing with the less fortunate. It may make me sound arrogant and rude, but Calida, you are not in the backwaters of Eleari anymore. This is High Court." He offered her his arm. With a sharp inhale, Calida reluctantly took it. The nobles expected it of her as a polite guest.

Doesn't mean I cannot seethe on the inside.

Dominic paused for a moment and gazed at her, appearing disappointed and confused.

"Do you really not remember me?" he asked.

Calida squinted at him. *What was he talking about? This was the first time they had met.*

T hey walked around the party, partaking in small talk. If it wasn't for the fact she needed to play the part of the companion, then she could fall asleep where she stood. Every noble they had talked to completely ignored her. Regretting her decision, Calida mentally cringed as the Duke of Eleari looked her way while talking to Lord Dominic. It wasn't even a peek of curiosity.

Lord Bartholomew Sullivan's beady eyes sent chills down her spine. They had a lustful glint, and if thoughts could be action, then she would be on her back this moment. The rumors around town seemed to be right based on his conversation with Lord Dominic. In Poramun Creek, rumors had run rampant for years about him and his wards. Not one of them left his home, at least not alive.

Calida had overheard a mumbled conversation once as a child that in the forest outside town lay a mass grave where the bodies of broken and used women were hidden. His lustful appetite showing in his eyes decided what he was in hers. *Never have I ever wanted to be invisible more than in this moment.*

"My mother always said I had a sharp tongue," Dominic said.

The duke patted his belly, which caused it to ripple. His body moved like a bath of muddy water, slow and smooth. The duke sidled a little closer to her. Calida laughed awkwardly, uncomfortable with the duke's sly examination of her frame.

"A man is only as good as his ability to use that sharp tongue to keep the stray in line." Lord Sullivan spoke as he wheezed from laughter and then took another peek at Calida while licking his lips. His gaze said *you will warm my bed later.*.

Calida tried to feign politeness as she searched for an escape. Her face hurt from the forced smile hiding her overwhelming discomfort. Everywhere she looked were more and more nobles, but not her parents. They still had to be here, though. It would ruin the reputation of the family if their only daughter was a social outcast because her parents decided to go home without her. No unwed woman who hadn't come out in society would be caught dead left alone at a social event. She would be written off as too unruly to be marriageable.

Out of the corner of her eye, she noticed a tall man who could be Lord Dominic's doppelgänger signalling for him to come over.

Lord Dominic nodded at the man, then he turned to Calida with a frown and said, "I will return in a moment. I must speak with my brother. When I return, I hope to share a dance."

Calida opened her mouth in protest, but before she could, he walked off and joined his brother. They exited the party through a back door, leaving her to keep a forced smile on her face and try to walk away from Lord Sullivan.

The oppressive presence of Lord Sullivan crawled up her spine and left her stomach feeling sick. He was right behind her and reeked of sweat, alcohol, and salty musk. She could almost feel his sausage fingers touching her skin and his beady eyes ogling every curve of her body.

"Now that we are all alone, we can have our own party. A private one in my chambers." His sour breath hissed in her ear and his eyes were like dark, endless pits. She held her breath and hoped he would lose interest and walk away if she stood still. The duke stepped forward until he was so close she could feel his belly pressed up on her back. He took one of his sausage fingers and slid it along her body.

Calida shuddered and tried to step away from him. His hand clasped her arm, and then something happened. She hadn't meant for it to happen but didn't regret it either.

A spark ignited on her skin and then shot down her arm and travelled up the duke's. As it spread up his arm, it left a burning trail behind it until he had charred clothing and an unending flame. Her eyes widened in surprise.

What had she done? She set the duke on fire for molesting her!

In amazement, Calida looked down at her hands and barely contain her maniacal grin.

Then, she saw the other nobles glaring or shaking their head in disappointment. The crowd gasped as Lord Sullivan panicked and dashed from here to there, hoping to dispel the fire. The noblewomen watched with detached interest. Of course it was interesting to them. Any fodder to feed the gossip pigs caught their attention.

His arms flailed in the air as he thumped around, the panicked scream growing increasingly louder as the fire licked at his over-the-top garments and jewellery. It was his squealing that almost broke Calida. She could barely hold in her laughter.

Just what you deserve, you hairless rodent.

As he thundered past the banquet table, looking for anything to take away the burning pain, the fire spread. One small touch and the flames licked at the banquet table, but this time, she didn't find it funny. *Skitr.* It was one thing to have a bit of payback on the lecherous creep, it was another to have it spread to innocent bystanders.

Calida whipped her head around, looking for a cloth or water. Anything to tamp the fire. The duke forgotten, she picked up a nearby goblet and poured it into the flames.

Instead of dousing out, the flame blew out into a conflagration of tremendous magnitude. Jumping back in shock, she stared and then stepped backward, away from the fire.

Whatever it was, it wasn't water. Why should she expect there to be anything other than alcohol at a wedding?

Foolish girl.

Tears pricked her eyes, and her chest squeezed tight. Frustration and anger bubbled up, but she shook away her overwhelming emotion and focused on the crisis at hand.

Above the crackling flames, the whispers of those pretentious old hags made it to her ears. Are they seriously gossiping in a moment like this? It was in that instant, as Calida had finally found a bucket with water which a servant had handed to her, Lord Dominic came back from wherever it had been that he had been. Seeing the fire, he rushed forward.

"Why are you all just standing around? Do you not have functioning hands? There is a fire!" Lord Dominic's hands gestured at the idle nobles' inept abilities. Many of them just whispered and looked at each other and then at him.

Those of luxurious lifestyles did not lift a hand to work or help. Many were hesitant to respond to Lord Dominic's enthusiastic rebuke of them. She knew they were as useless as a dead horse. Nobles grew up living like this. They wouldn't own up to responsibility or accomplish something that a commoner could just as easily do. Obviously, the Lord of Weommadran did not get the message. She held back the urge to roll her eyes, her thoughts so full of attitude that if her mother could mind read, she would never hear the end of it.

After some time, nobles like Lord Dale and Sir Vaughan stepped forward to help. Instead of coming forward, the others escaped the hall through the balcony doors. The crowd was now gathered outside instead of loitering about inside.

Calida frantically flitted from spot to spot around the banquet table in order to gain control of the fire.

Many times, she saw servants try to touch the things on the table only to screech away in pain, unlike herself, who could touch the fire without the sting. On one end of the table, she had successfully put out the flames. Her victory was short. The rest of the table was becoming a blackened mess as the fire licked down the table and onto the floor, undeterred.

The others were working their hardest to tamp down the flames, scorching everything they touched. The servants frantically beat the fire with cloths and fans. Calida jumped right back into the fray. At one point, she was toeing the line between dangerous and skin melting, and Lord Dominic dragged her away from the fire.

"Let me go! I need to put out the fire!" She desperately pushed at the arm he wrapped around her middle.

"There is nothing more that you can do, Calida. How do you plan on solving this on your own?"

"I... I can't."

Her face grew slack and the tears that built up in her eyes spilled. The nobles at the banquet would eat her up alive after this. She would feed the gossip vine for months, if not years, after this stunt. Normally not one to drink, for once she wished to scrounge up a glass of wine. Forget that, a barrel of wine. She needed to drown herself in alcohol for the next week to forget this event. At least she was blessed that after this she could go back home and, for once, be given the wished-for invisibility.

<h1 style="text-align:center">Three</h1>

Calida was still stuck at the party an hour later, watching Lord Dominic and her father talk animatedly about the difference between a knight with shining armour and the one who came battered. For once, a lovely smile graced her mother's mouth. If Calida didn't know any better, she would think that smile was a pleasant addition to the events. However, she did. Cressida had something up her sleeve.

Calida glanced at her father. His eyes sparkled and shone with pride as Lord Dominic spoke in grandiose gestures.

"Oh, shush, Meredith, it's not something you need to make a big fuss about." Lady Karin leaned in close and held her hand up to the other noblewoman's ear. Distracted, Calida turned an ear and an eye in their direction.

"It is just so upsetting to know such an eligible suitor for a respectable young noblewoman slumming with that common-er's daughter. I don't care if he's well respected. He is still not a *real* knight. His daughter would know nothing of noble life and what Lord Dominic's duties pertain," Lady Meredith said.

The man beside her was Lord Dominic. But were they referring to her? There's no way. They had only just met.

"Not to mention the fire at the banquet. I saw it come from that girl. Lord Sullivan was speaking with her one moment, and then the next he was aflame and running around in a tizzy. Among all the other things, she had the nerve to laugh at the tragic incident she had caused!" Lady Karin said.

If the old hag thought having sympathy for that pig of a man would earn her points in the high society circle, Lady Karin had to be off her rocker. That bloviating beast was the worse type to be around.

Calida clenched her teeth. If the nobles thought she was horrible for setting fire to a pervert, she felt glad not to stay long. If only she could leave for her paints now.

The conversation around her hushed, and the stares from the group brought her attention back to her parents and the earl.

"Pardon? I missed what you said."

Her mother clenched her jaw while maintaining her impeccable smile. "I said, we would like to formally introduce you to Lord Dominic."

Calida's brows drew together. Cressida smoothed her outfit and fiddled with her hands. Rayner tugged on his collar. They were more skittish than a newborn fawn. Her frown dropped from her face when she realized the truth. *Dear Eesa, please don't let this be true.*

"Lord Dominic, may I present my daughter, Calida." Her father turned her way. "And also, your betrothed."

Calida blinked once. Twice.

He is my betrothed.

No, she had heard it right.

"I beg your pardon... Mother?" Calida looked into her mother's eyes and saw only darkness. Cressida took her daughter's hands in hers and gave her a tight grin.

"You are engaged to be married to Lord Dominic."

All the events of the night and of the last several years caught up with her. She felt years older and envied infants who did not have the mind to even know what conversation was. Calida shivered in the chilly wind. Normally she would feel warm at any time of day... but it was like the fire inside her dimmed to a hot coal.

Slumping forward, she pushed past the crowd in search of the alcohol she had been only thinking about drinking until that moment. She paid no mind to her father calling out for her or the heavy footsteps behind her.

Calida stumbled into and around servants who bustled about with buckets to quench the fire. She had been ushered out by Lord Dominic around the time of the event. Calida had no time to rectify her mistake, but now she wanted to forget about her emotions. About her problems. About the attractive man who was dangerous to her safe lifestyle. Everyone around her moved at lightning speed while she tried to find something with alcohol.

After some searching, she found a skin, sniffing to confirm it was fermented fruit. Lifting it up, she threw it over her shoulder and carried it off like a bag of laundry to the nearest door, heading outside and toward the dock. The door closed behind her, and the large skin fell to the ground. Still holding onto it, she dragged it behind her as she hurried away from the banquet hall. Shoulders slumped and her hair spilling out from all angles, she collapsed on the wood near the end of the dock.

Her feet dangled over the edge, toeing the water. Calida pulled the wine onto her lap and gulped it down. Her head swam with the news of her own engagement, told to her as if it were merely a fact of nature. She had made an explosive entry into society at a nobleman's wedding.

She swayed with the lulling sound of the wind kissing the water. Her soul was at rest for once. The flame inside burned again. Calida couldn't discern if it was the half-gone wine or the fire simmering under her skin. Her mind felt relief. She sat in nature for what seemed the longest of time.

Even the little bits of what she remembered from when she was seven couldn't disrupt her mood.

Then, none other than Lord Dominic came barrelling onto the dock, sloshing the water all over her and disrupting the ambience. Calida slowly turned her head his way, holding the wine close.

<h1 style="text-align:center">Four</h1>

"How long have you been here?" His voice reverberated over the water, and he cringed as the echo hit him.

With a startled jolt, Calida clambered to stand up. The drink had thrown her balance off kilter.

"I just got here, milord." She hiccupped.

"Was there only half a skin of wine when you brought it out here?" Dominic glanced at the skin.

"It was fully delicious," Calida said.

Lord Dominic took the skin gently from her hands.

"You have been out here too long. The party is long over. We must get you home."

Calida sobered up a little at hearing that. Shaking her head to clear the cobwebs in her mind, she trudged back to the hall.

The trees hummed and whistled around Calida as she attempted to find her parents. Even if her mother was the type to think about abandoning her wretched daughter at an event, her father surely wasn't. Her father was stubborn when he could be. As Lord Dominic and Calida ventured up the hill, she stumbled once more. He reached out to assist, but she only pushed away from him.

Where were her parents?

"Your parents have returned already." Lord Dominic stopped in his tracks as Calida halted.

"I beg your pardon, Lord Goldwyn?" She spun and glared up at him.

His ability to hold her gaze vanished.

"It is up to me, your betrothed, to escort you home." Lord Dominic cleared his throat as he looked off to the side. He was seriously shy now of all times. What was wrong with this guy?

Her mind cleared as the alcohol in her system burnt off from the growing heat radiating from her being. Her chest heaved, and her sight seemed to grow brighter. Unbeknownst to Calida, the roots of her hair began to catch fire as if she were dry wood waiting for the right spark.

"I am not your betrothed! No matter what my parents and you have to say, I didn't agree to *that* arrangement!" Calida stomped closer to him, her throat closing as she yelped in anxious desperation.

Lord Dominic inched closer in order to calm her. She scurried further away. One gentle touch and all the anger would be gone. There would be no succumbing to any distraction that may come her way. He was too attractive for her liking. She would melt if he so much as looked at her sweetly.

In the shadows behind Lord Dominic, she thought she saw a moving shape stalk toward her, but it vanished as quickly as it had appeared.

Holding his hands out in a calming manner, he said softly, "I am your betrothed. But I won't force marriage upon you. I want more than just an arrangement. I hope you will change your mind. Whether you care for me is up to you."

Little shitty bacraut. Mentally, she tried to hold her emotions closer, like a slippery ribbon which would fall from the hand of the one who tried to hold too tight. With the passionate emotions gone, she felt vulnerable. She could no longer summon energy to rebuild the wall of hurt she had constructed to keep people out.

"You deserve the world, Calida. If you left the task up to me, I would search high and low to bring a spark to your eyes. To give you the rarest gems."

The compliment felt like a seed dug in deep into the soil of her mind. The hard, unmovable soil. It almost hurt to have someone compliment her so, a hurt she didn't want to acknowledge as a healing pain.

She looked down at her clenched fists, her frame shaking from the exertion. Don't feel it. It will sting more when the truth is revealed.

He is nothing but a no-good leasing-monger.

She took a breath and summoned up the energy to fuel her anger again, pushing off the relaxation he had created. However, the compliment took root. It would always be there, no matter how much she fought against it. Calida grumbled to herself. The frivolous nature of the heart was always a roadblock in the path of surviving.

Turning around, she tromped up the hill and focused on Lord Dominic's arrogance and cockiness. She'd received little education on the behavior and mannerisms of the elite. But if it was anything like the earl, then she wanted no part, especially with the impending tears fighting to stream down her face.

Lord Dominic followed behind her in silence. Both stayed quiet as they approached the banquet. Inside the hall, the servants were finishing up the cleaning, and Calida stepped forward to assist. Lord Dominic swiftly grabbed hold of her elbow and guided her to the entryway.

"Milord! At least let me assist in cleanup." Calida attempted to pry his hand off so she could earnestly try to make up for the mistake she had made earlier. *Not that I will ever forgive myself.*

"My lady, what do you hope to accomplish by helping? Are you looking for information? Wanting a servant removed?" He turned to her with a fierce stare. Calida's hand shot to her mouth as she gasped in shock.

"Lord Goldwyn, are you suggesting I would have ill intent by merely doing my part to help clean up?" She was astounded the nobleman in front of her would assume the worst of her. He still held her elbow as he leaned toward her, his presence overwhelmingly frightening.

"Miss Calida Rhodes, look around and see that no noble would stoop so low as to help servants with the job left to them."

Her glare furiously tried to burn through his head.

"They are the reason the servants are here. They wouldn't even *try* to lighten the burden?" Doesn't this just prove what complete zoilists the nobles are? They cannot even admit they have kept people chained at their sides. These... creatures insist on making servants work endlessly. No different from the ones in Poramun Creek, making them work until they are malnourished and falling dead in the fields.

Lord Dominic shook his head as if disappointed in her. If anyone should be in dismay, it was her. No caring human could dare act as if those under their charge were lesser.

No one intercepted them along the way. Calida almost wished something would happen. She didn't want to spend another moment near Lord Dominic, but seeing how her parents abandoned her into his care, she had no other safe option to get back unscathed. No matter how much she begrudged him, she wanted to return home safely. At least, by any consolation, the man was honorable. She wouldn't be murdered, robbed, or stashed away for seconds in his care.

Calida avoided his eyes as she stumbled into the carriage

waiting outside the banquet hall. The road was quiet, the courtyard empty, and the scent of dried maple leaves lingered. He had been right about the party being long over. The cushion was softer than the wood benches in the small carriage her parents had stashed away—if she sat on it wrong, she would get a splinter. Lord Dominic's was fancy, soft and comfortable enough to fall asleep on.

With the reminder of sleep, her eyes began to droop. *Oh no, no, no.* She was in the presence of someone untrustworthy. Sleep could wait. If it happened at all, it could happen in her own bed.

She cut off the yawn with her hand.

Lord Dominic sat comfortably on the bench.

"You must be tired. Feel free to take a nap. I will wake you when we arrive," he said.

She vehemently shook her head, attempting to fight off sleep as it pulled her under until all she could do was flop over and pass out on the bench.

With a gasp, Calida rushed from her bed. The light streaming in was too bright. She blinked and shut her eyes in pain. Her head throbbed mercilessly. Normally she wouldn't have so much to drink, but the upsetting news called for such things. If she admitted it to herself, it could have been far worse. However, she wasn't made for the life of a noble. She wouldn't allow herself to grow weak and vulnerable. It would only end badly.

She dragged herself out of bed and put on the outer garment she had folded next to her pillow, just like her mother had nagged her. All it took was one careless action for it to get chewed by pests. Calida tied her apron around her waist and headed to the main room of their home. Now that she was an adult, it was her job to take care of all the things her mother couldn't. In this case, almost everything.

Once upon a time, Calida had thought it would only be temporary. Just quietly complete the tasks her mother put on her. Some were strenuous for a child and not something she had been used to. Her mother had done everything until the incident. Then slowly it became one thing after another until, before she knew it, it was her job alone.

Her mother was already up and had started breakfast. It was at least one of the few on Cressida's short list of tasks. Many others in town didn't have the luxury of breakfast, but because of her father's job, her family could indulge in luxuries. Every morning, her mother would boil together a helping of grain and sausage. It was not the most lavish, but it was food. There was no flavor or spice. It was enough to have her fighting back the urge to vomit.

She grabbed the wooden bowls and spoons. Her father may be a member of the Elite Dominion, knights of their own making, but that didn't mean they received a lot of special treatment. There were some liberties taken, but a lot of other entitled reimbursements were overlooked. The Faction knights couldn't afford such things as silver spoons and metal bowls. It was normally reserved for those in the noble court and royalty. It was still something they were entitled to buy if they so desired, but the province officials would mutter about a lack of funds to hand out or how they already came to pick up their lot of the reimbursement. Her father frequently spoke in private to her mother about being left out of their share of government funding. Yet another case of the gluttonous nobles and their greedy eyes.

Her father came out of her parent's room. His eyebrows creased as he frowned.

"Darling, I do not regret my decision." His words didn't settle her down at all.

She turned her head around, refusing to address the issue. Her mother brought the food to the table. The three of them sat silently to eat.

"Calida—"

"No, Mother, I don't want to talk about yesterday," she said.

She placed the bowls in the right spots. Her mother looked her way and put a hand on top of hers. Cressida searched Calida's face, a range of emotion flitting across her face, as though she wished her daughter would reconsider. But the light in her eyes was still missing.

Her mother still looked her father's way when he wasn't paying attention. As if to gage whether he noticed Cressida's strained smile and "tender" touch. Even the feeling of guilt for being the wayward daughter wouldn't change her mind. Sometimes Calida felt like all she could do was wrong in every way.

It was like her mother wanted her gone. Even if Cressida didn't, Calida was too useful.

Her throat worked as she held back tears. When envisioning her future, an arranged marriage wasn't something she pictured. Having few prospects in town, she thought she would've captured the attention of a passing traveller who would either take her with him or would stay here in town. It was that or growing old helping her mother with the duties left to a woman. Calida had pictured it more as her growing old alone, perhaps selling paintings. Love had never been in the cards for her. She removed her hand from under her mother's and cleared her throat.

"Can't you just say no?"

Her parents might think they were acting in her best interest, but a marriage of advantage was truly heartbreaking. The realities of what could happen to her circled her mind. What if she was walking into a life of torture, or what if he was a horrible person who liked to share his wife with other men? Calida's face paled at her thoughts. Mentally, she shook off the horror. He seemed nice enough in person, but she could never really know until behind closed doors.

"No, Calida. Someone of our status doesn't just say no to a lord." She slammed her fist on the table. The slap on wood echoed in the room while Calida's heart pounded.

Her body tensed as she fought to straighten out the grimace on her face. Not once had her mother acted out in front of her father. She wouldn't start now.

Then Jetta walked in, looking around at the silent family. Calida breathed in through her nose and then out. She glanced Jetta's way and did a double take. Jetta's official armour had her staring. When on shift, she was expected to dress the part like the rest of the Crescent League faction. Like her father's faction, their reputation hung in the balance. The armour comprised black painted bamboo, shoulder plates, and a crescent league cape. The black and red lent a sense of harsh rigid beliefs.

The Crescent League often produced mercenaries. They believed in the greater good, but the members of the faction did not blindly follow the rules set in place. If there was someone in need of the faction, Crescent League would step up and help. A struggling mother who the nobles had abandoned because of the illegitimate child she birthed, or an elderly man thrown into the streets to die after an injury because he could no longer move.

The Elite Dominion had a different focus. They saw how the commoners were treated by those in positions as knights to the queen. The queen gave them a wonderful opportunity, but those in the higher ranks, specifically the knighted nobles, didn't agree with letting commoners have the same opportunities. Higher ranked knights strictly selected the newcomers and shunted commoners to lower jobs. The Elite Dominion gave the opportunity back for commoners. All commoners, not just the ones the knights could morph into their own little dogs.

"What is with the formal attire today?" Calida asked.

Jetta pursed her lip, then her eyes shifted from familiar to stranger, as if their years of friendship had been set aside.

"Milady, Lord Goldwyn has requested my presence at your side." Jetta saluted and took her position at the door.

Calida's face went slack with realization. He had placed Jetta as her guard. Lord Dominic had used her own friend against her and had her guarding Calida as if she were a lapdog. The very idea had her steaming in her shoes. She could feel more sparks gearing up to pour from every orifice of her body, but she swallowed the anger and addressed Jetta. A bead of sweat rolled down Jetta's face from the temperature change caused by her friend and now, charge.

"I won't need a guard today. You can return to Lord Goldwyn and tell him that." For the first time, she spoke formally to her dear friend.

She wanted to tell Jetta to warn him that Calida would yell his ear off the next time she saw him but knew it would get Jetta in trouble. Her selfish desire to do unspeakable things to her *betrothed* did not mean she should tell Jetta to play messenger and land her in hot water. Betrothed or not, a commoner doesn't threaten someone of nobility without consequences.

Jetta didn't move. Calida cleared her throat. Her mouth opened to speak until she was cut off.

"Milady, I am under the orders of Lord Goldwyn, not you. If I were to move even an inch away from you, then I would put the Crescent League's reputation at risk. The Crescent League is my life. I cannot afford to make a mistake."

Instead of calming her, the statement only riled her up more. *The bastard is truly despicable if he puts such harsh restrictions on her friend.*

"Darling, Jetta is just doing her job. Let her guard you." Rayner laid a hand on her shoulder.

Instead of letting him comfort her, she pushed his hands away and glared. "I do not need a guard and wouldn't subject my friends to such things if this—this arrangement hadn't happened! I-it's like you want to a-attack me…"

Rayner's face fell at her cutting words. Calida's gaze scoured the room in a desperate effort to force the anger out.

"I cannot believe you kept me in the dark about my betrothal! You may be my parents, but I would at least like to know about my obligations!"

Cressida stood from the table and strode toward Calida. She grasped Calida's shoulders with a stern look, a hint of the dark cold eyes staring back at her.

"We are doing this for you, Calida. Some day you will understand."

This was the way it was. Others expected a woman to marry for advantage. If Calida was a different woman, she would completely understand. She was under obligation to listen. They would receive an easier lifestyle and she would live in the lap of luxury. Calida *understood* perfectly. Life as she knew it would be a long suffering one from now on.

Cressida wrapped her arms around Calida and pulled her tight. She struggled to be free, but her mother held her closer as she fought against the crawling feeling that dug into her chest. *Stop. Stop. Stop!* Her skin itched as she resisted the urge to fight free. Her head swam as her mother's mouth touched her ear.

"How dare you be so selfish. Yelling at your father when he only wants the best for you." Her mother's hushed tone tickled Calida's ear. She fought to glare over her shoulder. "You are going to apologize to your father when we part."

Cressida released her. Calida's throat dried up as she summoned the anger back.

"Did you do something you weren't supposed to, father?" Calida gritted her teeth. "Are you in some kind of debt?"

Her father glanced at the floor.

Glaring at her parents, she stepped away from them and sat once more at the table to eat her breakfast. The conversation was most definitely not over, but the conclusion scared her the most. Giving up hope, happiness, and peace didn't scare her as much as being forever a prisoner under her mother's control.

Five

The rest of the day, Calida completed her chores in begrudging silence. Any time her mother tried to be affectionate, which she always did at the wrong time, she would glare and move away. One part of her felt ill while being so rude to her parents, but sometimes maintaining the happy cloud her mother wanted was impossible.

Calida's eyes stung with tears brought on by the overwhelming emotions.

She spent her day shopping for food her mother would use and sweeping out the house. She also skinned an animal and prepared it for dinner. Calida had learned from a young age to care for the family. Cressida did little to help, and the stresses of the household fell on Calida's shoulders alone.

Rayner couldn't contribute to a conversation at the same time as he was shining his shoes and armour.

Although Mother won't let him get a word in edgewise.

As a guard of knighthood status in his faction, the Elite Dominion valued his appearance, so it was vital that he keep his armour and shoes in good condition to represent the reputation of the country and faction correctly. The Queen would pay for the services of extra guards in the palace in moments of political gatherings. Otherwise, her father was stationed at base camp.

One time, he was focused on shining a dull spot he had missed when his wife asked him where his daughter was. Calida was fourteen years old and had just come of age. There were many dishonourable men in town, lecherous monsters who would rather take than ask. They were interested in her beauty, so Cressida was constantly monitoring her. Cressida called to Rayner five times before she received a response, each time sounding more and more harried until she was shouting. He had been so focused on his task that he had even tuned out his wife. It was not something that he meant to do; it was something that just happened.

The couple had spent a while searching for Calida before they found her on the side of the road that led into town. She had been looking at a bush of wildflowers as Cressida rushed up to her, followed shortly by Rayner in a jog. Her mother had been frantic by the time they had found her.

Calida had been so lost in thoughts she had not realized the time had flown by. Back then, she had been longing to have a true, loving connection. She had been sitting in the meadow, fantasizing about a man of tall, dark, and handsome features sweeping her off her feet. Then she would follow him on his travels around the world, always supporting him and at the ready when needed for something other than chores. As a young, fanciful girl, she had even sworn to herself she would do the dreadful chores for her lover, if that was needed. Calida made it clear she wouldn't nag. She would communicate clearly and reasonably.

The exact opposite of her mother's frenzied, irrational need to know every detail, to control everything.

Calida knelt beside the pot over the fire. Several hours had passed, and the sun was setting. The dark crept in quickly.

Dinnertime was around the corner, and the women were concerned. Jetta had left for her night guard shift at the Crescent League Chancery, leaving another guard in her place. Calida was still peeved, but slowly adjusted to the announcement of her betrothal. She didn't want to stay at Lord Dominic's side but accepted the fact that she needed to be wed to him for the sake of her parents. She had come to the bitter understanding it was not for the sake of love but for the sake of comfort. *At least she would be free to paint.*

Cressida served up the food even though her father hadn't arrived. Calida glanced down the road and then served a bowl for herself.

They were just waiting for Rayner to return. It was unlike him to come back so late, but she was determined to think positively. He could've been delayed.

ealtime had come and gone. They couldn't wait for him. Cressida had stored some dinner away in a cloth with salts so Rayner could eat it when he got back. However, the women were becoming less and less hopeful. Calida stood and sat down restlessly. Rayner would come home on time most nights but to be this late was unusual.

The remaining light faded, and they began scouring the pot when a soldier wearing the armour she had seen so many times before marched up to them. Calida shook her head. Other soldiers didn't visit their home. The timing was too perfect.

Father is not returning home.

The women stood frozen, bracing for the news. Behind him, Lord Dominic approached. What they hoped wasn't the situation was, in fact, true.

Calida's father, Sir Rayner Rhodes, was dead.

"I am deeply sorry to inform you of the passing of your father and husband, Sir Rayner Rhodes. May you be prosperous," the soldier said as Cressida wept.

Doom weighed on Calida's chest. She would never see her father again. The soldier implied that her father had confronted a thief in the palace and died. The motives of the thief were still unknown, but the knights would investigate.

Pressure built in her chest. Not a single tear fell from her eyes, but a deep, piercing agony sunk into the marrow of her bones. It was like nothing she had ever felt before. All she could think about was the fight they had that morning. How the words she spat at her father were so cutting and cruel. A blanket of guilt and despair sat upon her like weighted manacles.

Lord Dominic offered himself as comfort to Calida. Instead of hugging him, she punched his chest, the only expression of her inner turmoil. A grunt whispered from him, but he remained unmovable. Inside her mind, she screamed and writhed, scratched her eyes out and tugged her hair. On the outside, she was a statue. Lord Dominic stepped forward and held her. She stood there in utter despondency.

He whispered empty comforts and gently rocked where he stood. He hummed a lullaby until she cracked, then he restarted the whispering. A tear spilled down her cheek and the floodgates broke. *He's... gone.*

"In, in the stormy sea," Lord Dominic's softly sung to Calida. Her head pressed deep into her arms, shielding the sides of her face and burrowing as if the pain was too much for her to handle. "There is a song for me. It only calls the brave to sleep away the day." His low voice vibrated through the air as she wept harder. Not a sound left her throat.

The bush that stood by caught fire as Calida's pain pushed outward. Her body radiated so much heat that the dried leaves caught fire, and Lord Dominic broke into a sweat. It was a miracle he wasn't developing burns.

Cressida's weeping grew louder as she collapsed on the ground.

"Legends, the legends ring true. Worthy, it could happen to you," Calida weakly sang in response.

Commonly sung among those who lost a loved one. Parents taught it to children as they went to bed. The song was tragic. About a man and woman. Their forbidden love and their demise, thanks to their warring countries. As the two hummed the song, her mother wept louder and louder until neither could hear anything but her hollow, soulless screeching. Even in a moment like this, her mother desired all the attention.

After a long period of tears, they stood in shock. When the family returned to their senses, the soldier was gone. Lord Dominic stood at a distance now. *Thank Eesa he is staying away. If he tries to hold me again, I don't know what I will do.* She closed her eyes and inhaled deeply.

Calida rose and collected the food off the ground. Doing something would keep her busy. Keep her sane. Neither her mother nor herself would eat any more tonight. Calida refused to address Lord Dominic's presence or acknowledge he was there. Talking to him now when she was so sensitive was too soon.

She bristled at the thought of talking to someone about her feelings.

"Men are untrustworthy." Her mother had taught her that allowing a man to see her anything but smiling was unladylike. What she knew of being ladylike came from her mother's example. Cressida would decide what was important to do. What they must accomplish in life, but never did she run it by Calida's father. Her mother would choose for everyone while he wouldn't say a word in opposition. Not that Calida could

blame him much. Her mother would rip someone a new one if her choices were put into question.

Cressida and Calida turned in for the night, and Lord Dominic left.

I t was late in the day when the pair dragged themselves into the living area. Calida's face was pale from the lack of sleep. She slumped at the table in the living area, unable to speak out from pain of the loss. It hurt to think about her father. He would want her to stay with Lord Dominic.

In the late night, between exhaustion and delirium, she decided she would accept the betrothal. For her mother, and for her father. He had kept her mother from completely falling apart. Calida didn't want to be around to see that. The future of her family was at stake if she didn't make the right choice. This was about more than just her. Her obligations needed to come first, and that meant it was her responsibility to focus on what her family expected of her. Her father had wanted her to marry Lord Dominic, so it would happen, regardless of her desire.

A blunt knife twisted inside her heart, and emotions gripped her throat and staggered her breathing. Her chest hurt as her lungs fought to breathe.

Emotions are weakness.

As she grew more and more annoyed by her grief, Calida pushed aside the emotions that would weaken her. Maybe the soldier had the wrong man? There could also be a chance the knights finally went beyond mockery and Rayner hid after getting back at them.

Her father couldn't truly be dead.

That was when Lord Dominic made an appearance,

accompanied by Jetta and another guard. The other guard was tall, intimidating, and brooding. Not someone to meet in a dark alleyway.

Lord Dominic strode up to Calida and crouched beside her. She sat outside her home trying to drown her grief in work and picked at the stalks of wheat scattered around her. Normally, she would put it all on a large flatbed and then shake the grains off the stems so she could separate the wheat with ease and efficiency. However, today Calida had the *brilliant* idea it would be more appropriate to her cloudy mood if she were to handpick the grains. At first it seemed like a good idea, but with the heat surrounding her, she accomplished nothing.

Skreyja! This was a stupid idea!

As time passed, Calida took out her frustration on the grains. The effort was fruitless by this point and a screaming meltdown threatened, where she would kick and stomp on the grains.

It doesn't matter...I don't... Emotions are weakness.

Heat radiated around her, the familiar flame sparking inside.

When the trio walked up to her, it took everything she had not to set the wheat on fire. When she thought about it, she knew that was a bad move. She wanted to set fire to all her enemies, though.

"Calida, it's time to discuss the details around your father's passing," Lord Dominic said. She stood up and faced him.

"If, if he actually died." Calida wouldn't admit he was dead yet.

Lord Dominic looked at her in surprise. He gazed at his guards before he addressed her. Stepping closer, he motioned them inside her home. She shoved past him as he attempted to guide her with a hand on the small of her back.

This was her chance to do right by her father. She could find out what happened on her own.

Her shoulders rolled back as she realized could have a true purpose for once. Lord Dominic followed her in as she plunked down on a seat at the table. Cressida was inside and looked their way when Lord Dominic entered behind Calida. Instead of pulling on her "perfect" hostess smile or a passive aggressive greeting as usual, she walked out the front door with a resigned stare. *Not even a word?*

"If you need me, I will finish the sifting of the *discarded* wheat." Cressida's words cut through her daughter like a sharp knife.

As if sitting for a moment to hear about her father's death was selfish. Did her mother not want to hear what had happened to her husband? This wasn't the time to ask those types of questions. Rayner's death was the most important question now. If he was still alive, then she needed to be on the move. Jetta stood behind Calida as the other guard stood behind Lord Dominic.

"Milord, how could my father be dead? It's more likely they have the wrong man." *Or the guards were sloppy in their check to see if he was dead, and my father escaped before death claimed him.*

Lord Dominic folded his arms and then sternly gazed at her, taking a moment of silence to consider her statement.

"I have considered that possibility. But before anything else, you should hear what happened."

He laid out the scene. Rayner had been on duty, patrolling the hallway on the floor of the treasury room. Same as the hundreds of other shifts, it seemed uneventful. There were no noises, no suspicious characters around or items that seemed out of place. That had been his first mistake. The guard who informed Lord Dominic of this told him that her father had done a sloppy job.

It wasn't long before a man jumped him from behind and knocked him out. Rayner had awoken moments later, only to panic as he searched the rooms on his floor to make sure nothing had been taken. After checking three of the four rooms, he had become too relaxed. The guard assumed it was because the other valuable items were left untouched. This was Rayner's second mistake.

Whoever it was had much more interest in the last room of the floor. Rayner had been stabbed and choked within seconds of entering.

The guards for the next shift had found him there, deducing thieves looking to make a good paycheck had killed him for the Queen's valuables.

Rayner's death would thus be forgotten as a botched robbery.

"The only item taken was a common fire gem. Odd for a worthless trinket to be in the queen's belongings," Lord Dominic said.

A fire gem was a beautiful jewel discovered ages ago. They look like they held a tiny flame inside them, frozen in place. Soon enough, their value plummeted, and many considered them a useless trinket now. Calida wore one around her neck, something her father had gifted her because it was cheap enough that commoners could afford them. It was strange the queen would only have one in her belongings. When it was first found, it would have been of high value.

Calida smacked her hands on the table.

"You mean to tell me my father, an expert hunter and exceptional faction knight, was offed by a mere thief?! And just how did this guard know so much about the events anyway? How could he trace every step so easily?"

Lord Dominic sighed and wiped his face.

"A guard claimed to have placed a surveillance amulet on

your father upon his entry to the palace. However, no one can find it, and the guard has recanted on that claim."

Calida pushed out of her seat and paced while biting down on her thumbnail.

That guard is suspicious. How can he know so much but have so little evidence? My father's supposed death is suspicious as it is.

Six

Calida shook her head. Her heart throbbed painfully with the realization of what Lord Dominic said. It was never easy to hear about death. It's still possible he's alive. But the explanation made the chance slim. *Please let Father still be alive.*

Even if they framed him, all she wanted was her father back. He would stand up for what was right every time. That was exactly what she was worried about. *Dear Eesa, let Father be the one to walk away alive.*

She knew he couldn't live forever. Eventually he would die, but it wasn't like him to act like a burlufotr. He was a hunter and knew the craft well. She still remembered those special moments on a hunting trip together.

The leaves fell around them as she followed her father, trying to walk silently but failing miserably. However, instead of Rayner telling her to stay where she was, saying that she was too loud, and he would do it alone. Her father got her to walk the path alone as he snuck in the brush. *Just walk loud, darling. Do not worry about being quiet.* He startled her later down the path when the deer she had found ran away from her and right into Rayner's range.

He had taught his daughter how to stalk prey, using the environment and party members to her advantage. It was not only useful when wanting to hunt for food, but it was also useful when enemies were nearby. Even during the last couple of years where he was distant, Rayner's words stuck with Calida. Her beloved father was still in her thoughts, even when he spent more time working than at home.

The rule, he told her over and over, was *never dismiss the signs in front of you.*

No matter how much she felt like an idiot, if Calida saw the signs of game while she and her father were out hunting for deer, he praised the instinct. Most of the time, it was worthwhile, and they came back with a hefty slab of meat, but there were also those times where it was just a rabbit.

Those times reminded her that her father wouldn't just dismiss anything with the flip of a coin. Rayner being knocked out was the biggest red flag out there.

Whoever reported him didn't know about his instincts and intuition to sense danger. Whoever it was saw no harm in spreading such a ridiculous tale. *It wasn't him.* Her fists clenched at the idea of her father's reputation being tainted.

In Eonifond, reputation was everything. Some people would kill to keep an excellent reputation. That is why no one could admit how awful Lord Sullivan was. Calida had heard whispers here and there, but nothing that solidly proved his lustful habits. It was also why exemplary faction members rarely received the coin that they should . Nobles would get wealthier while the commoners would get poorer.

"That guard had to be daufi." Calida nibbled on her nails as she muttered under her breath.

"Hmm?" Jetta looked her way.

Calida shook her head and followed the lord's lead.

The four of them left her home. She peeked over at her mother once more before leaving, hoping for a heartfelt moment. It disheartened her to realize her mother was in the garden, looking the other way. As she watched, Cressida stepped normally and then pulled down at the last moment, almost like she was faking a limp. Even from across the way, it sounded like she was whimpering. Calida would have felt sympathy and told the others she would stay if it wasn't for the glimpses Calida caught before her mother whimpered louder.

Calida narrowly held back a grimace of disgust as the group walked away. How often had it been that her mother would play the sick and injured woman just so things would go her way? Calida remembered many times after the *incident* where her mother played this game of being crippled and ill, only to run around the house when Calida finished the work.

"It is only right to take care of me. Or was Mother too horrible a person to think of?"

The memory of when her mother said that haunted her. How many mothers pouted, then snarled when things did not go her way? She couldn't think of another. She had never met another mother personally to even know. Maybe it was normal.

Alongside their guards, Lord Dominic and she strode to the horses tied down nearby. What had made the most sense to Calida had been to mount with Jetta. However, Jetta took that choice out of her hands when she loaded packages of food and other necessary things onto her horse and then mounted.

"Must we ride together? Is it not possible to have me on a different horse? Or you ride with him?" Calida looked the earl's way as she gestured to the other guard.

Lord Dominic gazed into her eyes as he firmly spoke. "A single horse could not manage the weight of two fully grown men who weigh one cart of flour bags."

Calida folded her arms as she struggled to produce a solution, while the unnamed guard mounted his horse and joined Jetta on the road to wait for the couple. She would rather do anything else than sit with Lord Dominic.

Now, that is a lie.

She would love to sit on the horse in front of him. It was the scandalous feeling bubbling up in her belly she didn't want. It was foreign, and the unknown scared her.

They had only just met and were becoming acquainted with one another. Sharing a horse ride felt too intimate and personal. She was not used to sharing a horse with someone, not that she had ridden much. Neither her mother nor she had one, only her father. They didn't ride when he was home because he needed the horse for his job. Calida would never forgive herself if the horse got injured by her, like her mother always suggested would happen. Her body stiffened as she remembered what her mother repeated whenever the opportunity came up.

"Why isn't Calida capable of doing such a simple thing?"

"If only my daughter could do more."

She was perfect until the *incident*. It had her mother defenseless.

Emotions were weakness.

How could she get out of this one? It was not like she had much of a choice now that the only horse available was Lord Dominic's.

Her reluctance had absolutely nothing to do with the pull she felt toward him. Not anything to do with keeping herself from gazing longingly at his shoulders and wishing she were in his firm embrace. Desiring to stare at his blue eyes, so dark they resembled the water on the deep parts of a river. *He isn't my type of man.*

Calida mentally kicked herself. Would lying somehow change her body? With a grumble, Calida admitted he was downright gorgeous. And she wanted to punch him for it.

They had not known each other long enough for her to even entertain intimate thoughts about him. It was not even sensible to think they should be that close so soon.

Calida inserted her foot into the stirrup and launched herself into the saddle, hoping to collapse on it in such a manner that left no more room for Lord Dominic. As she fell forward on the horse, her body covered not only the back of the saddle but the rest of it and the neck of the horse. The hard ridges between the saddle seat dug into her stomach.

"Oops." She smiled innocently.

With a small smirk, Lord Dominic handed his horse's reins to the nameless guard who had somehow appeared in front of the horse she mounted. The earl gestured with his head.

The horse lurched forward, and Calida squealed as she scrambled on the saddle and gripped the neck of the horse, momentarily forgetting her attempt to keep the lord off the horse. As she hung onto the horse's neck to keep from falling off, Lord Dominic mounted behind Calida and let out a long sigh as he nestled in the seat.

He leaned forward and whispered in her ear. "Your attempts to keep me off my horse seemed to have failed, Calida." His voice, laced with humour, grated on her patience. Of course, the honourable Earl of Weommadran wouldn't be stopped by such a childish action. Why would a great and mighty man such as him fall prey to the scheming of a woman? Her eyes rolled mentally with the sardonic tone of her thoughts.

"I believe we can agree that we should head to Weommadran to talk with the nobles," Lord Dominic said.

She agreed they needed to head to the capital of Eleari, but that didn't mean she had to voice it. His ego was large enough. Calida felt his amusement coming off him in waves and folded her arms as she straightened up. *Even if I lean against him, it won't affect me. Maybe.*

Lord Dominic wrapped his arms around her.

"Don't—"

His hands moved the reins in front of her as he respectfully leaned back and spoke to her.

"Yes? You were saying something?" His voice was laced with laughter.

"Nothing, milord." She choked back a grumble.

An awkward silence settled over them, then he snapped the horse's reins, jolting her until she was leaning against him. The group set out on their journey down the dirt path through the forest. The surrounding trees all blended into the familiar color of home.

Before leaving town, the group stopped in town to gather supplies for their trip. Jetta slipped off her horse and started to walk off before Calida called for her to wait.

Turning around, Jetta walked over to Lord Dominic's horse. "Yes?"

"I want to come with you."

Jetta stared at her, then glanced at the earl before turning her attention back to Calida. She shrugged and helped Calida off the horse.

They walked the short distance to the noisy market. Staying close to Jetta, Calida tried not to get shoved by the busy buyers. It was still morning, so the new, shiny merchandise was still sitting on the sellers' tables. Calida grabbed Jetta's sleeve as a large man shoved into her, almost toppling her over.

Jetta glared at the man over their shoulders, then wrapped an arm around her friend. As always, Calida's best friend took on the protector role. Ever since they met, Jetta had been there to keep her safe. From that day forward, she had vowed her allegiance to Calida and became her shield.

Back then, a strange man had been about to drag off

Calida when Jetta had appeared out of nowhere and socked him in the groin. Jetta had berated her for being in such a dangerous part of town and muttered about having to stick to her like glue so Calida wouldn't come to harm. That was when she had vowed to her.

Calida had been startled and couldn't understand what came over her friend. It was one thing to promise, but another to *vow*. In the middle of a dirt road just outside town, her friend had gotten down on one knee and bowed to her. She held her hand to her collarbone and made the vow a knight made to the queen, like the ones mentioned in the children's stories she was told as a young girl. Chills had filled her as her friend bowed her head to Calida with glazed eyes. It wasn't like anything she had seen before.

Ever since, Calida rarely went to a market without her friend.

They stopped at a stall and inspected the fruit.

Jetta picked up an apple and turned it over in her hand. As she looked at it, the owner of the stall in conversation a step away saw Jetta holding his merchandise.

His face reddened as he paused his conversation and stomped over to his stall.

"Hands off the merchandise, *thrall*," he snapped as he ripped the apple from Jetta's hand.

Calida stiffened at the slur. *Thrall*. Her friend's dress and mannerisms showed just how wrong the man was. The slave market hadn't enslaved Jetta to anyone.

The fire inside her warmed as her ire grew. Those around here held a prejudice against the children who grew up in an orphanage. The chances of orphans making it anywhere but a grave were slim. If they weren't "protected" by Lord Sullivan, they were enslaved, became thieves, or died.

Jetta rose past all that and to be accepted in the Crescent League, a difficult feat. If you were delicate or meek, there was no surviving the Crescent League's initiation phase. Her friend had told her of the test she had to pass. It took her months, but eventually she climbed to the top.

"Mister, is this how you address customers?"

The man looked at her and his mannerism changed.

With an enormous smile, he said. "Ah, young maiden, you wish to buy this apple? Please keep your thrall's hands off my products. It would only spread dangerous energy."

Calida had been frowning, but now she was scowling thunderously. She tried to breathe in her nose and out to keep the fire at bay. The heat built in her belly as his words swirled in her mind.

Keep your thrall's hands off my products.

She had been so absorbed in her attempt at controlling the boiling anger that it startled Calida when Jetta gripped the man's tunic. Her face was just as thunderous.

The man looked between them with desperation on his face.. "Miss, please command your slave back!"

With an audible snap, the boiling rage Calida had tried to keep contained spilled out. The flame from her belly spread like it had at the wedding and lit her hair with a life of its own. Each strand took on the glowing orange, yellow, and red, soaking it in like a piece had been missing.

The man blubbered as his eyes widened. He was no longer speaking any sense. His body shook as he desperately begged Calida. The trader was still not paying attention to Jetta.

Others were paying attention now, and the customers and sellers stopped what they were doing. Several people tripped in the street as they stared at her glowing hair.

Shit. Too much attention.

While magic was a normal part of life in Eonifond, hair on fire was an oddity. A fire user could wield it through their body, but for it to stay on your body was unheard of. It had never been determined if a fire user could burn themselves, but Calida proved they could not. The magic of fire was fickle. Calida remembered hearing whispers from other townsfolk about accounts of people with fire magic or other elemental magic becoming victims of their own abilities.

What if her magic was unstable and she made herself a victim?

Calida inhaled sharply.

The fire in Calida's hair flickered larger. In every direction it moved, the crowd scrambled away. Many women whimpered as they held back their children in fear. The men either look petrified or were ready to jump in if they needed to.

Whispering echoed in the crowd. "Is that Zabul? The second coming isn't upon us yet!"

A woman yelped and the people surrounding her murmured. Some ran.

I'm not the false Eesian!

Her gasps filled her ears.

Calida's full attention was on the man in front of her. He had been reduced to tears and pulled at Jetta's hands.

"Please, miss, remove her hands!"

She stared him down as she said, "She has her own autonomy. Jetta Arundel of the Crescent League will remove her hands from your tunic when she has decided you are adequately apologetic."

The man's eyes widened as he looked at Jetta in fear.

"C-Crescent League? M-Miss, you are from Crescent League?"

Jetta glared down at the man as she clenched her fist tighter into his tunic and pulled him closer.

"Now that I have your attention, you *bacraut,* let us talk about *skreyja beiskaldi pik.*"

Calida took a deep breath, in and then out. The rage inside her clouded her eyes. *Focus.* She breathed in and out slowly. She didn't want to set another building on fire.

Her hair simmered down as she exhaled, but it still wasn't enough. Calida walked closer to Jetta.

"Jetta, I cannot call back my fire."

Her friend glanced over, then did a startled double take at Calida's hair. The anger fell away from her face, and her mouth gaped open in surprise. The surrounding people were staring and growing restless with Calida's presence.

Jetta reluctantly let go of the man's tunic and pushed him away from her. It disgusted Calida to even look at him for his behaviour. Mentioning Crescent League had been what it took to give her attention.

Jetta bit her lip and then gestured for Calida to take a step back.

One final whisper in the man's ear and her friend joined her.

"Ready to go now. Just going to leave with an incentive to come back."

The silent man gestured toward his merchandise, encouraging the girls to take whatever they desired. Jetta loaded up bags of fruit, bread, and preserved goods. Calida tapped her foot anxiously as the crowd grew louder. Any longer and they would start a mob.

The man didn't say a thing as Jetta carried the food to Calida without paying. Calida squinted her eyes in confusion as Jetta passed the bag of fruit to her. The man was in the wrong, but was it right to take the product without paying?

Her friend shook her head and guided Calida through the crowd toward the horses. There would be nothing else they could get from this market.

As they moved through the crowd, people jumped out of the way, as if she was contagious. She didn't realize that fire was a disease to be feared

Calida rolled her eyes as they shouted to expel Zabul from the "poor girl."

When the crowd dispersed to flee from Calida, Jetta dragged her to the local well near the market.

Luckily, there was no one around. Calida leaned on the stone wall of the well as Jetta threw a bucket down and brought the water up. In a quick movement, her friend dumped the contents of the bucket onto her head, dousing the fire.

After the adventure in town, Jetta and Calida arrived back at the horses, wet, tired, and holding food. Neither wanted to talk about how they came to be wet and why they both looked like they could kill someone now.

Silently, Calida mounted the horse in front of Lord Dominic again and ignored his raised eyebrows along with his expression, which implied, "*What happened while you were in the market?*"

Calida scowled at him and grumbled, "I don't want to talk about it."

Lord Dominic reached around her and snapped the reins to continue their journey. Jetta guided them on the back roads around the market until they left town.

After the incident in the market, Calida wished to just lie down and forget. And her hunger grew stronger the further they moved. As the group galloped the forest road away from Poramun Creek, Calida's stomach let out a long, gurgling protest.

Leaning forward, Lord Dominic pressed his warm body against hers. Calida had this desire to turn around on the horse and wrap herself around him. Her eyes drooped and if it wasn't for the last scrap of restraint, she would nuzzle into the crook of his neck, social etiquette be damned. Soon it was not only the warmth of his body, but the warmth of the blush on her cheeks too. They had only just met. It was unlike her.

"Braxton, Jetta, we will stop here for now. The horses need

a snack and some water." Jetta and Braxton looked their way and nodded in tandem.

So, his name is Braxton.

She was so delirious now that the earlier thoughts didn't even bother her. Calida was not the type to be so hedonistic, but she didn't have it in her to be horrified by it. *Must eat.*

She dismounted the horse and walked over to where Jetta was setting up a cloth with dried meat for them to nibble on.

Calida sat down next to her. She hoped by sitting beside her friend, Lord Dominic wouldn't sit next to her. Not only would he fluster her, but he would also affect her focus on refueling. His presence was very distracting, and while in this state, Calida didn't know what she might say. *Anything to get food.*

To put it simply, she could spill her darkest desires in this moment. She would love to have him in the crossfire of her ire. *No, that is not polite. He is nobility.* She didn't need to become like the nobles she despised.

Lord Dominic walked to the side with Braxton to chat about something privately.

Calida scarfed down several pieces of dried meat and then grabbed the charcoal and paper Jetta had packed. She loved to sketch whatever she could when she got the chance, especially nature.

Seated against a tree, she positioned herself so she could see the others and the horses.

She began sketching the area. Starting with Jetta, she sketched out her basic shapes and then blended and fixed it to her liking. Next, she moved on to the surrounding trees and the shrubbery. She kept drawing until she had completed the entire scene around them. She had been finishing Lord Dominic's features in heavy layers when she returned to reality, appalled by her incomplete detail on one part of the sketch.

She slammed it down and looked up to see Lord Dominic smirking at her. He lifted an eyebrow in interest at her constant attention on him. Suddenly embarrassed, she rushed to her feet and busied her hands with the blankets and leftover food, along with her drawings.

Calida packed it up, hoping to hide the drawing and how flustered she was. *Hopefully, he doesn't peek in the pouch.*

Her body no longer felt like it was eating itself from the inside out. Calida had continued to munch on the dried meat while she had been drawing. However, now that he had given her that look, her stomach was all butterflies and her heart felt fluttery in that way after flirting with a crush. The small part of her, the anxious part, worried about that type of gaze. She didn't have any experience with people who could belittle you with a smirk and the cock of an eyebrow, but it was that feeling inside her. That implication of what it could mean.

He could simply be amused, but she wouldn't know because it didn't exist much in her life. It could be the gentle teasing between friends, but she had never seen it before so she could only guess. Calida closed her eyes and clenched her jaw.

Lord Dominic is an arrogant prick. She tried to convince herself he couldn't be anything else in her eyes.

"If you are uncomfortable with sitting with Lord Dominic, we could switch." Jetta stood close, keeping the conversation private. She had always been considerate. There were times that Calida had envied how she had all the features to draw in a man. She had the shiny black hair and eyes that someone could see a soul in. Even though she was rough around the edges and tended to violence, Calida could see the kindness in her soul.

Jetta was capable of so much love. Love that turned Jetta's eyes dark. Calida's closest friend refused the best thing she could have, the most powerful ability. Something she wished she could open herself to. Something that she wanted to feel for herself, and now it was too late. *Who could love someone to blame for her mother's assault?*

Her heart hurt as the sensation of guilt and punishment fell onto her.

"I will be fine sitting with Lord Goldwyn. Thank you for the offer."

Jetta's mouth fell open. Calida could count on her fingers the number of people she used formality with. Lord Goldwyn was exactly what she would call him. If only in hopes that the distance in intimacy the title might offer would create a larger divide in her heart. That she could shut down the flapping of wings in her heart ready to fly his way. It would be too painful.

T hey continued on their way, making stops and having moments of rest until they reached Weommadran in time for dinner. There was no more confusion regarding her emotions about Lord Dominic. It was quiet the rest of the way.

Jetta took the reins of the horses and settled them in the nearby stable while Lord Dominic guided Calida toward the castle. The setting sun created a rainbow of colours across the sky. Calida didn't bother to ask who owned this castle because there were too many nobles in the court to even remember them all by name. Many who filled the court were also only courtiers, competing for the attention of the noblemen. Once chosen as a courtier, they could continue to visit the court on events open to them in hopes of seducing a nobleman. Within reason, of course. Only the most cool-headed, well-mannered, and proper bearing got chosen to be a companion.

Calida stepped into a grand foyer shining with metal on everything.

It seemed today the nobles were having dinner together to

celebrate. What they were celebrating, Calida didn't know. They found something every fortnight. Sometimes it was just the latest kill a nobleman accomplished. Noise echoed in the halls and laughter rang high pitch.

With the sun setting behind the trees, the air had a bit of a chill to it. She shivered. Lord Dominic glanced her way and produced the cape he had been wearing. With careful practice, he placed it on her shoulders. She opened her mouth in protest, but he stopped her.

"You may use my cape until you are warm." He smiled softly.

She knew he was offering her to use it for as long as she needed, but that didn't change her debt. She sighed and took his extended arm. Together they strode into the full hall.

Knives clattered against plates and conversation filled the room. Calida stood beside Dominic, listening to the noble's blather about boring subjects.

If there was any time she could fall asleep even while so tense, it was now.

There were some moments here and there where she brought up recent news and they just commented and moved on. The same noblewomen from the wedding were here and obviously displeased with Calida's arrival.

Lord Dominic escorted Calida on his arm farther into the hall. Near the closest table in the room sat two young women and two young men who looked to be Lord Dominic's peers. The two women had drastically distinct looks. The one on the left had dark hair and porcelain skin. Her clothes spoke of her wealth and abundance. The other woman had lighter hair, almost like copper, and a light tan, but her clothes were obviously worn and patched.

Lord Dominic released Calida's arm when they stopped at the table.

The dark-haired woman immediately stood up and fell all

over Lord Dominic. She invaded his personal space and gazed up at him with doe eyes. This woman had all her attention on the lord and didn't notice the company beside him.

"Milord, we meet again," the woman said softly and moved away. Without breaking eye contact, she curtsied.

"Lady Evaine l'Orphelin. Allow me to introduce my betrothed." Lord Dominic guided Calida closer with a hand on her back.

Lady Orphelin looked at Calida, stricken. Her lips parted and tears swirled in her gaze. Calida realized that she hoped to be Lady Goldwyn.

Lady Orphelin didn't respond again. This time, the lighter-haired woman spoke.

"If you are expecting a polite and cheerful response from Lady Evaine, milord, then you are sorely mistaken," the light-haired woman said. "You should know better than anyone that she was originally your betrothed." She stood up from her seat and laid a hand on Lady Evaine's shoulder. "Duke Goldwyn himself spoke fondly of Lady Evaine. He promised her you two would marry."

Lord Dominic's face was impassive and unmoved.

Calida wanted to explain she didn't think this would be permanent, but Lord Dominic's hand stiffened on her back, stopping her from any comments.

"Mistress Vaughan. My father may have said such things, but I am in control of my choice. I have chosen my bride-to-be for a reason," Lord Dominic said.

This declaration startled Calida. She thought her father had chosen him. That there was some debt to settle, and she needed to play her part for her family. She stared at him in bewilderment.

That Lord Dominic had chosen her made her uncomfortable. When would they have met for him to know she was marriage material. She searched her memory and came up with a blank. There was no one she knew who would have been around her long enough to form such a strong stance. Calida shook her head.

Little Calida laughed as she ran past her father at his post at Duchess Goldwyn's side. The grass brushed against the dress her mother made for her. It was still too big, but she liked wearing it like she was playing dress up.

A mess of blond hair stuck out from the bush up ahead and the four-year-old giggled as she tugged on it as she ran by. A yelp and a tumble followed while she ran past the flowers then circled around until she reached the blanket where Her Grace sat, and Rayner stood with his armor on.

Calida ran up to the blanket and snuck a honey-glazed pastry from little Dominic's plate. She took a large bite while Maud Lilla Goldwyn let out a warning cut off by a small body tackled Calida to the ground and squished her into the blanketed grass.

"That was my treat, my lady," a blond boy with piercing blue eyes accused.

A crumble-crusted face smiled on the blanket and then shoved more into her cheeks until Calida resembled a chipmunk.

"Hey!" the eight-year-old yelled out.

A pout formed on his face as Calida giggled with crumbs flying everywhere.

"My snack, Du-Nic!" she said.

Calida pushed away the vague image of a boy with blond hair.

Lord Dominic continued to speak with the two young women. Calida disregarded the conversation. Her attention wrapped around the confusing question blaring in her mind. *Who was the little boy to me?*

He led her around and asked the nobles about her father until his name coming from a woman caught her attention.

"Do you mean that low-life knight who couldn't keep his

fingers to himself? I think that's what his name was," the noblewoman drawled. She fluffed up her hair and adjusted her dress as she moved around.

She looked at Lord Dominic with a longing gaze. "What purpose could talking about him gain? He had it coming."

Seven

er teeth clenched as she held back her fist and the desire to sock the so-called lady in the face. *How dare this wench speak about my father in such a manner?*

Lord Dominic held her hand and squeezed briefly before letting it go.

"Isn't it odd that he would take that moment? Assuming he is guilty."

Calida gazed sharply at Lord Dominic. *What point he is trying to get at? If he is on my side, he should just say it.*

Calida clenched her teeth. His roundabout way of conversation grated on her patience. She wanted the answers to the niggling questions this second, but Lord Dominic had this irritating way of circling it strategically instead of asking bluntly. Rarely did she become this irritated and riled enough to forget all pretenses, usually because she didn't let herself feel any emotions at all.

The noblewoman sniffed. "The only thing odd was that the other low-life guards weren't on duty at the same time.

Luckless sacks, the lot of them. It would be foolish to think they were innocent."

She fluffed her hair again and adjusted the soft shawl draped on her shoulders. The woman didn't even acknowledge Calida, who was standing between her and Lord Dominic. Her lustful eyes examined Lord Dominic with disturbing intensity. The woman seemed to have completely forgotten that she had accused the guards on duty of being responsible for the incident. Calida stepped forward to waggle a finger in her face, only the earl's hand pulled her back. She had a choice word or two to say as well, but Lord Dominic spoke first.

"I say, my lady, how would you even know they were on duty or not? You don't look the type to consort with such people," Lord Dominic scolded.

Calida's eyes widened as she realized what he was getting at.

The bumbling idiot was actually deviously clever.

Lord Dominic had not only interrupted her, but now he was talking as if she and her class were second-rate. If it wasn't for the fact she saw the little details in the conversation, she would be bursting at the seams. And if not for her desire to hear what the noblewoman had to say, she would have pummelled the lady, damn the consequences, and then made a swift escape. A part of her understood she could only accomplish so much alone. It was not comforting to admit, but Lord Dominic held power and sway over the people of the court, unlike her.

The noblewoman leaned forward to rest a hand on his arm, then addressed Lord Dominic as if speaking a sultry secret. She puckered her lips out as she gazed up at him, attempting to look like a sexy but hapless woman. It was not a fitting look.

Calida was still pissed about the situation, but the pathetic scene was amusing. The lady's lips wrinkled and rounded like two lumpy sausages and her eyelashes fanned so vigorously Calida was afraid they would take flight.

Oh, Eesa. If she tries to use the "innocent waif" tone on him, I might punch her. If only because the powder on her face is smudging in with the wax on her lips.

"Normally, I would keep such topics private because of the scandal, but one of the younger guards has been visiting another noblewoman's chambers late at night. Her husband is never there, and her bed has been lonely. She disclosed to me that once, the guard had told of leaving duty for her warm embrace."

Calida's eyes twitched wide in shock before she contained herself once more. *Oh my goodness. That is unheard of.* Such scandalous behaviour was taboo and if the court caught wind of this, her husband could oust her into the streets for adultery. Some provinces still followed the practices of torturing their adulterous women. It was no longer common, not since the queen subtly tried to fix it, but several provinces were protected by the queen's council, who were backed by the Elder Sanctum, a faction which has existed for a century. Her Majesty's subjects found it odd that she didn't just decree it, instead letting them have their way. It left an odd taste in her mouth. Calida wasn't a political expert, but as far as she knew, the queen's word was law.

The noblewoman tried to attach herself once more to Lord Dominic before he pushed her away, making some kind of excuse to escape. Then he dragged Calida away. At that point, she was more than ready to leave.

After a bit more conversation with the other nobles, Calida and Lord Dominic exited the castle and joined Jetta and Braxton.

The guards reported back to Lord Dominic about the informant they had found in the local underground market, a place only people with suspicious pasts could find. As she and the earl had been talking to nobles in the castle, Jetta and Braxton had left the couple in the care of the castle's guards so they could do what Lord Dominic had ordered. Calida begrudgingly understood she needed to accept the fact he would be a mainstay in finding out what had happened to her father. His source of information could be vital.

Calida tapped her feet on the carriage outside the castle as the trio talked a step away from her. She was listening, but to stand still was nearly impossible. Maybe it came from all those years of living in the forest hunting with her father as a child.

Father. How she missed him already.

A part of her chest ached at the memory of the vibrant scent of pinecones and damp soil.

Calida's attention snapped forward as she realized they had stopped their private conversation and returned to the carriage.

The informant would meet Lord Dominic, but he had to be alone. Calida insisted she come too. Jetta strongly disagreed, reminding her she didn't understand this part of the world.

So, Lord Dominic and the two guards agreed Calida would stay behind at the local tavern with Jetta as Braxton followed him.

Calida mentally punched something at the idea of being left out. Yet again, she was not in control over her personal life. She wasn't used to thinking about her own safety or handing it over to someone else, let alone leaving it in Lord Dominic's hands.

The two women sat in the tavern across from the entrance.

Many people filled the tavern. The men drank and hollered; the women served them more drinks.

Calida flinched at a chair scraping. Her head whipped around, and she searched for the noise. The talking grew louder. A part of her wanted to wail at them to shut their mouths, but it would be far too contrary, and walking away unscathed wouldn't be an option. According to the men behind her, any woman addressing them would immediately be seen as fresh meat. *Filthy pigs, the lot of them.*

Jetta sat close to Calida, trying to provide comfort and security, but the men behind them would spill their drinks on them every time they cheered, chugged, and then thrust it over their heads to prove they drank it. Each time she would flinch.

The event seemed brutish and mind numbing, but they enjoyed it.

If only they could see how their manner appalled women. *Although they don't seem the type to give a single thought.* A time or two Calida caught the men at the table swatting the butts of the women serving them.

After one very enthusiastic chugging contest, one man threw his drink backward and hit Jetta.

Her hair and shoulders were covered in liquid. The beer soaked into her clothes and doused her with the scent of alcohol.

Jetta went to stand up, and as she did, her fists clenched. Calida grasped her arm.

"Jetta, you shouldn't. They're just a bunch of drunkards. Here today, gone tomorrow," Calida whispered.

She wanted to punch the drunkards too, but it was dangerous to take on a whole table of them.

"Just get a rag to clean up."

Jetta looked at Calida reluctantly. She shifted her clothing on her shoulders uncomfortably but didn't want to leave her post.

Calida gestured away with her hands. Jetta chewed on her lip.

"Do you still carry the knife your father gave you long ago?"

Calida gazed at her in confusion. "I would never leave home without it."

Jetta's shoulder slumped as she exhaled in relief.

"Good. Keep it on you. I will only be a moment. You won't even miss me."

She brusquely tromped to the tavern barkeep, leaving Calida staring at Jetta's back, urging to her return quickly.

After a few minutes had passed, Calida started to relax into her chair some more.

As soon as she did, she realized the rowdy drunkards behind her had stopped making noise. In confusion, she peeked over her shoulder. The drunkards now spoke in hushed tones and glanced around them. Instead of smacking assess and whistling at women, the drunkards seemed completely sober and clearheaded.

Her mind screamed at her to move or to do something. She felt like they were speaking about her, but Calida just scolded herself for being so self-absorbed. For all she knew, they were just whispering about their wives or mistresses. Anything other than what her mind was urging her to believe.

"Honestly, Calida, I am just as important. Not that you would care about focusing on your mother."

Calida pushed her mother's words from her mind.

Jetta still had not returned. Calida grew nervous, and the men behind her now glanced her way.

Another chair scraped, and she jumped in her seat. Frantically, she looked around and saw a person moving toward the front door.

Calida glanced at the table of men and saw they were now

talking calmly amongst themselves. They were passing around alcohol and food.

For the first time since she had entered, Calida relaxed.

She closed her eyes and rubbed the tension out of her neck, hoping to lose herself in the dark corner of the tavern.

Eight

Dominic grasped the back of Rayner's arm and let go when he had the man's attention.

"It's been a long time, Sir Rayner," he said.

"Milord, it has been some time. You have grown into quite the man in the meantime." Rayner bowed.

It was true. He had grown out of his need for his father's approval. In fact, he was set on earning his father's disapproval. His father wanted Dominic to continue the bloodline with other nobles. However, the young man knew better. He needed to have a loving marriage instead of one of convenience.

After seeing Calida many times while he was at the Poramun Creek market, he had grown fonder of his childhood memories of her. He had seen her be kind to young and old alike. He had watched her give her last apple to a child crying on the street and smile sadly to a wailing malnourished baby.

He could imagine tending to their children with her and spending time in the garden of his new home, upon obtaining his rites of adulthood. He would be going up to the mountains to train and then bond with his shadow to allow the physical manifestation to materialize. It would take him four years and then he would return for Calida. In the meantime, he hoped she would learn about their engagement and await his return. First, he had to convince her father to allow him her hand in marriage.

She had been the only one not to care about his position. They had many fun moments together as children, and he knew he wanted children who looked just like her running around the new home he inherited. Ones who would deserve to inherit his power and responsibilities.

"Sir, since we last saw each other, I have grown in my studies on literature, a-and my swordsmanship. I have bested the strongest guard on my father's payroll." Dominic stumbled over his words. Maybe if he convinced Rayner he would be able to protect his daughter first, then he could have one foot in the door.

Rayner eyed him like he knew what the young man was hinting at. With a frown of disapproval, he turned to the entrance of the Faction Knights' head office.

"I apologize, milord. I must be off. I have next shift." Rayner's back was to Dominic. He was going to walk away before the eighteen-year-old would get out the words.

"Please, wait, Sir Rayner!" Dominic shouted out and then cringed.

Rayner looked over his shoulder.

"I wish to ask for your daughter's hand in marriage," Dominic finally squeezed out, bracing for the man's response.

"You ask for my precious daughter to enter the world of nobles with your father as her greatest adversary?" The frown on the older man's face deepened.

Dominic flinched. He hadn't thought about that. It was true his father wouldn't approve, but the more he thought about it, the stronger the feeling to have Calida as his bride became.

"It would be difficult, but she would become a countess of the

House of Goldwyn. I could provide her with a good life and endless luxuries." He racked his mind for anything to convince this man he meant to keep her happy, safe, and warm.

Rayner shook his head and walked toward the entrance, obviously disappointed with the young man.

Dominic frantically glanced around before he dropped to his knees.

"Sir Rayner Rhodes, I, Dominic Goldwyn, son of Duke Charles Goldwyn, demand you fulfill your debt. I saved your life on the battlefield on the shores of Eleari, and you promised to repay the favor when the time arose!" Dominic shouted.

His head touched the ground as his eyes shut, horrified that he demanded this man let him marry his only daughter.

The sound of footsteps stopped. Rayner sighed and then shuffled around.

"You really are insistent."

Dominic kept his head to the ground. The man could still say no.

"Sir, please. I won't have anyone else but her," he said.

Rayner kicks some rocks on the ground and takes a deep, tired breath.

"I did promise," the man muttered to himself. "Alright, you may marry my daughter."

Dominic's head snapped up off the ground to stare at Rayner.

"But you must wait four years,." Rayner said.

Dominic stood up and grasped Rayner by the hand, shaking it over and over. He had to go to the mountains to train, anyway. He needed to become stronger for Calida's sake. He had no right to take a wife if he couldn't even keep her safe.

The darkness cloaked Dominic as he moved swiftly through the streets with Braxton following closely. Small lights twinkled in the distance as they walked down the alleyways and paths that could confuse anyone who didn't know their destination.

The dark houses looked worse for wear as they passed. As Dominic and Braxton strode closer to the lights, Dominic heard people mingling. Lamps lit every table or wall in the market.

Dominic moved past the crowds and merchants as if he had been here often enough. The sellers were peddling everything from stolen knives to kidnapped women.

If they came back tomorrow, it would all be gone. Only those intimately aware of the market's patterns could tell when or where it might appear. It was like a game of chance. If you could guess the right location at the right time, you would have access to the entire underground market.

Braxton stopped them near a turn off past the market stands. "It is over here, milord."

Dominic walked forward, expecting Braxton to stay back as he talked to the informant.

Braxton cleared his throat behind Dominic.

"Yes, Braxton?" Dominic asked, looking over his shoulder at the guard. He tapped his foot impatiently as Braxton paused. "We haven't much time."

Braxton's face grew firm. "Milord, as much as you may wish to go alone because he requested it, I must stay by your side."

Dominic's face twitched. "If you must, Braxton. But please stay in the shadows. I don't wish to scare off the informant."

Braxton nodded and then waited for the earl to continue. Dominic strode up the unlit path away from the underground market.

After a few minutes of walking, they arrived at the meeting location in the grove. Braxton blended into the trees, dagger at the ready but hidden from sight. The wind rustled the leaves, and an unsettled chill ran down Dominic's spine.

It took only another minute for a swish disturbing the brush to capture his attention. The moon disappeared behind a cloud as a short, slim figure emerged from shadows.

Silence filled the air. "Greetings to you, milord."

Braxton moved quietly in the bushes. If not for Dominic's heightened senses, he wouldn't have located the guard.

"Greetings to you as well," Dominic said. Gazing into the darkness around them, a sense of urgency overcame him. "As much as it would be proper to make niceties, I feel we should get to the reason we are here."

The man shifted in the dark. Clouds obscured his identity. Dominic tried to narrow in on his features but to no avail. Even with his excellent sight, the man's face was indiscernible.

The informant sighed. "The guard you wanted to know about; maids saw him leaving his post the night of the incident."

Dominic wanted to know how he got this information, but that wasn't part of the deal. The guard who was supposed to be on duty with Rayner, the guard who reported his supposed treachery, wasn't even there at the time of the event. No matter how he looked at it, it was all too suspicious. Even when he had talked to the guard who made the report, something about his statement didn't feel honest. The man would fidget all over the place and wouldn't keep eye contact, then would try to use too much of it. At least once, Dominic was certain his eyes would tire from the unblinking gaze.

"What do I owe you for this information?"

The man chuckled with a creaking cough to it. Dominic cringed.

"I don't require payment right now, but I'll contact you when it is due." Then, as quick as he came, the man retreated through the shadows.

Just as the last strip of cloth from the man's cloak was following him into the darkness, the moon reappeared and illuminated half a crest on the informant's cloak before the man was completely gone. The crest was unlike any he had seen before.

Nine

A hand clamped over Calida's mouth, and a man whispered harshly into her ear. "If you come quietly, I won't off you here and now." He grabbed her by the arm and pulled her up. "Good girl."

When she didn't utter a sound, he chuckled. A sharp knife pointed into her back to move her forward. With no other choice, she did.

Slowly, the two moved closer to the tavern door.

Calida scanned the room, hoping to capture the attention of someone, anyone, in order to escape. She couldn't even get the attention of the other patrons; they were all absorbed in their own little worlds.

It didn't take long for them to reach the door.

The man stood so close to Calida that his pungently boozy clothing invaded her nostrils. It was obvious he had nefarious plans once they passed the door. If it wasn't for his appearance and treatment of her, then it would be the small chub he pressing through his trousers into her back.

As he went to open the door, Jetta finally returned.

"What's going on here?" Jetta said.

The man let go of the door and faced Jetta with his arms crossed around Calida. She wanted to shout for Jetta to just kick him but stayed silent. As much as she struggled with trust and relinquishing control, she knew Jetta would come through.

"Run off with you, wench. I paid for her services fair and square." If it wasn't for the knife to her, his tightening grip, and the erection in her back, Calida would have laughed at his bold lie. Obviously, he wasn't being observant when he chose his target. Jetta mimicked his body language and glared straight into his eyes.

"Oh yeah? Did you make sure to ask her husband too?"

The man jumped back in surprise. In a second, his behaviour changed from threatening to intimidated, trying to figure out when Calida had found a husband. *What has him so confused?* Why would he think so hard about it when she assumed he had just picked her out of the crowd?

After a few moments, he grabbed Calida by the arm again, glaring at Jetta.

"Lies. This bitch doesn't have a husband. No woman with a respectable husband would even be near a tavern!"

The idiot didn't even know what a tavern was. They aren't just for drunkards. A tavern was a place of celebration, a place of rest, and a place of work. The barkeep could supply you with mail someone had sent you from travelling merchants who were dropping in. This man was confusing it with a brothel.

"Well, he is outside and about to come in to bring her home. Stay and meet him, why don't you?" Jetta said.

The man literally puffed out his chest and flexed his arms. "Well, the boy is about to be given a rude awakening. The two shall pay me and maybe he can even watch." The man grinned down at her.

Calida sincerely hoped Lord Dominic was out there. She

peeked at the door. A part of her wished he would show up, but her pessimistic side thought it was more likely he was a long way off. With her luck, it was possible. She hated to admit it, but she didn't want to see him hurt and wished he wouldn't show up.

A moment passed, and the door didn't move. Calida's hope crumbled. The man burst out into cackling laughter. He bent over as wave after wave left his mouth. The man wiped his eyes.

"Looks like the boy lost his nerve. Guess she is all mine now." He dragged her toward the door.

It burst inward, the wood splintering on the floor.

Standing on the threshold was Dominic. Dressed in his dark lapel jacket, white shirt, and brown pants, he stood out as a royal. His shining boots and clean skin stuck out like a sore thumb, but he moved onward like the penetrating stares of all the customers in the tavern weren't there. Dominic zeroed his sharp, steely gaze on the man who had been trying to steal Calida.

The feeling in her chest that had been growing tighter the longer she didn't see Dominic disappeared. It was like being without water, then suddenly supplied it. A sense of ease washed over her as she drank in the sight of him. It hadn't been long since they met, but somehow in that time she knew she could trust him. At least a little bit.

He marched up to the man who still had a hand on her. Calida stared, transfixed by the way he strode over with the full height of Eesa on his shoulders. The man who had been attempting to kidnap Calida stood small compared to Dominic. It felt like he was a warrior come back from war for her honour. *Way to make it straight out of a romantic tale, Calida.*

Lord Dominic's eyebrow creased, and his jaw clenched.

His gaze rested on the hand holding her. If she was trying to kidnap someone, she would want to disappear under his ire.

"You are going to remove your hand from the lady, and you are going to do it now," Lord Dominic said.

The man stared back at the earl, speechless. He had obviously not been expecting Dominic.

The man shook. There was fear in his eyes. Calida couldn't blame him. Lord Dominic wore a fierce face.

Whoever the man was, he had heard of Lord Dominic, Earl of Weommadran, and in wartime, the general of the queen's armies. He was well known, so it shouldn't be that unusual, but there were still ignorant people out there. Calida excluded herself because she hadn't been concerned with learning about the nobility. Instead she focused on helping her mother.

After a moment, the man slowly took his hands off Calida, never moving his eyes from Lord Dominic. She did not know what had his attention when Lord Dominic was right in front of him, but she was happy to be free.

Calida slowly moved away from the man until Jetta wrapped an arm around her and walked her backward.

"I didn't realize she was the wife of nobility, milord." The man bowed, still shaking. He clearly saw that her betrothed was not just a boy.

Calida's body shook and tingles prickled her skin. Tears pricked her eyes. Her chest felt tight as she finally breathed out. She wanted to scream out all the emotions bottled up. Lord Dominic was no ordinary nobleman. He had piqued her interest and it bothered her.

She stared at Lord Dominic. For the first time, she realized how alike he was to her father. She also noticed the things that made him different. His shoulders were broad. She could imagine wrapping her arms around his neck and resting on his shoulders. His arms were powerful enough to fend off attackers and soft enough to comfort her. He was unlike the other nobles she had the "pleasure" to talk to. He found the facts and based his decisions on logic and knowledge rather than those old hags who would gladly tarnish someone's good name for a lick of gossip.

Lord Dominic had been calm all the other times they had been together. Not much got under his skin.

The tight grip of his hands and the fierce glare on his face said it all. If he did punch the pig of a man, she certainly wouldn't stop him. Her respect for him grew with his self-control, though.

In their province, if a person found a woman kidnapped or interrupted a kidnapping, then the man of her household would determine the punishment. Now that she's betrothed to Lord Dominic, that made him the man of the household.

Our household. Calida mentally shook her head. That led down a rabbit hole she had no intention of burrowing into.

Lord Dominic grabbed the man by the back of the neck and dragged him out the door. Jetta stood in front of Calida, determined to do what she had failed at earlier. But Calida couldn't contain herself and rushed after Lord Dominic. She had a taste for the thrill of action and drama.

Dominic dragged the man behind the building. As he turned the corner, she tiptoed. She still hadn't accepted what had almost happened to her.

Her head peeked around the corner as Lord Dominic dumped the man in the middle of the alleyway, near the shadows cast across the wall. Calida squinted. He seemed to grow even larger somehow since coming outside. There was movement beside Lord Dominic in the shadows, circling the man.

The shadow slowly materialized, turning into a wolf. Lord

Dominic didn't seem surprised. The lord held out his hand, and the wolf crouched down as if ready to pounce.

Her heart pounded in her ears. Panic worked up her throat. She wanted to scream at the sudden turn of events. Not only was Lord Dominic a noble, but he was one of those mythical men from the clan of old legend. *It had to be. Who else could materialize a wolf in shadow form?*

A legend was told to the children of Calida's region. Once there was a clan of men who sought the world. They had the power to control the shadows and could morph them into the shape of wolves. The clan wanted total domination and destruction. They were thirsty for the throne, but before they could overthrow the queen, they vanished, leaving behind a barren land.

No one knew what had happened. Until now.

Calida's eyes widened in shock. Lord Dominic was hiding in plain sight. He was a great threat and could be just like the legends told. A ruthless monster of a man.

Her breath sped up as the panic warped her mind.

Lord Dominic glared at the kidnapper. The man knelt on the ground, shivering uncontrollably. The wolf growled at the kidnapper, targeting its prey.

"You have two options. Either you disappear and I never see you again, or Aither eats you." Lord Dominic's harsh and blunt voice grated on her ears. Calida shivered as she imagined a cold bloody knife instead of his voice.

The man let go of his bladder, blubbering and begging.

"Please, please, let me live! You'll never see me again. Never again!"

Lord Dominic growled. "You will stay away from my wife, too."

That comment jolted Calida. She wanted to turn around and run away but felt fixed on the scene. In the future, she would thank herself for learning Lord Dominic's true character. If she had learned later on, when it was too late, Calida didn't know what she would do. At least now, if she thought hard about it, she might come up with an escape plan.

"I will. I will. I did not know she was your wife. I have learned my lesson." The man bowed deeply into the ground, and piss and mud covered the filthy man's face.

Lord Dominic paused before gesturing, and Aither returned to the shadows. The man dashed away. He ran past Calida, not noticing or caring she was there.

Lord Dominic's body slowly shrank before her eyes, as if he had been morphing to intimidate the kidnapper.

Calida collapsed on the ground.

He spun around in alarm, ready to fight off an attacker.

Calida's eyes fixed on him like a frightened deer would stare at a hunter before the kill. He moved closer but cringed as she flinched away from him.

Calida didn't know what to do now. There was nowhere for her to go. If he was anything like the ravenous beasts in the story, then she could show up dead by her wedding night. Calida's mind raced as convoluted scenarios played before her eyes.

This stranger was her betrothed and a killer, no doubt.

He crouched and stilled himself. He was treating her like a jittery forest animal, but she didn't care. The only thing she could focus on was a way out. Her eyes frantically scanned around him but not too far away. If she let him out of her sight for a moment, who knows what could happen.

Jetta had been behind her. Calida had heard the crunching of leaves as she had tiptoed. Her throat grew dry as the silence stretched. *Why hadn't Jetta interrupted Lord Dominic?*

"Calida, you need to let milord explain," Jetta said.

Why was she siding with this monster? Was Jetta a beast like that, too? Calida mentally shook her head. *No, Jetta was not the same as him.*

Her friend couldn't possibly be a bloodthirsty monster who would prey on the women and children of every village. Jetta wasn't evil enough to tie up the bodies of previous mayors in every town and drain their blood to drink like a fine wine.

Ten

It took some time, but Calida reluctantly let her friend approach. Jetta talked her into listening. Believing in her own judgement, Calida hid behind the crouched Jetta.

"Yes, I'm a member of the Goldwyn clan in myth. Our birth, me and my brother, brought change and hope. My family is one of the few remaining of the clan. We had lived in secrecy and plan on continuing to live that way." Her betrothed spoke as he emerged from the shadows and seemed to shrink as the light of the moon hit him.

Calida couldn't believe that he was a member of such a vicious clan, nor that he was trying to sound like the victim.

"Milord, I have already heard the history, but why are you trying to portray your clan like anything other than killers? Your clan tried to overthrow the queen!"

Lord Dominic flinched at her formality and accusation. "Sometimes stories are just stories, Calida. Don't believe everything you hear just because it was the only story told."

Her eyebrows furrowed and her mouth hung agape. She couldn't trust Lord Dominic enough to just take him at his word. The stories were ingrained into her during childhood.

Lord Dominic stepped forward, and when she didn't recoil, he offered her a hand up. Calida stared at it for a moment before she grasped it.

At least for the meantime, he was protecting her. But she would keep a vigilant eye when he shifted to other motivations.

Crunching footsteps ran up to them. The three of them turned their heads, and Calida held her breath. Braxton jogged up.

She exhaled and stood up with Jetta. *With my luck, it could have been another assailant.*

It had been odd he hadn't been here to side with Lord Dominic.

He quickly told the women about his adventure tailing the informant. He told them about the visits to several public shops and inns, taking a suspiciously long time to leave each one. Not once had he removed his hood, so Braxton still had no idea who the informant was. Mystery followed him.

Calida ground her teeth as Braxton recounted the information to the women. He had only provided a piece, and they were no closer to the truth. Jetta's arm was wrapped around her as if to protect her from the world. Calida clung to her friend.

Her face went pale as she thought about the reality. *My father could really be dead.* She dug her hand into Jetta's tunic. It hurt to imagine him gone for good, but she could understand why the others would want her to see the truth. She just didn't know if she was ready, or if she ever would be.

The wagon pulled up to a large mansion that was a dark contrast to what Calida pictured. The ivory castle she imagined was nothing like the basic, functional mansion she saw before her. There was a step up to the wooden door. No ornate carvings or expensive plants. She hadn't realized he was so practical. By not letting herself find out more about him, she would be open to surprise. Her preconceived notions would be tested around every turn.

There she stood in front of a mansion of modest nature. She forced her jaw closed. Lord Dominic was making it hard to keep a callous shell.

Calida flinched as he smiled while guiding her by the waist to the door. She squinted up at him. A chill ran down her spine, but she had to fix her mind. It seemed to mistake the chill of fear for a zing of desire. *He is still from a killer clan, remember that, Calida.*

The inside of the house was just as surprising, but she didn't know what she really expected. Instead of floors so bright her eyes hurt and candlelit chandeliers, he had basic wooden floors that spread out into an open space. There were stone arches that showed a grand hall for events. No expensive rugs or ornate silver mirrors.

Calida carefully took several steps away from Lord Dominic, the image of his transformation still imprinted on her mind. She didn't know what was going to happen now. Calida was supposed to marry this man, but how could she if he had a predisposition for violence?

"I have other matters to attend, so Braxton will accompany you on a tour of the house." Just like that, Lord Dominic left as if he couldn't stand to be in her presence any longer.

She stared after him until she realized his aide was not by her side any longer.

Calida strode to catch up to the fast-moving Braxton,

attempting to stay close. *If there is a time to wish for longer legs, this is it.*

Calida looked around her and not only realized that Jetta had mysteriously disappeared, but the floor of the grand hall was not the same as the wooden floors of the foyer. It had tile of different colors and patterns, but all the vibrancy faded to the background when she noticed the large insignia on the floor. Two wolves stood on their hind legs growling at each other on either side of a sword laid across the moon. The intricate design had runes carved into the floor behind the moon, but when she squinted from a distance, she couldn't make it out.

"The stairs to the left lead up to the second floor." The quiet voice startled Calida out of her musings. Her head whipped around to gaze at Braxton.

He kept to a slow crawl until they reached the stairs. His crossed arms and unintelligible grumbles left a lasting impression in her mind. *Whatever chafed his armor seems to have him in a foul mood.*

Staring up the spiral of the stairwell, she realized just how much of a dunce she truly was. Calida hid a look of embarrassment. Lord Dominic's home was completely different from other nobles. Even Lord Sullivan had more frivolous bangles lying about than Lord Dominic.

"What's up there?" Calida asked.

The number of homes with stairs she had visited could be counted on one hand. Maybe less. The home she lived in was all one level and small in comparison. Lord Dominic's mansion was a like a glorious statue of ivory in a garden of perfect peonies.

Braxton sighed and walked up the stairs. "It's the way to your room and the tutor who is waiting to start your lessons immediately."

Calida whipped her head to stare at Braxton. Her mouth

flapped like a fish as she tried to conceive the words to say. *A tutor? I haven't even settled in yet*! She raced up the stairs to catch up with the fast-paced Braxton.

"W-what do you mean, tutor?" She had been informed of none of this. She thought for sure all this would be temporary. That Lord Dominic, too, would cast her aside and she could leave without a fuss.

Obviously, she was wrong.

As they travelled down the hallway to see her new bedroom, she couldn't help her curiosity.

"How did you come to be employed by Lord Dominic?"

Braxton glanced at her.

"I have known him for some time. He had come to the meeting place of the Crescent League and picked me out of the others who were sparring and practicing. I've been employed by Lord Dominic ever since."

Calida peeked at him before turning her attention to the doors they passed.

"It sounds quite forward to say, but I am rather curious about you. You have garnered the respect of a nobleman and Jetta," Calida said.

Braxton stopped and looked at her sternly.

"Jetta doesn't have respect for me."

She grinned. "Well, that's just not true. If she had no respect for you, then she wouldn't even entertain the idea of sharing responsibilities with you. You two work together in harmony because she respects you."

His eyes lost focus and a frown formed on his face. It was almost cute how out of touch he was.

"I know little about her, but from what I have seen, she reminds me of my younger sister."

Calida tilted her head. "You have a sister? What is she like?"

Braxton smiled with a twitch of his lips. It was a slight

gesture, but it was all he needed to bring light to his hard features.

"Alice is a handful. She is stubborn and smart and likes to do things herself. She is everything in my life. And I hold her close to my heart."

He clutched the necklace he wore. After a few moments of quiet, Braxton snapped out of his thoughts and returned to guiding her to her room, where she met her tutor. There she jumped right into how to integrate into high society.

Eleven

Calida shuffled around in an uncomfortable dress. It was left for her to wear, but it wasn't anything like the one she wore to the wedding. This dress had a stiff bodice and itchy underskirt.

Two days had passed since Lord Dominic effectively dumped Calida in the entryway to his home. Jetta had shown her around the rest of the mansion, introducing her to the servants, each one irritating her with their bowing and calling her "milady." It was like she was found and brought home, and now was supposed to settle in and grow comfortable.

Life with Lord Dominic would never be simple and comfortable. At least living with her mother, she didn't have constant gossip behind her back. She could take some paintings to the market to sell, helping her mother with the groceries and household duties. She could go out hunting. No cold nobles or fake smiles.

I must remain at a distance. For all she knew, he would kill her on their wedding night. In her heart, she couldn't believe he would, but the heart is a fickle thing. She had heard the stories, and it would be reasonable to listen to them. Those stories were widely talked about and there were so many variations, one of them had to be true.

For now, she had to learn the ways of being a noblewoman. The tutor she had met immediately schooled her on everything from how she slouched to the way she walked. Her hands throbbed from the smack of the stick to correct her posture. It wasn't until late in the night that she could sleep.

Not that she slept much, anyway. Her mind circulated around her father's death and whenever she shut her eyes, all she saw was Rayner's face, a bloody image of anger and torment.

Calida felt like she had fallen out of a tree and bruised every part of her.

The next morning, even though she had little sleep, who was there at the crack of dawn to start her lessons once more?

Calida's tutor. The small woman was as mean as a feral guard dog.

The woman's glare seared her intent into her mind. A shiver coursed down her spine at the memory. Perfect posture and conversation starters went straight over the head of the average commoner, and Calida was no exception. Even though her father was a guard assigned by Elite Dominion, she had never received such lessons before. If it hadn't been for her father, she wouldn't even know how to read or write.

As a Lady of Weommadran, there was much she had to learn. Like her tutor sniped at her, she had to know it all by heart. From how to use her social standing to become an influential member of the aristocracy. The moment she opened her eyes in the morning to the moment her door closed at night, it didn't end.

It overwhelmed her how much she had to learn. The servants put her into a warm, fragrant bath at once and then dressed her in clothes that felt as smooth as a newborn. They stitched the dress with vibrant purples and reds that she had never seen before, except in meadows near her town. It was sewn onto her body. As if it was meant only for her. Never had clothes been made just for her.

She wished she could run away, but Calida vividly imagined what her mother would say if she walked away from a chance to use her daughter as an easy path to luxury. The wealth that came with being the wife of an earl provided a luxurious life for her family, something she had become even more knowledgeable about after her lessons. She wasn't here for herself. She was here for her father, who wished they marry, and for her mother, who would criticize her harshly for being daft.

Calida stood in a beautiful dress of blue and green in the hall while practicing her lessons on delegating. She was directing the servants where to put the best napkins for a dinner party, based on culture, when she heard Jetta and Braxton bickering just outside the door.

She held up a hand to the servants, gulping when they stopped immediately while holding the beige napkin with the plate set for the Nydeawyr example. It was startling how fast the Goldwyn servants would listen to her.

Jetta and Braxton entered the foyer outside the dining hall. If she were standing beside them, her ears would be ringing from the yelling.

"Just because you're quick to answer, doesn't make you right!" Jetta said. Braxton growled something unintelligible.

Jetta huffed and then stomped away before slamming a door somewhere in the mansion. Whatever he had said, her friend didn't like it.

Peering quietly through a crack, Calida watched as Braxton pulled at his hair. He paced in short, firm strides in the foyer. The maid who stood near the door gaped wordlessly. Obviously, she had the first row to the drama. If it had been a few days ago, she would have been surprised too, but those two were more explosive than a heated coal, always igniting each other. She had been hearing their bickering on and off since they found residency at Lord Dominic's mansion.

Braxton walked away, leaving the maids to shuffle around, absorbing the incident.

The two servants whispered about the fights and conflict that had been growing since Jetta and Braxton began working on the same detail. One giggled and insisted they made such a cute couple, and the other hushed her about being overheard.

With a quiet snick of the door, Calida turned around and returned to her studies of the different plates, utensils, and napkins. She walked over and told the servants to continue with placing each plate setting for the different provinces, based on her advice.

Calida tried to stay focused, but she was reminded of when she had met Jetta at 7.

She and Jetta had been friends since the moment she had entered the market with her mother. There was Jetta between two fruit vendors, tattered and dirty. She had been trying to steal a piece of fruit to eat but couldn't find the opportunity. She had the look of a feral animal, like she had learned the only way to get what she wanted in life was to fight for it.

As the daughter of a knight, they had some extra coin. Calida had taken two coins from her mother's pouch and snuck over to buy a piece of fruit for Jetta. Her heart was set on doing something for the little girl who had nothing. When presented with the fruit, Jetta was skeptical why such a well-dressed girl was giving her food, but no child could stop the groaning of an empty stomach.

Jetta had snatched the fruit from Calida's hands and devoured it.

She had meant to introduce herself, but when she started to talk, she heard her mother's voice frantically calling for her.

Soon enough, it became a tradition until Jetta could fend for herself. She would buy a piece of fruit for Jetta and maybe take a moment to chat before she had to quickly find her mother.

From there, Jetta would come find her and they would spend hours playing outside her home.

Now, if Calida presented Jetta with fruit, a smile appeared on their faces. It was a sign of their friendship and trust in each other, and a reminder of simpler times. They had survived and nothing could separate them.

She was walking down the hallway to her room after finishing the dining lesson when she heard the whispers of the maids nearby.

"Any day now, I say! They're living together. Soon enough we'll be making their marriage bed for them," one said.

The other fanned herself with her hand. "It is exciting to think about, but milady hasn't even begun to warm up to him."

Calida cleared her throat. The maids whipped their head in her direction, both of their eyes widening like two deer caught in crossfire. Immediately they bowed to her.

"Milady, we didn't see you there," one maid said.

"I can tell."

"W-we were merely talking, milady, nothing crass, I assure you," the other maid said. Glancing up from her position.

"It's just that we worry, milady." the other one said.

Calida clenched her jaw and dug her fingernails into her fist.

"It's not your place to worry about my interactions with your master. He's a grown man, he can take care of himself," she said.

The maids bowed deeper, their frames shaking. "Yes, milady."

She hurried to her room and closed the door behind her.

While those in the household expected her to warm up to the lord, the opposite was happening, and she was nurturing it.

Calida would be cordial with Lord Dominic, but she didn't desire to learn more about him. There wasn't anything else to learn. She was his slumming whim, and he was a member of the Goldwyn clan. Calida couldn't believe she didn't see it before. Who would have connected a child's tale to a household name in high society, though?

The couple would have dinner and spend time in the library together. Lord Dominic was "teaching" her how to read and write. Apparently, no one told him she already knew. But she wouldn't be the one to tell him. Calida grinned as she imagined the look on his face when he realized she was literate, unlike many other commoners out there. In her spare time, when Lord Dominic wasn't looking, Calida would choose books on more advanced topics about leadership and how to act like a noble.

She sat down on her bed and picked up a book.

Lord Dominic tried to engage in conversation, but she wouldn't reveal more to him than he already knew. She could see his face fall every time she didn't share more. It hurt, but it was important. If he lost interest, then he would leave her be. She could continue to put on a facade until he found someone to replace her.

Her chest squeezed. She wanted him but her mind was right. The risk was too high. The idea of another woman standing at his side stung, but she wouldn't listen to the foolish ways of the heart. She wasn't the right type for noble life, anyway.

"Du Nic!" the small voice of her childhood rang out.

She whipped her head around. *Where had that come from?*

With a sigh, her fingers ruffled the pages.

Calida searched the book with a hand drawn picture about where the green napkin was placed. She had been going through all the information in the book about noble etiquette. Of course, Lord Dominic told her all of it, but she could read it by herself without issue. It was almost humorous how sure he was that she was illiterate.

I almost feel guilty for keeping up with it.

Each province had their own culture and traditions that stemmed from the times when they were all their own king- doms. For example, the province of Eleari, Calida's home, had rich blue napkins, a chalice on the right of the plate and an engraved mug meant for tea on the left.

Twelve

When Calida's study time had passed, she was free to do a hobby she enjoyed. So, she raced to her chambers for the painting easel she had placed there.

She pushed open her doors and rushed to paint right away. Calida covered her new dress with a smock and tied back her hair with the lace she had left on her painting easel.

Holding a paint brush finally, she found herself without an idea to paint. Sometimes this would happen and then it would just hit her.

So, until something inspired her, she painted random shapes and colour schemes, not aiming for any picture.

After just playing around, inspiration found her, and she painted without hesitancy.

Time flew by. It startled Calida when a knock sounded on her bedroom door.

She quickly turned around to open the door. Braxton was on the other side. He bowed to her.

"Milady, it's dinner time. Milord has summoned you to join him."

Calida hadn't realized so much time had passed. She thanked Braxton and sent him on his way. With the door closed, she set her brushes in their bath and then began cleaning up. By the time Braxton had come back to escort her, she was ready to eat.

Braxton offered his arm to her, and she took it.

"How long have you known Jetta?"

Calida snuck a peek at him. He was looking ahead and fidgeting around as they strolled. *So, he is interested in Jetta.* Containing a grin, she had half a mind to hold out. But decided it was too cute to resist.

"I had been a young girl. But she had been so small, I thought she was younger than I." She paused, expecting him to encourage her to continue, but he stayed quiet. Glancing over, she noticed his dark, furrowed brows popped out against his tanned skin. Calida didn't want to bother him from his musings, so she continued in silence, down the stairs to the dining room.

When they arrived, Braxton held open the door for her and announced her arrival.

Lord Dominic sat at the head of the table at the other end of the room. If this were the first time they dined together since they had arrived, the long, seemingly unending table and the grandeur of the room would intimidate her. However, they had been here for four days and five nights. The only thing that vexed her now was the imposing way Lord Dominic sat at the other side of the table. He fit the position like a king to a throne. All that was missing was his crown and staff.

She glided to her spot beside him with her head held high. It was another duty the tutors instructed her to master, the ability to look graceful when crossing a room. With her chin up, she sat down in the Madam chair reserved for someone in her position.

She searched the room to avoid his piercing gaze. If he

thought he was being stealthy, the lord was failing. It was as obvious as a spot of mold on an apple. Calida had no desire to make small talk with the confounding man. Like she would give another noble a chance to belittle someone in her station. After witnessing many from high society strolling through town and mistreating her people, she determined nobles were the real scum of the earth. The best example she had was when she was a child. There was a nobleman in her town who had control over the taxes. He was always on the lookout for his next wife and had a habit of wedding the youngest girls that he could.

Remembering sent a chill up Calida's spine.

"Please enjoy your food, Calida."

Calida's head whipped up and met his gaze. *Shit.* She hadn't meant to meet his eyes. It took a moment for his words to kick in. Looking down at her plate, she realized they had served food. Her stomach grumbled in protest. Picking up her utensil, she plucked at the food in front of her. It wasn't until the lord looked away that she could eat in peace.

The meal was quiet. Tension built in Calida's body with each bite. The silence was grating, and all she could think about were the times her mother would sit in silence when she was angry at Calida for an unavoidable mistake. Lord Dominic didn't fill the empty void with chatter and by the end of the meal, she wasn't only feeling homesick.

Her stomach twisted and turned as she thought about the lord being angry at her, dizzy with sudden worry. It could've been anything. She hadn't been that accommodating of a visitor. However, she knew she would end up being uncommunicative. Her head hurt at the conflicting actions.

As she stumbled to her feet, Lord Dominic grabbed her wrist gently.

"Stay. We need to talk."

She whipped her head around. *He wants to chat after that awkward meal together.*

He had not said a single word to her throughout the meal, but as soon as she wanted to be alone, he wanted things his way.

Fine. She could stay. It would be in silence, though. Calida could be petty like that.

Slowly, she sat down. He had her full attention.

"We both know that your father's death was more than just a botched robbery. It makes little sense. Any intelligent thief wouldn't target the palace."

Calida agreed with him. The well-guarded palace wasn't a suitable location for a flawless robbery. Didn't mean she would say it out loud.

"The irritating part is when I confront the guards. The palace authorities are sweeping it under the rug."

Just like those nobles. Nothing but snakes.

"How dare they insult my father like this!" Damn it. She was going to be petty.

Her hands warmed as her anger surged through her. Those bastards would pay. Determination filled her as insidious plans piled into her head. Calida had to hold back the maniacal grin from cracking her face.

Lord Dominic held out a hand and placed it on hers, which was clutching a knife suspiciously hard.

"We'll do it together. As we're soon to be married, this is something we will accomplish as a team," Lord Dominic said.

She stared at him for a beat, wondering if maybe he was actually in need of a bloodletting like she had thought at the wedding.

Calida was not used to someone who insisted on being involved in her life like this. When he jumped in without hesitation, her answer was no. While she hated conflict. If she handled it alone then it was her burden to take on alone. But to take on the blame of another person made her nervous.

Her stomach turned, and the meal fought to come back up. She didn't even know if she could trust this asshole. After some thought about when she saw him transform in the alley by the tavern, she felt silly for thinking he might harm her, but that didn't mean he was trustworthy. Who knew what his motivations were?

"Milord, I don't think you need to get involved any more than you are."

Lord Dominic frowned. Crossing his arms, he stared sternly at Calida. She pursed her lips and avoided his gaze. It didn't matter how he stared at her. Calida wouldn't take it back.

"I won't change my mind no matter how much you glare me down, milord."

Calida straightened her back and lifted her head high. If he wanted a fight, she was ready. She hated the idea of going against him, but she would if it had to be done.

"It's Dominic."

She whipped her head around and pointed accusingly at the lord, until she stopped short. *Wait, what did he say?*

"I beg your pardon?" Her eyebrows furrowed and her mouth gaped.

"My name is not milord or Lord Dominic or Lord Goldwyn. You are going to be my wife. You should be used to calling me Dominic."

A blush worked up her cheeks. Never had she called a noble by their first name. They would be husband and wife soon, but that didn't change the fact that it was awkward. It was even worse because he was attractive. How would she keep her composure if he insisted on things that left her tingly?

Lord Dominic smirked as the blush deepened on her face.

"Lo—Dominic." She cleared her throat. "I can handle this problem alone. Only I could do it right."

The smirk fell from Lord Dominic's face. He pushed up from his seat. His height was intimidating. Calida's breath hitched, and her hands fidgeted in her lap.

"My dear one, just because it's something you can do alone, doesn't mean you *should*."

She stood up and moved away from the table. "You don't know me." Calida's hands warmed as frustration built.

Dominic grabbed her arm. "Only because you won't let me."

She pushed his hand off and strode for the door. "It doesn't matter."

Dominic sighed heavily from behind her. "But your father's death does. We need to talk about that, at least."

She stopped in her tracks. *Bastard. Why can't he just let me walk away?*

With a deep breath, Calida turned around. "Fine. I'll listen for a bit."

Calida and Dominic moved from the dining hall to the library to talk about their plans. Arm in arm, the couple sat in the chairs in the corner.

"Just listen." Dominic gently caressed her hand.

Butterflies erupted in her stomach. She hated that a part of her was interested in him, but committing to him sent a wave of fear through her. She was too prideful to allow someone to hurt her.

"Fine, I got it. You have my attention for now." She shook off his hand and scanned the library. Anything to avoid his gaze. To distance herself from the vulnerability that came with losing herself in his eyes.

Dominic then went into a long explanation about setting up a ball at their mansion for the nobles, inviting those they suspected. Then making those people the guests of honor. He theorized with her that if they could get them to open up about the recent events, then maybe bring in the wine to loosen their tongues of the truth.

She started to chew on her fingertips. A party was the perfect disguise for finding answers.

She hadn't meant to, but when he started to pace the room and share all the details with her, Calida tuned out Dominic and started making a list of objectives she would need to complete for this event. She was already thinking about the food when he brought her out of her musings.

Dominic placed a hand on hers. "Calida, keep me involved. I can help."

Calida shook off his hand and stood up. "Milord, you won't need to lift a finger. It's only right that someone of lower class like me should handle this."

Before he could reply, Calida rushed out of the room.

The next few days, Calida ran from place to place to prepare for the party at the mansion. She surrounded herself with all the things she expected to be at a party.

It would be filled with nobles, but there weren't many books in the library about how to plan and prep a casual party for nobles. What she knew was for fancy events, the type at a banquet hall, with scented invitations and [too many people].

Calida imagined a party at the mansion to be like the gatherings in her village.

Every now and then, the commoners and peasants would bring out whatever food they could. Someone would bring a guitar and they would play games together. Whoever won the games would receive an extra share of food. People would team up and cheer when victory was obtained or dramatically sob when lost.

Calida smiled softly at the memories of the gatherings in her town. She hadn't made friends in those times. She was sad when sitting on the outside, never experiencing the laughter as children ran around and played.

As Calida tried to enter the kitchen to start making food for the party, the servants swarmed around her and pushed her out the door. Apparently, it was not her job to prepare food for a small party. It could just be a few people, what would the big deal be about her managing it alone?

Calida was sure it would be a small party, so she didn't put much detail into her dress. It was like the one she wore to the wedding. She didn't want to ask for something too fancy because the idea of asking for something for herself left her feeling ill. She didn't need anything else. Calida held up the dress. It was a simple flax colored dress, the type she would wear to the gatherings in her town. There had to be some similarities between commoners and nobles.

Jetta stepped beside her; her approach so silent that Calida jumped out of her skin. She was still on edge ever since the kidnapping attempt. Any time there was a dark corner, she skidded away as fast as she could, and if someone came up behind her, she would screech in terror.

"Calida, the nobles are very persnickety. If you wear that, they will feed you to nature."

Calida glanced behind her at her friend. She scoffed in her head. Jetta just wanted her to stand out. She didn't want the nobles to pick her out of a crowd like they did at the wedding.

Calida had been wearing a blue dress back then. It stood out but something to blend in wouldn't garner attention.

"They won't even notice me, Jetta. As always, they will be focused on their gossip and scandalous conversation. I'll blend in perfectly."

Jetta just shook her head and walked to the door.

Over her shoulder, Jetta said, "Lord Dominic is expecting you in the dining hall."

Just like that, she stepped out of the room. Calida joined

Jetta in the hall and jumped in surprise when she saw Braxton just outside the door, leaning against the wall.

What is he doing skulking around like that?

Normally, he escorted Lord Dominic, but lately it seemed like he was escorting her more and more. If this was the lord's way to gaining her affection, then he was failing miserably.

On her way to dinner, Calida prepared herself for another awkward meal with Dominic. The sound of laughter rang through the door of the dining hall. Confused, Calida entered. No one had told her there would be company, so when she saw a group of young men and women seated with Lord Dominic, Calida stopped in her tracks.

On his right sat Lady Orphelin. She was in the chair closest to the Madam chair. Lady Orphelin was fidgeting in her seat, glancing longingly at the chair reserved for the lady of the house. It was created for the purpose of displaying the lady of the house. The person who was supposed to be her.

But if Dominic moved on, Lady Evaine would be his first choice. Calida's face warmed as irritation filled her. The Madam chair was hers and hers alone. Even while indecisive, she was going to be Lady Goldwyn, not Lady Orphelin. As Lord Dominic's wife-to-be, Calida was within her rights to sit that close to her husband. In the history books, it mentioned that the seat closest to the lord of the home was a great honour. In the past, the wife was shown around like a trophy. While it hasn't changed much, it wasn't the same anymore. These days the Madam chair was a way to show respect to the lady. If someone wanted to disrespect the house, all they had to do was sit in that seat. They would also be claiming to have the lord's favor as well.

She felt silly for showing irritation over a simple seat, but it was harder to let go of the idea of sharing a life with Dominic than she thought.

Calida wasn't willing to accept her affection for Dominic,

but that didn't mean she wanted someone else to fill that position in the meantime. It was childish but that's what she felt.

Calida glided toward her seat as she realized Lady Orphelin wasn't the only one at the table. *Dear Eesa, she hoped she wasn't glaring.* Dominic glanced between the girls before tilting his head in confusion.

The same two men she saw last time when she had the "pleasure" of meeting Lady Orphelin stood in the room. The friend of Lady Evaine, Heloise, was also among the crowd. The odd one in the crowd was a man who looked remarkably like Jetta.

Calida couldn't help but stare at him. *Is he from Mirynd, is that why he looks so much like Jetta?*

Sitting down, she refused to acknowledge Lady Evaine or Lord Dominic.

Lady Evaine softly smiled at Calida.

"Hello, Lady Calida. How pleasant to see you once again."

Calida gave her a nod and then directed her attention to Lord Dominic. He stared at her with an eyebrow quirked.

"My dear one, we didn't get the chance to introduce you to my friends last time we saw them."

He gestured to the man who stood at the wall nearest Lady Evaine's seat and the one sitting across from her.

"This is Garrick Dale." He nodded his head toward the man sitting at the table with them. Garrick was a large man with dark hair and enchanting eyes. The same eyes and hair as Jetta.

"The one standing near Lady Evaine is her guard, Silas Mallory."

Calida turned around to greet Silas with a nod. He was just as enchanting. She almost wanted to do a double take. Tawny-gold and rugged skin, and thick dark hair with a powerful firm jawline. Not to mention as tall as a tree.

She could picture him with Lady Evaine, the two a dynamic duo. Her pale and dainty disposition compared to his darker complexion would pair nicely. If Lady Orphelin wasn't the woman who wished to replace her, then Calida could imagine them as a couple. Maybe even imagine being good friends with her.

"I guard Lady Evaine sometimes. Usually, I float between guard duties." Garrick said.

When extra security is needed, a guard on duty is assigned to float between stations, a term her father explained to her. Calida couldn't think of why Lady Evaine would need extra security at a time like this. It wasn't like she had any part in turbulent political agendas.

She met Garrick's eyes, and again Calida couldn't help but compare him to her friend.

"Are you related to my friend Jetta?" her mouth suddenly blurted.

Garrick looked over his shoulder and smiled. The sun shone through the window behind him and illuminated him in a very picturesque moment. His expression was so full of joy, she knew they had to be related. The dimples in their cheeks were identical.

"He is my brother, Calida," Jetta said.

Turning around in her seat, Calida glared at her friend.

"How come this is my first time seeing him?" What kind of friend was Jetta that she couldn't introduce her friend to her only brother. After all they had experienced together, Calida had hoped to be closer than that. "Was he at the orphanage when we met?"

Jetta's eyes glistened and she cleared her throat.

"No. The Dales adopted him before that."

The rest of the afternoon, Calida listened as the others talked. She didn't take part, feeling like the stranger once more.

Dominic discussed the ball they would host soon at his home. *Lady Evaine looks far too excited to see him again so soon.* Calida frowned and glared at her back.

She still didn't like the idea of Lady Evaine being so enthralled with him. She wasn't keen of the idea of liking him, either.

"My lord, what is it you fancy the most in your spare time?" Lady Orphelin batted her eyelashes. All her attention was on Dominic. She hadn't outwardly flirted with him or laid a hand on him, but it still made Calida uncomfortable. If they became a public couple, it would be easy for him to forget all about her. Her heart stung, shooting pain all through her. Wasn't that what she wanted?

The two were a few paces ahead of her as they walked through the paths in the garden of his mansion. Calida had done it on purpose. If she walked up to them, her emotions would be harder to control. Harder to hide. One moment she wanted to cling to Lord Dominic and insist that Lady Evaine find her own man. The next, she convinced herself it would be good they grew closer. It would make room for a replacement. *Her replacement.*

A sharp inhale from Calida suddenly gained the attention of Lord Dominic. He looked at her with concern.

However, just as he turned to talk to her, nurture her growing tumultuous emotions, Lady Evaine distracted him. With his head turned once more, Calida took the opportunity to slow her pace until she walked beside Jetta.

Her heart hurt at the image in front of her.

They shared a spirited conversation. Lady Evaine's beautiful smile lit up her face for everyone to see. Not even the blind could miss her love for Lord Dominic.

He walked with his hands at his sides, but Lady Evaine's floated out as if to grab his but would stop short and fall back into place.

At least go all the way. If anything, to give me a reason to be mad.

She couldn't hear their conversation anymore, trailing farther behind. Calida glanced up at the group from the corner of her eye. The more she slowed, the worse she felt. *It is normal, isn't it? Calida the outsider.*

Lord Dominic nodded, responding seriously to Lady Evaine, and she radiated in joy at his acknowledgment.

In a bittersweet way, Calida felt happy for them. If she forgot the anger gnawing away at her from the inside out. If she ignored the depression that set in when she thought of banishing herself to a life forever alone. Only then could she wish them a happy life.

Unlike her, who would more likely go back to take care of her mother.

Even though she felt angry and tired, Calida couldn't blame her parents. They didn't send her off to be miserable. It was almost like she wasn't supposed to accept her own emotions. Like holding any sort of emotion made her envision her mother's critique all over again.

A tear fought to fall.

This wasn't the place to cry.

She stopped, gripping her until they reached a turn and she caught up with Lady Evaine and Lord Dominic.

"Milord, it might be rather forward, but I had been happy when your father mentioned our engagement. It's not my place to decide, but in terms of who would do better in the role of Lady Goldwyn, wouldn't it be a noblewoman?"

Evaine's words hung in the air. The message was out there and there was no going back now.

Lady Evaine's eyes were glossy with emotion. Not exactly crying but wet with hope and emotion, as if wishing this could be her moment.

Calida's lips tightened, and her eyebrows creased. Her body tensed and her eyes clenched shut as she fought the desire to run off. Calida didn't want to hear his response but needed to.

"You're right."

Calida's heart stopped. Her lungs stalled and every fibre of her couldn't move an inch. *You're right.*

"It isn't your place, Lady Orphelin. I have chosen my bride and no argument from you or my father will change my mind."

Suddenly, Calida was sore everywhere. Her breath came back to her, and the drum of her heart returned to its rhythm. A tear spilled down her cheek, but she ignored it.

Slowly, she opened her eyes and the bright light surrounded her. There in the brightness stood Dominic, tall and strong, an unforgiving glower in his eye.

Lady Evaine l'Orphelin's eyes were now filled with tears.

Something Calida was also experiencing, but for different reasons. His firm statement devastated Lady Evaine, and what she meant to him hung in the air. At the same time, he had destroyed Calida in one sentence. She didn't truly know him, but he did her in with three words.

And brought back to her being with four. Free from the paralyzing stillness, Calida took off at a run for the mansion. Not caring the others had whipped their heads around to watch her take off for the security of her room. Not caring about Dominic's step in her direction, which was cut short.

Thirteen

The clinking of glass and stiff chatter echoed in the grand hall. Calida stood stock still, holding her breath as the party whirled around her. The last two weeks of planning had been chaotic. Several times she had been thinking about surrendering, mainly because the more Jetta and Dominic cringed as she included parts from parties in her town like festive food, the more Calida resisted. She hadn't expected the formal wear.

Noblewomen walked by her and stifled a laugh at her simple dress while she stood near the table with delicious food. It was nothing like the wedding where she met Dominic. She had expected something completely different. The stuffed pig on the table looked just like the one she would see at the gatherings she saw growing up if anyone could scrounge up one. It had a glaze on it that shone so brilliantly, Calida could see her reflection in it.

"Can you believe the slum rat chose *that* to wear?"

Calida's face flushed as a woman near her snickered as she walked away. *If only the ground would swallow me whole.*

The dress she wore was something she felt comfortable in,

but it wasn't up to date with new fashions. The others followed the trending fashion to have bright, enormous eyes and soft dresses, the ones displayed in tailor shops a commoner walked right by but wished they could purchase. No commoner could enter such a shop and hope to come out with something so expensive. At least not the average commoner. There were some rare ones who had come across wealth, but many were so close to peasant it was laughable. She was lucky to be marrying into a [better] position. Calida could depend on the lord to give her a stable allowance for necessities.

Dominic held out a hand and walked around the room, greeting every invited noble, a hospitable smile on him. He wore a tunic and vest which was not his usual dressed-up attire. He had chosen his clothes based on her plans for the party, as if to humour her insistence even after she turned away his protests.

Calida focused on the ground like an embarrassed child caught doing the wrong thing. In her mortification, she silently wished for her efforts to garner the attention to eat and enjoy. The men and women in the room would skim the table and then turn their noses away in derision. *Food was food, right? Apparently not.* There were some who glanced her way and scanned the options before looking her in the eye and scoffing with a smirk on their faces.

"See Calida, even mother can do better."

Calida touched the tablecloth. She had planned it to be casual, but she gazed around the room and saw the guitar off to the side was abandoned. There was no dancing and laughter. The women carried fans and covered the fake smiles on their faces. The men were boastful and puffing out their chests in pride about their exaggerated stories.

Why hadn't she taken Dominic's advice? She wanted to prove herself. That she was worth something to a nobleman.

He knew much more about the nobles and their palates than she did. Calida couldn't deny the foolishness of her bullheaded choices. But either she was a failure, or she wasn't. Her worth depended on her ability to assist someone other than herself. His help would mean she couldn't play hostess for a crowd of nobles.

Toying with a napkin abandoned on the banquet table, Calida sniffed her wet nose. It was the colour that her province would use. Tears spilled out of the corner of her eye. It was at least one thing she had gotten right.

In the middle of the hall was a spot reserved for dancing. Instead, the nobles stood around in small groups to sneak spiteful glares at each other. Joy wasn't the favorite past-time of these men and women.

The empty floor called to her, and Calida pictured herself walking up the dance floor. Lifting her skirt, letting the music move her like the folk in her town would at a lively gathering. Swaying and flittering about as if she were a butterfly caught in the wind. If admiration were that surface level, then the people around her would stop and stare as she danced so beautifully. Gasps and murmurs of awe would echo around her, and she would soak in the attention like a cloth absorbing water with a large, beautiful smile. She would hold her head high as the nobles clapped and cheered at her fluid movement.

Snapping out of it, Calida was fixed in spot, staring into space like a lunatic. Fantasizing about things that would get her laughed out of the grand hall. In reality, if she was to be so bold, the nobles would never let her live it down. Just another mistake from the foolish girl who clung to Lord Dominic.

Looking away, she picked up a roll from the table, slathered it in butter, and took a generous bite. Calida moaned as the soft bread melted in her mouth and wiped her tears away.

From the corner, she overheard some noblewomen talk as they passed her, not caring who heard.

"Did you see what she is wearing? What a poor, clueless country bumpkin. If only she had better taste." The one woman grinned as she fanned her face delicately.

The other chimed in. "Even then, it's just not right that they chained Lord Dominic to that girl from the backwaters of Eleari. She doesn't know the burdens of the title Lady Goldwyn."

She bit her lip to fight off the quivering. Those two noble-women were right about everything. Dear Eesa, she wanted to stop existing this second. Her mind swam as tears filled her eyes again. To think that this all started with Dominic. Rage bubbled up from deep inside. Calida clenched her fists as the need to stomp over to him and yell in his face surged through her.

"You're right." Dominic said.

Her ears rung with what Dominic said to Evaine earlier. Over and over, it played, until the nagging voices turned mocking.

The flames inside her had been doused. She wouldn't go over there to talk or yell at him. Like she hadn't the last two weeks. Calida knew she couldn't avoid him forever, but after her hasty exit in the garden, seeing him was the last thing she wanted. She would be the centre of his attention, and then what? *What if I make a fool of myself?* Calida was only seeing him again for the first time since the party.

In her self-pity, she ate her fill of the cooling food. She had given up resisting the desserts and buried herself in a flaky tart when he approached her.

His hand caressed her back, and Calida yelped. She jerked away and the flaky tart was squished in her fist. Then some of the swallowed tart got stuck, and she coughed to clear her throat. Coughing violently, it wasn't until Dominic patted her back a few times the tart came loose. Why was it every time he startled her, food got stuck in her throat?

After a few moments, the coughing passed.

Calida frowned as she refused to look up at him, gazing across the room as she massaged her neck.

"I haven't seen you at all this evening. How are you doing?" He stood close.

Calida peeked up at him. Earlier in the week, she would've kept her distance, her ability to trust a member of a vicious clan slim. They had talked little or had gotten to know each other enough, yet he was still kind to her. *Just what is his motivation?* She faced Dominic and in the silence, her eyes wandered.

She didn't want to admit it, but his height and size were alluring. He was almost built like a tree. If a foe came upon them, Calida was assured he wouldn't topple over in the wind like a twig.

"Eating the food. I guess I should have left the party to you after all. It seems like I just can't do the right thing around nobles." She lowered her eyes as her cheeks blushed. If she glanced his way, her willpower would be out the window. She didn't like the conflicting emotions.

Dominic grasped her chin and tilted her head back up to meet his soft gaze. A gentle smile creased the corners of his lips, drawing her attention for a moment, before she forced herself to look away. Still a moment too late because he saw her distraction. Calida tensed, but unlike when he would tease her before, Dominic stared at her, waiting.

"The party is exactly what you desired it to be. So, we must own it. Mistakes and all," Dominic said. "I am proud of you, Calida. You put yourself out there and planned a party. You put your heart into everything and that is amazing."

His compliment felt good. Tears pricked her eyes again, but she refused to let them pour. *I can't meet the standard.*

Her tears dried and her body tensed as a man dressed in expensive robes approached and struck up a conversation with Dominic. When the nobleman turned the conversation toward Calida's father, her interest piqued.

"My, my, you must have been around to hear about that incident in the palace the other day. Another case of theft. I felt sympathy for the poor man. It's not his fault. Can the impoverished help themselves when all they could have to live a long, good life was sitting in front of them like a fat cat?" He shook his head like it was a sad tale of the inevitable.

Calida's shoulders stiffened. The bastard spoke like her father was a pitiful whelp.

The hand on her waist felt like a weight holding her in place instead of securing her to Dominic's side.

Calida pushed it off and marched over to the door leading out of the ball. She didn't wish to inhabit the same space as the guests any longer. Not that they would notice, anyway. She had been the laugh of the party until the nobles moved onto something else to sneer about. Calida was practically invisible.

As she strode farther away, the quieter the mansion sounded and the darker the hallways became. Calida's throat closed as the shadows closed in around her. She clenched her fists, then rushed into her room. Slamming her door shut, she exhaled. Her easel stood on the other side of the room. It was still holding the painting from before, but she needed a way out.

Passionate slashes of paint covered the canvas until the frenzy drained from her and she collapsed to the floor, sobbing. The control she had from before broke, and tears streaked down. As she furiously wiped them away, paint stained her face. Calida's hair lay haphazardly against her neck, loosened from the braided bun she had put it in when getting ready.

Her chest hurt and it was like someone had viciously scrubbed bark against her face. The energy drained out of her. The floor became one with her body. This was one of those moments she wished it was possible to be anything but herself.

After a while of just lying there, she looked over at her most likely horrifying painting. Shifting a bit on the ground, she sat up, surprised by what she saw. In the dark contrast a hand reached out from the painting. Calida felt something stir within her. She stood and ran a hand over the painting as the feeling of comfort warmed her. She had used a mixture of vibrant blues and purples on the sleeve before it faded into the vignette she had created. The colors hypnotized her as she stared. They were all overlaying to create what looked like a realistic hand reaching out to take hers. *Something about the hand felt familiar.*

A vision of Dominic's hand flashed through her head. Calida gasped as she realized that the painted hand was his.

Shocked, it took a while for her to move. The likeness disturbing her greatly. Her hands shook as she cleaned the bristles. Her mind drifted to the party downstairs, and her throat tightened as she thought about returning to it. Conversing with those people was nerve-wracking. How foolish she had been to think men and women of high society wouldn't be so different from her people.

She didn't know how to host nobles. Calida didn't even know what the hottest fashion trend was. She could've left it to Dominic, but what would that say about the backwater country bumpkin?

Calida staggered down the stairs to rejoin the party, regretting her decision to turn tail and lick her wounds. She walked to the grand room across from the stairwell. The chatter of the nobles greeted her as she strolled through the threshold of the room once more.

Haughty laugher greeted her ears as she passed the banquet table. The food still lay almost untouched. The only noble who seemed to be hovering around the food was a round man. He piled up his plate with the cold food as he moved down the table and ate whatever was in sight simultaneously.

At least someone is eating it.

Calida frowned as she remembered the guitar she had provided so someone could play it. Growing up, it always seemed like someone knew how to play in the crowd of people attending the gathering. Calida had assumed dancing would be everywhere by this point, and she would at least feel a little bit better.

She strolled through the room, sighing as the noble-women's gazes landed on her. Their sneers twisted until it looked like they were the cats and she the mouse in a game of chase. Grins painted on the faces of the women with done-up hair and fancy fabric pinned to their bodies. Panting shallowly, she stopped in the middle of the hall. Unable to handle it anymore, she pushed through the crowd of people in search of escape.

Dominic was nowhere to be found. Calida grew warm as her anxiety climbed. *Out. Where was the door?* Pushing past a group of men in a serious conversation, her eyes focused on Dominic speaking to someone on the other side as she slumped forward. Then her breath halted when she realized who he was talking to.

Her dark brown hair waved down her back in elegant

curls, and the dress she wore had layers of purple and blue. Lady Evaine l'Orphelin looked like a beautiful bird on the arm of a warrior.

A chalky taste greeted her tongue as she gazed at them.

Even here she can adapt more than I can.

Her knees buckled as she turned her back on them. Calida wasn't surprised that they stood so close while talking merrily. *I am the outsider after all.*

The chattering around her faded away as she stared at the ground. A sharp laugh pierced through her loneliness. A woman from the crowd howled a grating cackle at the conversation she was having. No doubt it was about gossip. What else could it be? Calida had realized quickly that noblewomen's conversations were fueled by it.

They would demurely hide their mouth as they chewed or laughed, but the glint in their eyes was unlike anything she had seen before. It was dark and slimy, leaving a trail of evidence behind it.

Not all of them are like that, though. What about Lady Dale or Lady Evaine?

A rare outlier didn't make up for the seething underbelly of the court.

As much as she would protest, Lady Evaine was a part of it too. Every woman in the court was attracted to Dominic's upstanding character and position, and she wasn't the exception. The lady would flutter her eyelashes at the lord and try to worm her place in his life. Calida's betrothed had a position of power. Even the nicest of people would have something to gain from it.

Lady Orphelin didn't talk behind her back, though. She was upfront and kind. How could Calida judge someone so harshly who treated her with respect?

Calida shook her head. No, it didn't matter. They were in the wrong with their false smiles and muckspouting. It was the same noble who would grow resentful and then kill those who lose their usefulness. Like her father.

Rayner's smile suddenly flashed through her head. *"I love you, darling."*

She missed him. The security and contentment from one hug. She used to last a month on one hug. After the attack on her mother, Calida tried to separate her need for those annoying distractions. It grew uncomfortable to hug her father. Her mind would race, and her body would tense. She regretted her resistance to share her burdens and to be vulnerable with him. As she thought about him, all the things she didn't get to do flew through her mind.

Would his memory always be this painful?

It hadn't been long since Rayner passed away, but all her mother had left was a problem child. Neither could have accomplished much without him. He had been the light of their lives. And now it was snuffed out by the high society of Eonifond. She was left in this world without him, and it was their fault.

Who else? They are the ones who are always blabbing their mouths about every little thing and ruining the reputation of a man on a whim.

Calida walked toward the banquet table when she saw a group of noblewomen. Each of them was dressed in heavy fabric and rich colors. The women's necks were decorated in bright jewels and large bows. *Just the right crowd to eavesdrop for details about her father's death.*

She took a deep breath and then trudged to the noblewomen. Calida stood beside their group as she waited for them to start blabbering. The women snickered to each other, not realizing someone was listening close by. *Then again, they might not care.* Each had bulbous rings on their fingers and too many flowers pinned to their braided updos.

Calida waited in silence. Her body faced Dominic. Pain pulled strings in her heart. *Don't think about that.*

"Can you believe that the guards of the palace let a *faction* knight in? How could someone from a faction keep the palace safe without feeling greedy?" The noblewomen had their backs turned toward Calida. Another minute passed and the old bats still didn't seem to realize she was there.

"My lady, how do you cope? You have such a kind heart. The palace guards must see how generous you are." The woman fanned herself and flattened stray hairs back into place.

These old hags are so focused on their own appearances they don't even realize how shallow they sound.

One of the other ladies in the group cleared her throat.

"Someone from the Elite Dominion might as well as be a jester. They have no standing or dignity," she said.

Calida's eye twitched. *Those bitches.* She swiftly turned around and strode into their group.

"*Sir* Rayner Rhodes was given the title of Faction Knight because he was highly regarded in the Elite Dominion for his bravery, integrity, and loyalty to the crown," Calida said.

The women stared at Calida, realizing that they had been talking a little too loud. Calida stood tall even as the critical eyes of judgement scrutinized her. Her fierce stare met each of their sickly-sweet smiles hiding their disgust in their eyes.

"Rayner Rhodes was nothing but a peasant thief." The woman across from Calida shrugged her shoulders with her head held high. Calida stomped up to her and shoved her face into the noblewoman's space. She held back the urge to punch her.

"A thief? Like your underfed maids?" Calida asked.

Oh, how she wished to snarl and bite the head off the old bat. However, she was incapable of that. *What a time to wish to be anything but human.*

The woman's face reddened as an ugly scowl wrinkled her face.

"How dare you!" The lady stomped her feet.

Calida stepped closer until the women were almost face to face.

"Do you deny it?" Calida said. the older woman blustered as she swiftly glanced at her friends for help.

Calida watched in sadistic pleasure as the light of hope fell from her eyes. Her friends froze like prey. She might've brusquely pushed herself into this conversation, but it was definitely worth it.

Her mouth cracked open until a maniacal grin stretched into place. They were so easy to rile up.

"What is there to deny? The help is only as good as their bodies can handle."

Calida's grin fell. Rage simmered behind her eyes as she controlled her breathing. *Once a breeding bitch, always a breeding bitch.*

"Who are you to invade our conversation, anyway? You are nothing but a bedwarmer." One of the ladies snickered as she held a hand to her mouth. A spark lit from Calida's hand. Her mouth tightened. *Please say the wrong thing.* She silently begged for them to give her a reason to torch them.

"You called my father a thief. Why?" she said.

The ladies laughed in unison. Several shook their heads like Calida was a lost cause.

"*Miss* Calida, surely you know that *faction* knights are not given any regard in the court." The lady she stood in front of gave her a pitying look.

Calida frowned at her. Yes, many nobles would not call her father by his well-deserved title. They would rather laugh in his face for being a "wannabe knight." Knights for the queen are loyal to the crown and her advisors. Her father never told her if he tried to be a knight, but Calida knew enough that if he had tried, it would have been a near-impossible attempt.

Of those who tried to become a knight, nobles were favored in the choosing of new knights. If a peasant was chosen, they would have to be exceptionally intelligent and strong. Even then, they could be kept from reaching the moment of knighting.

Her father had once told her all about the Elite Dominion's pathway to becoming a knight like those under the crown with the same fight against the wall of privilege.

First, those who would want to take part would send in an application to their local tavern where it would be taken to the Elite Dominion base. Then they would be brought in and given a camp outside base to live during their testing. The participants would be pushed mentally, physically, and magically. The magical flow of people in Eonifond could be affected by the stress and strain of their life. Some would have a lower presence of magic when put under certain circumstances, leading many to drop out during the testing because it was too draining.

"Faction knights are not thieves, though, milady," Calida said.

"*Miss* Calida, they might as well be. They are a sad example of why we have high standards for the knighthood. *That* faction felt like they needed to replicate it for the losers." The ladies snickered behind their hands. Calida scowled at their hands. *If only I could just chop them off.*

"That is only because the knights of the crown are selected based on nepotism. At least Elite Dominion allows talented commoners to be exceptional." Calida clenched her fists to control her violent thoughts.

The noblewomen stared at Calida, their nonchalant expressions pissing her off. They didn't care that commoners didn't have the same chance as the nobles to be a knight.

"My father was not a thief."

"If he wasn't, then why would he sneak a coin or two when he thought someone wasn't looking?" a noblewoman said.

Calida's mouth opened in protest. Her finger pointed accusingly and then fell.

"Or when he would corner maids and caress their bosoms?" another said.

Calida ground her teeth as she listened to the ladies spin a tale of absolute shit. According to the old hags, her father walked around the palace on guard duty like he was a rooster in his prime. They recounted how he would walk up to married and unmarried women who worked as maids and pressure them to join him in bed. The fictitious version of her father would look down their dresses and touch their asses. In the end, the man the ladies described sounded nothing like her father.

Calida's face heated at the women's words, her eyes glaring with the temperature of a roaring fire.

Why do they insist on demeaning a dead man?

"He wasn't. He wouldn't." *Would he?* Calida stopped short. Her breath stalled. Was she questioning her own father? Mentally she shook her head. Calida knew her father. The rumors weren't accurate about him.

"Try saying that to the maids who loved his advances and found out he was married." A noblewoman huffed and folded her arms. Like a pebble being thrown against a wall, nothing Calida said seemed to get through to the women.

"My father was loyal to my mother," Calida said.

A chorus of cackling erupted from the crowd. They hid behind their hands as the noblewomen haughtily mocked Calida. She glanced at each of the women around her, surprised by the outburst.

"Just what's so amusing?" Calida glared at the noble-woman behind her laughing especially loud.

"You're so unbelievably naïve and ignorant! *Mister* Rayner Rhodes is not innocent and the stories of his affairs with unwed maids are infamous by now."

Calida's lips twitched in disgust. Her mouth opened to blast her again when a tinkling laugh pierced the tension around her. She whipped her head around and her eyes widened as she spotted Lady Evaine.

She was walking around the room on Lord Dominic's arm. The giggle that resembled a bell came from her mouth as she gazed up, entranced at Calida's betrothed.

"Lady Orphelin and Lord Goldwyn are going to be the talk of the town when they get married." The noblewomen turned their gazes to them. Several of the women sighed wistfully. Calida's fists clenched as the fire inside her burned. She absently rubbed her chest as the sting grew fierce. *Lady Evaine suited him.*

"She is a *far better* fit for a man such as him."

Tears stung her eyes. Calida looked away; her composure struggled to stay in place.

"Can you imagine the children they would breed? They could create a sinfully beautiful child," a noblewoman said.

It felt like a knife to her gut. Unable to handle it anymore, Calida pushed through the crowd. Her head tucked down low; she ran from the room.

Fourteen

Calida's bedroom door creaked open as Jetta slipped in and quietly closed it behind her with a snick. The only noise in the room was the rustle of clothing as Calida silently arose from her bed and dressed. Neither spoke as she readied to leave.

The night before, after she fled the grand hall for the last time, Jetta had stopped her for a moment. They made plans to visit the chancery at the crack of dawn to review the incident report of her father's death. Jetta added, "Before it is too late."

Calida had glanced sideways at her friend. Jetta thought that something might happen before they could get there. For the life of her, she couldn't think of anyone who would want to alter it when her father's death was not that complicated, but Jetta's hunches were usually sound, so she said nothing.

Goosebumps rose on Calida's arms as the chill of the early morning cooled her. She blinked her eyes as the darkness enveloped them. She fumbled about until she reached the door with Jetta at her heels.

With a hand on hers, Jetta stopped her.

"We need to tiptoe. I have already prepped the horse."

Calida nodded and nudged open the door, then snuck down the hall and down the stairs leading outside. Her friend was close behind her. In the calm rustle of the breeze and the absence of light, Calida looked over her shoulder as they hurried to the horse and departed for the closest chancery.

She couldn't avoid going alone to deal with this. Not that she wanted to talk to strangers all alone, but Jetta would sooner drop dead than to let her wander off.

While the actual chancery was in the palace, a decade ago the lord chancellor decided it was too annoying to have nobles coming to see him in the palace day and night. So, he had someone with object magic establish an office in each province. They enchanted a book to connect the chancery every few hours. Anyone could go from one office to another. It was something very experimental and unstable. They only gave it to the lord chancellor because he was becoming impatient. The object magic user had warned him, but he had dismissed it and duplicated it for every province.

The wind cut through the forest as the girls galloped on horseback. Calida held onto Jetta as they sped past the dark towering trees. Calida clung closer to her friend as the skittering of critters moved in the bushes. The darkness had always put her on edge. She couldn't remember where it came from, but the lack of light had always irked her. Being alone in the dark was even worse, while she was only anxious when with someone else. If she were alone, Calida didn't want to even imagine what would happen.

It was nearly daybreak when the two arrived at the Weommadran chancery. She dismounted the horse next to the building in the centre of the city. It was quiet outside, but with the day beginning, she could feel the rustling of townsfolk waking up from their night's sleep. The chill in the air warmed as the sun peeked through the sky. Jetta tied down the horse, and they entered the chancery.

Inside stood two guards who paid no mind to Jetta and Calida. No doubt they knew of Calida's betrothal to the earl of Weommadran. Even if they didn't recognize her, the Crescent League crest on Jetta spoke volumes. They were a popular faction to talk about in any community. They held themselves to a high standard and expected their members to treat others with respect and dignity. Not to mention, they jumped into the muddy mess of politics all the time.

Calida followed Jetta as they walked through the shelves to the back of the chancery. There were papers strewn everywhere, and it seemed like no one had been here recently to clean. Her eye twitched with the desire to tidy up the mess. If she had ever left it that messy at home with her mother, she never would've heard the end of it.

Jetta skimmed the books and stacks of papers until she came across one book that stood out from the others. Unlike the worn books and papers scattered about, this book was clean and pristine. It looked as if it had never seen the light of day before and the spine didn't have a crease in sight. Jetta picked it up and fingered through the pages until she reached the section she wanted.

"Before I activate the book, it might disorient you at first, so be prepared." Jetta pressed her finger to the page and mumbled something unintelligible.

"Disorienting? What are you talk—" A flash of light shot from the book and in an instant shaped an ethereal hook that latched onto something inside Calida and pulled her in. One second, she was standing beside Jetta in the Weommadran chancery and the next, her head was swaying as if on a boat. She opened her eyes and realized that she faced the wrong way. *Did it work?*

Then the swaying stopped, and she realized that the shelves and floor looked cleaner than before. The room seemed lighter, too. The surrounding shelves didn't have a stray paper in sight nor a speck of dust.

Calida panicked as she looked around and didn't find Jetta, but then another light shone from a book on the shelf beside her. It was open and the writing on the page glowed as if on fire.

There was an imprint resembling a finger on the bottom of the page, and then suddenly it grew brighter and brighter until she had to look away.

The next time she looked over, Jetta stood beside her in the aisleway of the shelves.

"You could've warned me," Calida said.

Jetta blew a stray strand off her face and brushed some imaginary dirt off her clothing.

"You would've protested against it if I did."

"With good reason."

Brushing off her clothing, Calida took in the shelves surrounding them. Her friend walked ahead and turned the corner with Calida close on her heels.

"Where is the lord chancellor, anyway?"

Jetta looked back at her friend, her eyes unreadable. "You will know when you hear it." She frowned as they walked through the shelves.

Why was she being so mysterious?

"When I hear what?"

They continued to weave through shelves and books until she heard a noise in the distance. It started as a small, irritating sound. A little whining over the stillness of the chancery.

"I don't care what you have to say! I should not have to wake up for some foot soldier!" A deep voice echoed through the hall of books.

Jetta and Calida looked at each other and then hurried through the last few shelves. The complaining voice grew louder as they moved toward it.

They passed the last shelf and saw an older bearded man standing in front of a hunched over elderly man. He was a tall, gangly looking fellow blanketed by a gold embroidered black robe. It dwarfed him until it looked like it was supposed to be worn by someone much larger.

"Lord Chancellor, Lady Calida from the house of Goldwyn has arrived." Jetta's voice pierced the conversation happening in front of them.

Lord Chancellor looked over at them and grimaced openly. *Who shit in his porridge this morning?*

"It's too early. Come back later."

Calida glanced at Jetta. Her friend was standing firm and undeterred by the grumbling response of the man in charge of all official documents of Eonifond.

"We won't come back later. Milady needs closure about her father's death."

Lord Chancellor scowled at her and then shooed away the man he had been talking to without a word. The man bowed deeply and then rushed out the door. The lord shuffled to the table nearby, holding a book.

"Why should I give any information about a thief to a woman who's not even married to Lord Goldwyn?" he asked.

Calida clenched her teeth at his tone. *So, she couldn't ask for information because she wasn't married and a countess yet.*

"I am living in the house of Lord Goldwyn. I am promised to be married to him and a lady in training. Is that not enough?"

The lord chancellor scoffed as he frowned in disdain. Evidently, he thought that was nowhere near enough. Couldn't she be enough as she was?

"Fine. You can have access to the papers." He flicked his hand to make them go away.

Calida suppressed the urge to roll her eyes at his dismissive tone. She opened her mouth to ask where those papers would be, but Jetta grasped Calida's arm and guided her back to the shelves and further away from the lord. The floorboards squeaked under her foot as they passed shelf after shelf. She was tempted to turn around and give the lord chancellor a piece of her mind.

"It's just right here." Jetta pointed to a shelf that had scrolls with the royal seal on them. In one section where the scrolls looked small and tattered, Jetta picked up the cleanest one in the section. Her friend walked over to the wooden lectern and rolled open the parchment. Calida walked up beside her and looked over her shoulder.

Incident Report
Queen's Palace
Faction Knight on duty
Description: Faction Knight Rayner Rhodes, on duty in the treasury room sector. He acted dishonourably to other guards and maids on duty. Faction Knight Rayner Rhodes was restless and snuck away for a long period. When Faction Knight Rayner Rhodes returned, he was cursing and clearly upset. Other guard on duty left post for a moment, bathroom break was required. He notified Faction Knight Rayner Rhodes of this, leaving him alone. When the other guard returned, Faction Knight Rayner Rhodes was dead. A jewel in his pocket and a list of accomplices in his hand.
Witness: Guard on duty Sir Sheldon Wood
Superior in charge: Sir Edward Frederick

There was a symbol in the paper's corner that looked like a crest with a snake wrapped around a skull. It was smudged and only barely legible.

"What's that?" Calida fingered the corner of the paper.

Jetta squinted her eyes as she frowned in concentration.

"I'm not sure. I have heard of tales about a fellowship of snakes…"

Calida glanced at her friend as Jetta stared into space.

Maybe the lord chancellor will have the answers.

Calida scooped up the scroll and dashed through the shelves to find the haughty man once more.

Jetta chased behind her, calling for her to come back.

She reached the same area he had been the first time and slammed the scroll down on the table in front of him. Calida got up close to his face and stabbed the mark on the parchment.

"What's this?"

Lord Chancellor met her gaze before glancing at the parchment. He grumbled and grimaced before he rolled his eyes.

"*Miss* Calida, that is a smudge. Do not waste *my* valuable time with such trivial matters."

"This isn't a smudge, and you know it. It looks too intentional."

She jabbed it as she glared at him.

It couldn't possibly mean anything, right? What a wild imagination she had.

He stared in derision and pushed it away.

"Please leave the way you came in. I won't continue speaking with such a dimwitted woman."

Calida's cheeks reddened as the flames inside her licked heat into her anger.

"I am not dimwitted, you insolent *oflati.*"

Jetta rushed over and wrapped her arms around Calida. She kicked out as her friend dragged her to the book that would send them back to Weommadran. Calida swore and wrestled to get free. She tried to press her heels down and stop Jetta's efforts but was rendered useless against her friend's strength.

"Let me go! He has answers!" Calida said.

"No!" Jetta stopped in front of the book. She let go of her friend and grasped Calida's shoulders.

"You are not yet married to Lord Goldwyn. You could get into trouble for causing an uproar with the official in charge of important documents for Eonifond," Jetta said.

Calida pushed the hands off her shoulders and clenched her fists.

"I'm entitled to know what happened to my father." Calida's fist spluttered with fire as the anger consumed her.

Jetta shook her head. "You already found out."

Calida opened her mouth to protest.

"Calida, you don't get it," Jetta said.

Calida closed her mouth and folded her arms as she begrudgingly listened.

"You're only entitled to what they *tell* you. Anything else is confidential and you're not on the need-to-know list."

Frowning, Calida didn't like the idea of information about her father's death leaving her in the dark.

"He's my father. I need c-closure." Calida hiccupped as her throat closed tight. Tears stung her eyes. She closed them briefly and took a deep breath, willing them away.

Jetta laid a hand on her shoulder as they stood in silence. After a moment, she gestured as ready and the two transported through the book and landed in the chancery in Weommadran. The sound of a bell rang in the distance, signalling the beginning of the day.

"I'll try to get the papers to you," she said.

The morning light shone through the window and warmed her face as she sat staring at the breakfast laid out for her. The birds chirped outside the cracked open window across the room.

Dominic sat at the head of the table, looking as regal and burly as ever. Calida squirmed in her seat as she remembered how uncomfortable the flex of his arms and the way they rested on the table made her feel. Suddenly, she felt this need to rub the ache deep inside her. *Would Eesa see this as an indiscretion? Maybe if I don't act on it.*

He glanced her way with a disarming smile. She could imagine him dressed in battle armor and mounted on a horse, riding into battle. Calida squirmed again. She needed to stop thinking about him. It was dangerous. He was dangerous.

"How are you this morning, my dear one?"

Calida rubbed her legs as his voice rang through her, as if it was humming from within. She wished he wouldn't stop using that endearment. It was wonderful and sent shivers down her spine, but it was keeping it hard for her to stay distant.

Although, that decision was draining as it was.

He could tell me what to do anytime.

No, she needed to maintain a distance.

Calida fought back a yawn as it came unexpectedly. After leaving the gathering yesterday, sleep was a long-lost friend. Her morning was dreadful and if it were possible to go back to bed, she would.

"It was uneventful, Dominic. Nothing to report." She pursed her lips as she lied. The morning was nothing short of chaotic. Not that she would share what she learned. At least not yet. She was still unsure if he was to be trusted. Maybe he would just start dictating her life like her mother. She wouldn't mind his demands. She didn't want to be caged in any longer.

Peeking up, she gasped when Calida realized he held a steady gaze on her as he leaned an elbow on the table, intensely focusing on her. *Shit. Was she that transparent?*

He quirked an eyebrow and smirked but returned to his meal. His thighs shifted under the table and brushed her knee. With a jump, she realized all her attempts to keep a pure mind had failed.

Her head spun as the ache grew almost unbearable. In her rampant imagination, she knelt and peeked up at him. Calida imagined herself naked and vulnerable as he stared down at her with shining golden plate armor on him. His glower left her tingly as the dim lighting took up the space around just the two of them. In her mind, shivers wracked her body, and he had a frown on his lips. If Dominic had spoken, she had no doubt a growly voice would greet her ears.

Calida shook her head to clear the fantasy before purposefully staring at the curtains and tablecloth, then the chairs around the dining table. *I am going to burn in the ethers for this.*

As the fluttering of anxiety filled her, a pregnant pause echoed in the room.

After a moment, she took a deep breath, and they delved into their breakfast. The warm air and stillness before the day began did nothing to tame the pulsing aching from within. After finishing her meal, Calida stood and walked away until Dominic stopped her. *Oh no, please let me escape this embarrassment.*

"We still need to discuss what I had found out at the party last night. While you had retired early, I asked around for more information regarding your father's death."

Calida inhaled sharply. She was still raw from the earlier encounter with the lord chancellor. She stumbled, as if a fog had descended in her mind. The sharp pain of grief was dulled by the sudden fatigue from the reminder of her father. Thinking about all the time spent with her father and what she would never get back flew through her mind, but the visceral pain attributed to it was missing. *If only I could crawl into a hole and forget I exist.* She had been sitting around here going to parties and living a luxurious life, but she had yet to avenge her father's death.

Dominic guided her outside to the garden. It was warm and bright and the gentle breeze influenced the flowers and grass all around them. Dominic let go of Calida's arm when they approached the bench. They discussed the guests. Some only wanted to gossip and sneer at Calida's plain choices for the party. Those that were not gossiping answered some questions about the incident, but none were sympathetic. What else had she expected, though?

Bushes the size of trees grew around the spot and no servant was in sight. Anything they spoke about would be kept between the two of them.

Dominic took her hand. "The viscountess had something to say yesterday."

Calida knew little about Viscountess Victoria Wallington. The woman seemed nice enough, but no one could truly tell. She had introduced herself earlier in the evening and had been a bubble of smiles and happiness with an aura of welcome and motherly instinct. She was sure the woman was the type who gave generously to others.

The viscountess had told Dominic about rumours being spread around that evening. She explained as one for concrete evidence, childish rumors meant nothing to her, but some nobles were spreading information about Rayner and wanted to confirm if it was true.

"The palace maids' testimonies about Rayner were damning. They claimed he was flirtatious and touching them inappropriately."

Calida's face went red with fury. That someone would gossip such awful things about her father! If she wouldn't get in trouble for it, she would punch in their faces.

"My father was loyal to my mother until the end. Anyone who knew them could see that." Calida gritted her teeth. She breathed out slowly, attempting to control her anger.

Staining her father's name like that, it was the greatest way to test her fury. None of it seemed true, but she didn't know who to believe anymore. As far as she knew, he was killed on a whim because some noble decided he had enough of another "lowlife rabble."

"Who would want to spread such things about my father? He has only been loyal to the Queen and all she represents. Isn't that like saying they don't believe in the crown?" Calida glanced his way. He just so happened to be staring down a bush in the distance.

With a sigh, she stood. There wasn't much point in making conversation with someone who wasn't paying attention. Dominic pulled her back to him.

"I don't know who would gossip about your father. He wasn't someone who would do such treacherous things."

Calida's eyebrows creased in confusion. He knew her father was honorable, but how did he know her father that well? She wouldn't argue the point, but it was still odd he knew of her father at all. *Just how did he come to pick me as his bride?*

"How did you know my father?"

Dominic avoided her eyes as she tried to keep his gaze on hers. She squinted and pursed her lips as the lord cleared his throat and tried to find something else to talk about.

"I talked to some other nobles too," he said.

Dominic told her about Duchess D'Airelle, aghast at the rumours being spread. D'Airelle was one of those nobles who believed in logical, reasonable thinking instead of filling her days with spreading and creating trouble. Calida had heard about the chats Rayner and the lady had about political topics. She hadn't understood a word of it at the time, but seeing her father happy to have someone who was willing to speak to him about his opinion filled her with joy. Even though her father wasn't nobility, the duchess valued his opinion. Apparently, she considered even a commoner to have more sense than anyone else in the court. Maybe it was because her father didn't spend his days ruining the lives around him.

A smile creased her lips as a weight lifted off her shoulders. Even if the other nobles didn't approve of her, at least she had one who wasn't so bad.

"Sir Colin Vaughan, Heloise's father, spoke to me as well. Your father knew him well and he took the news hard. Not to mention the terrible rumours being spread about Sir Rayner," Dominic said.

Calida had never met Heloise's father, but she had heard of him. The man was a good person. Sir Colin Vaughan was an honourable Faction Knight who worked day and night for his daughter. Heloise was all he had left after his wife died in childbirth. Her father often spoke of his kindness and generosity among the brethren in the faction.

The day his wife died, Calida and her mother had picked some fruit from the market for them. Cressida had taken it to the family as a condolence gift. The townsfolk and her mother spoke often about all that was heard from their home was weeping. She had wanted to do more to help, but how appropriate would it be for a stranger to offer comfort to someone who they didn't know well? She wasn't friends with Heloise. The only reason she knew of them was because of her father.

Lost in her thoughts, Calida jumped when Dominic suddenly embraced her. Tears trailed from her eyes.

She wiped them away in shame. Scolding herself, she attempted to move away from him. But he spun her around and pinned her to him.

"Calida, don't hide from me."

Calida's eyes widened. She hadn't thought she was hiding from him. If she was tearful, it had always meant she needed to practice better control of her emotions.

Her mouth opened and closed, speechless.

He caressed her face, his thumb brushing her lips. "If I could put a smile on your face every hour of the day, that would be my greatest accomplishment."

Calida's tears welled up again. His warm body against her was comforting. She was tempted to nuzzle his neck and sigh in relief like a contented cat.

If only for a moment.

Her eyes drifted shut until she hadn't even realized they had sat once again.

Before she knew it, she had fallen into a peaceful slumber on Dominic's shoulder under his watchful eye in the garden.

Darkness greeted her. *Where am I?*

Groggily, she opened her eyes. With a gasp, she remembered what she had been doing before she had fallen asleep. In a panic, Calida pushed off the bench and distanced herself. Her head was spinning as she tried to reorient the world around her. Clenching her eyes shut, she tried to breathe through the swaying.

After taking some time to stop the earth from spinning, she glanced Dominic's way.

He stood near the bench, his hands out and ready to help

her. His steady gaze met hers. Calida gulped. *Oh, dear Eesa, he had that wooing look in his eyes. Did he even realize that his eyes were mesmerizing?*

If he was thinking she would come closer, then he was a bigger *daufi* than she thought.

She wasn't going to venture into the unknown and no amount of intense staring that made her melt in the knees would change that. At some point, he had to realize that she wasn't suited for the noble way of life. She lived in the fields and the dirt. The forest was her home. Calida didn't have the habit of oiling her skin to preserve her youth or powdering her face to look prettier. The most she did was brush her hair. Not that any commoners had the luxury of keeping up their appearance for posturing.

If only she could summon enough anger to punch him in his arrogant face. Bacraut.

"Why didn't you wake me up?" Calida combed through her hair with her fingers.

With a peek his way, she whipped her head around when she realized he was smirking at her. Suddenly, her body was hot and cold, a vicious dichotomy as she inhaled sharply. *Oh, my Eesa.... What in the salacious sarding was he doing to her?*

She clenched her jaw as she took off out of the garden. Not wanting to look at Dominic's face, she feared the embarrassment would make her faint.

Hadn't crying in the presence of someone else been embarrassing enough? Apparently not, since she had also fallen asleep on his shoulder. *The asshole didn't even bother to wake me up.*

The last time she cried in front of someone else had been when she was a child and her father found Cressida in their bed, left for dead. She hadn't understood the implications then, but now she knew her mother had been assaulted. As a child, she didn't understand why her mother would no longer share in jokes or laugh until she overheard the complaints of other women in town about her being too emotional. They had said something about how a child who cried all the time wasn't a grateful one. They sympathized with a traumatized mother who had to deal with a child who wouldn't stop making demands.

She stopped crying in front of others then. What was the point if it was a nuisance? Calida had been processing her grief over losing the mother she knew, but it wasn't about her. She had realized that her mother didn't need a child. Cressida needed someone who could help her regain herself.

Calida had made sure her mother had at least one meal a day. Her father tried to stay home, but he couldn't be there all the time. Months would go by, with her mother being cold and blind to her own daughter. Some days, it was like Calida didn't exist. She wanted to believe it was only because her mother's sorrow consumed her. It had become her moment to take care of her mother instead. Her tears had no space in her responsibility. Taking care of her mother came first. She needed to be in control of herself.

Crying in front of Dominic was like admitting that she needed comforting. That would mean that all the effort she put in to be a dutiful daughter was meaningless. And she needed attention she hadn't received while her mother spent month after month weeping and wishing death upon herself. Calida would have to admit that her needs were valid and all the efforts she took to step outside her own head were wasted.

Dominic caught up to her and grasped her hand.

"My dear one, falling asleep on my shoulder is not something to be ashamed of."

Calida tugged to release her hand from his grasp, but he was stronger. As she fought, he pulled her into a hug. Tears threatened to pour once more, but she squeezed her eyes shut to resist. She couldn't believe the words of a man who didn't truly know her. After so many years of staying in the background, Calida couldn't just step into the sunlight that easily.

Dominic tilted her head up to look him in the eye. He captured her gaze, and she gulped in apprehension. His hair fell around his eyes, contrasting with their vibrant blue. With a shiver of fear, Calida pushed away from him.

All it took was meeting his eyes for her to hike up her skirt and take off running. She couldn't handle that look. Not when she was trying to be invulnerable. It was too wonderful and frightening.

She couldn't stay near him, not when what shone in his eyes was what she wanted most but wouldn't dare let herself have. Love.

She rode her horse for a long time before she stopped and rested in a nearby field. The grass swayed in the breeze and birds sang. The sky was clear and warm rays of sunshine touched Calida's face. She breathed raggedly as her head spun. The brightness stung her eyes and the noise of the wind and nature dug into her mind. All she could think about was silence.

Shut up. Shut up. Shut up.

Calida collapsed on the ground as she dug into the flesh of her chest.

Emotions are weakness. Don't feel.

She felt the need to scream at herself as tears of relief touched her eyes. He looked at her so lovingly. No words said, but it looked just like how her father would glance at her mother. Her chest tightened. She couldn't accept it. It was too frightening.

"Calida, do your chores this instant, you wretched brat! Do you wish to be sent to a mental asylum?"

Tears spilled down her cheeks. If she hadn't been enough as a child, how could she be enough now? She had to be more, do more. It was her responsibility to take care of her parents. What saddened her the most was her father was none the wiser. As far as he knew, Cressida was doing her due diligence. Calida played the perfect part until she couldn't.

Why would I be enough for Dominic if I wasn't enough for my own flesh and blood?

It took some time before she could calm down and dry her tears.

Calida got up to head back to the mansion. Returning was something she didn't want to do, but Dominic was the person who kept her safe now. Taking off on a run like that had been foolish. Women who roamed alone were likely to be kidnapped and never seen again.

It would be awkward, but it needed to be done. At least he wouldn't harm her.

Unless heartbreak counted.

She shook her head to discard her disturbing thoughts.

As Calida rode back, the sky grew darker, and she came across a tavern. It seemed mellow and inviting. Light poured from the windows and several men and women sat inside. The smell of freshly baked bread wafted her way, drawing her in. After the last incident in a tavern, she was reluctant, but it was outside in the dusk or inside with witnesses.

Calida dismounted, then stepped inside. She took a moment to close her eyes and breathe in the relaxing environment inside before she strolled to an unoccupied table near the bar.

"Can I get you anything?" A barmaid approached Calida.

Calida looked up at the girl and smiled slightly, holding up a coin. "Perhaps some information? Anything new in the grapevine?"

Pursing her lips, the barmaid glanced around before leaning forward. "The palace guards found a list of accomplices at the site of the robbery. There was even the name of a deceased faction knight on duty as a palace guard on it!" She shivered and rubbed her arms. "I've never been that scared before."

Calida kept a neutral face. It was hard to hear about her father, but it wasn't like the barmaid knew it was her father. Although a guard on a list of accomplices was strange. Calida's eyebrows creased as she thought about what it meant. *Why would they have a list?*

It meant there was previous planning. The entire explanation seemed off. No thief just went through such elaborate planning for some jewels they didn't even take. The biggest alarm sounding was that they would be in the palace. It was the most well-guarded places in the realm. Also, the only guard at the scene had been her father. The only one who could be on that list, unless the said guard, was the one that had been missing from his post. She paid the barmaid a bag of thirteen silver galatos and then rose from her seat.

She needed answers, but where would she find them? It all seemed to be leading nowhere.

Calida strode away and mounted her horse. All the opposition to the reputation of her father was enraging. *Why couldn't they just see he was a good person?* The people behind this were determined to taint her father's name. She didn't have the proof yet, but it would be found. They couldn't keep up this façade for long. The true colors of the person constructing this nonsensical tale to sway the people's judgement in their favor would be shown one way or another.

Her father's name had been the word on the street this past fortnight. If the barmaid knew by now, that meant that merchants and travellers knew. Their mouths were as loose as water. To reveal the truth and avenge her father, she needed to take extreme measures. It was only natural that people would be curious about the downfall of a guard, especially one connected to a private faction. Most people around the country silently watched the factions until they trip, then used that to their advantage to get ahead. Sometimes an innocent bystander would start a rumor without even realizing it. That was all it took for the fall of factions like Elite Dominion.

She grasped the reins and took off into the night for Dominic's mansion. The air was slightly chilly and everything around her was closing in to smother her. Not a speck of light from the setting sun remained. It seemed like the surrounding darkness was coming to life as she travelled as fast as she could. Flashes of her mother being attacked and whispers about other villagers being struck in their own homes had her urging her horse to move faster.

Her body clenched in her saddle as she tried to stop herself from whimpering in fear. A prickle of awareness nipped her arms and feet and hands. The overwhelming paranoia of someone coming out of nowhere and jumping her filled her until the trees closed in on her. She glanced every which way as she galloped back to Dominic.

"I just need to get back. I'll be alright," she said.

Calida focused on the road ahead of her, trying to not let her imagination get the best of her. Her chest hurt as her breath fought to come out.

Soon, a light spilled on the road up ahead. Slowly and gradually, it brightened. Some of the urgency left her, but she sped up to reach the light, as if it would make it all right. Up ahead, the trees broke, and the end of the path was visible. Calida gasped at what she saw.

With a candleholder in hand, Dominic sat atop his horse, waiting.

The light seemed to encompass more of surrounding wood than possible as she cleared the forest, but she didn't give it another thought. The light cascaded, causing a larger and more menacing expression. He frowned as she came closer. If he was anything like her mother growing up, then she would be scolded for not being on time, or for leaving in the first place. Her heartbeat frantically as she froze.

"My daughter, how lucky to be held to this standard. If it were I, returning at this time would be lazing around. Just think about the consequences of showing up late. Mother could be mocked by her friends for such disrespect."

Her mother had also drilled into her the dangers of men, but it was like all that had flown away when Dominic inserted himself into her life. He stared back at her, the light of the candle mirrored in eyes full of intense emotion. His gaze softened when she finally approached.

Her wide eyes prickled with tears as she loosened her shaking hands from the reins.

When she was close enough, Calida flung herself at Dominic, colliding into him with a force that would knock over the average person. Dominic grunted, then wrapped his arms around her and struggled to sit her straight on top of his horse. Moving her until she sat on his lap, he held her close while trying to keep the candle lit.

In that moment, the darkness that had been circling in to swallow her whole pulled back. The air was still and the tidal wave of emotions that she had been struggling with mellowed out. Somehow, Dominic was all it took to feel right again. Calida realized she had flung herself at him. That alone was embarrassing. Many people usually saved this intimacy for after marriage.

She remembered his expression from earlier. Calida had completely forgotten the reason for her mad dash out of the garden. Her face reddened, and she froze. Shit, what was she to do now? She had just flung herself at the man who she had run away from.

Her body was rigid as panic filled her and grasped at the last straws of her sanity so she could dismount his horse as swiftly as possible. What a brilliant feat she had accomplished now.

As she was about to slip off and make her escape for the mansion behind them, Dominic blocked her with his arm. He leaned his head forward and rested it on her shoulder. She thought he sniffed her but dismissed it out of sheer ridiculousness. What type of human man would sniff a woman? It was far too absurd.

"You scared me, Calida."

Her jaw fell slack, and she whipped her head up to stare at him. This enormous beast of a man was afraid? She couldn't wrap her head around that.

"When you ran off and didn't come back for some time, I thought someone had kidnapped you. It frightened me out of my skin. If something had happened to you..."

He was shaking, like the thought of her being kidnapped could send him over the edge. Dominic's arms circled her closer, plastering her slight frame up against his larger one. Not once had she thought it would affect him in such a way.

Her first thought was to escape. She wasn't used to someone being this concerned for her. Bottling her emotions just couldn't work anymore. The conscious effort to keep her feelings under control caused more to spill out. Slowly, she patted his chest in a soothing pattern. She was half tempted to hum a lullaby to ease him, but she couldn't remember the one he had hummed to her.

"I'm back now, though. Nothing has happened to me." She thought about mentioning the chatter in the tavern but decided tomorrow would be better. His ragged breathing showed just how he would take talking about anything at this point.

It took a while of him holding her in the darkness outside the mansion before he released Calida to slip away and lead her horse back. Concerned, Calida peeked back at him, then whipped her head around when she saw Dominic's fierce, longing stare as if being parted from her was hard on him. With a kick to her step, Calida made for the stable next to the mansion with her horse in tow. All the while, Dominic slowly trotted behind her.

Walking at a fast clip, Calida had her horse in the stable in record time. When she entered the mansion, she had paid no attention to Dominic and focused on the goal of reaching her room without further embarrassing herself. She tried not to be aware of his presence following her to her bedroom, only to walk to his own once she was in hers. As if he had to make sure she arrived at her room safely.

Under the covers in her bed, Calida shut her eyes and welcomed sleep, wanting nothing more than to forget all that had happened. The slow lull of nothing pulled her eyelids closed. She dreamed of her father and his laughter during the times he was at home. Dominic, and his complicated expressions. The desires that stirred inside her when they were close. All the nobles in her new life, pointing and laughing at her dream self. Their bodies turned into shadows that taunted her every breath. Until it was all just darkness and she fell into a deep slumber.

The next day, Calida walked to the library, where a servant had told her Dominic was. She knocked on the door and waited, then entered when he murmured, "Come in."

Dominic sat by the window, leg up on the cushioned bench and his arm resting on it as he stared outside. If only she could paint his portrait. Natural light shone in through the window with the tint of frost. The shelves of books behind him framed the background and added some chaotic colour. Dominic leaned forward in his seat, returning his focus to the book in his hand. A serious frown sat on his face as his eyes sped through the lines. A smile edged her lips as she watched him read the book. His frown would deepen at certain parts, but then his eyebrows would rise at other ones. If it wasn't already picturesque enough, he had taken off his boots and they sat on the red rug.

Calida stepped forward and cleared her throat.

Dominic looked up from his book, his eyes lighting up when he saw her standing there. Calida blushed but stayed on task. It wouldn't take long for the conversation she had overheard last night to wipe the happiness from his face.

"I apologize. I didn't tell you what I found out while I was away. You know, about my father." She bit her lip as she fought to tell him. For once, she didn't want to rely on someone else to get some type of resolution. Calida sighed. He insisted on helping. If Dominic was to help, then he would need to know.

"Hmm? What did you find out?"

Calida pushed a strand of hair behind her ear and sharply inhaled. "After I had run off, I went to a tavern for a rest when a barmaid came up to me. When I asked her for news, she told me something distressing..."

Dominic stared at her, waiting for her to continue.

"The palace guards found a list of accomplices in the room where the robbery took place. They mentioned a guard on the list. A faction knight guard." Just as she predicted, a scowl replaced the small smile on his face. She was just as upset.

Dominic pushed out of his seat and paced before he smacked his fist against the wall and rested his forehead against it. His shoulders shuddered as he struggled with composure.

"Your father was a good man. He didn't deserve this."

Calida's gaze shot to the floor as he abruptly spun around. She wanted to say she agreed, but her throat was as dry as the Syniel Desert. Her mother had never hit her before, but sometimes words felt like punches. He moved toward her, and although she tried to suppress it, Calida flinched. She didn't fear him, but erratic behavior made her skittish.

Dominic stopped. "Calida, do I frighten you?"

Calida shook her head vigorously. He frowned. Obviously, she failed to convince him she wasn't frightened of him, only the chaotic and unpredictable emotion that was anger. "Milord—my lord, it was a reflex. It meant nothing."

Dominic looked her in the eyes as his face grew serious. He wasn't buying it. *And why would he?* Calida nibbled on her bottom lip as she wrung her fingers in her lap.

He lowered himself into his seat, not breaking eye contact with her. Calida shuffled around, unsure of what to do. Many commoners didn't sit close to a noble like this. All she could think about were the times rude nobles in town would shoo away any commoner who dared sit too close to them. One time, this affluent noblewoman had plopped down in a seat at the local tavern and when commoners didn't get up and move or sat at tables around her, she threw a fit. It cost the barkeep his job.

"Feel free to sit anywhere you want."

Dominic gestured for her to sit next to him in the other chair, his eyes never leaving her. Calida scrunched her nose and glanced at him while nervously rubbing her hands on her dress.

"I know what we should do next. But you won't like it," Dominic said.

Calida bit her lip, then inhaled and exhaled.

"What's the idea?"

"It involves attending a ball."

Calida dashed for the door. After the previous two formal gatherings with nobles, she wouldn't listen anymore. Putting herself in parties was a disaster. *No way am I going to attend another event only to be mocked once again.*

Dominic grabbed her wrist and stopped her as her hand touched the doorknob. He moved her hand until she had to face him.

"Please, I know you dislike public gatherings with nobles, but this may be necessary to find out the truth."

Calida gritted her teeth. *Dislike.* That was so mild and didn't properly convey her hatred of balls.

"Dislike is for a type of food. Loathing is a far better description."

Dominic sighed and glanced at the ground before meeting her eyes.

"I apologize. I was watering down your anger about them. I get it. They are awful, but we need to find out more. Right now, our information is just not lining up."

Calida paused and closed her eyes as she thought. She really hated them. The nobles were so rude. Their cruel eyes drilled into her mind, judging her without mercy and leaving her feeling ill.

She should go, but that meant risking her own dignity and pride. Calida didn't want to volunteer to play the games noblewomen favored, becoming once more the insect caught in the spider web.

Did she really have any say in the matter, though? Lord Dominic was the one who had experience with nobles. Even her attempts to keep information from him were short. Calida's mouth fluttered open as soon as she felt guilty for not telling him every aspect of what she learned. He insisted on helping, and she was grateful, but that didn't silence the little voice in the back of her mind.

"Can't even complete a simple task. She couldn't even learn the first time".

Not to mention, as a commoner, what could she say against a nobleman? He had connections and a position of power. If he wanted to, she could be exiled to a pirate ship in the middle of the Primeval Ocean, gurgling six feet under.

Calida looked down. She gulped as the dark realization sunk in. He had all the power and if he was that type of person, he could do such a thing. Not to mention, commoners always got the blame.

"I'll do it."

"Calida..." His thumb rubbed on her skin in a circular pattern.

Tears fogged her eyes. His comforting voice grated against her. She took her arm back and escaped out the door. Her feet pounded on the ground as she left Dominic standing in the room.

Calida shook as the carriage clacked along the road, the snap of the reins urging the horses onward.

She had been painting, ignoring the tears that poured from her eyes after the encounter earlier in the day with Dominic in the library. Jetta slammed her door open in a rush. The list was found at Viscountess Victoria's home, and her ladyship had an interesting story to go along with it. The kind that demanded in-person conversation. At least it would be a pleasant conversation.

Viscountess Victoria also lived in Weommadran, so it was a quick trip to her mansion.

Rocks crunched as the carriage stopped in front of large wooden doors. Jetta exited first and held out a hand for her lady. Calida stepped down and breathed in the wind that rustled through the leaves of the surrounding trees.

"Greetings to milady Goldwyn." A man pulled open the doors and bowed to her.

Jetta bowed and gestured her forward.

Well, there is nothing like now to act like a lady.

She stepped over the threshold. Jetta followed close behind, surveying their surroundings. Another servant inside the pleasant mansion bowed to her.

"Milady Goldwyn, milady Wallington is in the back. I shall guide you through to the garden." She turned around and rushed to a door on the other side of the foyer.

Calida followed, trying to make it appear the polished walls and floor did not dazzle her. With a casual glance, she took in all the beautiful decorations and ornaments that she could while not appearing like a newborn babe in the wood. She may live in a mansion of this splendour now, but it still fascinated how amazing the homes of the nobility were.

The maid held open the door for her.

"Thank you," Calida said.

The maid's eyes tightened as she frowned at her in confusion. *Is a noblewoman not allowed to thank the maids? It seems like a natural courtesy.*

"We should continue on." Jetta cleared her throat and gestured her to walk outside.

Calida took one more glance at the maid, but the girl's gaze was fixed on the ground. She sighed and walked into the gardens.

Amid the flowers and brush sat Viscountess Victoria Wallington. The pinks and pastels flushed her pale skin, and the wind fluttered her blonde hair. However, even though surrounded by beauty, her eyes appeared sunken with bags under them, as if she hadn't slept in a week.

Calida strode the path through the flowers to the table in the centre.

"Ah, my lady Calida. To what do I owe this pleasant visit?" the viscountess asked.

Calida went to bow, but then the viscountess's hand shot out to stop her.

"My dear, we're both nobles. No need to bow." A demure smile appeared on Lady Wallington's face.

Calida glanced up and shifted nervously. She hadn't been alone with a noblewoman in this setting before. She grappled with what to do. None of the few books she had read about noble etiquette said what to do if you were alone with a noble and how to say or phrase the words.

Lady Wallington gestured to the seat beside her. Inhaling, Calida held her breath as she sat down.

"M-My lady, I don't believe we had a chance to speak at Lord Dominic's mansion," Calida said.

The lady sipped from her tea, then smiled at her. "No, we didn't, but I have heard about you. It's quite extraordinary, the nobles are obsessed with the topic of you." Viscountess Wallington picked up a small spoon and stirred her half-drunken tea.

Calida picked up a cookie from the tray between them and broke off pieces of it, then rubbed it between her fingers. She wasn't hungry. Why would she be when she was alone with a noblewoman? It was important that she stay calm, in order to get the information about the accomplices list. Before getting that, Calida couldn't fathom eating a bite. She didn't think she would be able to swallow anything. The anxiety of being in Lady Wallington's presence was enough to strangle a bear.

A sharp, carefree laugh cut through her thoughts, disrupting the spiralling turmoil in Calida's mind. With a cleansing breath, she felt some of the weight on her shoulders lighten.

"My dear, you look positively ill! Don't tell me I make you that nervous?" Lady Wallington chuckled into her hand. A warm, comforting grin that almost radiated maternal kindness shone on her face. Tears pricked Calida's eyes; the lady was the type of mother she wished she had grown up with. The last time she had felt such comfort...

Before the incident, her mother had been that kind.

"I-I... It's just I heard you have a list of accomplices that was found in your maid's possession."

Lady Wallington cocked her head to the side and gazed at

her quizzically. Calida bit her lips and fixed her eyes on her wringing hands.

"You see... There was a rumor that my father was on that list. I need to know. I need closure." Closure that something foul was afoot.

"Ah. Your father must be the recently deceased Sir Rayner Rhodes of Elite Dominion. Of course, you would want to see that." The viscountess snapped her fingers, and the servant nearby ran off toward the house, only to return moments later with the paper. Calida peeked up at it, almost tempted to rip it out of her hands, if only to get it faster.

The lady handed it to Calida. Her fingers brushed over it, as if to convince herself it was real.

Parts of it were ripped and it felt smooth. Her eyebrows furrowed as she realized it was an expensive piece of parchment.

It was stained brown but didn't match the stained paper many guards would likely have on hand. The papers her father had brought home had been grainy and brown with splotches of white. As if the person who made it had tried to bleach out the color, but it wasn't possible without compromising the fibers.

Calida read the words on the page to herself and frowned at the nonsense.

In the corner there was a mark that said "*SC.*"

Break in.

Find G.

Let nothing stop them.

Accomplices:

Sir Ralph Hughes

Sir Sheldon Wood

Sir John Rolfe

Sir Rayner Rhodes (Linchpin)

They all know their task.

HE is the key to this all.

Calida blinked. She didn't want to believe it, but it was there in ink. Whoever this was had used her father's death as a part of their twisted plot, which she still didn't understand.

The tears returned as a heavy weight struck her chest hard. Something felt off, but she couldn't quite figure out what. One of the other names sounded familiar, but for the life of her, she couldn't remember why.

She looked up from the paper, her eyes fogged by tears.

"I didn't want to believe until now... but there it is," Calida said.

Lady Wallington laid a hand on hers as Jetta slipped the paper from her fingers to examine herself. Calida bit her lip as she fought back the tears.

"My dear, this must be truly awful to find out. And so soon after his death." Tears welled up in the lady's eyes as she held onto her hands. The sting of longing lashed Calida's heart like a fresh wound. Hunching forward, she only barely held back to lay her head on the table to sob. It was too embarrassing to cry in front of others.

Lady Wallington stood up, dragging Calida up with her. Her hands clutched Calida's shoulders and hugged her close. Warmth and softness filled her limbs like the sun on skin until it poured over her aching heart. Calida wrapped her arms around her hesitantly, then grasped her tight. The onslaught of tears dampened the lady's dress.

"Yes, yes. Let it out. I'm here for you, Calida." Lady Wallington gently patted her back.

A smothered sob escaped her mouth as she wept over the death of her father, the accusations against his honor, and her promise of marriage to Dominic. Her life had changed in an instant, and all she could do now was cope.

For several minutes, only Calida's sobs filled the air.

Her shoulders shook until the energy to cry left her. Calida separated from the lady and wiped her eyes.

"I apologize for dampening your shawl, my lady." She cleared her throat. "I didn't expect *that* at all."

Lady Wallington softly smiled at her. Calida grimaced as she realized her failings. She showed such weakness in front of a noblewoman...

"Foolish girl. Showing emotions is manipulative and rude."

Calida fought back the urge to apologize and beg for the woman to forgive her for being so awful.

"If you need to cry once more, you know where to find me. My door will always be open to you." The viscountess squeezed Calida's arms and then guided her back to her seat.

She froze. The lady didn't see anything wrong with a girl like Calida breaking down into tears. Wasn't she wrong to show something so malicious?

After a few minutes of idle chatter, Calida and Jetta set off back to the Goldwyn mansion.

In the carriage, Jetta was the first to speak up. Concern twisted her face as she watched the scenery pass by.

"Milady, something was strange about that paper," she said.

Calida glanced at Jetta and continued her perusal of the busy roads of Weommadran. Ladies in flashy hats walked the streets and merchants yelled about their products from each street corner.

"Maybe. I don't know what, though." Calida nibbled on her finger as she tried to think of what bothered her about it.

Jetta frowned at her. She held her chin in what Calida knew to be deep thought after years of friendship. It took a few moments before Jetta's eyes flashed in realization. Her eyes whipped up to gaze in Calida's direction.

"The initials at the top of the page."

Calida squinted. *Why would that be important?* She remembered it, but it wasn't anyone she knew.

"What if it's a place?" Jetta said.

Even though she racked her mind, for the life of her, Calida couldn't think of a place named *SC*.

Then she remembered once reading about an obscure cave in Syniel called *Sollicitatis*. It had been in a dusty book she gotten for free one day in the market. The lady had sold all her products that day and only had the dusty book left. Most of its pages were torn out, but among the few left, Calida had read about hidden places in Eonifond. Places that the book said held special powers.

"What if it means the name of a cave?" Calida said.

Jetta furrowed her eyebrows and frowned. Giving it a thought.

"I don't know. I guess we will have to investigate further."

Soon, the creak of the carriage was the only sound in the silence between the young woman again. Her mind wandered back to earlier. It would seem as of late she was crying more. Calida frowned as her friend's eyes bore an imaginary hole in the side of her face.

Please don't bring it up.

"What cave do you mean, by the way?"

Calida inwardly sighed in relief.

She gazed Jetta's way once more. She told her friend about the cave.

With a shake of her head, Calida pulled herself out of her thoughts.

"I was thinking maybe *SC* means *Sollicitatis Cave*."

The next morning, Calida and Dominic were at breakfast. The clanking of cutlery was the only noise to greet her ears while trying to avoid Dominic's eyes.

"Would you like some more food?" He gestured to the plate of hard-boiled eggs, cheese, and bread. Calida hummed in agreement, then snatched a piece of bread and took a large bite that would take a while to chew. Dominic's eyebrow quirked at her bloated cheeks.

She had a feeling he wanted to talk to her about earlier, maybe give her comfort that would make her feel all warm and smitten. Neither sounded pleasant. Her emotions were all over the place and truthfully, it was giving her whiplash. Calida was downright alarmed at her willingness to be so sensationalist.

The maid strode in and whispered to Lord Dominic. The mail had arrived. She handed the bundle to her lord and then left the room.

Dominic opened the first letter and read it through. His face stared it down with intense concentration. Then without a word, he passed it to Calida. She blinked. Having grown up with someone who desired control in every aspect of her life, she hadn't expected him to show her.

She examined the paper. It had the official insignia of her majesty, the Queen of Eonifond. Calida was so stunned, it dropped from her hand and landed on the table. It was an invitation to the palace ball hosted by the queen.

We cordially invite you to attend a banquet at the Ember-fall palace.

Please wear formal attire and have a flower ready if you are coming alone. You shall give it to the queen at the allotted time. Invited guests are free to stay in the palace for the week of the banquet.

Queen Bedelia Ida Milena Eleonora Severina

Her skin crawled as she realized that the party Dominic had been talking about was likely this. Even more reason to say no. If she made a fool of herself in front of the queen, the noblewomen would remember it for sure. Their cackles rang through her mind like a curse on her soul.

As she clenched her teeth, Calida peeked over at Dominic, only to realize he was no longer seated. Instead, he was pacing.

His presence grew heavy and unsettled, as if his mood could affect the environment around him. He crinkled the paper held in his hand. Calida swore she heard a growl under his breath as he scowled.

She stood up slowly.

"My lord, what was on the paper?"

Dominic glanced her way, fury brimming in his eyes.

"I have told you to refer to me personally. Are you still not comfortable enough to do that?"

Calida stopped short, her mouth agape. It was obvious he was upset, but did he have to be so rude? She stared at him in shock. It was the first time he had been so foul. If he had burst out like that when they first met, she would have chalked it up to being a haughty nobleman, but Calida had gotten to know him. This wasn't like him.

"I apologize. I should not have said something so rude." Dominic took a deep breath and closed his eyes. With a staggering exhale, the lord rubbed his face. "The paper's a threat."

She looked at the paper and snatched it from his hands. Dominic clenched his fist as he held onto the back of a nearby chair.

The paper was dirty, and the writing was messy but legible.

Nobles aren't as safe as they think. Even they fall prone to accidents.

A chill went down her spine. Calida suddenly felt ill at the thought of what it meant. Whoever sent this obviously felt threatened by their investigations into her father's death, but she still felt the need to peek around every corner to make sure she wouldn't be kidnapped. She might not be a noble, but that threat was directed at her.

Dominic's head hung down.

"If they are sending threats, then we're doing something right," he said.

Calida dropped the paper. Suddenly, she didn't want to be anywhere near it.

Dominic reached for her hand.

"I know this is frightening, but I promise I'm here to help you," he said.

Calida gulped and warded him off as he backed up.

"I can't do this. I-I need time to think."

Calida bolted for the door and pounded up the stairs until she was in the security of her own room. There, she painted until her arms went numb. Only then did Calida collapse on her bed, exhausted.

Sixteen

Four days passed uneventfully and before she knew it, the day of departure was upon her. A servant gently shook her awake from an afternoon nap.

"Milady, milady... You must get up! Lord Goldwyn is waiting for you downstairs. The carriage to take you to the palace has arrived." The girl pulled Calida up. "We must get you up and dressed in your best. Everyone will be at the palace."

Calida rubbed her eyes and stood up. She shivered in the chilly air, still half asleep. The maid guided her to the warm water she had brought for her to wash her face.

Using the cloth the maid handed to her, she wiped her face slowly, revelling in the warmth and wishing she could pour it all over her body.

After spending a moment absorbing the heat of the cloth until it was cold, the maid guided her to the dress laid out for her. It had a silky undergarment with two underskirts and a corset. The dress itself was a deep green. It reminded her of the forest she would hunt in with her father. All the bushes and leaves were the same deep green.

"Milady, you'll look most beautiful in this dress. I can just hear the compliments and murmurs now."

The girl sighed as she gazed off for a moment. With a smile, Calida put her arms through the arms of the dress with the help of the maid.

The woman braided her hair into a crown on her head, snug and not a hair out of place. The dress she was in had been designed for a noblewoman to snag the heart of a man because it fit so well that the curve of her breasts and hips were exaggerated in the right way. The fabric was endless, and the corset was firm. It was odd that the dress had no shoulders, though.

After slipping on her shoes, she left her room with a coat and a pair of gloves in hand.

Jetta and Braxton were outside the door and escorted her to the foyer, where Lord Dominic awaited her arrival.

At the top of the stairs, she looked down and gazed at Dominic. His back was to her, so he had not realized her arrival. He had not confirmed his feelings for her and that was something that comforted her since she didn't want to address what she felt, either.

The fear of the unknown was a powerful thing.

At the bottom of the stairs, Dominic was speaking with the carriage driver. He towered over the stout man like a mighty tree. Calida walked down the stairs. The conversation ended and he turned around. She bit her lip and fidgeted as he stared her down. What did he want?

Maybe he wants to order me around. Her eyes widened at her thoughts. If only she could jump into a hole. Such close attention of a male was uncomfortable. Growing up, the boys her age left her alone, but the older men stared as she grew into her body. Dominic's expression wasn't disrespectful, but it reminded her that there were men out there who were.

"My dear one, you look divine."

Calida blushed. It was the dress, not her, obviously. She tucked her hair behind her ear.

It would be foolish to expect it to be anything more. It was hard to be disappointed when there was no expectation. If she was more, then she would resemble Lady Evaine, a true noblewoman in the making.

Dominic called for a maid. "As much as I love this dress on you. It's probably not best for the first trek of our journey." He instructed the maid to change Calida into a riding dress.

A knot formed in her throat. Yet again, she didn't do the right thing. But why was it so important that she do exactly the right thing? She couldn't remember anymore.

Pulling herself out of her thoughts, Calida cleared her throat.

She changed, and the maid packed her dress into her luggage. "Let us be off."

She swiftly walked out the door to the carriage, where the footman waited to help her. Jetta and Braxton were quietly discussing something behind her, and she strained to hear. Dominic followed close to check the luggage in the back of the carriage to make sure it didn't come loose. The others loaded in, and the group was off.

The journey to the palace was two days and one night. They had a long trek from the mansion. After several hours and an uneventful dinner filled with idle chatter, the sun was getting low, and Braxton declared they must make camp.

The carriage pulled over to a spot near the road surrounded by trees, and there they set up for the night. Jetta went to gather firewood as Braxton hunted down game for the fire.

Lord Dominic stepped out of the carriage and held out a hand for Calida. She hesitated for a second, then took it to help her down. She pursed her lips as she stood in front of the carriage, unsure of what to do. *Was she supposed to fill the silence?*

They hadn't talked much so far on the trip. Her mind had been actively fighting off the depressing thoughts about her inadequacies in high society and how her favorite person was dead. Jetta and Braxton had been on the carriage's coach bench in the front. So she had been left alone with a brooding Dominic. She hadn't realized he could do such a thing. She thought he was the type to tackle something head on spontaneously. Although, when swimming in the poison-filled rivers of dark thoughts, it was hard to start a conversation, so she left it alone.

Calida brightened as she remembered what she could do.

Quickly, she grabbed the dagger her father had given to her and found some twigs on the ground. Dominic stared at her in bewilderment. She took some vines nearby and sculpted something from her childhood.

When Calida finished, she turned around and offered the finished item to Dominic.

In his large hands was a dainty bird with carved spirals that wrapped around and looked like large feathers. The beak was hooked, and it had feathers on the top of its head too. It looked so small that if he closed his fist, it would break.

He gazed at her as if to say, *What is this for?*

"It was something my father used to make a lot when I was a child. He would give it to me as a way of making peace or understanding. It was something that I learned how to make from him and have grown to appreciate."

Dominic looked over at her and then back at the bird.

"It looks like a phoenix," he said.

"Most likely a coincidence. They represent peacefulness and justice, but I don't think my father was looking too much further into it."

Braxton and Jetta returned with their findings. Before

long, they had a fire stoked, several rabbits cooking, and berries to eat. Calida sat down on a blanket and ate some berries.

Jetta joined her while Braxton and Dominic discussed strategies by the carriage. Her eye twitched as she hated being left in the dark. *He better fill me in later.* But at least for now, she was too sleepy to care. Before she knew it, Calida was out like a light.

When she woke, the fire burned low and Jetta sat by it watching a portion of food set aside. Her heart warmed at the sight. She hadn't meant to fall asleep, but here was Jetta, saving some food for her while watching over the party. If Jetta let her, she would hug her, but knew better than to do that. Last time she tried that, she almost lost a finger. Jetta was not a hugger.

Calida sat up, took the rabbit off the fire, and ate.

"Would you like to practice sparring after you're done eating?" Jetta asked.

Calida nodded mindlessly.

Jetta stared into the depth of the smouldering coals. Calida gazed at her.

"How do you and Braxton know each other?"

Jetta glanced her way, then back at the fire.

"Other than being in the same faction?"

"Yes."

Jetta poked the fire with the stick sitting next to her. She frowned as she took a moment.

"I met him once when he was shopping the market with his family. They had newly accepted me at Crescent League, and I was looking around the market for a suitable weapon." Jetta stared into the distance, caught in her memories.

"I had noticed him immediately because he was wearing the same cape as me. I had thought nothing of it, but when I got into a conversation with a weapons dealer, Braxton showed up at my side. He told off the dealer for attempting to scam me out of my money." She shifted a bit and grabbed some of the leftover food from the bowl on the fire and held it in her hands.

"I had been considering a sword I thought looked of reasonable quality and coin. I had just been hoping to get something cheap and then get something sturdy later, but Braxton scolded me for my choice. He said that it was something that wouldn't see me through battle or life's struggles. I had argued with him, claiming it was all I could afford. I just wanted to save as much money as possible now that I had gotten some."

"Why was he so insistent it wasn't a reasonable choice?" Calida said.

"The metal. He claimed the blade was made from weakened metal and would more likely get me killed than help me win my battles." Jetta glanced at her friend.

Calida's eyebrows rose in surprise. Braxton had the know-how to tell the quality of a blade? She struggled to even hold up a sword, let alone study one.

Dominic moved in his sleep, and their conversation halted for a moment.

Calida moved closer to Jetta and whispered, "How did he know?"

Jetta gave her a quick smile, scooped some food into her mouth, chewed, and swallowed.

"His magic is earth. He can tell when certain swords aren't good quality."

Calida pursed her lips. It made sense. Every individual in Eonifond had magic, and it was explained in detail to every child. How her father had explained it to her was that everyone had a hidden talent, and everyone manifested it in different ways and at different times in their childhood. He had drawn in the dirt outside their house the symbols commonly used.

A sword for object magic. A hand for healing. The fist was

for physical magic, and the tree for elemental. A skull was for death magic, the ritual circle for ceremonial magic, and the flow symbol was for nature or natural magic.

Rayner had drawn out a diagram of how magic worked in Eonifond, starting with physical, object, healing, and ceremonial.

Each symbol faced each other, and then he drew branching lines outward from them. The line over physical branched into two different sections, elemental and nature. Healing branched into death magic. Ceremonial branched out into black magic, and object magic branched out into charms and enchantments.

Rayner told Calida how each magic had the potential for both good and bad. Calida remembered being fascinated with the structure when she was a child. Learning something new back then had always been an adventure. Now, she knew several magic types were more likely to be evil rather than good, especially ceremonial. It wasn't that far away from black magic.

Calida focused on Jetta and remembered her question from before they got off track. "Yes."

Jetta looked quizzically.

"Yes. I'll spar with you."

Understanding dawned on Jetta's face.

"Well, let's do that, then." She stood up and offered a hand to Calida.

They walked over to the gap between the carriage and their campsite. Calida still had her dagger on her, and Jetta pulled out the spare dagger she carried in her boot.

Normally, Jetta sparred with a sword and only sparred with a dagger when practicing with Calida. Her friend had greater finesse in battle compared to her, but it was inspiring to see her in action. Calida hadn't used her dagger much because Jetta had always been there to protect her. Her friend insisted they practice, but Calida didn't see how it would come in handy with Jetta by her side. But Jetta urged her to do so shortly after they arrived at Dominic's home.

Jetta took her stance with the dagger, and Calida took hers. When they were both ready, Jetta charged. She tried to hit Calida with the flat of her blade, stabbing at one side and then another. Jetta went in again, but Calida blocked with her sheath on the forearm. Something her friend had taught her. It only worked with the daggers. They didn't have enough power to break their sheathes.

Calida cut upward and Jetta jerked back to dodge. Feet grounded and stance firm, Calida charged forward and stabbed at Jetta. Her friend tripped over a log that they had cut for the fire and fell.

Calida burst into laughter. It felt wonderful to laugh after such serious focus, and once she started, she couldn't stop. She collapsed on the ground in laughter, and Jetta joined in.

After a moment, when they had calmed down, Jetta got up and helped Calida to her feet.

They walked back to where the men were sleeping and joined them in slumber. As Jetta passed Braxton, she kicked him to signal the changing of the guard. Only when he was sitting up and awake did she lie down and fall asleep next to Calida.

Seventeen

Leaves crunched as the carriage drove through the palace gate. Calida looked out the window as the guards patrolling the top of the wall and ground level shifted position. The well-maintained wall stood without a crack in sight. There were arrow slits along the top and wrought iron spikes along the bottom of the wall.

Calida stared in wonder as they passed through the residential housing. The people who lived here were servants, or anyone else of commoner status, with a job in the palace. It was also home to the largest market in the region. Merchants and peddlers from all around could gain access to the stalls by speaking with the guards, whom they had to vouch for.

People passed by them, gazing and staring as the carriage moved through the streets. The people here would have seen many a carriage before, but Calida could imagine how exciting it would be to look from the outside at the beautiful carriages arriving. Each an artwork of their own, as it was quite common for the nobles to hire popular artists from all around to decorate their carriages frivolously. Each region was home to a distinct style.

The one she was in was very plain, but Calida hadn't expected anything else from Dominic. He wasn't the type to take part in that. It was jarring to not be on the outside, staring in awe as the beautiful carriages passed.

It was nothing like she had experienced at home. Her small town was more like a hamlet with few people and only one or two nobles, including Duke Bartholomew Sullivan. While she had never met him before the Marquess's wedding reception, that did not mean she didn't know who he was.

His castle overhung the river's bed on the other side of town on richer soil. Anyone passing it saw the women constantly coming and going from his house. Calida had never seen it for herself, but the gossipers around town had no qualms about spreading the word. The women rarely left but when they did, it was to return with a man on her arm.

When the carriage pulled up to the palace entrance, Calida's eyebrows rose as she realized the guards were heavily armored and stationed everywhere. If there were so many around every corner, then how did her father die?

She was amazed by the stern gazes on the guards' faces as the group gathered their things. Not even her father's status could give her access to the palace. Calida couldn't attend anything until she was fourteen. As an unwritten rule of coming-of-age, a girl can attend her first party with her parents at the age of fourteen. She vividly remembered the first event she went to.

Lord Sullivan had invited several townspeople to his home for a gathering. It was very peculiar and the people serving were all women. The strangest part was her mother had insisted on their attendance. Her father was reluctant about going to the duke's event, with good reason, but no one could prove just how perverted he was. So, they agreed to attend, along with many other men in town. There were a few young girls her age there, but the girls seemed to wear the same outfits as the women serving. Since Calida had been at such a young age, she was confused why they looked so frightened. It may have been four years ago, but it was imprinted into her mind. None of them lived in town. According to the word around town, they were Lord Sullivan's wards. The men in town, particularly the less reputable ones, claimed the women were there for asylum anytime someone whispered a conspiracy theory about trafficking.

It had been odd, quite like the invitation to the wedding of the marquess. She assumed it was because of Lord Dominic. After the event, she had confirmed that the man who ushered Dominic away from her side that day had in fact been the marquess, his brother. So, it was likely a condition of the betrothal, which had her mood souring that even his brother knew before she did.

Damned bastard.

The footman opened the door and let Jetta and Braxton out. They surveyed the area for a moment, then Dominic exited and helped Calida out of the carriage.

Steps led up to an enormous door with engraved wood, dark brown against light grey stone on the ground. The guards were stationed on each side of the door, their hands on their weapons and staring into the distance without moving. If she didn't see their chests rise and fall, Calida would think they were statues.

Dominic took her arm in his and guided her up the steps. The guards opened the wooden door and allowed them through. As they walked down the hallway, the doors behind them closed with a boom that echoed against the tile floors. The couple walked down the clean and sparkling hallway. It almost hurt to look at the walls. Calida peeked over her shoulder and craned her head to get one last look at the guards with the shining armor.

"They are willing to take a sword for you," Lord Dominic said.

"That's rather morbid, don't you think?"

"I'd like to think of it as being prepared." Dominic gazed down the hallway, stoic.

Calida couldn't think of what he would want to be prepared for. The palace was heavily armed, and they stationed guards at every entrance and exit. A merchant couldn't set a foot inside the palace walls without someone of authority knowing. It was incredibly confusing her father could die in such a fortress.

Dominic guided her to stairs leading to a pathway. On either side stood two more guards. The height of the building was impressive. With a gulp, Calida followed her betrothed through the passageway of stone. On the other side, she gaped at the sight before her.

To the left, a wall with arches and doorways stood, allowing anyone to peer through to see a court of stone and grass. The wall to her right looked similar, but inside the court was a stone table the size of a water-house wheel.

Calida followed Dominic as he maneuvered through the courtyard, stopping for a moment while the door at the other end had to be opened by the guards. She gazed everywhere, unable to stop herself from admiring the inside of the palace. On her left was a stairwell with iron window panels latched into place along the wall. Calida stared at the immaculate stairs from the distance. She hadn't seen many homes with stairs. These were stone and somehow lacked a single speck of dirt.

The dimness inside temporarily blinded her. The stone was similar but had a more polished look to it. Tapestries covered every wall. The floor was stone. More stairs stood in front of them, this time leading to an iron and wood door with embedded spikes.

It was then she realized Jetta and Braxton were no longer

in their company. She looked behind her to get a glimpse of them, but it was fruitless.

"This way, my dear one." Dominic wrapped an arm around her and gestured forward.

They found yet another level to navigate. She could only imagine getting lost in this place. Grasping her hand, Dominic walked them to the stairwell off to the side and ventured up to the second floor. Calida's heart sank as she saw the identical doors all along the hallway. *Does Dominic even know where he is going?*

The two travelled down the hall, only to climb another set of stairs at the other end. A few moments later, Calida had convinced herself that he was walking blindly but didn't want to admit it. This was too overwhelming to remember. If she was going dizzy from it, how well was Dominic doing?

"We are stopping here for now. Before we get too comfortable, we need to talk logistics." Dominic stopped before a door like all the others. He pushed it open and ushered her in.

It was a small room with a table and chairs taking up most of the space. On the far side was a small endpiece that contained a pitcher of water and a bowl. Calida hurried over to use it. Since arriving at the palace, all she could think about was how filthy she was. A commoner like her was no doubt muddying such a beautiful place.

"What are we talking about? Who else is coming?" Calida poured the water into the bowl and washed up quickly. She took a moment to enjoy the refreshing coolness before centering herself for the upcoming conversation.

"Braxton and Jetta will join us in a moment. We'll discuss what's important to discover while we visit."

Dominic moved closer and stood in her personal space. Normally, such proximity irked her, but somehow he relaxed her instead. She shouldn't have such a calm nature around him. Was she even staying with him that long? An intense gaze met hers. Calida nibbled on her lip as a blush rose on her face. If only his focus on her wasn't so embarrassing. *It probably wouldn't embarrass Lady Evaine.*

Her blush faded, and the smile at the corner of her lips disappeared. Calida frowned as she locked her eyes on the interesting pattern of stone on the floor.

"What happened?" Dominic examined her as he moved closer and grasped her chin. "Why do you have that look on your face?"

Calida didn't want to admit that it hurt to think that Lady Evaine might be a better match, but it did. They were both nobles, for goodness' sake. While Lord Dominic had brought in a tutor to teach her all the information she would need to know as the lady of the house, it only scratched the surface. She hadn't enough time over the last week and a half to learn how far one must curtsy or the right angle of the head to nod when greeting another noble. The tutor had covered some books on the history of the wooden bowl and other such nonsense, but that didn't help her with knowing exactly what to do with a salad fork.

Not to mention emotions! Nobles love to antagonize and then twist an outburst against their enemies.

She needed to get ahold of herself. What did she truly know about this man? She was just a speck in the wind of his life.

Calida tensed as she mentally constructed a wall to protect herself. Dominic's frown deepened and his eyes grew dark. Her eyes deadened as she fought her feelings. He was upset again. *It's all my fault.* Calida shook her head, refusing to comfort him. She wouldn't give into that urge. It wasn't her place.

And yet, it is.

It was too late now, though. After some panicked breaths during her spiralling emotions, Calida took back her control.

"Whatever do you mean, milord?" Calida stared over his shoulders. She refused to meet his eyes. If she did, her resolve would crumble.

His face grew sullen as he crossed his arms. Dominic looked not only disappointed in Calida but also tired.

A part of her cried out for him to not give up, but she couldn't say it. That would mean risking the pain of rejection. She wasn't courageous. She didn't have the boldness to face pain head on. The fear of the unknown was a powerful concept. And the concept of being open to someone else was daunting.

Dominic opened his mouth, but a knock sounded on the door, interrupting the moment. Pinching his nose and putting a hand on his waist, he took a moment to calm down and then answered the door. At the door, Braxton and Jetta looked at the couple for a moment, then at each other. Calida sat and refused to admit that it would be even more awkward with him. After the moment between them, she would have to struggle to act nonchalant. There was paper sitting on the table and immediately, she brainstormed what they could do.

More like what she would do. She had never been the type to include others in her plans.

She thought she would insert her well written idea into the conversation, but Braxton came up behind her. She jumped and held the paper to her chest.

"You scared me." Calida's voice squeaked as she clutched the ideas in order to hide them before she was finished.

Braxton murmured an apology as her cheeks reddened in embarrassment. *Just like me to overreact.* She reluctantly offered the paper to him, but Braxton didn't take it. He just stared at her.

She stared back and asked, "Don't you want to see my idea? Isn't that why you came up behind me?"

Braxton shook his head. "Milady, I can't read."

Calida's face fell in shame for asking him if he'd like to when he couldn't do something she was privileged to do. How could she be so rude?

It's not like she knew, though.

Jetta took the paper from Calida and read it. Immediately, Jetta shook her head. "This won't work, milady."

Calida narrowed her eyes at Jetta. Just why wouldn't it? It was her father, she needed to do something.

"It's too tame. We need to be bold to get answers. But we need to be stealthy as well."

Lord Dominic took the page from Jetta and agreed with her. Apparently, Calida at the focal point wasn't acceptable. Again, the poor country bumpkin couldn't simply demand the truth from the nobles.

"In order to learn more, we need to play on their level, Calida."

"Then what are you *suggesting* we do, my lord? That I go guard to guard, asking them questions? How else will we get answers unless I go straight to the source?" Calida folded her arms as she grumbled.

If only she could hide in a corner. She wasn't used to having a group of people to talk to about her ideas, so the rejection stung a bit. Normally, she made her own decisions. Calida wasn't a team player. There hadn't been much point if she could accomplish more alone than with others.

"If anyone should try, then it should be someone with sway over the people at the party." Dominic said, sitting down at the seat at the front of the table in the room.

"No," Jetta and Braxton said together.

"If you talk with them, then they'll know something's up. Not to mention the other nobles would pay close attention to your sudden interest in the habits of high society, milord." Jetta shook her head. "No, we need to do something else."

"I still think my plan is fine. It's not like they would give much credence to the little commoner from Poramun Creek." Calida scowled as she stewed on the hard shutdown of her idea without a single explanation. If only she could confidently state her opinions.

Jetta glared straight in her eyes. "Enough of this mopey, 'woe is me' mood from you. Regardless of whether you like it, you're noticeable now."

Calida's eyes filled with tears as her friend ripped into her with harsh words. It wasn't like Jetta to beat around the bush, but that didn't mean it hurt any less.

Just as melodramatic as ever.

Calida lowered her gaze to the table, unable to say more. There was no point. Her friend had made it clear and arguing any different would be a waste of breath. People didn't change themselves for the weak.

"Calida," Braxton interrupted Jetta with his deep voice, "the best solution would be to switch off talking to guards. Jetta and I will take turns guarding the both of you while the other talks to the guards."

Dominic gave a murmur of agreement. "That could work."

Calida looked up and saw Dominic nod to Jetta and Braxton. With nods in return, they exited the room, leaving her alone with him once more.

"Calida, you know Jetta cares for you." Dominic left his seat. He stepped closer and placed a hand on her shoulder. An urge to flee his comfort spread like wildfire. And yet, her heart whispered to let him hold her.

"I wish to go to my room now." Calida avoided his eyes. Her tone resembled a frigid winter night. She couldn't take his loving nature while she was trying to be strong.

Dominic sighed, but then moved away to allow her to get up. She rushed out of her seat and through the door, only to stop when she remembered she needed him to show her where to go.

Peeking around at Dominic, her heart tweaked at the hurt on his face. "I don't know where my room is."

Dominic looked away for a moment and then, when his gaze returned to her, the hurt in his eyes had vanished.

"Of course, my dear one." He guided her into the hallway. "If you will come this way, I'll show you to your room to freshen up."

Her room was another few floors up and completely astounded her with its size. The room was larger than her chambers at Dominic's mansion and for sure greater in quality than her parents' home.

It was also all stone, but it had a darling fireplace with a fire burning, and the bed was made for a queen. Rich in colour, the sheets were luxurious, and the armoire was spacious. Was it expected she would show up with an entire wardrobe instead of a single outfit? One dress should suffice, if it was in good condition. Then again, she was nobility now, which meant she needed to learn frivolity because that's what would surround her.

"Thank you for escorting me to my room, my lord." Calida turned toward him, staring up into his eyes before curt-sying. If only she had it in her to apologize to him. But it was a weakness. She couldn't allow for weakness.

"Of course, Calida. I wouldn't say no if I can help you feel happy, safe, or warm."

A moment passed before their eyes. The silence floated between them, waiting for the close. Heat rose on her cheeks and as her lips parted, his gaze shifted to watch.

Suddenly, she blurted goodbye and shut the door before plopping onto the bed amid the luxurious room. Her mind swirled. Dominic had been on the other side of the door, within easy distance to touch or kiss. Shaking began in her arms and then took over her chest as the exuberance flowed through her. If only she wasn't so weak.

As if she were decades older, a sudden fatigue weighed her down until she lay on the bed and the darkness crept into her eyes. It had been a long several days, so her body won over as she passed out.

Eighteen

Jetta lounged on the chaise in the bedchamber while Calida sat across the room having her hair styled by three palace maids as the first rays of morning light broke through the window. One maid brushed her hair, another held stray hair and the other braided everything together. Calida's friend shifted many times on the chaise while waiting for her to be done with the powder and pins. None of it was ever in Jetta's style. She was the type to throw on her closest tunic and pants, then run out the door while struggling into her boots. Unlike the society Calida was entering. Even the servants were dressed better than her friend when off-duty.

The maids worked quietly and soon enough, they were done.

Calida's hair looked like a painted masterpiece. It delicately swept by her ears and was pinned in the back while they carefully constructed braid upon braid on the back of her head. The maids had curled some of the stray hairs with a hot iron from the fireplace, which startled Calida. She kept completely still out of fear of a burn. They pinned up as much as they could around the buns at the nape.

Never had she felt so dressed up and clean. The maids had taken it upon themselves to put Calida into a bath of heavenly water. The tub was made of polished wood and varnish with decorative flowers and birds on the outside. Before she would bathe in the river in her dress, but now she had a luxurious bath where maids scrubbed her skin until it was pink. By the time she was pulled out, Calida felt so fresh that she was scared to walk on a patch of dirt. Although, at first, it felt intrusive how active the maids were in helping her.

After pulling Calida out, the girls lathered her pink skin with a mixture of oil and roses. The scent filled the room and lingered until all she could smell was floral, reminding her of her father in the meadow. A smile tilted her lips.

Her skin was so clear it was shinier than the metal on the guard's armour. After making sure her hair wouldn't move with a set of powder and oil, one maid brought out her dress for the evening.

"Milady, the Duchess D'Airelle handpicked this for you!"

She hesitated to accept it, but it didn't seem to bother the maids, so she dressed in the slimming gown without a word. Normally, a dress would come with two undergarments and other attachments for vanity. This beautiful rich blue gown had only an underskirt. She frowned at how quickly she slipped it on, then asked for the maid's help with doing up the back.

They giggled, and one said, "Milady, you won't be needing help with the back on this dress. There's no back."

Calida paled. *Shit.* What was she to do now? If she became the focus of entertainment for the evening again, she didn't know what she would do.

There was a hidden rule about showing skin in public. It was akin to perversion. Modern ideas were not accepted well as the populace was run by traditionalists. Calida was a maiden of Eleari, and any respectable woman in Eonifond wouldn't sell themselves away like so. Any commoner from Poramun Creek who didn't want to be assaulted by drunkards refrained from doing so.

She shook her head frantically, the panic rising in her throat. Her arms stretched to the back in an attempt to pin the sides of the dress together.

"Please no, I couldn't bear it if I became the brunt of the joke again." Calida was barely holding back tears now. She wanted out of this dress, and she wanted out now.

A maid approached and hushed until her breathing slowed. "Milady, you are most beautiful. They wouldn't dare make fun of you. They would be hypocrites as this style is very popular amongst the noblewomen these days. Many will probably come dressed like this."

The panic subsided a bit. But she wouldn't just accept a maid's word. How would she know for certain?

One of the other maids scoffed. "That is because they only have one thing on their minds."

Calida squinted questioningly at the girl. What was she on about?

"The noblewomen showing up are vying for the attention of the queen's suitors. More so to fawn over their handsome features."

The queen has suitors still?

She didn't know her majesty was still being offered like a pig at auction. Many moons ago, the queen's council argued hard to have someone beside her on the throne. She rejected each suitor who came up. None were suitable enough. None were the right man to rule by her side.

"Milady, didn't you know what you would walk into upon arrival?" The maid gazed up at her with clear, sweet eyes.

She was a small girl with braided hair and well-kept clothing on.

"No, I didn't think about the details regarding the ball. My mind was busy with other matters." The death of her father and all the conflicting emotions she had felt for Dominic had taken up her time.

"May I ask what the other matters were, milady?" Her eyes glittered in curiosity.

Jetta walked over. "No, you may not. Anastasia, you know better than to ask a line above your station." The tone of her voice was like the snap of a whip. Harsh and cold.

She bowed her head as a sullen look passed over her face. "Yes, you are right, Miss Arundel." Then she turned to Calida and bowed further. "I apologize, milady. I didn't mean to step out of line."

Calida was about to comfort the girl when Jetta interrupted. "You all must be off now. There is still much to prepare for."

The maids left her room and shut her door behind them with a soft click.

Calida looked at Jetta and said, "You were rather harsh with her, don't you think so?"

Jetta folded her arms and glared at her charge. "Calida, you must grow a steely spine now. I know you are compassionate and loving, but the people with whom you will associate are a different breed. They mustn't see you being friendly to a maid. You may see it as a good deed, but it will oust the maid and she will be the target for bullying."

The statement hit her like a punch. She stepped back as a horrifying, morbid understanding cleared her mind.

Even being herself among the maids would cause more harm than good. She could stand up to the noblewomen, but a maid couldn't. It would ruin her livelihood. And if it was serious enough, the noblewoman could have the maid killed.

Not a single person in the palace would blink an eye at the disappearance of a simple maid.

Calida stared at the ground in stark horror. Even the maids had it hard here. She couldn't offer special treatment or words of encouragement. A vow to suffer in silence was all she could do when she saw someone of the lower class struggling.

Tears pricked her eyes. This time, she didn't stop them from flowing.

Jetta was right. She needed to get her act together and realize this was a different world altogether. A world of nobles. Nobles like Dominic.

Nineteen

DOMINIC

Dominic strode down the hall, excited to see Calida. He wasn't one to focus on dresses and frivolous items, but his imagination got the better of him when thinking about the girl he had known for so long.

Little Calida laughed as she ran past her father at his post at Duchess Goldwyn's side. The grass brushed against the dress her mother had made. It was still too big, but she enjoyed wearing It like she was playing dress up.

A mess of blond hair stuck out from the bush up ahead, and the four-year-old giggled, tugging on it as she ran by. A yelp and tumble followed, and she ran past the flowers, then circled around until reaching the blanket where Her Grace sat, and Rayner stood with his armor on.

Calida ran up to the blanket and snuck a honey-glazed pastry from little Dominic's plate. She took a large bite while Maud Lilla Goldwyn let out a warning. It was cut off as a small body tackled Calida to the ground and squished her into the blanketed grass.

"That was my treat, my lady," a blond boy with piercing blue eyes accused.

A crumble-crusted face smiled on the blanket and then shoved more into her cheeks until Calida resembled a chipmunk.

"Hey!" the eight-year-old yelled out, pouting at Calida..

She giggled and crumbs flew everywhere.

"My snack, Du-Nic."

Dominic blinked away the memories.

While he was much better suited for the battlefield, that didn't mean he wasn't concerned about just how much attention Calida would garner. In the end, he might have to fend off men who were too *courageous.* Eesa, bless his soul. He hoped it wouldn't lead to bloodshed, but Dominic knew how the men were.

A hand slipped through his arm. He glanced to the side and found Lady Evaine attached to him. Dominic's eyebrow quirked. It wasn't the first time his childhood friend had wrapped herself around his arm. As always, he could only see the snot-nosed little girl he had known as a child. The one who would run by him and squeal his name before clinging to his arm and demanding he be the knight in her game of pretend. Which was why her keen interest in his marriage to Calida was concerning. He had humoured his father for a bit, but when it seemed like Lady Evaine took it to heart, Dominic knew he had to act.

"My lady, my greetings to you. How are you this evening?"

It was rather unorthodox to have her on his arm. A gentleman would bow to his company first as was the common courtesy in the court, but his friend stood too close and made it difficult to complete the proper greetings.

Lady Evaine smiled up at Lord Dominic. "My lord, I'm jittery. These events are always so exciting and to see all the interesting people is thrilling. Do you find yourself enchanted by the people coming and going from the parties thrown by nobles as well?"

A smile twitched the corner of his mouth as he stared at his friend with amusement. They didn't interest him unless it was something out of the ordinary. Like Calida. She was unique, and she didn't even realize her own spectacular idiosyncrasy. Even if the tutors tried to form her into a *perfect* lady, Calida would be a run for their money. She was wild and refreshing with a creative intuition. Her spirit was one that wouldn't easily break.

In comparison, the nobles at court were nothing but lazy buffoons surrounding themselves with short-term pleasures and unaware of the implications. The small conversations in the darkest corners of the land had their consequences unbeknownst to the nobles. Even in the palace, there were spies who spoke lies and smiled with false intentions.

"No, I don't have much of an interest in the parties thrown by nobles. I am too busy studying military strategies and the management of Eleari affairs."

She slid her hand up his arm and rubbed it while she stuck out her bottom lip in a pout. "That is quite like you, isn't it, Dominic?"

The setting sun dimmed the hall as the two strolled at an easy pace.

Dominic smiled gently as he thought about the man she would marry. He would be lucky to have such a kind woman. Lady Evaine was like a sister to him in many ways. He remembered how she was as a child. Nothing had changed. She was considerate of those around her and still smiled in the darkest moments.

Lady Evaine had been there right after his childhood friend departed from his side. He had been friends with an enchanting and outspoken little girl before Lady Evaine entered the picture. When the girl didn't come for an entire month, he had met Evaine, who had offered her sympathies and spoke about other things to distract him. They laughed about Lady Dale's kitten's antics and pulled pranks on his twin brother, who was always studying everything from how to read the stars to how magic manifested itself in the body.

He had never felt close enough to tell her about Aither. Never found himself able to let her know about the hidden secrets of his family that only one other outside his parents and brother knew. Something always kept that part of him and the Goldwyn's homeland locked away.

Lady Evaine stopped walking for a moment and turned to him.

"I recently learned a joke. Care to hear it?"

He raised his eyebrow and nodded. As he agreed, a smile dawned on her face. He picked up the pace once more, and her arm attached to him again.

"What is the favorite pastime of the peasants?" Her voice was light and airy, as if what she had said would have no meaning.

He stiffened slightly. Unfortunately, the bigoted side of the court influenced Lady Evaine too much. Like her father and his cronies. Lord Dominic inwardly cringed at what would come next. While he was also a noble, comments that belittled the lower classes didn't sit well with him. What was a good kingdom without the backbone? It only made sense to support the people below so that everyone could flourish.

"I don't know." His voice controlled, trying hard to not give away his frustration at his naïve friend. As they turned the corner, Evaine grew childlike in her giddiness to complete her distasteful joke.

"They absolutely love to serf!" Lady Evaine said.

Her hand flew to her mouth as she giggled. A forced laugh escaped him as he tried to hide the anger. He had to take part in the activities even if he hated it. It was expected of nobles to keep up pretenses. Once upon a time he might've been open with his friend, but these days the nobles dazzled and influenced her far too much .

They reached the top of the stairwell.

He looked down and there stood Calida. Her amber eyes sparkled with an inner flame as she stared up at him, a wash of emotion drained through him too fast to discern. A twitch of a smile turned into a frown as soon as they entered the stairwell. Lady Evaine was on his arm, but his beautiful betrothed, dressed in an alluring outfit, waited at the bottom of the stairs.

The lady let out another giggle that was loud enough for Calida to hear. He whipped his head around to Calida as he squeezed Lady Evaine's wrist to silence her.

"Be fateful for wealth." She gave a departing kiss on the cheek. The common gesture said in parting made no sense, and even in his etiquette classes no one explained why it was phrased that way. But it's just what was done.

His mouth dropped in surprise. Calida sped away from the stairs, but not before he saw the tears. Dominic was still learning the customs his bride-to-be grew up with, one of which was noble or not, kissing someone else's partner was unacceptable. However, he hadn't thought Lady Evaine would do so in front of Calida. Surely, Lady Evaine should know that his betrothed would misunderstand.

Shit. He was in trouble now. Just what did his friend hope to accomplish by doing that?

Dominic let go of Lady Evaine's arm and rushed down the stairs, wanting to fix whatever had just happened.

Hopefully, Calida trusted him enough by now.

Twenty

Calida waited for Dominic at the bottom of the stairs. She craned her neck, fruitlessly searching for him. As a man of propriety, being on time was important.

A moment passed when she could hear his voice making its way down the hall. She didn't know who he was talking to, but his laughter as he turned the corner caught her attention.

Dominic appeared at the top of the stairs, with Lady Evaine on his arm. Suddenly, the stairwell felt like it led to an altar and she was a mere pebble. If her comparison was to the lady, how much could she accomplish?

Calida Rhodes roughed up her hands from washing laundry and helping her mother. She had put her head down and blended into the background. She had learned to say "yes, milady," instead of, "yes, my lady." She had only a handful of dresses in her wardrobe and two were given to her by Lord Dominic. Her fingernails were nubs and the skin of her hands scarred from hard labor.

Lady Evaine giggled at something had Lord Dominic said,

and it stabbed into her heart. She was jealous; it was as simple as that. There was no point in denying it.

What cemented all her insecurities was Lady Evaine leaning over his arm and gently pecking Dominic's cheek. She had learned some basic customs of the nobility, including the act of a farewell kiss on the cheek, but where Calida was from, a woman didn't kiss anyone other than her husband. It was a great way to have your name tarnished as a bedswerver. Not that it meant much for reputation, with all the philandering men in town.

The act was an innocent affair to the nobles. Calida realized just how much she had to know to fit in, but seeing the Lady Evaine's dainty lips on Dominic's cheek felt like a short drop and a sudden stop on her hopes.

If only she could run up the stairs to avoid him, but Calida still had a duty to fulfill. She had agreed to attend the party so Jetta and Braxton could ask questions without arousing suspicion.

She rushed to the door leading to the foyer in front of the ballroom. Anything to avoid the two people descending the stairs.

Dominic sidled up beside her and gently murmured, "Calida, it's not what you think."

"I believe it was, milord."

Dominic gently tugged her hand to his chest.

"Calida..."

His mouth opened again, but then the doors in front of her parted and the guards announced their entry. She tried to remove her hand, but he held it tightly. She gave it one more tug, hoping to escape out of self-preservation, but when he didn't let go, she sighed in resignation.

With a deep inhale, Dominic took Calida's, arm and they entered the room. The door was wide open and when she looked down at the dance floor, she saw dozens of people chattering, dancing and laughing.

As the maids had said, there were several women with dresses that had the open back like hers. Letting out a breath of relief, she felt lighter, knowing that burden was off her shoulders.

Why must she keep holding back? While nothing good came from letting others know what she truly thought, wouldn't it be less painful to just go up in flames, damn the consequences?

How many times did she have to push people away before she grew tired? How would she know when it was the right time to open up? What if he was waiting until her guard was down to ruin her and leave her defenseless?

No. Lord Dominic is too honourable to leave me so mercilessly.

Her shoulders rolled as the flame of her spirit rose a little.

Dominic looked over at her and she froze, realizing they still hadn't descended the stairs.

The guard leaned forward and took Calida's shawl to be hung up. "What would you prefer to be announced as?"

"Lord and Lady Goldwyn," Dominic said.

Calida whipped her head to stare at him, gaping in shock.

What the ever-loving shit was that? She was prepared to be announced as Miss Calida Rhodes but as Lady *Goldwyn*? Her cheeks reddened as the fire in her roared to an impressive height. On the inside, she was shrinking and expanding. She wanted to hide somewhere and never leave, but also dance around the ballroom with exuberance. To encapsulate her name in his household already, basically he was telling everyone she was now deemed a Goldwyn.

Just what is going on in that mind of his?

In a daze, she silently followed Dominic as he towed her down the stairs. Calida couldn't take her eyes off him. Before, she couldn't force herself to look at him. What she had seen on the stairs and the emotions she felt now gave her whiplash.

He seemed to grow taller before her eyes and his shoulders grew broader. Nothing realistically changed, but everything until this moment shifted her view of him as it all pieced together. The question that stuck to her now was, did he care for her, or was he like the man on the stairs? The one who ruined his reputation in exchange for pleasant kisses from unwed maidens.

As she stared at him more intensely than she ever had before, Calida realized by denying herself an opportunity to be hurt, she was also denying herself a chance to love. His eyes never shifted away as they completed the last step on the stairs, conveying a message of their own. It felt strangely intimate, but his lips still drew her in like all the other times she had caught herself staring. Firm, but they could easily melt her until she was a pile of mud. She didn't know if she could ever think or speak the same now.

Seeming to sense her speechlessness, Dominic walked her to the middle of the dance floor. There he placed her hand on his shoulder and put his on the middle of her back. His eyes grew darker as he clenched his jaw the moment he realized her back was exposed. She barely held back a giggle, and her breath sped up as the bare skin tingled from his warm touch.

Dominic spun her around and then pulled her closer to him. Their faces were inches away. His breath fanned over her face and his lips were within reach. The desire to reach across and experience bliss tempted her. Imagining his warm lips on hers and then trailing down her neck made her knees shake. If she hadn't been pinned to him, she would've fallen to the ground.

His arm pressed her closer until Calida was flush with his chest. A fierce ache blossomed suddenly as his fingers spread to touch every inch of her back.

Dominic spun her around and walked away a step, then the couple joined again to circle one another in tantalizing closeness. They stepped away and around other dancers to join again. His eyes burned with desire as his hand found her back once more until all that kept the ache at bay was her slow methodical movement with the music. She swayed and swished as the dance entranced her until their hands met once more.

And his lips were a hair apart from hers.

He inhaled sharply and shut his eyes. Calida whipped her gaze up as Dominic pulled away and stood them a distance apart, fists clenched at his sides. She gulped and tried to control her panting. If they had stayed where they had been, he would've surely kissed her.

Turning away, she patted her cheeks as she came to her senses. If they had kissed, it would have changed everything. And that would be far more humiliating. Calida would have to admit she wasn't immune to Lord Dominic's charm.

The moment broken, both stood in silence. The couple held each other an arm's length apart as they continued to dance, not looking at each other until the song completed, and then he escorted her to speak with other guests.

His friends were close by and chatting up a storm.

Near a table set with plates and napkins stood Lady Evaine and her friend, Miss Heloise. Guarding each side of the women were Sir Garrick and Sir Silas. There was a new member of the group she'd never met before. He looked to be the same age as the others and had beautiful slicked back blond hair. The man was engaged in a conversation with Lady Evaine, who was politely smiling and nodding, while his hands would flail every which way.

Dominic and Calida walked toward them.

"I swear it's the truth, my lady." The man grinned widely.

"Come on, Weston, you have to be joking." Lady Evaine

giggled.

Weston just shook his head with a smirk.

"Am I interrupting?" Dominic said.

Weston looked at Dominic. Suddenly, his eyes sparkled.

"My lord! No, not at all! I was just engaging in some light conversation with Lady Evaine about the whereabouts of Lady Dale's cat." He stifled a laugh.

"Where is her cat?" Calida asked, curious.

Lady Evaine's hand flew up to her mouth as she stifled a giggle. Weston faced Calida.

"Lady Dale's maid found her walking around in her lady's undergarments. Somehow the cat managed to get its legs into the undergarment and was strutting around the mansion proudly with them around its hips."

Calida's hand whipped up as a bark of laughter almost escaped.

Unlike her, Dominic let out a free and loud laugh. She abandoned her one attempt to hide her laughter as she stood enchanted by the lord. In her peripheral, Calida realized she wasn't the only one fixated on him.

Evaine watched Lord Dominic laugh as if he were the only being in the realm. A small smile creased her lips as if she were a sunflower, living every moment waiting for the sun to rise on her again.

Braxton slapped Jetta's outstretched hand as he took her place and she strolled off to talk to the guards about what happened in the palace the night Calida's father died. Braxton had talked some while Calida and Dominic danced. Jetta stood by the couple and surveyed the crowd until it was her shift of questioning.

"I don't think you have officially met my betrothed, Weston." Dominic gestured to Calida. "This is Calida Rhodes. Soon to be Lady Goldwyn. She and I are planning our marriage."

Weston gave her a generous bow. "Good evening, my lady! I am Sir Weston Raleigh, soldier of the Elite Dominion and friend and comrade with not only Sir Silas, but yours truly, Lord Dominic."

Calida glanced at Dominic, who had moved over to talk with Lady Evaine and Miss Heloise. She looked back at Sir Weston, but he had mysteriously disappeared. She twirled around in search of the missing man and when she couldn't find him, Calida stepped closer to the circle around Dominic as they chattered animatedly.

"And then Lady Dale said to Garrick, 'My boy, what did you mean your friend has switched bodies with somebody else? Is that something that is even possible?'" Miss Heloise said, holding back a giggle.

Calida inched closer to Dominic's side as he chuckled.

"Miss Heloise, you said the joke wrong!" Lady Evaine held her mouth to keep from laughing. Heloise's eyebrows creased as she stared at her friend in confusion, then cleared as they exchanged a secret conversation with their eyes.

Lady Evaine grinned and then stared at Dominic with big doe eyes as she huskily told the correct joke. "Garrick was talking to Lady Dale and said how hard it must be to be a woman. His mother then agreed and said that the burden women must carry was great. He corrected her and said, no, no, my friend switched bodies with a girl and the first thing he did was fondle her breasts before they returned to normal. Somehow, she figured it out and sought him out. Then the woman slapped him, and in a huff, she ran off." Lady Evaine tucked a hair behind her ears, the longing coming off her in waves.

Calida stood off to the side, an outsider, as her heart squeezed. The tentative smile from the conversation deflated as she realized she once again was no longer welcomed. Or maybe she was just invisible.

As if she never existed by Lord Dominic's side.

As Lady Evaine stepped closer, Heloise nudged her forward encouragingly. "Of course, Lady Dale didn't see what that had to do with the burden of women and lectured him on proper manners. It was in that lecture she said, my boy, explain how your friend could switch bodies. That sounds utterly preposterous." Her lips pursed as she imitated Lady Dale's voice.

Dominic and Weston broke out in laughter at the silly voice and nonsensical behaviour. It was like Calida was being dragged away from the group and yet there she stood beside them, playing the outsider in this intimate moment.

Among her generation, she assumed it was normal to find such confounding things humorous, but she couldn't see it. Then again, she was more likely to be called a poor sport than a fun partygoer. Sir Weston had joined Sir Silas in conversation nearby, leaving Calida standing alone. She could just join one of the groups, but an overwhelming sense of doom filled her. *Once more, I am all alone, the shadow to the light.*

How often was she the visitor to a friend's group only to be listening as they regaled each other with tales that sent barks of laughter far and wide? Too many times to count. Even in the village, friends didn't come easily. Any time she had a group she thought she could call her own, it was like being at an inn and Calida had gone in to grab food while the others stopped for a sip and continued without her. A piece of wood in the forest of trees.

She could guess it was as simple as going up to the group, making a spot for herself and boldly sharing something she had learned, but even the times she had tried that...

How many times was she unheard or ignored? So many times. Peers would say or gesture something wildly and force her away. Peers would talk over her as if her mouth didn't even recite a sentence. People would look at her with disgust because she dared shared anything at all.

Possibilities swarmed around her mind like a hive of busy bees, thinking up the most cruel and unrealistic scenarios. They could snub her for joining a conversation. Or what if, instead of being included, they ignored her when she tried to include herself?

It would be better not to even try, to save herself the humiliation.

Her mother wasn't the sole tormentor of her childhood. The children her age had been just as cruel.

Calida looked down at the ground and held back the wash of emotions once more. It was all self-inflicted, but that didn't make it any less traumatic.

Dominic and the others were happily talking away and having a grand time while Calida stood on the borders of their conversations, unable to summon up the courage to say anything at all.

With her heart in her throat, Calida couldn't take standing outside the group any longer. She made a dash for the table off to the side, where there was food to munch on and drinks to partake in. She put her entire focus on admiring the foreign dishes available. Though she was used to more of a farm-based meal, the items available had everything from fresh apples to fruit soup. At the end of the table, she saw the largest swine she had ever seen. It was at least the size of three average pigs back home.

They had charred it with a golden glaze that made it look like fresh tree sap. The cooks served it on an enormous platter filled with other delicious meats. Calida saw birds and lamb served as well. Two types of meat she had only seen in the market but never tried gave off a mouthwatering scent. The food available seemed fit enough for a king, or a queen in this case.

Overwhelmed by the selection, the choice became daunting.

Calida swayed between trying some of the meat or having a fresh apple. She could not rightly remember the last time she had fresh fruit. Peasants had little in the way of fresh produce. As a well-off commoner, she had more ability to get it, but it was still something that was savoured. It wasn't an everyday occurrence to even hold fruit, so to see so much unblemished brought tears to her eyes.

Someone walked up behind her. "I recommend trying the apples. They are from the orchard nearby and I have been told they are the juiciest batch this year," the woman said.

Calida jumped as she looked at her. Her eyebrows furrowed as she tried to figure out where she knew the woman from. There were far too many people in the court to remember them all. Not that she remembered any of them. Stunned, Calida stood speechless at the beauty of the woman beside her. Her luscious black hair was pinned up in a high updo, and the maids must have powdered her face and added some tint to her cheek because she looked as fresh as snow. The woman's eyes sparkled with life as she stared at her.

Then Calida remembered. *She is speaking of the apples.*

"It has been a long time since I last ate an apple," she said hesitantly.

Slowly, she picked up an apple, almost waiting for someone to tell her off for daring to touch the food.

With the apple in hand, she looked back over at the woman, who was still staring with a smile on her face. Calida didn't feel odd or uncomfortable next to this woman. In fact, her eyes held so many mysteries that Calida wished to learn all she could. If only she knew how to strike a conversation with such an illustrious woman.

She opened her mouth to say something but fell silent

instead. The idea of talking when she felt so depressed felt like the burn of salt water up the throat after nearly drowning.

"What a lovely evening, isn't it, Calida?" the woman said.

Calida whipped her head to look at the woman in alarm. "How do you know my name?" Then she quickly added, "If you don't mind me asking?"

The woman let out a light, full laugh.

"Calida, who doesn't know you now? Especially after the incident at the marquess's wedding. That was quite exciting, don't you think?" An air of calm stillness came from the woman. If it wasn't for the anxiety of doing something wrong, Calida might've been relaxed by her presence. But the idea of accidentally stumbling upon the queen and offending her left Calida jittery. And the reminder of the events at the wedding was enough to bring that choking feeling back.

Her gaze stuck to the ground.

The woman gently tilted her head up and gazed softly at Calida.

"Dove, please don't lower your head in such a manner. There is nothing for you to be ashamed of." She nudged Calida's shoulders straight and tilted her chin until she held her head high.

"There, that's much better. Be sure to keep that up for the rest of the evening. I wouldn't be pleased to see you slacking. Otherwise, I might have to give you a stern talking to." The woman pulled a small little pout and then turned Calida around in Dominic's direction. "I shall have my eye on you, my sweet dove. You shall never be truly alone. Now go be merry with your friends."

Calida glanced behind her to question the woman, but she had disappeared.

She looked back in Dominic's direction. The group was talking and laughing. Weston had poked at Heloise like a schoolboy, and she took off in a chase, clamouring on about how he would regret it. A smile graced her lips, and without another thought, she approached them.

Along the way, more nobles talked to her and stopped her momentarily on her way to Dominic's side. Some were pleasant in a distant stranger sort of way. But there were one or two who stopped her to snicker at her misfortunes, all too glad to have her on display.

You shall never be truly alone.

The woman's words repeated in her mind as the villainous mockers made her the jester until Calida made it to her betrothed's side. Finally, she was able to disregard the hateful opinions of the other nobles.

As if the words held no meaning.

As she stopped beside him, Dominic finished his conversation. He promptly faced her and reminded her of the conversation awaiting them with her future father and mother in marriage. Calida felt nauseous about having a conversation with at least one of the nobles who most vehemently was against their relationship.

With a gulp, Calida linked her arm in his.

He strode over to a couple on the other side of the ballroom, a tall man with tanned skin and dark hair, and a small woman of a paler complexion than her husband. Her platinum blonde hair piled up high on her head was stylish and curled to the perfect look for the noblewoman who didn't want to look positively out of date.

As they approached, Calida's stomach dropped. Sweat clammed up her palms with nerves. Duke and Duchess Goldwyn were very prestigious and could send her to the ends of the world if they so desired.

She and Dominic stood quietly in front of his parents. His mother had a soft and curious look on her face as she gazed at Calida. His father was not so kind. Duke Goldwyn's face was aet in a deep scowl. His eyes, nearly slits, glared her down. The two hadn't even spoken, but already Duke Goldwyn had decided.

"Mother, Father, may I introduce Calida Rhodes of Poramun Creek," Dominic announced as he gestured to Calida.

His father grunted, not glancing again at Dominic's betrothed, and searched the crowd. When he found the person he was looking for, he strode in that direction. Calida peeked over her shoulder and saw Duke Goldwyn striking up a conversation with Lady Evaine. His expression softened at her excitable banter. Her smile was as wide as the moon and her arms flailed about like a dancer.

Calida's face tightened, and then she looked back at Duchess Goldwyn.

"My dear girl, you must forgive my husband. He doesn't adjust well to things not going his way," the duchess said, her eyes soft and welcoming. Calida relaxed a little and forgot the stress caused by Duke Goldwyn.

"I-I…. I-it is alright, Your Grace."

The duchess shook her head. "It isn't, but you didn't come over here to discuss melodrama." She looked at her son and smiled sweetly. Duchess Maud Lilla Goldwyn stepped closer and placed a hand on her son's face.

"My son, you have a lovely bride." She gazed at Calida. "I look forward to visiting with you once more, Calida."

Her mouth opened to speak again, but before she could, a lady off to the side called out for the duchess. Lady Maud Lilla glanced her way and then returned to talk with Calida and Dominic.

"I must go now to converse with the others, but I look forward to many meetings with tea and conversation." Looking at Dominic, she said, "I shall see you later."

Then she was gone, leaving a flowery feeling in her wake. Duchess Goldwyn, a vision of kindness and grace.

Twenty-One

Calida stood beside Dominic as he talked with Sir Weston and Sir Silas.

Sir Silas was telling the story of how he landed himself with a bear rug for his sleeping quarters at the Elite Dominion base.

"Then, just as I had expected, the bear rounded the boulder, and I jumped it. The two of us tumbled about and I was getting tired, but I grabbed the knife on me, which I had enchanted earlier in the week, and stabbed it in the neck." Sir Silas ended his tale by demonstrating the stabbing motion of his kill.

Just like when I used to go hunting in the forest with Father. They would scavenge what they could and made traps to catch smaller prey while talking about strategy. None of the strategies was quite like Sir Silas's, though. Her family didn't have an affinity for enchantment and the price for one was too steep when saving was a foreign concept to her mother. The woman insisted on purchasing expensive items, like the crystals her mother said were grown in the nest of a phoenix. Cressida refused to believe they didn't have medicinal properties.

Because of her mother, her father had to work tirelessly.

The realization hit her. Calida would never see her father again. His words of encouragement were the only memories she had now.

Her mouth parted as the breath escaped. She didn't think his death would affect her, since she had been trying so hard to keep people out for the longest time. She had assumed she had reached the point of emotional indifference, even though he had been her hero growing up. After the *incident* when he became distant and drowned himself in work, she thought it would dull the pain.

The possibility of her father dying as a traitor to the crown was enough to boil her blood. Rayner Rhodes was the most honourable man she had ever met. Once, when they had been out for a stroll on a day off, Rayner had seen a woman being kicked out of her home by her husband.

The woman was very stubborn and had always excused her husband's behaviour. She kept to herself and wouldn't engage with anyone except women. Her father had noticed several times the woman would sneak away to go to the market. Her father had acted without thought and berated the husband for his deplorable behaviour. The husband had gotten upset. He threatened to beat her father within an inch of his life.

He called Rayner a home-wrecking hoodlum and should stay on his side of town. The fight between them had allowed the woman enough time to make her escape. She ran into the woods.

It had been the last time Calida had seen her.

A sharp sting shot through her heart.

Calida blocked out everything around her until she heard a noblewoman mutter something behind her.

"I can't believe that backwater bumpkin is still around the earl. She's just a disaster."

The inflection of the woman's voice sounded familiar.

Calida's eyelids fluttered as she realized it was the noble from the wedding who bad-mouthed the Dales. Calida froze as indecision flooded her. *What should I do? Should I act as if I didn't hear her? But isn't that cowardly?*

"Lady Welch! You ought to be ashamed of yourself! To say such treacherous things about someone you haven't even talked to." Lady Evaine's voice rang out behind her.

Calida sucked in her breath. The girl who wished for Dominic's attention stood up for her. Why would she do that?

It was hard to be angry or jealous of the lady when she acted so honourably. The lady was showing kindness by defending her, but it could be a façade. Calida didn't know her true motivation.

Was she truly defending Calida on her behalf, or was it all a ruse to win Dominic's affection?

Calida looked over her shoulder to see the action, but something else caught her attention across the room.

In the crowd near the door, she thought she glimpsed the man who attempted to kidnap her standing near Lord Sullivan, whispering to him. Both men glanced her way separately until she couldn't handle watching any longer and turned away. She feared Lord Sullivan approaching her, even with Dominic by her side. Last time they met, the duke's interest in her was greatly disturbing, but Calida couldn't summon a reason he would still try.

Why would he approach her, anyway? Wouldn't he be the type to cower after her display of magic? Or lose interest in prey that wasn't cowed after a single inappropriate touch?

She glanced over once more as a couple passed by, then as suddenly as she found them, the man and Lord Sullivan were gone. Her heart thumped as her palms grew clammy. Her mind raced as it tried to piece together what she had just seen. Calida had hoped to never see either of them again, but certainly, she never expected them to be acquainted.

Was it possible Lord Sullivan was more involved than she had thought?

She whipped her head around hoping to catch another glimpse of them, but it was all in vain. The surrounding room had people from all over Eonifond, including nobles from the elusive Mirynd and Nydeawyr. There was no hope of finding two people, let alone one. The only group not in attendance were the elves from Oburynn, located in Nydeawyr. They didn't attend events hosted by human nobles. Not that they weren't tolerable and sociable with humans, but they didn't socialize with the idiotic, lazy nobles.

She caught Dominic's attention, and he looked at her with worry.

"Calida, are you alright?"

"I'm all right," she murmured.

"Please tell me. I can't help if you don't talk."

"Just thought I saw something. Duke Sullivan—no it couldn't be. Must have been my imagination."

Dominic searched her eyes and then surveyed the party. He didn't find what she had seen, but instead of just dismissing it, he summoned over Braxton and Jetta.

"Search the crowd. Your lady saw something," Dominic said.

Her head whipped around to stare at him, startled. What was he doing? Just because she saw something that didn't mean he had to listen to her. What if it was just a hallucination, and she was mocked for wasting his time?

Calida stayed silent as he commanded her only friend like a noble's lapdog. Before, she hated how he would order Jetta around, but now understanding was dawning on her. He had the power and authority to do so, and now that power was also hers. Calida realized just how much power was hers for the taking as well. As the wife of an earl, she would be a countess and could obtain the things she never had as a child.

She could have anything from her wildest dreams in the luxurious life of a noblewoman.

The real question was, did she want it at all?

Jetta and Braxton took off in opposite directions, weaving in well-practiced teamwork. Calida stood in awe of their swiftness but found it all so silly. She was already second guessing what she saw. There was no plausible reason she could think of for the duke to be talking to the man who tried to kidnap her.

Dominic moved closer and pulled Calida into his arms. If she wasn't so consumed by her thoughts and emotions, she might have pushed him away. Instead, she rested against his chest. Her mind was too crowded to think about keeping people at arm's length.

If that man and Duke Sullivan were working together, then what almost happened that evening in the tavern was no happenstance. It meant she was in more danger than she had originally thought.

Calida collapsed into Dominic's arms as she took in one shaky breath after another. The light in the ballroom was suddenly brighter. She couldn't reason when they added more candlelight. Panicking, it worsened. Her head spun, and she worried about whether she was floating. In the background, she could hear her breath speed up. It was like it wasn't her breathing, yet she knew it was. Heat poured from her until flames flickered on her body at random intervals.

"Calida?" His voice sounded far away, as if they were across the room from each other. After a moment, he realized she could not respond, and he sang soothingly, trying to calm her.

Dominic's lips gently touched her ear as the lullaby for sleepy children rang through her. "In, In the stormy sea. There is a song for me. It calls only the brave to sleep away the day." Her eyelids drooped as the hard block in her chest loosened.

"Legends, the legends ring true. Worthy, it could happen to you."

The tune calmed Calida into a slumber she had not expected. The darkness pulled her under, and she finally achieved peacefulness. No anxiety or conflicting emotions, or overwhelming thoughts.

In the darkness, a light stood at a distance. It was coming straight for her. The light spread out until it formed wings lit with flames. They continued to spread outward until it was encompassing all that Calida could see. There was a body attached to the wings, long and slender with a beak and a sweeping tail.

The colour of the flame and the intense heat licked at her face.

She locked eyes with the bird as it whispered into her head.

"Phoenix Child."

The bird faded away, and the darkness receded. This time, when she looked up, Calida saw Dominic. He had an intense look on his face, and his hair was unkempt. She glanced around and realized they were no longer in the ballroom. She tried to stand up, but a hand appeared on her shoulder and pushed her back down.

Jetta hovered over her. "You should rest some more, Calida."

Undeterred, she pushed Jetta's hand off her shoulder.

Calida swung her feet off the couch and stood up. Dominic rushed to her side, but she didn't fall again. She wasn't in her room. This one was larger and had rich colours on any available surface.

"We're in my room. It was the closest without causing a scene." Dominic jumped forward to answer.

Calida blushed. While this wasn't his real room, only the one he was using in the interim, that didn't mean her mind didn't conjure up images of him walking around in any manner of undress.

Don't be such a loose-thinking whore. Your mother taught you better.

It was like a drug induced state, and she couldn't help but to stumble as her mind imagined him confidently walking around his room while as naked as the day he was born. She wondered if he was just as breathtaking with his shirt undone.

Maybe she could take a peek later.

Realizing her mind was wandering into dangerous territory, she shook her head. Hard. Hoping it would shake loose some sense so she could focus on the matter at hand, but it seemed like she was a lost cause. A blush was still hot on her face, and Dominic stared at her with a fierce gaze dripping with sensuality and amusement. Like he knew what she was thinking about.

How could he possibly know what I'm thinking? Is my face that readable?

Trying to feign nonchalance, Calida said, "That'll do well enough." Looking away from Dominic, Calida directed the rest of her conversation at Jetta. "Did you learn anything?"

Jetta paused for a moment and exchanged a glance with Braxton.

"Well... many of the guards had heard from the others about a rumour concerning your father spreading around the palace." She spoke hesitantly, like she didn't want to share it. Calida's red cheeks deepened in color as her body grew warm.

"What was the rumour, Jetta?" Calida clenched her teeth.

Jetta opened her mouth, but Braxton interrupted her. Walking forward, he stood beside Jetta with his arms folded. He looked intimidating, and if it wasn't for having spent the last month by his side, it would have cowed her into a corner. The presence of a fierce warrior flowed off him in waves. A mere stance could frighten away a stray bunny.

"Someone passed along the maid's story about Rayner being unfaithful and forceful. Some said your father made attempts to bed them. Also, Rayner apparently looked shifty around high-value palace items. One had seen him shove something into his pocket before returning to his post."

Calida's hair caught fire as the wave of fury bubbled up.

Her laboured breathing was the only noise in the room, and she was clenching her fists so hard they were white. Everyone had been dead silent and then burst into motion to put out her hair. Jetta stumbled to the washbasin and grabbed the pitcher of water left by the bed. Braxton fetched a blanket while Dominic grasped Calida's hands.

"You need to calm down, Calida." Dominic's voice wavered as a flicker of flame licked his arm.

If only she could stab the bitch who spreads nonsense about her father.

Sir Rayner Rhodes? A philandering kleptomaniac? Never in a thousand years.

"Calida, your hair." Jetta shuffled closer step by step, ready to dump the water on her head. Braxton tried to wrap the blanket around her hair, hoping to pat away the flames. The fabric started to singe and a lick of flame burnt Braxton. He jumped away, flailing his hands while swearing, "*Sarding* wench-like creature".

Calida's chest tightened with fear as the heat of the flames filled the room.

The guards exchanged a look. Jetta inhaled sharply, then dumped the water on Calida's head, drenching the fabric at her feet. A sizzle of steam escaped as the flames went out.

Calida pushed Dominic's hands off her.

"I'm alright, Dominic." Her tone was indignant. Calida didn't want to admit that her hair catching on fire freaked her out. She could be strong. She had to be.

She had never had her magic light up her hair completely,

at least she couldn't remember it doing so. At the wedding reception, it had been only a little bit. *Or had it?*

Patting her shaking hand on her head, expecting charred bits, she was greeted by soft hair that was slightly warm instead. She gripped her hair and stared at the unblemished strands. How was that possible?

Fire is destructive. So why didn't it damage me?

"I don't think your powers have been that intense before."

"I-I... No. I didn't expect it to do *that*. I'm not hurt though." She frowned.

Dominic searched her gaze and scowled when she tried to hide her fear. If her powers were so intense now, what did it mean?

"What about the rumours? Were you able to find out who find out who spread this?" Dominic looked in Jetta's direction.

Her friend nibbled on her finger, and her eyes shifted between Calida and Dominic. "The maid might be at the debutante ball. It's rather strange that all other accounts are mysteriously missing though." Jetta walked over and picked up the singed blanket and patted Calida dry.

"We should head there, then." Braxton rubbed his hands and stared at Calida from the corner of his eye, as if uncertain how to take her hair bursting into flame.

"The party invitations should arrive soon." Dominic's eyebrows creased as he looked away in deep thought.

Jetta wrapped the blanket around Calida before picking up some stray linen and tearing it into a wrap. Then she took it over to Braxton, yanked his hand to her, and wrapped the linen around it with fierce tension. He hissed in pain.

"It's odd. The nobleman asked the palace guards to protect his daughter for that night. Apparently, there had been a persistent suitor that neither of them want around. He was showing up and trying to steal her away. Once he nearly got her out the door," Jetta said.

Calida's eyes grew wide. *The suitor tried to kidnap the nobleman's daughter? Was he insane?* One of the nobleman's daughters just turned fifteen years old. The party was a ball in celebration of her coming-of-age ceremony.

Calida put on her cape from the couch she had been lying on, preparing to leave. "We need to be there all the more, then."

Dominic came forward and put a hand on her shoulder. "I know you dislike events with nobles. You just finished going to a large one. We could figure something else out. Maybe I could go by myself."

The offer tempted Calida, but she knew it was the perfect opportunity. There was a good likelihood that the guard who was there when her father died will be at the debutante's ball. Like Jetta had said earlier, she needed to accept that this wasn't her world anymore. It was time she blended in.

"We should head out now while we can." She walked to the door.

"Maybe you should rest some more. You fainted only an hour ago." He frowned at her.

Calida shook her head and turned around to look at Dominic.

"No. Let's get going. We have preparations to make, and we have no reason to stay for the rest of the festivities. I don't think any of us are interested in seeing if the queen actually accepts a suitor tonight." Jetta stepped beside Calida.

"I would be," she said.

Calida side-eyed her friend. Just because Jetta was her sister in spirit, didn't mean she wouldn't throw a punch at the girl. She was getting out and she was doing it now.

"The only thing I can't figure out is how no one noticed what happened. The palace is a well-guarded fortress," Jetta said. "Your father's death and these rumours. It couldn't be someone else other than a regular at the palace." Jetta's last comment left the group with a damning realization.

Someone close to the court had done this.

The four of them set out from the palace. Eventually, the walls faded from sight as they headed back to Dominic's mansion. The densely wooded forest was calm as the nestling of critters fled from the road and the disturbance of their movement.

The wooden carriage creaked and rattled as they travelled down the road. Jetta stared out the window beside Calida while Braxton sat across from her, polishing his hand-axe. Dominic sat across from her, his leg bouncing up and down. They had all agreed to plan how they would accomplish their goal at the party in Baekkioron as they headed back to Dominic's mansion. With several days before the debutante ball, they dedicated as much time as they could to planning. Nothing could go wrong. They needed answers, and no one was giving them enough information. They had the report and some accounts of what happened, but the pieces were still not aligning. While it wasn't proper protocol, the group departed from the ball early, using the excuse of her fainting to leave.

"Hush, hush, child. It's not safe here. You'll be alright. Eesa will be close by. The morning in you will hide. Hush, hush." Calida crooned the tune stuck in her head since that dream she had when she passed out at the palace. The moon cast shadows around them in the forest and the muggy air hung heavy like just before it broke into rain. Jetta gazed her way. Her eyebrow quirked in question.

"Where did you learn that?"

"Did you just make that up?"

Jetta and Braxton spoke at the same time.

They gave each other annoyed looks but turned to stare expectantly at Calida.

"I guess so. It was just something that keeps repeating in my head. I think I would've gone insane if I didn't hum it out loud at least once."

"I liked it." Dominic smiled.

Calida blushed, then cleared her throat and looked away. She didn't want to admit that she liked it when he complimented her. Her heartbeat sped up whenever he looked her way, let alone smiled. Not that his smile affected her or anything. Why would the dimple of his cheek when he smiled make her feel like jumping out a window and squeal like she was a giddy girl?

They stopped to camp the night, then continued to Dominic's mansion.

The next day, they arrived in Weommadran when the sun was at its highest. Calida's stomach grumbled as they made it back. It had been a long trip and her desire to eat was growing with each passing hour.

Dominic guided her toward the dining room.

"Because of your long journey, we thought you would appreciate food and rest," Lucy, the maid, said. Calida was still familiarizing herself with the staff and household, but Lucy had been kind to her and unforgettable by Calida's standards.

Dominic nodded and held Calida close to his side. She jumped in surprise. His hand caressed her back gently, tickling her, and she hadn't expected it. Though it was just like him to be considerate, she still didn't expect him to be nice to her. It would take a lot to unpack all she was taught growing up. A real relationship with him could be fun. He could give her unconditional love and attention. Her life would have an unlimited supply of adventure and fun, instead of depressing chores and criticisms.

But what held her back were the noblewomen making her

life hell. Many didn't approve of the backwater *whore*, in their words, being within touching distance of Dominic. They deemed him the most eligible suitor. Whichever lucky lady married him was in for a pile of judgement the size of a mountain.

She didn't want to take on that judgement. Yes, she was slated to take on the role of Lady Goldwyn, at least for now, but the other noblewomen who were far too obsessive for her taste would make sure she failed every step of the way.

Calida's smile dimmed at that reminder.

"I think we would love a good meal. Right, Calida?" Dominic stared her down intensely, like he had interpreted her thoughts.

"R-right. Sure. Food would be nice."

Dominic pulled out her chair for her at the table in the dining hall. He sat in his usual seat and then turned to stare intently at Calida.

"Calida..."

She looked his way tentatively.

"Are you willing to try?" Dominic said, the hidden meaning obvious as he stared at her while scooping the food onto his plate.

Calida didn't know how to answer. In her mind, she could confidently think, *Please Dominic, make me your wife as soon as we can.* Damn the consequences. However, she knew realistically she didn't have it in her.

"I-I... What do you want, milord?" Calida cringed inwardly. By this point, she recognized he hated when she referred to him as "milord," but it was almost second nature when she felt insecure. Whenever embarrassed or unsure, she seemed to call him by his title. If she could stop herself, she would, because Calida hated how it upset him.

Dominic's eyes grew darker.

"Please, don't call me that again." His tone was firm.

She tensed and stared at her plate. If only she could beg him to be happy again. Anything but him getting upset with her.

"Yes, sir." Calida spoke softly as she glanced at him quickly before returning to gaze down at her hands. All she wanted to do was crawl into a ball and hide.

He sighed. "Calida, look at me."

Calida looked once more.

Dominic braced his hands and stared at the table.

"I desire to make you my wife eventually, Calida. But for that to happen, I need to know you want to be. Not because of the arrangement, but you wish me to be in your life."

Calida floundered with what to say. She was used to passive words and people who went back on what they said. Empty promises were familiar, and a part of her hoped he would disappoint her, too. That he would be just like the others who didn't keep their word. For her own sanity.

He could touch her wherever she wanted if they married.

Calida's breath hitched.

A maid knocked on the door, interrupting the couple at the table as the girl approached.

"Milord, the mother of our lady is at the door. She wants an audience with her daughter and you." She bowed then. Calida and Dominic exchanged a glance.

Why was her mother here?

Calida hadn't seen her since that day she learned her father was dead. It wasn't like they were comfortable to share letters with one another.

The clicking of heels echoed until the door to the lounge room opened and Cressida walked through. The maid closed the door quietly behind them. Calida and Dominic stood up.

Her mother rushed over and flung her arms around the shocked girl.

"My baby, it's been forever, and I hadn't heard from you

in so long." Cressida caressed her face and swept Calida's fringe out of her eyes. Her thumbs stroked her skin comfortingly. She gazed at her daughter; her eyebrows creased in concern. Tears welled in the corners of her eyes. Calida's mouth parted in surprise.

"I-I... Well..." Calida said.

Dominic stepped forward and wrapped an arm around Calida's back.

"She and I have been working hard to give your husband a proper send-off. There has been a lot to cover," he said.

Cressida looked over at Dominic. Nodding silently as she stepped back and wiped her eyes while turning around to sit down on a chair.

"Yes, yes. There's much to be done. I have just missed my sweet daughter. It's been hard to cope without her steady nature by my side."

Calida tensed at her mother's words,almost like she could hear the bitter undertone sewn into the sentence. She had never coped without her responsible daughter there to observe her. *Like a child.* If she thought Calida would accept this quietly, Cressida had another think coming.

"Yes, well... I couldn't possibly stay home and get what needed to be done out of the way," Calida said, hoping her mother would catch the bitterness in her tone.

Cressida stared at her. A fresh mask of wounded emotion slashed along her face.

"Its time you returned though, my darling. You have been away for too long. You have a duty to your family." Her voice beckoned her to feel guilty for "abandoning" her family. It was like before. She was under the whims of her mother who did as she pleased, and Calida couldn't second guess the decisions. It was also just like her to use the same endearment her father had used. Always the unnecessary competition with all of those around her. Almost like if she used that name, Calida would immediately favor her. Even now there was no one else to favor.

As she stood there in silence, her mother's face cleared slightly. Almost like she realized her daughter wasn't falling for the bait.

Cressida gazed at Dominic.

"There's duties Calida must do around the house. I cannot take care of them at my age."

Calida clenched her fists. Her mother reached into her pocket and pulled out a handkerchief.

"Please, my daughter. Don't continue this quest to find some type of meaningless closure to your father's death. It's in the hands of Eesa now. He will guide your father to his rightful resting place." Cressida blew her nose and held back a sob as she peeked up at her daughter.

Dominic glanced around the room, for once unable to address a situation straightforwardly.

Calida closed her eyes for a moment, trying to hold back the heat inside her. She didn't want to roast her mother alive. *That's a lie.*

Yes, she did, but it would be far too messy and the consequences..... Calida couldn't live with them.

Calida peeked at Dominic. Her sudden switch seemed to not only stun her, but him, too.

"I have things to do here. Not to mention, the engagement..." Calida said.

Cressida gripped the sides of her arms. She shook her head slowly with a frown.

"No, no. I need you back home. The engagement was your father's idea. As his wife, I had a responsibility to submit to his decisions. You can come back now. We can repay the earl for the time you spent with him." Her eyes pleading.

Calida's throat dried as the guilt weighed heavily on her. As she stared at her mother, she noticed the deep lines creasing on her forehead and mouth. *Could someone age that fast in a such a short time?*

Her mother's frame was thinner than she had ever seen it and the way she walked—it looked like she hadn't eaten in ages.

The girl nibbled on her lip. The part of her that was trained to listen only to her mother said to go home with her. But Calida knew she would be miserable.

"Actually. It wasn't his idea. It was mine." Dominic said.

Calida's head whipped to gape at him. *What in the shitting sard?*

She had always assumed it was her father. But it had seemed strange though. How would someone of lower rank have the power to match his daughter with a noble?

"Still. I need her back at home."

Her eyes shifted around as she shot up out of her seat.

Calida jumped as Cressida grasped her hands.

"My darling. Come back now. Are you going to leave your mother all alone in that empty house?"

Her chest squeezed. Cressida's hands shook as she held Calida's. The strained smile on her lips disturbed her daughter.

"I'm not leaving you alone. I can send coin back with you. It'll help." Calida looked over at Dominic, and he nodded in agreement.

Dominic held onto Calida's back once more, his steadiness anchoring her to say what needed to be said next. She needed to stay in the Goldwyn manor. For her own happiness. Calida was taking her first hesitant step forward. She hadn't thought of herself in such a long time. It felt wrong. And yet, right.

"I'm not coming home with you, Mother. I'm needed here." Cressida's eyes flickered. She stepped away from Calida as if she had been burned, a look of horror on her face.

"So you have decided to abandon me," she said.

Calida inhaled sharply. "I'm not abandoning you. I'll help give you what you need, but I can't return." Cressida's lips firmed and then wobbled.

"I need my filial daughter back at home, taking care of the home and me."

Dominic stepped forward then.

"Madam, you are not so old to insist your only daughter stay at home watching over you as if you're an invalid. You haven't even a single grey hair yet."

Calida's stopping breathing. *Shit. He didn't pull his punches.* She appreciated the support, but Calida already tensed as she could clearly see the backlash.

"I have been disabled since the accident twelve years ago. She is needed at home. You cannot hold her hostage." Her tone shrilled in a screech.

Dominic moved forward and Cressida moved backward, a face of fear painted on her. Her eyes darted to plead for Calida's aid, as if Dominic was going to pounce on her and hurt her.

"If you are disabled, I know of a caretaker who can stop by regularly to help. The townsfolk are more than willing," he said.

Cressida shook her head wildly as she moved backward until she jumped as her butt met the edge of the seat next to her, then moved behind it.

"The townsfolk are riddled with demons! They are of no help to me! I wouldn't allow such evil entities into my home!" Her voice was growing louder.

Dominic reached out, but Cressida shrieked and darted away until her body met the door to the lounge. Her frame shook as she tried to get Calida to help her. Her eyes widen in terror as if Dominic were a ferocious monster.

"Madam, I know of very lovely townsfolk who aren't

following Zabal's teachings...." Dominic stopped where he stood, his hands out in front of him.

Cressida's hand searched desperately for the doorknob.

"You are trying to trick me! The lot of you. You vile demons have corrupted my own daughter."

Calida watched in mild confusion. While it was odd she would get so worked up, it was like her mother to twist the situation into her own control. She sighed heavily.

Cressida gazed at her daughter once more, tears forming until the moment she realized Calida wasn't moving. Her daughter wasn't comforting her or trying to aid in Cressida's mental stability. There was no help for a lost cause.

Cressida scowled as the darkness in her eyes unmasked.

"My daughter has chosen the side of the *high and mighty nobles*. She has done nothing to stop her corruption. May Eesa condemn you!" she shouted.

Dominic scowled at her mother.

"Madam, I will not have you besmirching the names of this household. You must leave now." He stepped to the side to ring for a servant. All the while, he never let her mother out of his sight.

Cressida shook like a bull readying to charge. Her eyes locked on Calida. Her mouth gaped open as she darted forward, only to have a servant on each side of her. Both girls held onto her arms and pulled her out the door.

The entire time, her mother screamed as if she were in agony. Wailing about the demons coming to destroy her only daughter. How she needed to save her from the monster and discipline her in the ways of light.

As the door closed, Calida nearly collapsed as she held onto the chair in front of her. Somehow, being in the same room as her mother consumed every ounce of energy she had reserved.

Dominic rushed over and helped her up. He held her close as her eyes closed.

After a moment, they returned to the dining room.

"I'll think about it, Dominic," Calida's said softly.

He looked over at her strangely.

"About being your wife."

Dominic inhaled sharply, then sighed deeply.

"Thank you for at least giving it some thought."

Then slowly they ate their food, even though she was no longer hungry after the encounter with her mother. The frustration and unrest coming off Dominic was palpable, and she blamed herself.

If only she had been clearer. More direct.

Later, Calida picked up her paint brushes and got lost in another painting. Normally, she would have to wait a long period between being able to paint, because the money her father earned couldn't buy her as many art supplies as she would have liked. She never demanded them from her father, but that didn't mean she didn't fantasize what she could do with unlimited supplies. It was one reason she had switched to charcoal, because she could use the leftover remains in the fireplace.

Dipping her brush in an intense green, Calida painted the background of a canvas. At first, it was intense and jumped out at her. Then she brushed in lighter tones, blending and painting over mistakes until the finished result.

Hours later, after devoting much time and energy to it, she finished.

From one side, Calida could see her father. He was in a dark, brooding light that cast a long shadow. Then the lighter side was Dominic. He was bright and all-encompassing. His painted face took up so much of the canvas it was overshadowing her father's face. Rayner was in the shadow of Dominic in her life now. Her heart pounded as she stared at it. It was disturbing to see the blending and how it felt natural. She hadn't expected her father would get forgotten so easily.

Tears formed in her eyes. She couldn't think of a way to keep him as the focus of her life, as if it was natural to switch to Dominic, even though she didn't want to. How could she remember him, when life moved on and her heart had a mind of its own? Her mind knew better, but on the inside, she wanted to cling to stability and security. To cling to someone because of the things she lacked as a child.

After cleaning her paint brushes, Calida left her room to walk to the library on the other side of the mansion. As she was walking there, she felt like someone was following her, but when she looked behind her, no one was there. Easily dismissing it, she continued her path. Sitting down at a library table, she brainstormed on what she could do while at the party in Baekkioron.

The others and Calida had agreed to plan together, but if she didn't do it this second, she felt like she would pull out her own hair in frustration. *"The point to working is to get it done right away. Otherwise, they're a failure."*

Calida sucked in a breath. She hadn't even realized her mother's words were ringing through her mind. *Had she been away for so long she could see the difference?*

Calida wrote her thoughts and ideas in order to clear her mind.

The proof of the rumours still wasn't clear, and everything else surrounding her father's death was a mess. Something was missing in this puzzle, but she couldn't think of what it was for the life of her.

Calida clutched her head and growled in frustration before resting her head on the table. No matter how much she thought about it, she didn't know enough people in

Dominic's world to make a fair assumption about who was behind it. Calida stomped her foot under the table. Nothing she did got rid of the feeling inside her. *Find out who it was and now!*

She was on edge. Dominic drove her crazy, and Rayner's death consumed her. Calida wanted to try being Dominic's wife. And that didn't mean a marriage of convenience. She wanted it all. His love and comfort. His heated gazes and light-hearted moments. Let him in and feel happiness for the first time in a long time. It was a daunting concept, and she was so close to the answer. But she was still reluctant. The nobles of the court would show great disdain for her. It didn't suit someone from higher status to fraternize with someone of her station.

Calida was a piece of half-eaten raw meat compared to Dominic, whom would be a premium cut that was fattened all its life.

Her eyes fixed on the table; her lip wobbled as sadness consumed her.

She was ready to just give up on the fantasy of living a wonderful life with Dominic. She didn't know if they could void a betrothal with an earl, but maybe something else could work.

If they married, maybe she'd be the wife no one ever talked about, and Dominic continued like they had never married. It would hurt, but he'd start a relationship with Lady Evaine, someone far better suited for him. She could live in the wood-work and never brought to social functions, never addressed as Lady Goldwyn. Lady Evaine would certainly love to take on that title. The lady's desperation was palpable.

Just then, the door to the library creaked as Jetta stepped in. Halting her depressing thoughts, Calida stared. Her closest friend was someone who wouldn't stand for her throwing in the towel. Also, the one person she didn't want to see right now.

Jetta looked at Calida sternly. Was her face that readable?

"You have a look of utter despair on your face. Don't tell me you're thinking what I think you are?"

Calida frowned. "What am I thinking of?"

Jetta frowned and strode toward her. When she focused all her attention on Calida like in that moment, all she wanted to do was run.

"You're thinking like a coward."

Calida's eyes flashed up. How dare Jetta call her a coward? She was doing the right thing.

Was she? The little voice in her head whispered.

She held her hands out in front of her. They had signs of hard labour and calloused from long days. They were nothing like the hands of the women she had seen at the events the nobles hosted. The weight on her chest grew heavy again. Calida bit her lip. It was all she could do to keep from crying.

Suddenly, her mind went blank, and a white light took over her vision. Then an image came to her. It was his face, smiling down at her. He was vivid and colourful in the vision. Nothing else but his face. A serene look was in his eyes. Somehow, she knew she caused it. A ray of sunshine that was her love spread warmth through her.

Just then, all other thoughts left her mind. Any anxiety she had about their relationship disappeared. All she desired now was to hide in Dominic's arms. To escape the judgement world and have contentment. To trust that Dominic could take over the thinking for her and just hold him. *She was tired of the pain.*

"What's your answer, Calida?" Jetta interrupted her thoughts.

Whipping her head up, she had forgotten Jetta was there.

"I want Dominic, but I'm scared. What about when the nobles disapprove of our relationship?"

"What would you expect the nobles to do? Shake their finger at you?" Jetta scoffed as she mocked the gesture. Calida slouched down.

"What if they convince him I am no good and he listens to them? The thought of him suddenly treating me coldly... I'm so frightened of heartbreak I don't know if I could be attached to him." Calida didn't think she could handle if she was made the fool and left in the dust.

Jetta leaned down and planted her hands on the table.

"My friend, it's far too late. You have flown past unattached. If you don't do something, I will have to take drastic actions." Jetta scowled. The creases on her face deepened in a way Calida had never seen before.

Then she realized all of this was affecting her friend, too.

Jetta hadn't shared her opinion about it, but it was obvious what she thought about it. Calida had spent so much time worried and waiting. Moping about her inevitable return to her previous miserable life. At first, she almost wished for it, but the idea was foreign now. She couldn't imagine spending every day for the rest of her life without him. To wake up and never see him beside her at breakfast. Wouldn't be able to walk into the library and catch him draped at the window seat, absorbed into a book. Never dream of time away from guarded companionship.

Jetta's blossoming relationship with Braxton, or whatever it was, was strained because of her. Though their passion was clear, the two would argue and bicker with one another, as if they had to choose sides. The way they would tweak each other about the intimate details a friend certainly wouldn't notice. *How was she able to see such a perfect match in them, but not for herself?*

Calida felt tears well up in her eyes, but she held them back.

"I don't know what do to do now. I... I care for him, but I cannot think how to move forward."

Jetta's face softened into a smile.

"Go to him, Calida."

Her mouth parted. She couldn't think of what to say. Her feet moved first. The chair clattered behind her as Calida dashed for the door of the library.

She stopped for a moment. "I had been considering letting Dominic have an affair with Lady Evaine after we married. She would've been a better fit, anyway."

Jetta sucked in a breath. "You should know by now, Dominic is far too honorable to even consider cheating on his wife. Love or not."

Calida's chest loosened as she realized how selfish her thoughts were.

It went against Dominic as a whole.

She left in the library as she rushed to the one spot on her mind without a single idea of what she would say upon arrival.

Her feet pounded the floor as she ran toward the study where Dominic told her he would be. Maids bowed as she moved past them, and she skipped steps as she hurried to find him.

Before long, she came to a halt in front of Dominic's study. The door was closed and there was only silence on the inside. The guard at the door opened it for her and waited for her to walk through before closing it behind her.

The room was dim and only lit by a few candles that were spread around the table where Dominic stood. It held a map of Eonifond. He still hadn't noticed her. Dominic pinned markers for strategic placements in battle on the map.

He looked up and briefly smiled her way.

"What brought upon this sudden visit, my dear one?"

Calida rushed forward to give him a hug, her arms encircling him. She had not a single worry about him possibly refusing her attention. Dominic shifted and placed her in his arms, softly stroking her hair as he smiled gently at her. Murmurs of comfort and contentment escaped from him. Calida pulled him closer, unable to part from him again. He held the back of her neck with his hand as the arm at her middle wrapped around her. An idyllic moment at last.

The door opened, halting the conversation. With a quick glance, his eyes clearly said, "We will continue this conversation later."

The guard at the door walked in. His hands clenched a piece of paper and his mouth was set in a firm line.

"What is it, Mr. Winslow?" Dominic asked, suddenly alert.

The man handed him a note. It was a small paper that looked meaningless.

"Milord, milady, please read what it says." The guard went back to his post.

Calida peeked at it as Dominic folded the paper open.

There on the page was a sloppily written note.

Stop looking into your father's death.

Then a line down, *Your undergarments would look best stained in virgin blood.*

Dominic's face went dark with rage. Calida stumbled back into Dominic's chest. The desire to expel her stomach overwhelming. She was sure they were on the right path now. But the last line was unexpected.

Twenty-Two

ominic slammed the paper up against the door. She flinched in surprise. He wasn't the type to get angry. He could walk away from an argument with someone without raising his voice at all.

One time, a maid set out his favorite jacket on a bench and it fell into a bucket with red dye. It was ruined. If it had happened to Calida, she would've been fighting back the need to yell. However, Dominic took one look at it and dismissed it. Not a single note of strain or anger was clear.

She had been thrown by it. All she knew was if something she owned or was responsible for became damaged, her mother would badger her with endless questions until all Calida think about was what she should have done better. After some time, she had learned to defend herself against anything that might be an offense to her character.

"Keep your voice down! Do you want to be sent to an orphanage?"

Her mother had a loud temper and didn't mind sharing it. She would throw her temper at Calida, and Calida would return the same. It was on the days she was drained of energy that she was quiet. It was the experience Cressida gave her that taught her to be compliant. Anything more could bring attention to the small girl who sat in the shadows. She wasn't truly abused, nothing like some of the little girls in the small towns in her country. Noblemen from all over had a fondness for little girls, the men perverted enough to whip children.

In comparison, it wasn't so bad. She could still go on with her life without wishing to die like the traumatized girls who lived at the cruel hand of their abusers in the realm. Yes, she found it incredibly difficult to converse with another person without the constant worry whether they secretly hated her or found her annoying, but there was far worse out there.

And Mother wonders why I don't want to spend time with her.

"These blasted criminals and their threats. If only I could find out who it was."

His breath shook as he clenched his fist and then swiftly turned around. Calida eyed him carefully as he took methodical, deep breaths, eyes closed in concentration until they snapped open. His fierce attention returned to her.

"You came in here for a reason. I'd like to know why."

The sun had already set as she had run from the library. Anyone who didn't have sex in mind wouldn't go searching for their significant other after dark.

She blushed as she thought about her instinctual search for him. She didn't know why she came here. The comfort of Dominic's arms had consumed her mind. She hadn't given social niceties amongst couples a single thought.

Calida glanced away from him, his unnerving stare suddenly unbearable.

"I... I... my answer is y-yes."

Calida could feel his gaze burning through her as she stared at a particularly interesting wall. Dominic prowled closer. With a gasp, she stepped back.

"What question are you answering yes to? I don't remember asking you a question just now." He took another step forward.

Calida's body temperature spiked as she fought between gazing at his eyes and the wall. Her heart was in her throat. He was acting far too much like the cat on the hunt for the mouse, and she was the mouse. Calida's foot edged back. Before she knew it, the table caught her leg, and with a squeak, she lurched forward. Her eyes slammed shut as she braced for impact. Instead of the ground, a pair of hands grabbed her by the waist and planted her on her feet.

An eye cracked open, greeted by endless fabric. Dominic's large hands encompassed both her arms and back, holding her against him. She really wished it didn't make her feel a tingle all the way through her body. Calida couldn't find it in her to move away, excluding the fact a table was right behind her. She was trapped.

Calida took a deep breath and summoned some courage. She blurted, "I, C-Calida Rhodes... L-Lady... of Weommad-ran, will be Lord Dominic's wife." She held her breath as she cringed. *That wasn't the most elegant. Please don't laugh.*

Her statement hung in the air. He didn't respond. His face froze, not even a blink. She began to doubt if she should've said that. *Maybe it was too awkward. He wasn't laughing, but Dominic rejecting her was worse.*

"You may not be a Goldwyn yet, but on our wedding day, you shall be the most beautiful." A smile grew soft on his face as he gazed at her. His hands grasped hers, brought them up to his mouth, and he slowly kissed the backs of her hands with delicate care.

A flash filled her vision of Dominic in formal attire, spinning her around in the air. Both looked overcome with joy, and she was in the most beautiful dress she had ever seen. A wedding dress.

Dominic hugged her close, stirring her out of the vision. His hands softly stroked her hair, and his head rested on her shoulder.

"Thank you, Calida." he whispered into her hair.

Looking up, she moved back. "Why are you thanking me?"

Dominic paused for a moment. "For changing my life."

Changing his life? She might have made his life harder, but changing it seemed impossible to her, unless it was for the worst.

Dominic stared at her blankly, almost like he was stuck in the past, and a smile grew on his lips. The same ones that reached closer and closer until they rested on her forehead. The warmth from him lingered on that spot for several moments. Her insides melted from it like she had been frigid until that moment. Even as he pulled away, the feeling of his lips had her frozen. If it weren't for sheer willpower and his arms still around her, she would've collapsed onto the ground. If it was possible for someone to transfer affection through physical contact like that, then she deemed herself a victim.

Calida stood in the middle of her room as the maids worked on her dress for the Baekkioron Ball. This time, she assigned her maids to prepare the outfit for her because the last time she did it herself.

The dress they currently worked on was a deep purple with lacing on the front and a heavy skirt that flowed outward in the back. It was elegant and warm. She worried about overheating, but the maids assured her it would be fine.

They had mentioned something about an outdoor event, but Calida had only been half listening. By the time she had returned her attention to the conversation, the maids were talking about something different.

The arms of the gown bunched up at the elbows and shoulders. The neckline was appropriate for a married woman.

She guessed it was due time she started dressing like one. It would be reality soon. She had secretly thought about wearing beautiful gowns and playing house when she had been a child. Being a girl with dresses and play toys had sounded so much fun. It didn't hurt that the idea of getting all dolled up still excited her to this day. It was thrilling to get dressed up for an event.

As a maid pinned up a layer of the dress, Jetta burst into the room with Dominic and Braxton followed. Calida turned just as Braxton stopped behind his lord.

"There's been a development." Dominic said.

He paused as he realized Calida was occupied. Then Jetta shooed the maids away, telling them to come back later. Dominic stepped up and took Calida's hand.

"The guard that we had hoped to catch at the ball in a few days died in a forest fire last night. No one has confirmed it because it had been burning hot and was hard to control. The palace put fire breaks up all around their walls, but no one can find a body yet."

Calida's eyebrows shot up. Did that mean they had no reason to go to the ball now? She would be happy not to attend. They were draining and all she would wish for was a drink. The spreading fire was concerning, though.

What if it was near her hometown? But what did it matter? Her life was here.

Jetta held out a hand, which Calida took as she stepped down from the pedestal she was on for the dress fitting.

"Will we still attend the Baekkioron Ball?" Calida's voice almost held back the giddiness.

Braxton stepped forward. "We can still go to the ball, milady. Many other guards who heard the rumours will be there. Also, I have heard that Lord Sullivan will be in attendance. He has been on the list of untrustworthy men for a while. Milord hopes to find out more from him."

That name sent a shiver down her spine. He was the last person she wished to encounter. Flames and panicked screams filled her mind before she shook away the memory.

Dominic came up behind her and cradled her shoulders. No words, only the steady shelter of his arms. The tingle of his previous kiss on her forehead warmed her as she melted on the inside. The only evidence of her traitorous thoughts was the blush on her cheeks. Jetta glanced at her friend with a smirk.

I need to control that damned blushing.

"I don't believe he's dead." Jetta's tone was as prickly as a pinecone. When she was stubborn, nothing could deter her. Calida prayed that this time it was well founded.

"How would that change things?" Calida said.

Jetta looked at her friend. "Then we could find out more from the guard if he survived."

Braxton scowled. "The facts and evidence would prove otherwise. The guard was last seen encased by fire."

Jetta shook her head as she folded her arms. "A body has not surfaced, so nothing has proven that assumptionto be true."

Braxton moved closer to Jetta, frowned, and folded his arms. He looked rather intimidating, but Jetta stood her ground and glared at the man towering over her. Jetta looked like a small nymph compared to the giant oak of a man. She still glared at him as if he were an insect on the ground.

"You insist on questioning the evidence. Hard, cold fact is all the proof you need. A body can only provide so much. A fire was surrounding him, and a body has not shown up, therefore he has died," he grumbled.

"Sometimes you need to loosen up. Or else you will miss something," Jetta said.

Calida eyed Dominic as he stifled a grin. In retaliation, she threaded her free arm under her other one, entangled in his, to reach the fleshy part of his side, and then pinched hard.

All she heard was a sharp inhale as he cringed away from the pain. Then he cast a sly glance at her, saying, *He shall get her back.* Calida's cheeks puffed out as he held back a chuckle from the guards' amusing bickering. With horrifying awareness, she stiffened as it dawned on her. There was only so far she could push it with a nobleman like Dominic before he would retaliate and put her in her place. Like the place of a servant. Or worse. Jetta was at the point where she was flailing her arms about.

"My routines are perfectly adequate. My plans are far more organised than your unwieldy chaos. I don't see you looking for the post with the best advantage." The two guards' voices rose significantly. Braxton's face grew redder as the pair continued to argue their sides. Dominic's shoulders shook with the effort to hold in his amusement. Calida was aghast at his audacity.

"Just because you make your post as closet to the latrine as possible without stinking does not make you a master schemer!" Jetta shouted.

It was at that moment the laughter Dominic had been fighting burst out in peals of laughter. His cheeks reddened as he roared. He collapsed on the ground with shoulders shaking.

Braxton and Jetta stopped arguing to stare in bewilderment at their lord.

"Y-you..." Dominic wheezed and coughed. Taking a couple of deep breaths, then he cleared his throat. "I apologise. I couldn't help it."

He stifled another bout of laughter with his hand. Dominic rose from the floor and straightened his coat.

"When Jetta mentioned the l-latrines. The both of you fight as if you're old and married." He held a fist to his mouth to fight off yet another round of laughing.

Jetta blinked as a blush reddened her cheeks. Her ears

tinted pink as her eyes shifted nervously. Calida squinted at her friend. *Interesting.*

"How is that funny, milord?" Braxton inquired, still looking pissed off at Jetta but trying to pull off a calm manner for his lord.

Jetta was not the type to jump into an argument with such fervour before. Calida's gaze shifted between them with curiosity. She wanted to see how her friend would react to the large man who most definitely had an interest in her.

"In the time I have come to know you two, it's quite fascinating how *open* you are about your feelings with each other." He wiggled his eyebrows.

Stunned, Calida found it hard to not nod her head in agreement. If she said or did anything, her closest friend would slice her to bits. Everyone held their breath for a moment. The guards stared at Dominic in a manner that could either kill or get them killed. Though the more she thought about it, Jetta would pair well with Braxton. Maybe she could even pull a sneaky little move and play matchmaker. Calida pursed her lips to hide her smirk at the thought of setting up her friend and seeing her flounder for once.

Jetta looked at the ground and crinkled her nose. If Calida wasn't close to Jetta, she wouldn't have noticed the slight movement her friend made. Jetta took a step away to create distance, which Calida knew by now meant she was feeling cornered. It was hard to affect Jetta like that.

"Milord, I don't mean any disrespect, but you have made Jetta uncomfortable with your teasing," Braxton stated.

Jetta whipped her head to look at him, her mouth agape. Calida's eyebrows shot up. They were always bickering, so to see Braxton defending Jetta was intriguing.

A distant ringing from the foyer said mealtime was ready. An audible breath sounded, breaking the awkward pause.

Dominic gently touched the small of Calida's back as they

moved toward the door. She halted when she remembered. *This dress will be a beast to sit in.*

"I need to change out of this dress first," Calida said.

A spark of playfulness shot through Dominic's eyes. A smirk struggled on his face as he tried to keep a neutral expression. Calida stared at him in bewilderment.

Jetta cut in as she glanced intently at the earl. "I will assist you in dressing in better eating attire, milady."

Dominic looked away as he cleared his throat. "I shall be in the hallway waiting for you."

He glanced at her once more, leaving her feeling naked. Dominic grasped her hand and pressed a featherlight kiss on it before leaving the room with a soft snick of the door.

Calida wondered if someone could perish from flirting. Her face was red, and she lifted her hair to cool down. Dominic had made his intentions clear, and it was enough to set the giddiness in her belly free like a running deer. Not to mention the tingling left from his lips against her skin had her crossing her legs in heated discomfort.

How could one simple kiss affect her so?

Turning around, Calida realized Jetta was behind her.

"I saw that sly move the lord made. How was it?" Jetta smirked at her friend, her arms folded as she watched..

"I did n-... Just what are you implying, Jetta?" Calida stammered with indignation.

Jetta walked up to Calida and turned her around to undo the dress in the back. Then she leaned over Calida's shoulder and said, "He taught you how to ride, did he not?"

Calida kept a neutral face as she tried to appear innocent, forcing herself to picture riding a horse as a child and being taught what was customary for commoners. *She would not think about the type of riding only a man could teach.*

"Whatever do you mean? R-Riding is strictly a practical

discipline. Not that Dominic could teach me anything like that." She desperately failed to maintain a neutral tone.

Jetta stifled laughter from over Calida's shoulder and took a deep, quivering breath in as she fought not to laugh again.

"Ah, to be innocent of mind. I cannot wait for the day the earl changes that. Your decline into corruption will be a fast fall."

Calida looked over her shoulder at Jetta. "What corruption? Miss Arundel, I believe you need to get yourself checked by a healer."

Jetta undid Calida's dress as her friend fought a smile.

Maybe it wouldn't hurt to take "riding" lessons from Dominic.

Calida nearly fell where she stood from the direction of her thoughts. Her face was aflame at the possibly of even being alone in his chambers with him, let alone being naked. This was all very new to her. How often did she think intimate thoughts about a man?

"Why, Lady Calida, I wonder what would happen if I mentioned your *curiosity* to Dominic?"

Calida gasped and glared at Jetta. Her friend suggested revealing her innermost thoughts about Dominic and his physique. *My dearest friend, you had better watch your back carefully.*

"You would not dare," Calida said.

Jetta walked over to the armoire as Calida stood there, holding her dress up in place. She felt all too naked, and it was not just because of the unsettling conversation.

"Maybe I will, maybe I won't." Jetta shrugged, feigning indifference.

Calida glared at her head, unsure how she would get on the same level of ground to keep Jetta from spilling. Then, Calida's mind grabbed at the reminder from earlier. A sly grin dimpled her cheeks. *Two can play this game.*

"Braxton seems pretty handsome," Calida said.

Her nonchalant tone had her impressed with herself. It was rare she could respond without stammering when she was so embarrassed. Calida stared at Jetta's back while her friend rummaged for the dress she could wear as her back stiffened.

Jetta stood up straight and turned around with a dress in hand. Calida smothered her laughter at the constipated look on her friend's face. She stood there with the dress clenched in her fist as she tried not to glare at Calida. In fact, it was like she was trying to feign no interest.

How amusing.

"I mean, I guess so. Although it is not appropriate to be looking at other men while betrothed." Her voice croaked as she spoke.

Mm. She is about as unaffected as coal on white cloth.

"I guess, but imagine being *married* to such a man. Like you said earlier, *your decline into corruption* will be a fast fall." Calida smirked. "What a joyous day it will be when you become *staked* and forever lose your cantankerous celibacy."

Jetta glared at Calida, marched over, and stuffed the dress over her lady's head. Clearly, she did not like that her friend could play the same teasing cards as she did.

"You better watch yourself, Calida Rhodes. I will get you for that one."

Calida poked her head through the dress and stuck her tongue out at her friend.

A few moments later, Calida left her room in a much plainer dress with Jetta beside her to join the waiting men in the hall.

Dominic held out his arm and Calida took it with her head held high. Trying to keep the previous thoughts about his "riding experience" out of her mind, she refused to look Dominic in the eye. She desperately wanted to run into a burrow and never return. His eyebrow quirked in question, but he didn't say a thing.

As they walked toward the dining hall, Dominic stared curiously. "With the chaotic events recently, we haven't had a moment to talk with one another. I am rather curious about you."

Calida squirmed. Sharing about herself was unusual. Talking about others and her parents was normal. *What could she tell Dominic that would please him? That would leave her in the good terms with her benefactor of sorts.*

"What would you like to know?"

"Everything you want to tell me," he said.

Calida's head spun at the open-ended question. That didn't tell her what to say. *What did he want to hear? Why couldn't he just tell her what to say?*

He patiently waited in silence.

"I-I... don't know where to start."

"What was it like when you were a young girl?"

"It was like any other girl, I assume. I had a mother and father. Both were loving and played with me." Calida downplayed it, not wanting to voice out loud the difference between her younger self and the one after *that* incident. The effect it had on her parents and how she picked up the leftover pieces. Or how it wasn't until recently she noticed the difference between her mother and other mothers.

They continued down the hall and turned a corner.

"When I was a small child, just barely able to walk, I remember my mother being a radiant, splendid light to anyone around. She often had a smile on her face and whispered words to the wilted flowers. Laughter and sunshine seemed to follow her, no matter where she went." Calida reminisced with a small smile on her face, staring off as she remembered the times before everything else.

How her mother would tell her made up stories off the

top of her head. Nights she spent wide awake with her mother tucked beside her as they lay beside the fireplace. Her mother packing her skinning knife and dagger into her pockets as she prepared to leave before the incident. Her smile dimmed to a frown.

"It didn't last long, though."

Dominic's eyes met hers, urging her to continue. Clenching her teeth, Calida refused to get emotional about the story. She couldn't let herself cry in front of someone else.

Pattering footsteps hit the ground as her father ushered Calida home.

"Everything changed one day."

Calida eyed her friend's frown from her peripheral. While Jetta hadn't been there that day, she had heard the story. Jetta had been there for Calida as she suffered alone. She refused to listen to Calida's attempts to push her away when she had needed a friend the most. The day they had met in the market was pivotal for Jetta. If it hadn't been for Calida, Jetta would have died. That day, she had gone one and a half weeks without a single piece of food and had lain in a deserted part of the market, unable to move, just waiting for death to greet her.

"Growing up was rather uneventful for me," she sighed. *Find a way to finish the topic.* "I would spend most hours either foraging for food or making sure my mother ate."

Shaking off the melodrama, Calida looked up at Dominic and smiled.

"What was your childhood like?"

Dominic stared at Calida, silently asking for more, but she was done. Any more and she would cry, something she didn't want to do. When he realized she was trying to change the subject, he let it go.

"My life was the typical life of a child growing up in the nobility."

He trailed off, and Calida gestured for him to continue.

"I learned how to fight with any sort of weapons available and how to jump off my horse in battle to save myself time. There was a time I remember having toys hand crafted for me, but that's a distant memory. My father was insistent that I learn everything I can. He was a strict man who didn't show mercy when you made a mistake." Dominic looked off as if in a far-off place with a tight smile. Several moments went by without continuing.

They made it to the stairs as he realized he had been musing.

"I am a few minutes younger than my brother. He was more of the artistic type. While I would go on running in the woods, he would study literature and poems. I would master the sword and he would be accomplishing his own written work," he said.

"You didn't play with toys?" Calida gazed down as they descended the stairs.

Dominic shook his head.

"I had toys to play with if my mother was the only one in the household with us and my father was out of town on business. She would let us play with wooden horses and knights that we used to ride down the hallways of our childhood home. I spent those times playing like a child with my brother."

Just as he finished, they arrived at the dining hall.

Dominic guided her through the open door as Jetta and Braxton took up guard posts on either side of the dining hall doors.

Calida sat down in the Madam chair beside Dominic's at the table as usual.

As they got comfortable, the door to the kitchen opened. The maids brought out dish after dish. They prepared roasted pork and glazed bird. The stewed vegetables smelled heavenly and warm dinner rolls steamed in their bowl. It was all prepared on several platters and piled high.

How could she eat so much? Not to mention the scent had her stomach growling. It had taken some time to realize just how different her food had been in the town. She had to grow used to the food served to nobles. The flavours were much richer and the finest ingredients were used to please the noble's appetite. The food was left warm for longer. Each ingredient was prepared with precision, instead of necessity. The look and smell of commoner food in comparison was rubbish.

Calida looked at Dominic, who gestured to the food.

"Please eat what you want, my dear one."

"You eat first." She couldn't eat if he didn't first. There may be lots of food, but her childhood ingrained it into her to eat last. *The needs of others came first.*

Dominic picked up a piece of food and put it on Calida's plate. "Your needs come first, Calida," He said, almost like he read her mind.

Calida froze, unable to pick up the food. Tears pricked her eyes as raw emotion settled in her chest. The decision over-whelming, her body almost rejected eating at first. Calida hadn't even realized it was so bad. She picked up a leg from the bird and nibbled.

Dominic smiled as she took the bite. Then he nodded like it was alright to load up his plate now. With great enthusiasm, he piled up his plate until it was a small mountain.

Her mouth hung open. In all the times they had shared a meal, she couldn't remember if he always piled his plate up so high, but before she knew it, he had. As she slowly took bites of her meat, she watched in amazement as Dominic tore through the food on his plate at a record speed. Yet the entire time, he still used table manners. Not once had he just torn into the food like a savage beast. He had used his utensils and cup and the blue cloth napkin to clean his face.

When he reached the bottom of his plate, she expected him to be stuffed, but the maids in the kitchen brought out dessert. He still looked interested in eating more. Calida couldn't understand how he kept his physique with how much he ate. She was filling up from just a bit of meat but he was eating the amount of a beast.

The bowl the maid held looked to be made of the shiniest crystal she had ever seen. It had detailed designs on the outside, leaves of different sizes and vines twisting about, creating fascinating patterns. As Calida stared at it with complete enchantment, the maid put it on the table in front of her. The light from the chandelier bounced off the crystal, creating a pattern that looked like feathers made from light.

It reminded her of the legend of phoenixes. The people of Eleari believed in their power and majestic abilities. Eesa gave them healing. Many believed feeding ground up phoenix feathers would heal dying patients without a sign of illness left behind.

Phoenix Child...

A whisper tingled in her ear. She had thought she heard something, but immediately forgot about it when she looked up at Dominic.

"Dominic, this is breathtaking!" Calida exhaled as she admired the enchanting bowl in front of her.

Dominic leaned an elbow on the table as he moved closer. His face lit with joy as he stared at her.

"It is yours, *Kona*."

She looked up. "What does *Kona* mean?"

Dominic's lips quirked, then he deflected by pointing to the dessert. "Have a look at the dessert, my dear one."

She squinted at him before looking down at the bowl once more. She had been so mesmerized by the bowl she hadn't even noticed the dessert inside. Tiny balls that looked to be small, golden-brown pastries were sprinkled with sugar.

"What are these called?"

Dominic looked in the bowl. His eyebrows shot up in surprise and then grinned widely, clearly amused by the turn of events. "Ah... we call this Dulcis Pila. It is a pastry ball that is made for nobles as a way of congratulations." The corner of his lip twitched. The sparkle in his eyes left her squinting in suspicion.

Calida tilted her head to the side. "Congratulations? What does it congratulate?"

Dominic put a fist to his mouth to stop himself for a moment before speaking.

"It is in congratulations to a couple for completing their consummation." Dominic grinned slyly at Calida, his eyes playful.

Consummation.... Consummation? that doesn't mean that the maids thought she... and him... had a good ole sarding!

Calida's face turned beet red, then a flame left her and caught her hair on fire.

In alarm, several maids ran into the room to extinguish her hair. Many of them ran up in a panic, squeaking, "Milady! Your hair!" before rushing off to find a blanket or water or something. Bodies moved around the room in a blur of action as they scoured the room for something to put out her flaming hair.

The head kitchen maid ran in to see what the panic was and recognized the dish in front of Calida. Her face paled, and she squawked out. "Oh my, milady! I beg your forgiveness! The younger maids didn't realize what they were presenting to you!"

Calida sat there, her mind swimming as she tried to think straight. The heat from the flames only increased the blood flow to her head. And her *other* area, reluctantly, at the thought of sharing a bed with Dominic. If she could melt into the ground or throw herself in an icy stream nearby, that is exactly what she would do.

This was precisely why she didn't want Jetta to tell Dominic.

At the reminder of her good old friend, Jetta, and the *wonderful* teasing she had pulled last time had Calida wanting to get back at her. Now she knew how.

And how perfect it would be.

Fighting back a widening impish grin, she looked at the head maid straight-faced, which was impressive, given the circumstances.

"I apologize, you must have been so confused, you poor dears. I believe the couple you should congratulate is in the hall. Just fair warning, the woman is very shy and may not react well. It is only because she is so very much attached to their new bedchamber and hates to part from it. You know how newlyweds are." Calida winked as she took the dish and passed it along to the young maids who had fallen to their knees at this point.

"I would appreciate it if you kept the dishware intact. It is dear to me," Calida said to the one who had given it to her. She snickered to herself as the maid got off her knees and strode to the door.

Dominic stared quizzically at Calida. He would understand soon enough.

The maid who had delivered the dessert looked back worriedly at Calida as if to ask, *Are you sure, milady?* When she gave an enthusiastic nod of approval, the maid headed straight for the door and went through as the guards on the inside opened it.

As they were closing it, Calida gestured for them to keep it open a bit.

The guards looked at each other and then held the doors

open a crack as she waited to hear Jetta. Calida was nearly jumping out of her seat in excitement.

It took a moment. The silence was almost deafening, and then suddenly we heard a screech coming from the hall. That made it all worthwhile.

Calida held her hand to her mouth as she heard Jetta wail in the hallway.

"I am not married to that cretin! I can hardly stand to be within five feet of him!"

There was a mumble of the maid responding, followed by, "Just because we have similar interests doesn't mean we're married!"

Then a rumble came from Braxton.

"You wouldn't object to it, but that doesn't mean I wouldn't! The maids cannot just assume!"

She heard the maid clearer as she moved back toward the door as she said, "Then it's not true that you couldn't wait to return to your shared bedchambers?"

There was a moment of silence, and Calida could almost picture the look on Jetta's face. Pushed enough, her friend would blush a brilliant red. When things don't go her way, sometimes she had this habit of stomping her foot like a child. She would get frustrated and aggravated by the maid's assumptions, and Braxton's non-reaction would make it even more amusing.

"Of course, that isn't true! Wherever did you hear that?" Jetta's voice shrilled.

Another rumble came from Braxton tinged with amusement, followed by another screech from Jetta, before the maid rushed back into the room and ran to escape her wrath.

Poor girl, she felt awful for subjecting the young maid to such a terrifying task.

Calida looked over at Dominic.

"Am I a horrible person for enjoying that?"

Dominic held back a large grin.

"Calida, if you are a horrible person, then we shall be awful together because I, too, found that entertaining."

They broke out in loud laughter, and for once, Calida felt free and content. The moment only needed one more thing to complete it. A good dessert.

Another dessert was served up, but this time it was a pillowy cake that wobbled as it moved. Calida had her eye on it the entire time it made its way across the room. Dominic's muffled chuckle was barely noticeable over her fascination with the delectable dessert.

The door to the dining hall opened as Jetta peeked in. Calida glanced over, smirked, and gave a little finger wave. Jetta squinted at her and shook her head. She gestured, saying, *I have my eyes on you. Watch your back.*

Calida knew Jetta would get back at her, but it would be exceptionally sneaky now that she was someone of higher status. She would have to keep her guard up so Jetta didn't get the drop on her.

Once when they were children, after Calida had tickled Jetta and had her screeching to high heaven, Jetta came back later with a bucket of icy water and dumped it on her. Thankfully, it was summer, so she didn't freeze from the chill. Still, it had been unexpected, and she had chased after Jetta for an hour. After that, they pranked one another again and again. It had been a long time since they had pranked one another and they were due for a good pranking war.

After enjoying the wonderful dessert, Dominic led her back to her room, strolling leisurely through the halls

"My dear one, I once heard that you are an exceptional artist. However, I haven't seen a painting of yours."

Calida looked up at him and thought about it. Normally, she wouldn't show her paintings to just anyone, but this man was going to be her husband soon. The idea of letting her anxiety win this battle disgusted her.

"I can show you a painting, but please promise that if you have negative criticism, don't laugh," Calida said.

She tried to be brave, but she was already predicting his reaction. It was too easy to imagine him laughing at her work, even if it would be unlike him. It would crush her if he hated her work, but she would never show it.

He isn't like that, though.

Dominic frowned and stopped them in the middle of the hallway. They had one turn left and then they would be in front of her room. He grasped both of her hands and looked sternly into her eyes.

"I am sure that it will be exceptional. It doesn't need to look like a masterpiece. It just needs to have your love and care."

Her heart pounded at his words, but she did little to sway the irrational fear in her heart. Words were one thing. Actions were everything.

Calida walked the rest of the way to her room without holding his hand, hoping if he found it ridiculous that it would create some distance between them. The only sign of her inner anxiety was the wringing of her hands.

She opened the door to her room. The light was now dimmed by the setting of the sun. Taking a breath, she entered with Dominic close on her heels. He paused by the door as she walked over to the candle to light the room. Calida called upon the fire inside her, praying for its power, but nothing came of it. She sighed. With the flick of a match next to it, a flame rose and filled the room with light.

Calida walked over to the painting sitting on the other side of her room on the easel. She removed the covering swiftly, then turned toward the window, hoping that by looking the other way, Dominic's judgements would be less painful.

"It is rather interesting. I'm not much of an artistic person myself. I would much rather spend my days in the outdoors. But this is something I would hang on our walls," Dominic said.

Calida had been expecting a negative reaction so much, she faltered where she stood when he complimented it. *He likes it.* Her hands maddeningly wrung the cover before she rushed over to the painting to cover it back up again. A blush stained her cheeks. Now uncomfortable, Calida only wanted to sit in a corner and forget it all.

It wasn't truly embarrassing, though. He complimented it. She just didn't know how to take a compliment.

"I'm sure there are other paintings far more suitable to hang on the walls of a nobleman's house," Calida said, downplaying the work she poured her soul into.

Her feet shuffled on the ground while her eyes had become magically affixed to his shoes. Polished brown boots without a single sign of wear or the slightest crease, the mark of a nobleman with wealth. Dominic stepped closer.

"You are very talented, Calida. Art is in the beholder's eye. Those who don't see its beauty should move on because the beauty of your art clearly explains the same of your soul."

His words were gentle and kind. But nothing could truly convince her of her own worth anymore. He may see her as a beauty, but the awkward length of her arms and her wild mane of hair put her in the category of less. She wouldn't wake up feeling different and enchanting to the young men who gazed upon her. Her body was once flat as a twelve-year-old boy and had stayed such a way until she had been sixteen.

Maybe it wouldn't have bothered her so much if the children in town she only saw on walks to the market didn't mock and laugh at her boyish body. She had come into her womanly curves late, but the damage had already been done. Calida saw the other girls in town who were gaining the attention, the ones with a large bosom and hips a man could grab. She saw her small chest and narrow hips that eventually grew out but still looked small compared to theirs. The mockery rang in her ears for years until she couldn't form her own thoughts.

"I-I guess," Calida said.

Dominic sighed and took her hand to kiss it before he left her room, leaving her to retire for the night.

Twenty-Three

Calida lay on her bed, the sheets as chilly as the air around her. Sleepiness was the last thing on her mind and her company in her chambers insisted on it. His hands caressed her exposed skin and left a trail of warmth behind.

She gazed up and met Dominic's eyes. He leaned over her on the bed, watching her wriggle and writhe. His eyes left a trail just like his hands had, feeling almost physical.

She lay under him, undressed. Dominic's blue jacket was strewn on the bed, his white shirt open and his pants undone. Like he had been messed by a lover.

In contrast, she felt vulnerable, having shown her body.

Calida wanted to tug off his clothing, but her hands wouldn't cooperate. So, she used her legs. Wrapping them around his middle, she tried to pull him closer. Yet as much as she tried, he didn't move. Here she was on fire for Dominic, and he rested on the bed, not moving an inch.

His eyes pierced hers as she returned his gaze, which beckoned her to reveal all her darkest secrets. To submit to him and what he could offer. Calida's mind was trapped by the thoughts of what he could offer in the moment. Not venturing further, even when a fleeting voice had said something to her.

"Milady…" he said.

She mumbled something incoherent, and she continued to ogle the man in her bed. He had now magically become naked and crawled closer to her. It was a sight to see and left her curious to touch.

"Milady." His voice was off. It didn't sound like him. His voice was normally lower and rough, but this voice was higher and reminded her of tinkling bells.

Light punctured the world around her. Little bits here and there like a flame to sheets of paper. The dream she had been having suddenly disappeared, and Calida pulled herself back to reality.

"Milady." A feminine whisper came from the side of Calida's bed. She buried herself in her blankets after the raunchy dream. It left her wistful and lustful.

"Milady…" the maid whispered once more.

Calida murmured but wouldn't rise from her warm, comfortable bed. Now that she was waking up, the horror of someone hearing the noises she might have made washed over her. *I would rather join Lord Eesa in the skies.*

"Milady, please do wake up. The maids must get you ready."

Calida peeked out from under her blankets.

"I remember nothing on the schedule for today," she said, unsure what had them so insistent.

Calida had thought the day would be an uneventful one, unlike her days as of late. It had already been a week since she attended the palace ball. She had spent the days reading, losing herself in stories of knights and giggling girls from the large books in the library. It wasn't educational, but she was giddy with the excitement of doing something for herself without watching over her shoulder. Of no one criticizing her for doing something that had no gain.

A giggle sounded from across the room. The maid shushed the others and then held back a smile. She knelt next to Calida, so they were speaking face to face. *Lord Eesa, there are several maids in the room.* How could she escape this? If she had been making noise, Dominic was bound to know by the end of the day. Who's to say what his reaction would be?

An image of Dominic pinning her to a wall with a passionate fervour filled her mind, the vision coloured in sensual red and pinks licking the image like a piece of paper consumed by flames.

"Milady, one of your lady's maids overheard milord's plans to ask you on an outing!"

Calida peeked out. It didn't even surprise her anymore that the maids would know first. Since moving into Dominic's mansion, she had several moments that made it obvious the maid's words spread like wildfire. Once, the day after arriving at Dominic's mansion, Calida had been in a lesson with her tutor. The tutor was lecturing about the virtue of an innocent mind when Jetta mimicked her behind the tutor's back. Calida had to keep from laughing. The maid nearby also found it funny. Maybe a bit too much because she shared it with another maid and then that maid shared it. It eventually came back around to the tutor, and Jetta paid for it with a night missing sparring practice because the tutor had her researching the sinfulness of a secular mind and thinking inappropriate thoughts of an unmarried man.

With a grumble about moving in a cold room, she trudged out of bed to wipe off the sleep.

Calida washed her face with the bowl of water always in her room, and the maid assisted her into a blue and black dress. The straight style allowed flexibility while riding on a horse. It was simple, but if they were going to be outside, it made the most sense. She put on her black boots, freshly polished, just as a knock sounded on her door. A maid answered for her as she gathered her belongings for the day and walked to the door.

On the other side stood Dominic. He wore a cloth lapel jacket in deep blue and tight black pants that stood out against his white shirt. The fabric hugged him, making him look like he could crush a rock. It had her remembering the dream the maids awoke her from, and her cheeks flared. His outfit looked like the one in her dream too, except it wasn't wrinkled. Like he was supposed to be appropriate and not sensual.

Well, of course he wasn't supposed to be sensual in public.

Her lips rolled inward at the old noblewomen Meredith and Karin seeing Dominic in anything inappropriate and then fainting from a heart attack. Although she couldn't decide if it was out of lust or dismay. Calida understood why they would faint out of dismay, though. His presence commanded a room better than anyone she had ever seen. Any woman who saw him walking down the road in a billowing blouse with his jacket unbuttoned, allowing the wind to blow his shirt any which way, would be sent into a fit of insanity. Not that she had seen many people capable of that. The men she was used to, outside her father, were drunkards who tried to snatch up young women, or even small girls, as wives.

Dominic gazed at her. His eyes darkened with every slow second he stared at her in the simple dress. It wasn't anything fancy, so she couldn't understand what about it could capture his attention. She wasn't awe-inspiring. Calida stopped in front of him and waited.

"Another day to experience your beauty, my dear one. This time I'm delighted to know we'll be spending it together without... distractions." His mouth quirked as his eyes stared intently.

The maids snuck through the door past them, giggling. They had heard every word. Dominic looked behind her as they scurried away while he grinned mischievously. She blushed and looked away.

"The maids said you had an outing planned, my lord?"

He pursed his lips and squinted at her. Calida held back a shout of laughter as she realized he was pouting. The corners of his lips twitched as Dominic fought their downturn.

Surely, she was hallucinating because the next second, the pout disappeared. Dominic had wiped away any sign of it and with it, Calida's control to not laugh.

She muffled a laugh as she realized what she had done wrong.

"I apologize. I meant to say Dominic."

Dominic pinched his lips. "I guess I wasn't clear enough. My attempts to woo you fell flat."

Calida whipped her head to look at him, her mouth gaped open. *He had been trying to woo her! It wasn't just a nice compliment?*

With a smirk on his face, Dominic closed her mouth with a finger under her chin.

"*Kona,* if you don't want to lose use of that pretty little mouth of yours, I suggest keeping it shut. You already look rather tempting."

In need of a gust of cool wind, Calida closed her mouth with a snap. A shiver travelled down her spine and the temperature inside the home seemed to shoot to the heavens. The suggestive statement set her on fire and then travelled down her arm and caught on a nearby curtain.

As they walked arm in arm, Calida's head spun from the intimate thoughts replaying from her morning dreams. The maids panicked to put out the fire, their rushed footsteps thumping in the background. Their shouts for more water and the sizzling turned into white noise as Dominic pulled

Calida along. He led her down the hall, and she had no idea where they would be going. It seemed he planned to throw her guard off for the rest of the day if he could.

If only he hadn't said what he had when I came out of my room. Maybe I wouldn't be so off balance.

Dominic snuggled in close and whispered in her ear.

"I could have said something else if you had desired. You need only ask." It was like he had read her mind.

Calida opened her mouth, then realized she had accidentally spoken out loud. She looked at the ground in embarrassment.

Dominic stood in front of her, grasping her hands and looking deeply into her eyes. "The fairest maiden, if ye proved to be thine saviour. Thine steady sword and courageous battle-cry shalt vanish, grant your warrior a wish of splendour and might. Let us be a destiny's fate akin to Ordellius and Aviana, the star-crossed love that came to be and had always been meant to be."

She was silent for a moment, her eyes large as she gazed at her betrothed. She couldn't think of anything to top the words from his mouth. He bent down and kissed her left hand with a smile. If she could always remember it, Calida wished it was possible. Her eyes closed as she thought about the poem and smiled. She recognized it from a book she'd studied in Dominic's library.

As the couple walked outside their mansion, a guard jogged up. He was young and full of energy as he gave his message.

"Milord, Milady. I have a message from Mister Braxton and Miss Jetta. They were called to their home base across town for an emergency."

Dominic tensed.

"Did they say what the emergency was?" he asked with a note of concern in his voice. Maybe someone in Crescent

League needed backup but it wasn't something for a nobleman to be concerned about.

Calida laid a hand on Dominic's arm and made eye contact. The hard, commanding presence seemed to pull back as he remembered she was there. With a sigh, Dominic covered her hand with his and turned to the guard.

"Let me know the moment they get back. We will be in the next town over."

Calida's eyebrows rose. The next town over was hers. Dominic was taking her back home?

Then she envisioned Dominic walking through the market with her. He was leaning over a stall, deciding on a brooch he thought would suit her. The sun shone on them and a smile lit up the space between them.

The image spread excitement through her. Calida couldn't wait to show him her world. The market and the river and her meadow with precious memories of better times. For once, she would be the one familiar with everything.

Twenty-Four

The hooves of their horses clopped as they rode their way to Calida's hometown. The couple had agreed to stop by to pick up her belongings on the way. Now that she lived with Dominic, it was only right to have some things to remind her of home.

The leaves in the trees rustled in the wind as they moved through the forest. Nature shifted around them. Off to the side, a bunny hopped into a burrow and a fox stalked it. The natural cycle of life showed even in the smallest settings. Life, hunt, and death.

Her hair flowed behind her as they trotted along. No loud complaints from snobbish noblewomen or demands from a tutor. She could just be.

"This is peaceful," Calida murmured to herself, shutting her eyes and enjoying the warm breeze.

As they cleared the forest, they came across a meadow. It was not just any meadow, though. This was the meadow her father and Calida would frequent.

Calida could hear laughter joyfully ringing through the meadow. A voice from the past. The twirling and colourful flowers everywhere. His grin flashed in front of her like a daydream until it faded before her eyes.

"We can stop here for a moment," Dominic said.

Calida dismounted and walked to the field, the nostalgia carrying her into the midst of it. She heard the familiar birds singing to one another and crickets chirping happily as always. Everywhere she looked, flowers surrounded her. It was almost like she remembered, except the flowers weren't so vivid and the sky didn't look so far away. She was taller now, but the memory of her meadow was not quite the same. The dimmed colours around her were uncomfortable. Like having a wonderful dream, only for it to be dashed by reality.

The sky was clear today, and yet she wasn't so happy.

Being back in this meadow was bittersweet. The beautiful memories with her favourite person whom she would never see again were heart-lifting and devastating. And the last time she had visited the meadow had been when she had been seven years old.

It's my fault.

She couldn't help but blame herself for what happened. In her mind, she could hear those around her trying to give her false reassurance if she vocalized how she felt. Saying things like, "Such things just happen," but that didn't mean blaming herself was any easier to stop. It was about as simple as turning the flowers grey.

Dominic joined her in the field, holding a basket and something behind his back. As he stopped beside her, he took the item behind his back and showed it to her. In his hand was a set of charcoals in perfect condition, nothing like hers from home, and a lovely leather-bound book.

She looked up at him in question.

"I thought you may like to draw as we enjoy this beautiful day in the meadow."

Calida smiled sweetly at him as she took the book from

him. He had remembered her love for drawing nature and scenery. Her heart warmed at the wonderful gift.

"Thank you, Dominic."

He smiled at her. "Let's sit on this blanket as we enjoy the warm breeze." Dominic guided her to a flat spot and laid out a blanket, then placed the basket down.

She sat and quickly opened her notebook to sketch the flowers near her.

Their colours were cheerful, and Calida almost resented they could look so happy. Back when she was a young girl, she could lie in these fields and admire the radiance around her, happily swaying with the flowers bending with the wind. Now that she was seeing them as an adult, it only reminded her of the mistakes she had made that day.

Dominic's smile fell as she searched her face. "What's wrong?" He sat near her and gently nudged her chin to look up at her.

Calida's eyes watered. She wouldn't explain to him about that day yet. Her chest tightened as she imagined him being disgusted by her actions. Calida couldn't take it if he behaved like her mother did.

Dominic pulled her into his arms. "Someday, I hope to hear about it, but I'll let it go for today."

Calida sighed in relief. A part of her ached to tell him everything, but she simply couldn't do it. Not yet. Everything was too soon and too traumatising. The last thing Calida wanted was to be so vulnerable.

"Well, instead I'm going to have to share stories about my childhood," Dominic said.

Calida settled in to hear tales about him and his brother.

"In case you didn't know, my brother and I are twins." He had told her before today, but it had escaped her mind. *What is it like to be a twin?*

Were they close and could share secrets with one another?

She wished only a little that her mother had given birth to a sibling. Maybe then she would understand what it was like.

"When we were younger, we were very close. Spent every waking hour playing with one another. Sometimes we would play knight and princess together. Without a princess, Ansel had to play that part." Dominic chuckled, and Calida smiled as she thought of his brother in a dress. From her glimpse at the wedding reception, he was rather similar to Dominic, only skinnier. She didn't think he would like to wear a dress all that much.

"He obviously hated playing that role. Like any young boy, he would've rather been the knight. However, the only girl we grew up with was Lady Evaine, but she was normally much too busy to play."

Calida looked down at her book as she pushed away the feeling of inadequacy that came from hearing Lady Evaine's name. The only name that reminded her Dominic would fit better for someone else.

He chose me, though, didn't he?

"There was another childhood friend I had, though. One who Ansel didn't meet. This friend and I spent time together every week until the day my father realized my mother had let me socialize with a commoner." He stared deeply into her eyes. Calida held his gaze for a moment until it was too much and then suddenly fixated on the flowers closest to her. How he was wonderfully kind about his friends and family threw Calida off balance. Dominic was considerate and sweet but straight-forward, the best representation of nobles all around. Yet she was only a muddy commoner from Poramun Creek, playing pretend.

Her body hurt as the guilt smothered her.

"Growing up, I didn't have others to play with. You had your brother, but I didn't have anyone. I watched the other kids in town running around, playing, just not with me. It was me and my toys," Calida said. "I would draw on the ground with some sticks I found as I watched them run around, chasing each other and laughing joyfully. I never got invited to play."

She knew she was putting down the mood with her sorrowful thinking, but there wasn't anything positive Calida could find to talk about. She hadn't had a life as amazing as his and had nothing to share. Laughter was scarce for her and even now, she was a rather serious person in comparison.

Dominic paused.

"I have something to show you. Would you be interested in seeing?"

She hesitated, and the lord looked her in the eye and gently smiled.

"Have I given you any reason to not trust me?" he said.

Calida thought about it for a moment. From the beginning, Dominic had been direct with her, never holding back the truth or buffering harsh words. The lord had been kind to her and loving. In fact, the only time she had seen him be frightening was that time in the alleyway. He had grown larger and menacing. It was frightening, and she had just been about to be kidnapped, so overall, Calida hadn't been thinking straight. Eventually, she had realized how silly it was to think he would harm her. Her assumptions about him being a killer were unfounded.

It seemed ingrained in her to assume he was a killer because he behaved like the ancient clan of legend that pillaged, assaulted, and destroyed all over Eonifond. The clan's founder, Ordellius, had been a brutal man. Everyone knew what had transpired. The knights had searched all over for him and when he was found, he had been hanged for his crimes. To this day, people still celebrated the day of his death with a festival, the Ordellius Festival. Just like him, the crown found his clan and killed them for the safety of the people. At least, that was what Calida had been told.

Was it possible something connected him to Ordellius's clan?

Slowly, Dominic stood and closed his eyes as if concentrating.

At first, she saw nothing, but then his body grew slowly. Little by little, his arms and legs and neck grew larger and darker. It was almost like he had summoned a thicker skin to inhabit for a moment. His skin grew tanner and his stature bulkier. His shadow expanded out from him. Calida rubbed her eyes because if she was wrong, then she needed some bloodletting. His shadow pulled off the ground and stood on four legs of its own.

She must have spent too much time surrounded by the fancy paints at Dominic's mansion, inhaling their fumes.

Soon enough, what stood before her was the same thing she had seen in the alleyway after someone had almost kidnapped her. The wolf had frightened her then, and still frightened her now. Her heart pounded as she stared at it, unblinking. Calida's palms grew clammy as she saw the creature form eyes that stared right into her soul.

Her body didn't move a muscle. She struggled to stay put after Dominic asked she trust him when she felt the overwhelming desire to take off for the woods.

Dominic opened his eyes again and turned toward her. He moved closer to her once more and reached out to caress her hair. The lord's hands were larger than before. And she must have gone insane because fantasies of him pinning her down with them overwhelmed her. She imagined him kissing her while his larger hands caressed her, instead of crushing her like they probably had done to his enemies. She stared him in the eyes and recognized the piercing blue. Transformation or not, he was still looking at her with kindness and love. A smile softened the grim lines of a warrior's face.

A squeak escaped as she cleared her throat.

"The wolf. Is it the same one who attacked my kidnapper about a month ago?"

Dominic frowned and nodded his head. "Yes, I thought it prudent to introduce you to my shadow wolf. It would be hard to bond properly without having met him."

Calida peeked at the wolf but swiftly moved her gaze back onto Dominic. The wolf looked just as feral and wild as a normal wolf. As much as she wanted to keep staring at it in case it bit her, her eyes stayed focused on Dominic. He took her hand and gently patted the wolf with it.

"This is Aither." He nodded toward the wolf formed from his shadow. A rumble came from the wolf. She tensed as Aither gazed at her like he would bite. Calida jumped and tried to pull her hand away. His hand kept hers from moving away.

"He won't bite you," he said.

"How can you be sure? He looks so wild and feral." Her voice quivered while her hand sat on Aither's soft fur. Neither Calida nor Aither moved a muscle.

Dominic smiled softly.

"That is the nature of a wolf, to look wild and feral. His character is a different story, however. Not to mention I formed him from my shadow. He couldn't harm anyone I hold close to my heart."

Calida froze at his words. *His heart.* Was he talking about her?

It seemed like from the beginning Dominic had never treated her differently. Even in moments when fear paralyzed her, he was there to push her forward.

Dominic directed her hand to pet Aither's fur. Its softness was soothing, though she was unsure about it. Aither relaxed against her hand. Even though he was a fabrication of Dominic's shadow, he was solid.

Aither's fur was soft in some spots and grizzly in others. Slowly, Dominic helped her pet him until he removed his hand, and she was petting him alone. The more she did, the calmer she felt until Calida looked Aither's way and realized he was right up beside her.

"How is he solid? He was your shadow," Calida said.

Amazingly, Aither enjoyed Calida's touch and laid his head on her lap. If a wolf could purr, that was exactly what she was hearing. A pleasant sound came from him as he relaxed, and her fear was long gone.

"He still is my shadow. He's also a living creature," Dominic said.

Her shoulders relaxed. He was a companion and a loving one at that. Aither had cuddled up to Calida and let out a contented sigh. She muffled a giggle at the similarity Aither had to a dog in need of a tummy rub. Dominic smiled at the interaction.

Eventually, Calida picked up her book once more to draw as Aither lay on her lap. Enjoying the warmth of the day, they cuddled up like she had known Aither all her life. She completely focused on her drawing and rested against Dominic, who was gazing over her shoulder at her sketch. The flowers swayed in the wind around them as Aither peeked his head up and then stood. Neither of them gave any credence to Aither walking into the field and staring at the trees.

Satisfied with the progress of her drawing, she looked up to show Dominic when she realized he was already looking her way, transfixed by her lips. His eyes were dark and his lips moist. By this point, he had morphed back, no longer as large as a tree nor as hairy as a beast. It was almost like she had bewitched him. Calida's lips felt suddenly dry, so she licked them. If she could relearn how to breathe, this was the moment because Dominic had inched closer, and she held her breath in anticipation.

Her gaze locked on his lips as they approached. Their breath mingled together as they were a hair apart. She felt Dominic's warmth from this distance, even though she wasn't touching him. A tingle coursed through her. She could already feel the firmness of his lips and the knowledge they were going to kiss cemented into her mind.

Slowly, her eyes closed along with his.

Until Aither let out a vicious growl that startled them away from each other.

Calida looked at the wolf, alarmed, but he was glaring into the woods. He had been facing the forest the entire time and at first, Calida had thought it was just him being an animal. She had forgotten he was no ordinary creature.

"He saw something," Dominic said, the desire in his eyes replaced with awareness. He stood and held out a hand to help her to her feet. Dominic walked away and left Aither at her side as he strolled the edge of the field.

He returned to her side a few minutes later. "I found nothing near the forest. Whatever it was, Aither must have scared it off." His voice was tight.

Dominic and Calida exchanged glances. Their moment had passed, and there was nothing they could do to bring it back. Aither was still and looking toward the forest, but nothing stirred. The couple packed up their picnic and headed out. Even though Dominic saw nothing, they both agreed to leave without a word.

As they mounted their horses and continued their journey, Aither disappeared into the recesses of Dominic's shadow. This time, neither of them enjoyed the countryside. Dominic sat stiffly on his horse and searched the surrounding trees. In the back of her mind, she thought back to the attempted kidnapping, but it had to have been a freak incident. She shook her head free of the paranoia. Like she was special enough for someone to target her. It was more likely Dominic would be the target if there was indeed someone following.

"Does he come and go as he wants, or do you need to summon him?" The question erupted from her.

Dominic looked behind him.

"I must summon him. He's a part of me. So, like when an object magic user summons a blade, I too must summon him."

Calida had never heard of someone capable of summoning an animal. The type of summoning used in battle was typically by those proficient in object magic. An augmentation of their embedded magic could summon a weapon forward. A person couldn't summon just any weapon, though. It had to be one that existed in the physical plane already, so it baffled Calida that Dominic could summon a wolf. No less, one that didn't exist on the physical plane.

There were rumors the clans of ancient times could do something of the sort, though. But they were only myth. Their ability to command armies and will the wolves at their sides to fight couldn't be real. *Right?*

They trotted down the road at a slow pace. Awkwardly, they recounted stories about their childhoods and compared their education until they arrived in Calida's hometown. Dominic shared about his duties on the political side of things. Syniel merchants had been showing up in the odd corners of Eleari, selling anything from a stolen necklace to a kidnapped girl. He told her about his concerns because the province, Syniel, had been showing more and more signs of corruption, but no one else could prove it. One time, he had talked to a guard who had seen firsthand what Syniel had been up to, but when Dominic had arrived at the guard's post, the man was gone. His home had been left in shambles. Even the man's employer acted like he had never existed.

Calida heard chatter from the market as they entered Poramun Creek. The sight of the bustling town relieved her tension from earlier. Many faces were familiar, and some stopped to greet her. The villager's women had always been friendly and compassionate. If they saw her trying to get food by foraging, they would sneak food into her foraging pack. She was too proud to just accept help, but somehow they helped, even if it was just some dried fruit.

"Miss Calida! You're back! How nice to see you again!" a villager said. She gave a loaf of bread to Calida with an enormous grin and walked off. Calida tucked it into her horse's satchel and continued on with Dominic.

Another stopped for a moment.

"My oh my, how you have grown into a beautiful young lady!"

Calida chuckled and thanked the woman before she continued on her normal routine.

An old man stopped the couple.

"Miss Calida, I hope you have returned and intend to marry my son. You would warm his bed nicely." His chest puffed out slightly as he looked over her body.

Calida frowned and walked on as if the man didn't speak. Dominic, however, had another idea. His fierce glare spoke loudly of the bodily harm he wanted to commit on the old man. Calida cleared her throat and gestured up the road. He paused and followed her.

After strolling through town, Calida and Dominic stopped in front of her home and dismounted. As she walked in, her eyebrows rose in realization that her mother wasn't home.

It was rare for her to leave. Even as a child, Cressida would usually leave only when someone else was with her, which was why they would go to the market together.

The inside of the home was falling into disrepair. The

walls had holes in them, and someone had knocked the dining table over, spilling food on the ground. A stained cloth littered the floor. And in the corner, there was a pile of rotten food.

What happened in here? Where was her mother? Was she out back?

Calida walked outside and examined the courtyard behind the house. There was a bucket filled with dirty laundry and water, but no Cressida.

It had been a long time since the home had been in this state of disrepair. All her years as an adolescent, her mother would push for an orderly house. She insisted Calida keep it up to her standard lest she got sent away or worse. She had been threatened with an arranged marriage to a man three times her age.

Calida walked to the front to join Dominic, who she found in conversation with their neighbour.

As she approached them, her former neighbour noticed her.

"Ah, Calida—Lady Calida now, I believe. You have come back."

"Good afternoon, Matilda. I hope I am not too forward, but do you know where my mother is?"

Matilda sighed and shook her head.

"I am afraid everyone in town knows where she is."

Calida's eyebrows scrunched in confusion. She was missing something. Abandoning her home was odd behaviour for the woman who had lived a certain way for years. Her mother had been distant and critical, but to give up on the things her daughter wouldn't do anymore seemed unexplainable. Calida had hoped her mother was only being lazy and would finally take care of the house instead of insisting she return.

"My dear, you weren't told because you were so young, but at the time of the incident so many years ago... Your mother had been with child. She had been showing just as the *event* happened."

Calida stepped back in shock. *Mother had been pregnant.*

She had been only a child, so she had no way of knowing, but that didn't mean it wasn't disturbing to only find out now. Having been the one to take responsibility at a young age, she naturally assumed it was her fault. The one who selfishly kept her father from being home with her mother so she could have some fun. It was something she had blamed herself for years. The news felt like another brick in the wall of guilt on Calida's shoulders.

Was she really to blame, though?

"Sh-she had been pregnant?" Calida's voice stuttered, shell-shocked by the news.

Her knees buckled as she processed it. Dominic frowned and wrapped an arm around Calida, comforting her.

Matilda glanced in the direction of the old well down the road on the other side of town. They had abandoned it because of contaminated water and unsafe ground around it.

"Your mother has been visiting the old well almost every day," Matilda said.

Calida stared off in the same direction. It was rumored to have once had flowing water so clear, some had sworn they saw the spiritual realm. Once upon a time, the people in Poramun Creek had a thriving life where they could see jars of the water from the well. That was ancient history, though. It hadn't been like that for at least a century.

"Many have offered her comfort and condolences. She has sneered them away," Matilda said.

Calida's shoulder slouched as she realized she felt sympathy for the woman who she had lived with. Cressida had been traumatized and while she could've been better, that didn't mean she couldn't feel pity for the woman.

"Perhaps I should talk to her."

"No!" Matilda said as Calida stepped in the well's direction.

Dominic gripped her arm until she halted. Calida glared at both of them.

"Why shouldn't I talk to my mother?"

"Milady, she has been cursing your name," she said.

She explained how Cressida was bent over by the well, weeping every day and crying out for Rayner and her lost baby. Sometimes it was confusing because it she would say two different names for the baby. Many villagers assumed she hadn't picked a name for the dead child and so she wept in the names that came to mind. Matilda didn't know why she would subconsciously choose the names Casimir and Jabez, though.

"Matilda, please explain. My mother is cursing me?" Calida was almost in tears now. She had always longed for her mother's affection growing up and when she rarely received it, it left a mark. She had always thought it was her fault, that somehow she was to blame for being disrespectful or something. As always, she was the problem.

What could she have done to cause her mother's anger?

Matilda looked at her in sympathy.

"Many have approached to comfort her and ask how you are, but she has spat at those who dare utter your name. She claims she had no spawn of such name and even if she did, she would leave them to rot in the forest."

Her breath quickened. Everything surrounding them suddenly closed in her. Her chest squeezed as she struggled to breathe. A tear fell down her cheek as she took in the news.

How is any of this fair?

It wasn't, but such was life. Dominic stood behind her just before she collapsed. He comforted her with whispered words as she struggled, sobbing against him until she contained herself.

After a moment, Calida scrubbed her eyes and thanked Matilda.

"Please, dear, don't take the words of a broken woman personally. She hasn't [truly] been your mother since that incident." Matilda grasped her hands gently.

Calida knew what she was trying to say and commended her on trying, but this was something she needed to work through on her own.

Dominic took Calida by the shoulders and directed back to her old home. Too consumed by her thoughts, she obeyed without comment. She walked past all the mess and entered her former room. It was untouched, and a layer of dust covered everything. She picked up the scarf she had left and a pendent she wore when she was a child. Everything else, she left. Those two items were far more important than anything else.

Calida braced herself for Dominic to question her lack of items.

As she stepped up to the horses, she held out the two items. "Here is everything."

For a moment, Dominic's eyes seemed to darken, but it must have been her imagination because when he looked up at her, he was smiling sweetly.

"Are you ready to depart, my dear one?"

Calida looked back at the house. She could hear the laughter from her and her father fading along with all the other memories she attached to this house. Slowly, she felt the bond to this house severing. She still hurt, but this downward spiral was inevitable.

A little lighter, she took a deep breath.

Calida took hold of her horse's reins and walked beside Dominic. The couple trudged down the beaten path that led out of town when they encountered a woman on the road. She was short and skinny, her cheeks hollow and her face gaunt.

Her blonde hair hung limply, and the soul in her green eyes looked half-way to death.

Cressida looked up, and her eyes turned cold as ice. Her hand clenched around the metal bracelet on her wrist as her face contorted into a sneer.

"The prodigal daughter returns home at last. Has the *honourable* Lord Goldwyn cast you out of that highborn gilded cage?" Her mother spat at Calida's feet as her lips pinched in disgust. Calida's mouth worked as she tried to think of what to say.

"It's only the way of the world for a harlot to be thrown out after being pounded in any way they desire," Cressida said.

Calida's eyes teared up at the words. Dominic took hold of her shoulders and held her close.

"What kind of sadistic wench are you? Speaking to your daughter like that!" Dominic said.

"It was all her fault, anyway. From this moment onward, Calida Rhodes doesn't exist. I disown you." Then she stormed down the road, leaving for the last time with the final word.

Together, the couple left her hometown. Calida's mind was consumed by what had just happened. Her mother had cast her out of the Rhodes family. Abandoned by her own flesh and blood, the only one she had now was Dominic.

For some time, she had considered leaving on her own but to have her mother throw her out still hurt. When she was younger, Calida had hoped if she just put some space between them and she came back maybe her mother would revert to her old self. Now, she knew there was nothing that could change a woman who was content with being miserable and making others the same.

The only home she had now was in the mansion of her betrothed. At least he had tried to defend her.

A tear spilled once more.

What if her mother was right? Should she even be by a

noble's side? How many others would think she was just a money-grubbing harlot?

Dominic held her close as they rode on his horse. After what had just happened, she was incapable of riding alone. So, she mounted with the lord and tied her horse's reins to the saddle. Quickly, she wiped her tears away.

He frowned down. "My dear one, are you crying?"

Calida looked forward, unable to meet his eyes. She didn't want to worry him any more than she already had.

"No, I am n-not." She had been successful in keeping calm until the last word quivered.

Curses.

Dominic slowed down until he could stop and took her face gently in his hands. He wiped her cheeks. "You have been crying, Calida. Please don't hide from me."

Slowly, he lifted his wet thumb to his mouth and licked her tear off his finger. The emotions overwhelmed her and her tears fell without a measure of control.

"Please try to lean on me." His eyes pleaded with her as he took her hand.

The floodgates let go and Calida wept hard and loud into his jacket. She wept for losing her childhood, wept for the loss of her father and then finally wept for the loss of her mother.

Twenty-Five

Calida leaned against Dominic on horseback as they arrived home. She was drained from weeping, and before she realized it, he had placed her on his horse and towed hers behind them. Rather than arguing, Calida leaned against her betrothed as the horse cantered up to the entry. Just as Dominic slung his leg over the horse, a servant came running up.

"Milord! Milord! There has been news!" He waved a paper.

Dominic glanced at the servant before taking the paper.

"She's been found," the servant said.

Calida gazed curiously at Dominic.

"What are you talking about?" Calida asked.

Dominic glanced at Calida, and a sheepish grin slid onto his lips.

"Well, after all the whispers about the maids and guards who came forward against your father, I thought it would be a good idea to find out where they went."

Calida inhaled sharply, anxious anger boiling inside her until her hands warmed once more with the familiar flames.

"Without letting me know?"

Dominic scratched his head as he gazed down at the paper. He looked uncomfortable, but Calida couldn't care less. She had been left out of the loop and it was not alright.

"Yes. I was going to tell you later."

Calida forced out a deep exhale. *He didn't mean to keep you out of the loop.*

"You are not privy to every little detail. Stop being so needy." Strange that even after disowning Calida, her mother's voice still harped at her.

She shook her head as the breathtaking weight on her chest wrapped around her.

"I...I... You should've... Of course, leave me out of the loop again."

Dominic grasped her hand and held it to his face.

"I apologize for unsettling you. We needed to find her as soon as possible. The two of us should visit together now that we know where she is."

She closed her eyes as the panic subsided. Her head slowed from her dizzying breathing while Calida lightly leaned against Dominic.

He clicked his tongue, and the horse took off again. Calida held onto him as they headed down the road the same way they came, this time making a turn headed out of town in the opposite direction.

As they moved, he handed her the paper the servant had given her.

It was crumpled and only barely legible.

T*o Lord Goldwyn, I have found what you were searching for. There was a maid who was close to the one who reported Sir Rayner and then suddenly went missing. She is just outside of Weommadran. Safe travels.*

. . .

It was signed by one of Dominic's guards.

"I truly didn't mean to keep you in the dark, Calida. I wanted proof first before getting your hopes up, for them only to be crushed," Dominic said.

Calida's heart squeezed as he whispered words in her ear while they rode to the maid's home. An arm circled her, pulling her close to him. Close enough to feel every part of him. It was moments like these that reminded her of how small she was compared to Dominic.

"I wouldn't want to dim your smile and replace those sensual looks with daggers."

Her cheeks flushed as his breath tickled her ear. *What is he talking about? I don't have sensual stares... right?*

After several hours, the horse slowed when they reached a rustic shack with a wooden fence in front. Dominic dismounted and held out a hand, assisting her off the horse. She slid off while the two held a stare.

They stood for a moment in silence as the door of the shack creaked open. The couple walked up to the woman peeking out of the house.

"Can I help you?" She glanced around cautiously.

Dominic walked forward and gave a curt bow. "Miss, we are here because of a maid you knew while in the palace. May we come in and have a word?"

She looked between them and bit her lip. It seemed she didn't feel inclined to speak about the palace.

"If it would help, I am the daughter of Sir Rayner Rhodes," Calida said.

Dominic shot her a cautionary look. She glanced his way before returning to the maid. Yes, she knew it was a risk. For all they knew, she believed her father was a despicable human being, but Calida would take that risk if it meant getting some answers.

The former maid let out a breath of relief before she held open the door for the couple.

"Come in. I can tell you more inside. Outside... The trees have ears."

Calida and Dominic glanced at each other in surprise. *What would have her saying that?*

Calida entered first with Dominic following closely and shutting the shack's door. The maid put out a cold cup of steeped herbal leaves.

"I apologize. If I had known of your arrival, I would have prepared a warm cup of tea. I'm afraid all I have is this." The green leaves sat at the bottom of the stained water in the cup. It reminded her of the cold cups of pre-steeped leaves that the mothers in her town would give to the children. It didn't have much substance to it, but it rejuvenated someone quickly.

She went to take a sip, but Dominic took it from her and casually sipped it, then carefully held it to her lips for a drink as well. Her cheeks heated as her lips parted and the cold, bitter brew poured in. His eyes never left hers.

The maid sat down across from them and sipped her own drink, contemplating.

"I often worked in the same sector as your father."

Calida turned her attention to the former maid. She was playing with the cup in her lap and staring at the water with a distant gaze.

"He was a very wonderful man, and when I found out about his death before I left the palace, it was devastating. He was protective of us servants."

"What were your reasons for leaving?" Calida leaned forward and placed her cup on the table.

The former maid glanced up at her for a moment before continuing to search the depths of her cup.

"The maid who went missing. She wasn't only my closest friend, she was my cousin." The woman sighed deeply. "She and I were originally from Syniel. In fact, we were from a well-recognized family in the area."

Calida glanced Dominic's way, her eyebrows furrowed in question. *Why would someone from a popular family end up a servant in the palace?*

Servants usually were indebted for a particular reason or employed through friends. Many nobles would send someone to a local tavern to scout recruits. However, there were some rumored cases where servants were kidnapped from their homes and sold to a house. It wasn't something the queen approved of, but that didn't mean it didn't happen behind closed curtains.

"What part of Syniel are you from?" Dominic leaned down and picked up Calida's used cup of cold tea. Her cheeks flamed as her attention focused on his lips, which touched the exact spot hers had. She silently gulped as she grew uncomfortable in her own skin. Like every part of her was itchy and a deep hole inside of her was void. Calida fiddled with her hands as she struggled to hold still.

"I came from a town a walk away from Fluccatia. It was called Summerthor, and it had an oasis that kept our town from going thirsty. I remember there was a desert flower near the well my cousin and I met at as often as possible." The maid smiled as she continued to stare off in the distance, wrapped up in her past.

"How did you end up in the palace, then?" Calida asked.

The woman looked up, her face suddenly aware of them in the room. Her smile fell away, and sadness came to her eyes.

"My cousin and I were taken. One day, my cousin didn't meet up with me at the desert flower, so I went to her house, only to find her being dragged out by two men."

Tears filled up her eyes as she remembered the frightening moment.

"My uncle was selling her in exchange for the money for his gambling debts. I jumped in to try to save her, and my uncle added me to the deal. We were eventually taken together." The woman tearily inhaled as she tried to control her emotions.

Calida felt an urge to hug the woman, but they didn't know each other. She hesitated to comfort her, so instead, Calida took out a handkerchief and held it out with a small smile. The woman took it and dabbed her eyes dry before handing it back with a nod of gratitude.

"Were you sold to the palace?" Dominic gazed at the woman in alarm.

The former maid shook her head vehemently. She placed her tea down and rubbed her arms.

"No, I was sold to a nobleman who recruited me under the guise of working of my free will. It was Sir Rayner who found out and somehow freed me."

"What about your cousin?" Dominic said.

Calida felt even more confused by this news. It was just one thing after another. None of it seemed to connect properly anymore.

The woman looked at her hands with a conflicted gaze on her face.

"She was given to a faction. When I saw her again, it was in the palace. I had been so overjoyed, but when I tried to talk to her...she had changed. Then I heard she witnessed against Sir Rayner. I was so upset, and she was convinced he was a pig." Tears spilled down her cheeks and dark stains formed on her apron.

"I couldn't believe my own cousin could accuse an innocent man of such heinous things. When I went to talk her out of her confession, I discovered her room in the palace ransacked. She just vanished, leaving nothing." She bit her lip and kneaded her hands. "All that was left was a necklace I had never seen her wear before."

"What was the necklace?" Dominic said.

Calida leaned forward, silently waiting for the answer. The former maid reached into the recesses of her dress and pulled a necklace out of her pocket. It was braided leather and had bloodstains on it. The insignia on the medallion was the same as the one of the incident report Jetta and Calida had found. *SC.*

"This was in your cousin's room?" Calida took the necklace from the woman's outstretched hands. It felt heavy and ominous against her fingers. Something about it was wrong, but she couldn't put her finger on it.

"You may take it. I want nothing to do with it. My cousin is gone, and I have no way of finding her. However, if you do find her, please tell her I love her. She is my family." The woman broke down into sobs.

Dominic gazed at the necklace and took it from Calida's hands, and along with it, a heavy burden she hadn't even realized existed.

"It has been magically infused. You can feel the connection to the item." He inspected the threading around the braided leather. Calida looked closer and noticed the smallest shift of shadowing on the bracelet. Like when Aither was in Dominic's shadow.

Dominic's head snapped up suddenly and thanked the woman for her information.

"If we find your cousin, we will send someone to notify you," he said.

He grabbed Calida's hand and rushed her out the door. On her way, she thanked the woman once more before he hurriedly mounted her and himself on the horse and took off down the road back home.

"What happened? Why are you hurrying?" Calida tried to look behind her to talk to him, but he turned her head around and continued snapping the reins of the horse.

"We shouldn't be holding this necklace for long. I am surprised she didn't feel it, but it has dark properties, mind-bending ones. Magic that can make someone paranoid or worse—a shift in personality!" The horse panted as he snapped the reins once more. They were moving faster than she had ever gone before, but what worried her was what he had just said.

Personality change?

Being paranoid was one thing, it could make shadows jump out at you, but a personality change could have very dangerous potential. If someone with a hidden resentment got hold of it, who knows what they could do?

"How deep was the darkness embedded?"

Dominic leaned close to her ear. His panting breath from the horse ride tickled her hair and set her nerves on fire. Pins and needles pricked at her in wave after wave.

"As deep as the night is dark. I could feel it bleeding into me by holding it for only a moment."

Calida's eyes widened in alarm. They needed to take it to a safe location right away!

"How far away are we? Are you touching it still?" Calida's voice pitched higher as the panic rose from the depths of her mind.

"At this speed, we will be back in two hours, excluding a rest stop for the horse. Realistically, we will be back in three hours." The sun was already beginning to set, and they weren't even close to home yet.

The darkness crept in as they stopped at a grassy plain an hour and a half later.

The horse ate some grass and drank some water. Dominic and Calida stirred restlessly.

They wanted to take off right away, but they had to consider the horse who had been carrying them around all day. It was a living being with limits as well.

Calida tried to stay close to Dominic and ignore the unsettling paranoia from the darkness in the forest. She tried to shake off the creepy feeling from the shadows she imagined slithering about in the grass.

The winds rustled the leaves and grass around them, which would be comforting in the sunlight but eerie on a moonless night. Even if there had been a glimmer of moonlight, she would feel more at ease, but it would seem this was the night Eesa decided to cast the sky in clouds.

"Another few minutes and we can take off again." Dominic grasped Calida's hands and squeezed them. Some of her jitters melted away when she remembered he was nearby. If she were in danger, Dominic would keep her safe.

She exhaled in relief and focused on the fact they would soon be leaving for the party in Baekkioron.

After a few more minutes of restless waiting, the horse had drunk and eaten enough to continue.

Dominic grasped Calida around the waist and lifted her onto the horse's saddle. His hands lingered for a moment, and they gazed into each other's eyes. Her cheeks flared red as his gaze grew heavy the longer they kept eye contact.

Calida whipped her head around to look at the path ahead of them. Dominic mounted the horse behind her and snapped the reins. She breathed out slowly. Now that they were on the move, the prickly paranoia pinching at her neck subsided.

It was late in the night when the couple returned home. Outside stood their guards and a few servants waiting up for them. Jetta's face relaxed when she saw Dominic and Calida arrive, obviously ready to sound the alarm if they did not return in time.

Twenty-Six

Calida exited her room to find Dominic waiting patiently for her. His formal attire suited him nicely. Jetta and Braxton were there in their formal faction uniforms. Holding her betrothed's arm, she walked to the ballroom, with Jetta and Braxton on opposite sides of their charges, protecting them. The guards were.

She was excited this time. The other two events she had attended with Dominic were awful, filled with snobby conversation and many noblewomen treating her akin to dirt. Although she would love to grind *them* into the dirt, her father raised her to be honourable and respectful.

Calida looked down at her dress to smooth any wrinkles in sight. The deep purple dress the maid had put her into contrasted with her fair skin. The maid had gasped in awe at her enchanting beauty. She didn't feel like herself in this fancy dress but less uncomfortable than when she wore the plain one back when she first met Dominic. There was no doubt in her mind this time she would look like she belonged. It was just a matter of pretending like she did.

The couple walked to the door leading to the ballroom.

The herald was there and waited for their arrival so he could announce it.

They stepped into the room.

"The Lord and Lady Goldwyn have arrived."

There were a few who turned to look as Calida and Dominic entered the ballroom, but they immediately returned to talking with local dignitaries. Calida peeked behind her and noticed Jetta and Braxton were glaring intermittently at one another.

Dominic led her into the crowd by the hand. Both bowed in greeting to those they passed. Several were quite respectful and talked to Calida as an equal. She had little to contribute to conversations about war and strategy, but she enjoyed listening to them talk.

"My lady, have you ever heard of such a manoeuvre? A frontal attack by the experts and then a few of them led the fresh warriors to the rear with supplies to barricade!"

"No, not at all, sir. I am but a simple lady." Calida grinned, amused.

The dignitary puffed out his chest and told her a long-winded story about how such strategies were much too modern for his taste. He preferred the old times when a man could just run into a field to kill his enemy. Or when women weren't so modern and spoke their minds.

It was at this point she ignored his conversation and hummed and nodded when needed. If he had talked about art, she would be much more intrigued.

Soon enough, another noble came up and took the dignitaries' attention away from them, and she could move on without hesitation. Somehow, the man had made the art of killing people a dull talking point.

Jetta and Braxton had taken opposite sides of the ballroom at this point. Neither were talking and if they passed each other, someone would say something to get them arguing again. It was one thing to be glaring at one another... but to be so obviously not on good terms was troubling.

Dominic led Calida onto the dance floor, and they wrapped their arms around one another, swaying in place. The music and atmosphere around them relaxed her and a smile appeared on her lips.

"What has you so happy?"

Calida mentally shook her head. She focused back on Dominic and saw his bright gaze locked on her.

"N-nothing. I was.... It's been a long time since I have felt so... content," Calida said.

Dominic smiled softly and twirled her as the tempo changed.

Dominic and Calida swung around on the dance floor, her skirt flexing and flowing as she moved. The layers of deep purple material moved as fluidly as water. As Dominic dipped or lifted her, she felt as lightweight as an elegant fairy.

Maybe she could be beautiful? Could her emotions be exciting?

The air had warmed significantly. Dominic and Calida were huffing by the end of their dance. Smiles spread on their faces as some nobles applauded them.

Dominic held her in his arms as they stood there, regaining their breath. She gazed up at him, lost in his eyes. As they stared at one another, her desire to kiss him became overwhelming. The more she learned of him, the more she wanted to cling to him and never let go.

Should I cling to such a marvelous person, though?

Dominic pulled her into the hall. The air was much cooler and the noise of people chattering was significantly quieter. Calida peeled the front of her dress off her a little to let some air flow. She fanned herself as she tried to cool down. The dance had been very exerting but quite fun.

Dominic stepped closer and took her hands.

"My dear one, are you enjoying yourself?"

Calida smiled and nodded. "Very much so."

He smiled with relief. "I'm glad. Maybe in the future we can try more events. Hopefully, the ones we attend will be just as enjoyable as this one."

"How kind of you to suggest. We'll have to wait and see." Her tone was purposefully flippant.

Dominic grew serious as he gazed upon her. The conversation shift was obvious, and she could already predict what he wanted to discuss. She had brushed him off again. Maybe this was his breaking point. That was it, he was going to toss her away.

They would have to talk about it soon. Just, she didn't want to. That meant facing possible rejection.

She opened her mouth.

"Dominic... I—" Hesitation took hold and froze her tongue in her mouth. Doubt swarmed her mind.

What if I say it and merely imagined his feelings? Am I sure he feels the same?

Dominic's face cleared as her emotions grew twisted with worry. Slowly, he leaned forward and kissed her forehead.

"Don't worry, Calida. I won't talk about us yet. You have more time."

He grasped her hand and dragged her to the ballroom to resume conversation.

Suddenly, a blood-curdling scream rang from the ballroom. Dominic and Calida looked at each other and ran toward the commotion.

As they arrived, the crowd separated them. Dominic focused on finding the source of the scream while Calida tried to stay out of the way. There was nothing she could do to help.

Duke Sullivan was on the ground, kneeling as he clutched his chest. His face was red, as if he was exerting himself by keeping his position. Calida stayed off to the side, hidden and obscured from the rest of the group. It was stealthy. No one else seemed to notice, but it sent alarm bells ringing in her head. Duke Sullivan had been looking her way for a suspicious amount of time. It could have been her imagination, but she thought he had winked at her. She moved closer to the door, the idea of being close to this man was overwhelming.

A hand wrapped around her mouth and pressed in. An arm snaked around her middle and dragged her out of the ballroom and down the hallway. A swift punch to the head knocked her out.

Twenty-Seven

DOMINIC

Nobles gathered around Duke Sullivan as the maids came to his aid. Dominic narrowed his eyes as the duke returned to normal and the clutching and shaking in pain disappeared.

The duke stood up. "It's alright! I am alright! I must be short a good leeching." The crowd slowly resumed what they were doing.

Dominic looked around and realized that Calida wasn't next to him. He looked toward the banquet table, expecting that she got some food after the crowd dispersed.

A crowded banquet table was off to the side, but no sign of Calida or her red hair.

Panic creeping up, Dominic dashed to Braxton and Jetta.

"Just because you think wildfire killed that guard does not make you automatically right!" Jetta growled at Braxton.

Braxton snorted and folded his arms. "The wildfire was inescapable, therefore, dead."

Dominic interrupted their *discussion*.

"I can't find Calida. Have either of you seen her?"

The guards glanced at him, immediately alert. "No, we last saw her with you as you left for the hallway," Jetta said.

Braxton gazed guiltily at his charge. "Yes, and we didn't see her come back in behind you." The two had been swept up in arguing more than keeping an eye on Calida.

Dominic pulled at his hair. He had been sure she had been behind him. The panic of losing her overwhelmed him. He had not told her, but earlier in the week, Jetta had reported Lord Sullivan's growing interest in Calida. The duke had gotten sloppy. He started talking about a new ward he would be accepting into his home soon. Dominic had known for some time that the women there were not his wards, but he couldn't just go forth and accuse him without proof. The duke was not only of higher status, but it would fall under the queen's jurisdiction. He had no right to step in as the accuser and punisher.

He regretted not telling her the truth.

Dominic searched the mansion, attic to cellar. He upturned tables and beds but not a sign of her was left, like she vanished into the night.

He crouched over a map as he barked orders at each guard he summoned. The party had moved outside, leaving him to use the ballroom as he needed.

It took too long for him to realize she was gone, and now he blamed himself for it. It was his duty to protect Calida. She wasn't only the woman he had grown to love, but she was his direct path to renewing his clan. When the party took their events outside for jousting and lawn games, Dominic realized Calida was gone. *His Kona.*

He wouldn't give up on finding her. Even if it took the rest of his lifetime, he would get answers. Whether or not she was dead.

Do not go there. Focus.

"See what happens when you do not heed my words!" Braxton said.

"Sorry? My best friend is missing! You didn't even bother to open your mind. It was all straightforward to you, with no room for anything else. Calida's safety was at stake, and you couldn't have cared less!" Jetta glared sharply at his guard as she bellowed.

Dominic had ordered the guards from the mansion and surrounding noble homes to join them in the search for his future wife. Not even one let a moment's rest for fear of missing something.

Dominic's head swam. *She could have been in the depths of the black market by now. What if they plan to sell her as a slave? Or worse, they will sell her to Lord Sullivan at a hefty price.*

Braxton and Jetta's bickering grated on his nerves. If he heard another comment from them, he might not keep his composure. Calida needed him to, but his chest squeezed painfully.

Why did I hesitate to tell her?

Dominic wished to tell her he loved her at least once. Now that chance could be gone.

Dominic sat at the edge of the blanket, grumpily refusing to participate in the tea party his mother had fashioned on the trimmed grass behind their home. He wanted to look tough. Not a little mama's boy who would sip on mild tea and sweet pastries.

"Du-Nic, have juice?" little Calida said.

Dominic pouted and snapped his head away.

"No. Men drink mead," Dominic said.

Duchess Maud Lilla put down her teacup and sharply glanced at him. Rayner peered over from several paces away, just out of hearing range.

"Dominic," she admonished.

"What? That's what father said." Dominic crossed his arms and glared at the pastry on the ceramic plate in front of him.

Father said tea parties and sitting around wasn't what boys should be doing. That he should be productive and successful. Whatever that meant.

His father even frowned when his brother would study for days in the library but seemed to approve when young Dominic practiced with his wooden sword. Not that he could tell. He hadn't ever seen his father smile or show affection. The most Duke Charles Goldwyn had done was a stoic nod.

"What's mead?" Calida tilted her head.

"Nothing you can have. You're too little." Dominic scrunched his nose at Calida.

Calida's eyes widened and grew moist as her lip wobbled.

"Dominic! That's not okay, up to your room. Now." Maud Lilla pointed toward the mansion.

His face scrunched up and he folded his arms.

Father barely listened to Mother so why should he?

"No," he said.

His mother's face clouded over and suddenly the air grew chilly. Her eyes grew that sharp motherly glare that said, "wait around and find out."

Young Dominic's stomach bottomed out and knew now was the time to make his escape.

With a stomp, he got up and ran for his home. He pouted as he plopped down on his bed,

He was a big boy who could take sips of his father's mead offered to him by the duke himself.

The sun had set when Dominic snuck out of his room to find a snack. He had sulked in his room so long that his father had stepped in. Either he grew up and be a big boy or miss out on supper. He had refused to say sorry since his father had been the one who told him about big boys drinking mead. He didn't understand why the duke would say differently now.

He was hungry from no supper, so he waited until the last maid went to sleep before he made his way toward the kitchen.

As he passed his parents' room, he heard his father's booming voice muffled by the door. Dominic snuck up to the door and held his breath.

"He shouldn't have been around that porpari. He is going to be a man of distinction. Next time I catch them close you better believe, Maud, I will be relentless." the duke growled.

"She is a lovely girl, Charles. Her father is a revered Faction Knight. It would be a worthy match for our second child." Maud Lilla's quiet voice sounded soothing to the ear.

"Whether Dominic or Ansel takes my position is not up to debate and no child of mine will be with the child of someone who couldn't make the cut to become a knight of the crown." Dominic heard his voice move past the door and then further into the room, as if he were pacing.

Dominic slowly backed toward the stairs, unsure how to feel. Calida was a good friend. Even if she was a little dummy who tried to make him drink sissy tea.

He had gotten his snack and fell asleep with a piece of bread in hand.

Jetta and Braxton's bickering continued until Dominic could not take anymore.

"Enough!" Dominic boomed. His voice resounded off the walls and ceiling with a great vibration that brought everyone in the room to a halt. The command froze every guard, servant, and maid in their steps. He rubbed his face and took a deep breath in and out. Slowly, calming down enough that the command would release the surrounding people.

Jetta and Braxton, now silent, stood in shock.

Dominic kept his powers a secret, but this was one of those times where he couldn't control it. Who could blame him when the woman he loved had gone missing?

He leaned on the table in front of him. They had been

working on plans to find out more and canvas the area after no success at the mansion. He had assumed they would come across something if only they kept searching. It had not been that long, and she could not have gone far without being seen.

It had only been several hours, but he looked like a man who had crawled on the ground for hours upon hours. Cobwebs littered his pants, and his hair was no longer pressed down smoothly. His hands had fingered anxiously through it. Whenever he paced back and forth, Dominic would tug at his hair, looking like a madman as he muttered nonsense.

Taking in a deep breath, he said, "We can't fight now. The past is the past. Calida is our top priority." Braxton and Jetta looked at each other and reluctantly nodded in agreement.

They focused on the map. Several pieces surrounded the mansion on the map. There was a dock beyond the mountains they would want to look at, but it was difficult terrain. Forest surrounded them and Baekkioron was right along a river. He prayed desperately to Eesa she hadn't been killed and dumped somewhere, but the alternative was just as haunting to think about. *Think about her safe. Nothing else.*

The scrape of metal on the floor set him off. Dominic twisted around in an instant, from calm to erratic. Jetta and Braxton looked at each other in concern. It was very unusual for him, but his thoughts were consumed with an image of Calida trapped and chained, maybe even being whipped while he just stood there. Dominic twitched with the need to get something done. To move or something. Anything.

He placed a hand on Lord Dominic's shoulder. The lord's body temperature had risen abnormally. Braxton face didn't betray the likely discomfort from the heat. His temperature spiked. Though Braxton knew what his lord was, this was the first time he'd touched him as heat flowed through his body. Dominic's jaw clenched as he breathed to control his thunderous rage, and it was all he could do to keep from collapsing in his fear.

Calida needed him. He didn't have time to dwell on what-ifs.

"Milord..." A guard ran up beside him.

"Yes?" Dominic said, his eyes never leaving the map in front of him.

The guard cleared his throat and said, "Lord Sullivan, who we had escorted to the infirmary in the mansion, has suddenly vanished."

After the incident, Lord Sullivan had convinced several maids and guards to escort him to rest. He seemed a bit too eager to leave the ballroom. *Please Eesa, let him not be involved. What could an earl do against a duke?*

Dominic understood the desire to leave a drab party, but the man had been almost hopping with joy. Which was peculiar, since something had supposedly injured him a moment before. Dominic had dismissed it, but now it had him second guessing.

What an idiot I am!

The duke had become known for his fascination with younger girls and women. There was a rumour of him having a dungeon filled with women and girls who were his personal sex slaves. It disgusted Dominic to even think about, especially after hearing the word from an underground informant that the rumours were true. He'd had an interest in Calida from the beginning.

It had been hours. Dominic paced the hallway. He had sent out guards to different areas, places that were most likely to hold a woman and man in the area. None had returned.

He was sure Lord Sullivan was behind this.

His interest in her was too disgusting to ignore. It would be one thing for him to take her for political reasons, but

Calida was not from a wealthy or socially popular position. There were only two reasons Lord Sullivan would take her.

He was either involved in the death of her father or he intended to make her his newest slave. Maybe even both.

Thinking about it dried his throat, making it hard to swallow.

Jetta and Braxton were back to glaring at one another.

"There are times to accept defeat..." Jetta said, her voice biting like a dog. Braxton crossed his arms and looked away. "This is not one of those times."

"Both of you, cease being uncooperative! It angers me you would rather focus on your petty disagreement than finding Calida." Dominic's head pounded.

"I am just as concerned about Calida as you are! She is like a sister to me. You would never grasp how closely bonded we are, milord!"

Tears threatened in Jetta's eyes. Her arguments with Braxton were not helping anyone, and it was time for them to end their childish fighting. If nothing else, he would use his title to calm them.

Not that. It was not the time.

Dominic moved through the mansion and exited. Finally, a guard he had assigned to scout the area returned. The guard ran up to him as he cleared the last step.

"Milord! I have returned from the east! No sign of the duke or milady!" The guard saluted and ran off.

Dominic bounced on the balls of his feet as his restlessness filled the silence, as did Aither's from within his shadow. He had grown attached to his shadow wolf, something the elders of his clan had forewarned him about. His clan was unique, and for the sake of his clan, he couldn't get attached to his shadow wolf. The elders of the Goldwyn clan had been around since the collapse of the six kingdoms. They had told each generation born about what they suffered as children.

The children of the son of Ordellius had told Dominic and his brother the same thing they told their father—their shadow wolves were a tool to be used for their own power. It was the key to vengeance against the treachery committed against their clan.

Jetta and Braxton followed him as he made a last-ditch effort to find her around the outside of the mansion. Many of the other nobles would snub a nose at his behavior, running around like a chicken with its head cut off. At this point, Dominic didn't care. In fact, he cursed his title. He was a noble, yet he couldn't find Calida. He had the armies of Eonifond at the ready, yet he couldn't find one person.

What good is my title if I can't find the most valuable person to me?

His thoughts turned dark once more. If he found her and she was dead...

The faster he ran, the larger the darkness grew in his mind. No one would escape his wrath if she were harmed. He had learned to keep an even temperament, but it would all be for naught if she was not there by his side. The anger he had reined in for years felt uncomfortable, but he knew who to direct it at to calm himself. The one responsible for taking his *Kona*. Lord Sullivan. *He was sure of it.*

As soon as Dominic found him, the perverted man would rue the day he took her away.

He soon left Jetta and Braxton far behind, so focused on finding Calida. Dominic searched every nook and cranny for her. He gave up, and by the time his guards found him, they seemed to have come to some sort of truce.

Dominic had run around until he wore himself out. When they approached him, he was on the ground, breathing heavily and tearing at the grass. Sweat poured from his forehead and stuck to his hair as he wiped it away in frustration. Green stains covered his pants and shirt, along with twigs and dirt. If anyone from the party had come by at that moment, they would be aghast at his appearance. It could affect his reputation, but he could be naked for all he cared.

Two other guards sprinted up to him, one the lord had sent to the north, and another he had sent to the south. Immediately, they started talking over one another.

Dominic held up his hand, then stood up.

"Tell me one at a time."

"No sightings, milord," the guard from the north said.

"That is because they were in the south," the other said.

"Speak."

"There was talk about a suspicious carriage in the area. It was rundown and wobbly. The women in the nearby village are superstitious and thought it carried the dead to Zabul." The guard from the south rubbed his hands on his pant legs. The sweat on his forehead beaded as he stumbled over his words.

Dominic could guess it was most definitely not a carriage to Zabul. It was the only lead he had, and it was the one he would use. He was running out of time and his patience grew thin. He needed to find Calida. And no man would stand in his way, lest they feel the wrath of Aither in his battle-ready bite.

Twenty-Eight

Calida woke up disoriented. Her head was ringing, and the side of her face felt like it was on fire.

A slight chill surrounded her.

She cracked her eyes open and looked around. It was dark, but wherever she was the the wind blew past in a hollow squeal. Her eyes squinted shut as confusion flooded through. Clearly, she was outside, but the surface she lay on was firm and cushioned.

Slowly, she sat upright and cradled her head as a throbbing pain shot through her.

Looking around, she realized she was in a carriage. The events from the previous night flooded back.

She panted heavily as her hand shot to open the carriage door, only to find it locked. Calida pulled at the door harder and harder until her breath was dizzying and her vision blackened worryingly.

She was most definitely not in the same place anymore. Her mind swam as Dominic's security and protection felt like a fever dream. Being alone again was much more frightening now than it had ever been in the past.

After some time of trying to tug open the door, she returned to the other side of the carriage.

The door finally opened and Lord Bartholomew Sullivan, the Duke of Eleari, stepped in. Her face paled as she realized just how badly the situation would go. All she could do was pray to come back whole and alive.

As the duke sat down beside her, the carriage sped off. Her body was thrown around and she was forced to sit on the bench beside the duke.

"I didn't appreciate what you did last time, bird. Burning me is not the right way to get attention." Lord Sullivan licked his lips sloppily.

She held back a grimace. The fact he had kidnapped her so easily was unnerving. If he could grab her when she was inches away from Dominic, where would she be safe?

The carriage was suddenly too small for them, and she wished she could just jump out the window. With a sudden spur of motivation, she made a break to jump, but the duke grasped her arm roughly and ripped her backward. She hit the backboard of the seat with a hard thump.

Calida cried out in pain. *Don't cry. Don't cry. Don't cry. He will only use your tears against you.* She couldn't let this vile monster of a man have that satisfaction.

Her hair fell in front of her face as she tried to think of what to do.

The duke pulled her hair back and held it roughly at her neck, forcing her to look up at him.

"Now..." he said with a lick of his lips. "We are going to give you some discipline. Any good slave needs to be taught her place right away."

Calida's eyes widened at Lord Sullivan's words.

She was even more desperate to get away now. She could see in his eyes that he wouldn't kill her. He had far worse ideas in mind, something far more torturous. Living with the knowledge that she would be forever tainted would be far worse than anything a blade could do.

Calida tried to pull away to make another attempt at escape, but his grasp was too firm. He tightened his grip again, and she whimpered.

"How many times will it take until I break you?" Leaning close, the duke hissed into her ear.

Calida's vision went blurry. The overwhelming fear nearly blinded her until she was close to fainting, but he slapped her cheek to keep her conscious.

"Ah, see, I didn't give you permission to pass out on me yet. We have yet to get to the good stuff." He clicked his tongue in dissatisfaction.

Calida's voice croaked and then a cough scratched up her throat. She wanted to stay quiet and be brave, but her mind was quickly slipping into that state where she was that scared little girl. The same one Cressida traumatized.

Please, Calida begged in her thoughts for Dominic.

"I think the first thing we must get you to do is learn the art of pleasing a man." He licked his lips and grinned at her fiercely.

Calida tried to shake her head vigorously. She would rather drown in the Primeval Ocean than do what this lecherous asshole wanted.

He released her hair but pressed her neck down until she was kneeling on the floor. If she could, she would fight against him, but his grip was remarkably strong. Even though she grew up doing many laborious activities, she was not nearly strong enough to resist.

He untied the front of his pants and reached in to grab his dick. His beady eyes stared at her with a ravenous hunger.

A large bump broke his grip on her neck. He fell sideways in the seat and took a considerable amount of time to get back up. It put him off from what he had planned, and from that point, she tried to stay out of reach. He wasn't willing to move more than required, and that was a good thing. It kept his slimy fingers off her.

He huffed in frustration before he sat back and waited in silence.

Soon enough they stopped, and a man opened the door, the same one who had tried to kidnap her the first time.

"You!" She pointed at him accusingly.

The man sneered. "Yeah, me, bitch. I'll get you back for that little stunt you pulled, no doubt."

He reached in and dragged her out, not caring if she fell on the ground as she exited.

Calida landed with a grunt, her knees and the heels of her hands scraped up from the stone beneath her. With a quick thought, she pressed her hands further into the rocks. If nothing else, it gave her a sense of accomplishment. At least she left a part of her behind in case she was never found again.

The possibility of Dominic finding her was a wonderful fantasy, but she needed to face reality.

A tear threatened to fall, but she held back.

No crying. These vile men don't deserve my tears.

Pushing herself up, Calida stood on her feet. She would try to resist when she could, and prayed she'd stay hopeful.

Twenty-Nine

A hand roughly grabbed Calida. A dark, damp cave stood in front of them. Rocks stuck out from all angles in the cave. As they walked up, it looked like an enormous gaping mouth wanting to swallow her whole.

If only she could stop where she was. However, Lord Sullivan had hold of her hair and dragged her along whenever she didn't move fast enough.

He held her close to his side. As he moved, the duke's woolen outer coat smothered her as he kept her hair high and tight in his grasp.

"I am halfway tempted to just start right here with you." He dragged her up so he could whisper in her ear.

She gasped at the sting on her scalp. A shiver ran through her. He meant what he said. His lust was palpable. It came off him in waves as thick as the ocean.

As they moved further into the cave, he dragged her past prison cell after prison cell. An ache spread through her head. There was no doubt she would lose her hair after this, but at the moment, losing a few strands would mean nothing if she didn't escape.

They arrived at a cell deep in the recesses of the cavern. It was poorly lit and had a musty smell. Lord Sullivan shoved her in. She turned to him, if only to find a way to escape, but Calida knew if she did, what came next would be nothing compared to the punishment. It wasn't the time to escape yet. If there ever would be.

Eventually, Dominic would have to find her.

What she feared the most, though, was her betrothed not finding her before she had been touched. The path on the mountains separating her from Dominic was a hard path to follow. She and Lord Sullivan arrived when they did because of shortcuts and roadways that few knew. She had heard murmurs about them before but dismissed them as myth, but she now realized they were as real as anything else.

Bandits and black-market dealers apparently used the roadways, Lord Sullivan and his minions included.

He licked his lips and grinned sinisterly, taking a step forward into the cell. Calida scurried backward. What was he going to do now? Her heart raced and her mind flooded with images of him jumping on her and of never escaping in time to save her virtue.

If there was a time for her magic to work, now would be it. *Maybe it would.*

Shakily, she stretched out an arm, hoping to set him on fire once more. Duke Sullivan paused to see if she would produce something. She concentrated hard, praying for something, anything, to come out.

Nothing came forward.

Not even a glow appeared.

As she struggled, the lord broke out in hideous laughter before shuffling forward.

"Maybe I can get a small nibble in before the boss arrives." The duke rubbed his hands in excitement. Whoever "the boss" was didn't sound any better than Lord Sullivan.

Her arms shook as he reached out for her leg, and she tried to move away. Calida's head shook side to side, her lips soundlessly mouthed, *no.*

He kept advancing on her.

Her back struck the wall at the far end of the cell. Calida scrunched herself as close to the wall as she could, hoping to keep him from touching her.

It didn't work.

His sausage fingers reached around her and pulled her arms up, pinning them in place. Her eyes fixated on the door to the cell, trying to muster up the strength to overpower this monster.

Calida struggled against him, trying to push his arms off her with all her might. She panted with the exertion. His face stretched with a wide smile and the more she squirmed, the larger it got. It was a terrifying nightmare.

Lord Sullivan pulled down his pants. If he had succeeded in the carriage ride over, she would've tried to bite his shrivelled little dick. A swift death in a carriage was more appealing than this nightmarish creature using her body for the rest of her life.

"Now, remember not to squirm too much. This is your first time. I'll be *gentle.*" His large grin stretched out as if he were insane and bound for the asylums.

Calida pinched her eyes shut. If it happened, she didn't want her eyes open. If she kept her eyes open, it would be all too visceral. If she was alive after being used by him, she wanted it to seem like a bad dream, rather than remembering every little detail until the end of time.

Someone called down the hall for Lord Sullivan. "Milord, he has arrived. Quickly, you must greet him!"

The duke groaned in annoyance but got up, anyway. She pried her eyes open. Calida had halfway expected him to continue even though he was summoned.

Duke Sullivan tidied himself up and then walked to the door of the prison cell.

"Don't think I am finished with you yet." With a steely gaze, he wiped his mouth with the back of his hand. "I will pick you apart like a ripe cherry for harvest."

Calida froze where she was as he closed her cell down and walked away.

Hours had gone by and there was no sign of Duke Sullivan. She had moved around her cell, scoping out whether she could escape. Even tried the door. But no amount of pulling or shoving opened it. She couldn't remember the duke locking up behind him, so there had to be some type of device holding her in. She tried to find a lock, but to no avail.

The walls were intact. There wasn't even a single hole. With a hopeless sigh, she confined herself to a corner of the room and sat.

A devastating ache spread through her at the thought of never seeing Jetta again, or Dominic. She had been just getting to know Braxton, but he seemed decent. She could only imagine what they were doing. Her mind swirled with all the conflicting emotions inside her. A part of her believed they had forgotten about her. She had no meaning to them, and theywere laughing and spending their lives in luxury.

However, the larger side drowned out the doubts. Why wouldn't they look for her? It wasn't reasonable to assume the worst.

Calida's mouth quirked as she pictured Jetta being her cantankerous self. She would bicker with Braxton and rage on about the delays in finding her. Her friend would barge through the cave with guards flowing in behind her. Calida could see Dominic rushing forward and wrapping his arms around her.

It was so visceral the dream could've been real. She would

savour the fantasy of the two who meant the most to her barging in.

The smile faded from her lips.

As much as seeing her love and her friend rescue her would be a dream come true, Calida needed to face reality. The chances of her being rescued were as high as her chances of escaping. Almost none.

She shifted in her spot. After the close call earlier, Calida didn't want to give the duke many more opportunities. Her strategy was to keep out of his reach for as long as she could. While he was slow and accustomed to sitting on his ass, Calida was agile and familiar with frequent exercise.

Speed was on her side as long as he didn't grab her.

Why try to fight him off? He will get upset, and I will pay the price. It's not like Dominic will come for me.

Calida shook her head. Her anxiety was once again trying to get the better of her. She knew that wasn't Dominic. He was kind and caring.

Who's to say he isn't wrapped up in Lady Evaine as we speak?

Calida clenched her teeth in anger. The thought had her seething with jealousy, but then she let it go. A deep breath left her body.

That being true would upset her, but he wouldn't do that to her. Dominic was a good man and to connect him to such distasteful acts ruined his honour.

At first, she thought it was utterly horrid to be married off to a nobleman. Any she had met previously treated commoners like scum of the earth and constantly mocked her father. She had expected him to be the same, but then he was charming and dignified. Calida had tried to deny her attraction, but it was impossible when she was around him all the time and the smile he flashed at her nearly dropped her dead. Words flowed out of his mouth and any thought of filtering what she should and shouldn't say vanished in the wind.

If anything, one part of her wanted to stand up and declare, "You, man. Me, woman."

She was strong enough to be his bride.

There was a bit of her, a part she most definitely never wanted to admit out loud, that longed to have him do all the thinking. Where she stopped thinking and worrying for a night. The idea left her blushing and on fire. It was a wonderful fantasy.

Calida moved her legs so she could rest her head on her arms. Thinking about such things kept her distracted. It kept her from suffocating in the overwhelming fear that came from Duke Sullivan's plans.

The walls closed around her as she lost control. Her breath quickened, and her eyes darted from wall to wall. If only she could escape the smothering.

Dominic came to mind again.

An image of him in brilliant light, a smile on his face. It was almost like she could feel his arms wrapping around he,. the comfort from his large hands encompassing her.

Her heartbeat slowed as the vision calmed her. The crawling darkness subsided. It was welcoming now. It would make her more invisible to the eye, and it was just what she wanted.

Eventually, she passed out in exhaustion, lying on the cold floor as the night darkened. The regret of not saying the words she had meant to say at the party in Baekkioron hung heavy on her. A tear slipped out as her eyes shut.

Calida startled awake from a nightmare about being kidnapped and molested by Lord Sullivan. He had been ripping off her tunic as she screamed in protest, and she woke up in fright.

The darkness around her and the faint creak of wood and

steady drip of water in the distance reminded her of the nights she laid awake back in Poramun Creek. With a steadying breath, she rested her head back on her legs.

After the nightmare, Calida didn't want to fall asleep again, not that she could. At any moment, the duke could return, and then it would be completely hopeless. Escaping with her life would be impossible.

Her fate was sealed the moment Duke Sullivan brought her here and locked the prison cell. Calida tightened her jaw at the thought of being stuck to rot with Duke Sullivan. Even if he kept her alive, his boss most likely had other plans.

If they thought she knew more than she did, it would spell bad news for her. And how would they believe her? Cruel men like them only listened to their own voices.

Even if she tried to convince him to let her go, there was no chance he would let her walk free, especially after being taken here.

Calida got up and paced the room.

There was also the fact Lord Sullivan was a duke. If Dominic rescued her, he would put his own title at risk. Few nobles would do that. She didn't think Dominic would be bold enough to risk estrangement from his family for one woman.

A sense of bittersweet despair washed away the momentary elation she felt.

Calida stopped in the middle of her cell. Dirt covered the ground, and the walls were all bricks, with no windows. The gaps in the bars showed more cells on the other side of the cavern. A hiccup escaped and the tears suddenly wouldn't stop. The anguish flowed through her.

Her shoulders shook as the tears fell, and she collapsed on the ground and curled up in pain. Whimpers escaped her mouth with every hiccup. The agony flowing through her was so intense, Calida would try to scratch it out if she could.

Her fingers dug into her face and body as she attempted to dispel the anguish. Holding herself back from making too much noise, Calida cried out with all her might in her mind. The memories of her childhood drifted through her. The suffering she endured and the blame she put upon herself. All the responsibility she had owned up to that was never hers to begin with.

She tugged at her hair to relieve the pain, and her thoughts shifted to the pain of having pure, unmanipulated love from someone for the first time in a long time. A gnawing guilt chewed away at her until she felt she would go insane.

Then the pain lessened, her heart hurt from what she had endured, and her shoulders shook as she curled inward.

"Please make it stop." A whimper escaped her.

Slowly, her arms relaxed, and the pain was only an ache. She was only now realizing just how much she could have had. The delay of the beautiful result that could have made her life bright once more, like it had been as a child. She hadn't told him she loved him. Now she would never get that chance. With resolve, Calida sighed as she stretched out her legs. This would be her final resting place.

Soon enough, she would be with her father. If not by the duke's hand, then by hers. Because she refused to stay in the hands of such a monster.

Thirty

Calida woke to the sound of her prison cell opening and the jingle of the keys. She shot up off the ground, the sight of Lord Sullivan filling her with fresh panic.

There were men behind him. *What do they want from me?*

The duke seemed to be the type to keep his prizes all to himself. Doom settled on her shoulders as the duke and one man entered her cell.

"Well, bird, I have returned. I hope you weren't too lonely without me here." He rubbed his hands together while leering at her.

Her stomach fell as he moved closer. He had a hand on the front of his pants as he eyed her, his horrifying plans transparent.

The man beside him stepped forward. He was taller than Duke Sullivan and looked at her differently. His hair was as dark as coal, but his skin was pale, like he had never stepped into the sun. His stature was intimidating and deadly. The look in the man's eyes promised death. Her death.

He put a hand on the duke's shoulder. "We need to begin. You can have your fun after getting answers."

Her limbs grew cold as she stared into the man's eyes. There was no empathy or caring in them. She was nothing more than a mission, and whatever else they wanted from her, she would end up dead.

Calida whimpered but didn't protest. If she did, he would smack her across the face and then beat her within an inch of her life.

She groaned as the man painfully gripped her hair. Calida wished she could disappear as she tried to pull away.

The man dragged her behind him as he led her out of the prison cell. It was dark everywhere, and she flinched from the subtle noises around her. Tears sprung up in the corners of her eyes.

"What do you plan on doing to me?"

The man stopped in the hallway and loosened his grip.

Another man answered from the shadows. "We know you have been investigating your father's death." His voice drawled in the accent of a noble.

Her eyes widened as she realized she had been monitored. Obviously, it ran deeper than she had thought. She could vaguely make out an intricate golden thread woven on the shoulders of his jacket. His stocky build towered over her, and the darkness obscured his face.

"I didn't find out much. Your people stopped me every time I tried to find more information." Calida said.

The man folded in his arms and shook his head. "It wasn't my people who stopped you."

Her beating heart threatened to burst from her chest as Calida leaned forward, hoping to appeal to this man.

"I haven't found out anything different from what everyone else knows, I swear!" If this man could effortlessly snatch her from a heavily guarded party and bring Lord Sullivan to heel, then he was a dangerous person to cross.

The nobleman sighed and knelt. "Little bird, I don't believe you."

Calida's eyes widened as she stared at him in disbelief. She had spoken the truth, but it didn't work. Looking down at the ground, it upset her for even hoping it might work. What an daufi he was. Her body shook as the damning sentence beat down on her.

He grabbed her chin in a bruising grip.

"My mercenary will get the answers from you even if you aren't willing." His voice was a sharp hiss.

Calida shook her head frantically. She didn't have any answers and no matter how much they tortured her, she never would.

The mercenary grabbed her hair harder and dragged her as he walked steadily faster along the hallway. She grunted and tried to stretch her neck up to lessen the pain. The man twisted his wrist around it until it was tighter, leaving her crouched over as the group walked.

Calida whimpered. At this rate, she wouldn't have any hair left.

The hallway was dark and smelled of piss. After an impossibly long walk, the man turned to the right and stopped in front of a beaten-up door.

He opened the door soundlessly and pulled her in.

The duke followed quietly, which was unusual because he couldn't help but gab when it was just the two of them. If it wasn't for everything else, that would have been frightening. No one else had the ability to shut up Lord Sullivan—that she had seen.

In the room, blood covered objects were strewn around. They hadn't bothered to clean them. She would die with a dead man's blood on her body. Tears slid down her face freely.

What was the point of resisting now? She might as well as learn to let go of her pride.

There was no pride in death.

If it wasn't for the overwhelming fear controlling her body, she would've been furious at their gall to hold her captive and threaten her with such disgusting tools.

Several were torture devices that the queen had made illegal. The one closest to her was a cross meant to stretch a person to death. What terrified her was the one in the corner. The Zabal's Stake, a painful device reserved for a woman who committed adulterous acts. She would be displayed in a public square where others would look down upon her for being naked in front of someone other than her husband.

It hadn't seemed so scary when she read about the device in Dominic's library.

What does it matter? There isn't any hope now.

"I'm not going to kill you... right away."

Her head whipped around to stare at the mercenary with wide eyes. He walked over to prepare the first device.

She was still in her ball gown, though it was dirty now. They had ripped the hem up the side. Her leg was clearly visible, but it was at least keeping her covered.

The man untied the buckles on each side of the wooden beams. He came over and wrenched her to her feet and then pushed her up against the cross. As the breath escaped her in shock, her instinct to fight kicked in.

Calida pushed and screamed at the man as he struggled to clip her in. Using her feet, she kicked out and landed a good one in the middle of his chest. A surge of adrenaline flowed through her. He staggered back, stunned by her powerful kick. The man sneered at her and then shoved her into the buckles.

"You won't win!" Her voice wailed with a shrill screech. A force of heat flared from her and sparked her hair like a flame to kindling. The whine of her voice turned into a cacophony of air, forcing the man to step back. The air around her boiled as her emotions grew more frantic. There was no way she would allow herself weakness in this moment.

Phoenix Child...

A catch in her breath stalled the power around her. A feeling of disappointment, not her own, filled her.

Calida tugged against her restraints with all her might. She glared at the hired man with a fierceness unlike anything she had ever summoned.

The flames on her head grew as the man stared, taken aback for the first time since they had met. The fiery tongues licked at the wood. It didn't startle him for long, though. With dead eyes, he pulled out a bucket of water from beside the door and threw it at her. Her hair sizzled as it soaked in.

Her deadly glare met his nonchalant stare.

"You're wrong, Calida. I will win," he said.

She froze. *He knew her name.*

The rage inside her was transformed into a paralyzing fear. If he knew her name, then what else did he know and what was his motivation?

The duke stood at the door, nervously peeking around.

"I still want her alive in the end. I want her as my slave." His voice wheedled. The lord's beady eyes watched as her gown slipped down her breasts. He licked his lips. "She needs to learn how to service a man."

The man turned to the duke with his arms crossed. "If she lives after we get the information."

The duke stepped further into the room and glared down at the mercenary. "She had better be alive. If I brought her here, she would be mine. That was the deal."

A wave of nausea flowed through her at the thought of these monsters using her as currency. Quietly, she tried once more to tug at the cuffs.

With a swish of his hand, he effectively dismissed Lord Sullivan. The man turned his attention toward her again.

"This can wait until after. I need to start right away," the mercenary said.

Calida looked around in panic. If only there was a way out without pain, but everything that might be helpful was out of reach.

The man pulled a knife from his boot and examined it as he walked closer to her. Now quiet, she couldn't summon up the ability to resist. It was like her energy had drained from her all in one fell swoop.

He dragged the knife along her cheek as he observed her silently. That was enough to unsettle her. His slimy stare grossed her out. If only she could run or die this second.

The hired mercenary dragged it down her neck, then slowly cut the front of her dress. Panic set back in.

"If you answer swiftly, maybe it won't hurt."

Calida glared at him. She had already said she knew nothing. What more do they want to know? She never found out who was behind it.

She let out a muffled groan as her bonds wore on her. The cuffs cut at the skin on her wrists and ankles.

The mercenary shook his head and clicked his tongue. "I see you want to be difficult. I will get the answers from you eventually."

"No!" Calida's voice cracked. "I am not being difficult! I have nothing to tell you!"

The man's cold eyes just stared at her blankly. Regardless of whether she had information to tell, he would torture her. He was in this for the money, and he would get his money's worth.

Sullivan stood by the door, glaring at the mercenary. He folded his arms like a petulant child. If it wasn't to whom she was referring, she would be in complete disbelief at the way these men acted about someone about to be tortured.

The mercenary pulled out a bag that clattered as he dumped it on the ground. Calida eyed it cautiously. Whatever it was, she was apprehensive.

He looked up at her quickly and noticed her expression. Smirking, he drawled, "Oh, don't worry. I won't be using this bag of goodies until later. After we have stripped you out of that dress."

Calida shivered. She had almost forgotten the duke wanted her naked, and the man saying that didn't help to erase it from existence.

From the bag, an odd-looking object came out. A crooked metal bar with a wooden handle. It didn't appear deadly or sharp. How did he expect to torture her with something dull? She didn't want to find out. His chilling smile was enough evidence of just how much pain she would be in.

He walked behind the wooden cross that held her arms and legs apart and attached it to something behind her with a click.

He twisted the handle in a circle, and a chill ran down her spine. Her limbs pulled uncomfortably as he twirled the handle until he reached the amount he wanted. He stopped and walked around to start the interrogation.

He stretched his neck back and forth and sighed. "Now, let's begin with a simple question."

Calida didn't want to answer. Maybe eventually he would realize she knew nothing? It wasn't likely, though. She had already discarded the possibility of getting out of here alive. It would be amazing, but this cold-hearted man would kill her before a guard could step in the room.

"Do you agree your father died as a traitor to the crown? Yes, or no."

Her hair flamed once more.

The man smacked her face hard. Tears spilled from her eyes. If her arms weren't pinned down, she would've died trying to burn the bastard alive, even though he frightened her to no end.

Out of nowhere, a splash of water hit her, and for a moment, she couldn't see.

Looking up, she saw the mercenary holding an empty bucket with droplets spilling from it. Her hair sizzled.

The wood beneath her creaked as she lost her strength to hold her position.

"My father is not a traitor," she murmured.

Water dripped from her hair as she leaned into her cuffs. The discomfort was on the painful side now.

The man shook his head in disappointment. "Even among the mercenaries, we know your father as a spitless, shifty man."

Calida panted in exertion.

He pulled the lever to wind the devise tighter, her wrists feeling the burn now. She gazed at the ceiling as the room spun around her.

The mercenary glided the knife along her skin, creating small lines of pain and blood.

Calida inhaled. It wasn't unbearable. Just uncomfortable.

He questioned her more about her father and what she knew. Calida answered negatively each time.

"Hmm... I know you know something. How many people were on your father's list of accomplices?" he asked, edging his knife under her thumbnail.

Calida shook her head vigorously.

The man clicked his tongue. "That is not an answer."

He put more pressure on the nail, causing her to groan in pain.

"I-I don't know! I don't know anything!"

In her head, she screamed for it to stop. Her mind grew

fuzzy with the anxiety and fear, all thoughts clouded by the pain of the knife under her nail.

The man frowned. "I don't believe you!" he growled.

Tears spilled from her eyes. She was a people pleaser, so she innately felt disappointment in herself when someone else was disappointed in her. It was only a nail, but not knowing what to answer made it worse.

Suddenly, his knife ripped off the nail and Calida screamed in pain as she fainted.

Lights flashed and darkness surrounded her as she arose from her fainting spell.

"Finally awake again." The mercenary got up from his seat on the other side of the room. Calida looked up with heavy eyes. She shook away the cobwebs in her mind.

Her nail bed throbbed as she looked around the room, gaining awareness of her situation again.

"Now, let's move to another question." He prowled closer, his knife held casually in his hand. Her gaze focused on the knife.

He roughly grasped her chin and forced her to look at him. His cold eyes stared into hers. "What do you know about the Soldiers of the Cobra?"

Calida looked at him in confusion. She had never heard the name before. It did not sound like a group to be trifled with, either.

They had kept Calida on the cursed device for hours. He tried to wring out every bit of information she knew about what happened to her father. Eventually, she told him she knew a guard was connected to what happened. She didn't believe her father committed the crime.

The man laughed harshly in her face. His mockery spit on her and ran down her cheek.

Calida squeezed her eyes shut.

The mercenary had tightened her cuffs, adding more pressure.

Her shoulders felt stretched and sore. It wouldn't be long before her arm popped out. The thought had her stomach dropping. The nausea from the idea of such acute pain almost overwhelmed her.

He paced back and forth in the corner as he rubbed the front of his pants, his gaze locked on her. A chill ran down her spine as he inched forward, hoping to get even a touch in.

In a panic, she whipped her head around to look at the hired mercenary.

She had no hope for him to show her compassion, but he seemed to want to get answers first.

The man was cleaning his knife with a cloth as he turned around.

"Would you like the honors?" He held out the knife to Lord Sullivan.

She watched the exchange between them closely. They seemed thrilled with what would come next. She wished for a swift death before that pervert touched her.

Calida was intelligent enough to know that the duke had sexual intents, but she had hoped that the mercenary had only been interested in torturing her.

Even the brutal pain of a knife or torture devices could not compare to the long suffering that would come from her body being bought by this vile man standing before her.

Duke Sullivan was a perverted man with a driving need to wet his twig with virginal blood and tears.

She wished there was courage and strength left in her veins. If there were, Calida could imagine her kicking him to the ground and slamming his head into the stones.

It was a pleasant fantasy. Impossible, but nice.

"I can have my go now, Stalson?" Duke Sullivan's expression brightened, almost like a kid with a jar of candies.

Though she didn't believe the man's eyes could get any colder, the mercenary glared at the duke so fiercely it was a miracle he didn't keel over.

"Do not call me by my name in front of the bitch," he growled.

Duke Sullivan's mouth closed with a snap. Obviously, his emotions had gotten the better of him, but that was good news for her because she knew the mercenary's name now. She still had no hope of escaping, though. Calida silently sighed in despair.

The two advanced on her. The desire to escape created a sense of anxiety deep in her soul. They pointed the knife in the duke's hand her way, and she didn't like the look of it.

Stalson was grinning for once. She tensed. The man that had been growling and intimidating her now looked like he could kiss her. Which wasn't good. At all.

Suddenly, the duke slashed down the middle of her dress. The fabric split and fell from her. They had cut off everything but her corset and never was she more thankful as she was now for complex corsets that needed to be undone by many people. This was specially designed by an elf who had woven the fabric himself from vines in the Nydeawyr forest. They had no hope of slashing it with a knife such as theirs. In red hot spite, she almost grinned.

They had ruined her dress, but at least she wasn't completely naked.

The duke growled in frustration as he looked closer at her corset. It had a faint tinge of green from the vine, something that was only noticeable if you knew what to look for. As a man of nobility and sexual immorality, Lord Bartholomew Sullivan would know what a corset from Nydeawyr looked like. Not able to stop herself, Calida smirked at him. She might as well have tied a chastity belt to her upper body. And from this stiff position on the stretcher, he couldn't get on her lower half. *Just try to be a sarding pervert now.*

Stalson proved her wrong by turning the handle until everyone in the room heard a pop from her shoulder. Blinding pain followed, searing into her brain. For a moment, everything went white as her arm went limp and fell out of the cuff.

Calida screamed in anguish as Stalson growled, "Don't forget where you are, bitch!"

Her shoulder ached as it moved limply. After the pop, the perverts decided to move her to another device. She feared what may happen now because of her arm, but there were far more pressing matters. Because the cross could no longer hold her, Stalson was moving her to the one thing that had her gulp in fear.

It was something that she could not bear to even utter the name of.

It had three sides that all pointed to one sharp edge, used for women or men to sit on. Either that or the wooden pony with a penis carved on it. It was rough and prickly, and a thousand moons ago, executioners used it to torture adulterous women in the town square. The queen understandably made it illegal.

The device they were prepping for her was very similar, except instead of an oversized wooden penis ripping apart her virgin vagina, a sharp edge would slowly poke into her as ropes weighed her on it.

Sweat beaded down her back as she stared in acute fear at the thing that could end up ripping her apart.

Now placed on the ground, Calida watched Duke Sullivan slowly inch toward her with a look of lust in his eyes. She held her limp arm as a shiver spread through her. What started as a small shake spread until tremors controlled her movements.

Her teeth chattered together as Lord Sullivan knelt in front of her and pulled down his pants.

He had no concern for the priorities of the hired mercenary. The duke seemed to have grown impatient and needed some relief now.

She tried to move away, but he pinned her skirt down with his knees. The once lengthy skirt was now a rag on her body.

"Mm... I cannot possibly wait another moment to break in my new slave, bird." He dug his pelvis into her hip as he showed her what he intended to do.

The feeling nauseated her like nothing else.

Stalson came over and shoved Duke Sullivan off her. "Can't you keep your lust on a leash? I haven't gotten the answers I need."

He grabbed Calida by her good arm and dragged her closer to that monstrous contraption.

A shuffling noise sounded from outside the room. It had been dead quiet until now.

The duke left the room to check out what was going on. Stalson continued to drag her as if he hadn't heard a thing. Calida didn't have the strength to fight against him. He ripped off her skirt, causing her to yell in protest.

There she was, half naked in front of a man she had never met before. Shame and guilt weighed her shoulders down. The one person who should have seen her naked form was Dominic.

Thirty-One

With a boom and a crack, someone kicked in the door. In a flash of motion, the room went from almost empty to filled with guards, including Braxton and Jetta. Following behind was Dominic with a fierce look in his eyes. Calida had never been frightened of him before, but the deadly expression was bone-chilling. She desperately tried to cover herself with the dress discarded on the ground, ashamed of her inappropriate appearance.

Jetta stepped forward with a blanket in hand, but Dominic stopped her in her tracks with a hand out, expectant. Hesitating for a moment, she placed the blanket in Dominic's hand.

He strode over to her, past her kidnapper. They pulled the mercenary off her and threw him to the ground. Another two grabbed Sullivan and restrained him with his pants around his ankles.

Dominic collapsed on the ground beside her. Calida shook as tears spilled down her cheeks. She had thought she would never see Dominic again. His face was twisted with anger and pain. She couldn't tell if it was because of her. Her hand reached up and grasped Dominic's face gently.

"D-Dominic…" Her voice was overwhelmed by emotions. His arms wrapped around her and squeezed tight.

In a gasp of pain, she tried to move away from him.

He moved backward a bit.

"Calida, what hurts? Please tell me!" His hands gently patted her body as he searched.

She grasped her arm once more. The pain now settling into a deep ache.

Calida glanced at the device they had strapped her to that popped her shoulder.

Dominic firmed his jaw and his gaze darkened.

A part of her wanted him not to know, but he was smart enough to come to his own conclusion. She peeked over his shoulder and tensed as the guards' eyes, while desperately trying to appear absent of mind, couldn't help gazing her way. After experiencing such lustful activity from her captor, it sickened her. A wave of nausea hit her like a ton of bricks.

A growl erupted from Dominic.

"Turn your eyes away before I send a message to the queen about why the men stationed by my side are suddenly blind. Do not stare at my wife."

Calida squirmed in discomfort. If it wasn't for the pain in her arm, then she would have thought more about his reference to her being his wife. And how thrilling his commanding tone was. *She was a disgusting mess, if she thought that tone was arousing after how she had been treated.*

It made her happy, but at the moment she was prioritizing not passing out again.

She felt the blanket drape over her body, the warmth from it seeping deep into her.

"They hurt my arm," Calida murmured to Dominic.

Dominic's face tightened in anger. Without looking away from her, he barked an order to Braxton. "Kick her kidnapper in the balls. Feel free to let your foot... hesitate on impact, too."

With a savage grin, Jetta held Stalson's head back as Braxton marched up and swung a forceful kick to his groin. Stalson grunted and groaned as he endured the blow. It was obvious he wanted to curl into a ball on the ground, but Jetta and the other guards held him in.

Dominic put his arms around Calida's back and legs and carried her out without looking back. All they could hear was the sound of Stalson being beaten by Braxton and Jetta, followed by the high-pitched squealing of Sullivan as the other guards kicked his genitalia over and over.

Dominic returned to the mansion in Baekkioron. It wasn't somewhere she wanted to go back to, but they had healers who could help.

She sat in the healer's ward, clean and covered with a thin dress. But the feeling of being dirty was still there no matter how much she scrubbed. The window across the room was open and the sun had risen. A warm breeze wafted in, and the atmosphere spoke of calmness and tranquillity. The room was peaceful, but her mind was chaos.

The one thing she couldn't stop thinking about was the name the mercenary had dropped.

Soldiers of the Cobra.

Dominic had not calmed down since he had rescued her. He paced quickly and anxiously behind her. It was like Dominic now and Dominic before she was kidnapped were night and day.

She should have expected something to change, but this was not at all what she hoped.

Dominic muttered to himself until the door opened and the healer walked in.

A woman with wrinkles and a limp approached. She wore clothing that resembled elvish wear except no elf grew old.

"Milady, I apologize for the wait," she said.

The healer walked over to a table beside the bed that had herbs and tools laid out. Her hand hovered over them and then she looked up at Dominic.

"What is it you see me for today?"

Dominic strode to the bed and addressed her in a formal tone.

"Healer Buffy Smithson, we have come to you so you may attend to Countess Goldwyn's arm. It was injured and will need readjusting."

Buffy Smithson bowed and walked over to Calida.

She cradled the arm Calida had been holding until it was straight out. A groan escaped her mouth as the healer fiddled with it.

With a jolt, the healer pushed the arm back into its socket. Calida shouted and collapsed on the bed. Her vision went white and a high pitching ringing replaced all sound.

Eventually, she came to with the sound of her panting.

Dominic slid gently onto the bed, trying his best to not move her too much. He kissed her forehead.

"You're going to be alright now, Calida. I'm not leaving your side again." Regret and relief were clear in his quiet voice.

Calida got up from the bed and the healer stopped her before she left.

"Milady, we must wrap up your shoulder with a cloth. It is best to let it rest for some time."

Calida nodded her head and waited a moment. No one moved.

"Milady, you need to take off your dress."

Oh...

Calida glanced at Dominic and hesitated. Her good hand

attempted to push the sleeve off her shoulder, but she hissed in pain. Dominic walked around the bed and held out a hand to her.

"Allow me to assist you." He gently grasped her hurt arm and brought it up to the other shoulder to rest.

Calida held her breath as he fingered the neckline of her dress. Her heart sped up as his fingers brushed her skin. The warmth imprinted in her head. Slowly, he pulled down the sleeve of her dress and then stepped back to let the healer wrap her up.

Calida sat in the carriage with Dominic as they travelled to the palace in Eleari. He hadn't done his noble duties in a while, and he was due to appear for those responsibilities. The taxes and fines needed to be collected.

Jetta sat across from Calida as they moved, and Dominic had refused to leave her side. She could feel his anxiety and stress because of the kidnapping. She felt the same, but being back with Dominic calmed her. The security that came with being attached to him was euphoric.

Calida looked out the window and watched as a snowflake fell and landed on her cheek. The chill in the air nipped at her nose.

"When we arrive, it is imperative for us to move all at once," Jetta said.

Braxton nodded. "Your safety is most important."

Dominic put an arm around Calida and pulled her closer. He buried his face into her neck, taking deep breaths in her hair.

"I don't want to let you go again." His voice was muffled.

Her heart swelled with the feeling of Dominic close. When

he was this close, she could remember exactly why she loved him. His gentle touch and considerate nature drew her in. It healed her soul like a salve.

Calida grabbed onto his jacket. He had never been so close before, but she would not complain. It was something she had desired more than anything.

Maybe now I can tell him.

That thought pulled her out of her dreamy, comatose state next to Dominic. She could picture herself telling him and the positivity radiating off him, the smile on his face shining with such brilliance Calida could faint from the heat.

A smile touched her lips as she thought about it but disappeared just as fast.

He had just as much likelihood of rejecting her or misunderstanding her. Calida could picture him removing his arm and drawing away from her, causing tension and discomfort in the carriage. Tears to sprang up in her eyes.

No, she knew Dominic better than that. He had shown signs he felt the same all that time. Calida took in a deep breath and willed herself to form a layer of courage on her skin. She looked into Dominic's eyes. Closing hers for a moment, she summoned up the courage, and then blurted it out.

"Can we talk sometime about us?" she muttered quietly for the two of them.

Dominic squinted at her in thought. "Yes, my dear one. Of course."

She felt relief that they would talk, but his stare on her was never-ending and penetrating. Calida wiggled in her seat, uncomfortable with the undivided attention.

"Later."

Hours later, they arrived at the queen's palace.

The carriage halted at the steps to the palace door. As she arose from her slumber, the surroundings slowly became clearer. The grogginess slipped from her mind and suddenly she realized her head was leaning on Dominic.

Slowly, a sigh escaped her as she rested on Dominic, pretending to sleep as he gently cradled her head. His lips kissed her cheek as he leaned in close.

"Time to rise, my dear one," he crooned. "We must walk inside, but then we can head straight to bed."

His hand stroked her hair soothingly. Calida groaned quietly in protest.

He chuckled softly. "I could carry you in if you wish."

The fog of sleep was claiming her once more. Any hesitation or desire to walk into the palace on her own was almost as daunting as lifting her head. She mumbled in agreement.

There was a moment of silence. Calida sighed in contentment. Then Dominic shuffled her around until she lay on the carriage bench and he picked her up.

The fog of sleep was still affecting her. Calida sleepily grinned up at Dominic. As they stepped out of the carriage, he looked down at her with his dishevelled hair and unkempt beard. He smiled softly.

The contrast of dark and light defined his face until he looked like a carefully carved sculpture with the most beautiful lips and eyebrows. It shadowed his eyes until they shone like the moon up in the sky.

Calida stared at him as she drifted further into sleep, her eyes closing, but somehow acutely aware of everything around her. She distantly heard the shuffling of feet and the crunching of gravel as Dominic walked up the stairs to the main foyer of the palace. Jetta and Braxton had exited the carriage behind them in a groggy state but were slowly gaining their feet as they walked.

The chink of armour as the guards moved to salute resounded beside them as the door opened and the group walked through.

Calida moved her head closer and clutched the front of Dominic's shirt. On the ride over, he had removed his jacket, leaving him with his tunic.

Off to the side, Calida vaguely heard someone approach.

"Milord, normally it would be customary to greet the queen upon arrival, but she has announced that you and your betrothed can hold off your greetings until the morning."

Calida cuddled closer. There was a pause and then Dominic walked again.

Her mind was surprisingly empty after having been tortured.

Tortured....

It was in that moment her mind snapped into clarity. She had been so drowsy and comfortable, but the reminder of what she had just come back from set her mind on edge. Calida struggled to get out of Dominic's arms.

They were in the hall near the guest rooms for distinguished members of the court. The carpet and walls were extravagant and glittered with polish.

She pushed to get up. "Please let me stand!" Calida pleaded.

Dominic held her closer.

"No!"

His voice echoed down the hall, freezing everyone who stood near them. Her shoulders jumped. He was never so uncontrollable before. It was so unexpected, it startled her.

Dominic's shoulders shook as he held her closer to him, head buried in her hair. It took a while for him to calm down as they stood there, but it was then she realized he was crying.

Wet droplets dampened her hair and cheeks as tears of sorrow escaped him.

"I was so close to losing you." His voice broke in a hushed tone.

Calida's throat tightened, and tears escaped her eyes as

well. They had grown closer than she had ever expected. Sorrow blossomed in her chest as she remembered her time with Lord Sullivan and Stalson. All of the pain and devastation she had experienced.

A hiccup escaped from her as she could barely hold back the feeling to scream and wail.

Dominic walked a few feet farther, and then Braxton and Jetta held open the door into the bedroom. The two stood stoically outside, guarding their charges.

Dominic and Calida collapsed in a heap on the other side of the door. Her hands wrung his tunic as her wails broke free.

Tears stained him while the realization of the events leading up to this moment washed over her. Calida's shoulders shook as she fought to catch her breath. The wails of pain and sorrow emptied from her mouth with no signs of slowing. Dominic patted her head and held her close, his tears falling silently.

Their friends were dutifully guarding them on the other side of the door, but she barely cared if they heard her. The memories of being held captive, not knowing if she would ever see Dominic again, harpooned her in place. The image of her arms and legs being bound stilled her breath and her wails. She couldn't make herself move a muscle. The mere memory had her frozen.

It had only been hours ago that they strapped her up so Lord Sullivan and Stalson could do their worst Their names were like a poison in her mind and sat on the flat of her tongue, threatening to choke her.

Calida shook in Dominic's arms as he tried to squeeze the

fear out of her. It didn't hurt, but she knew they could never remove the trauma now.

After sitting there just holding each other for a long time, they moved to the bed. The kidnapping and torture had taken its toll on Calida. She needed rest more than anything else. Being careful of her arm, she lay on her side and rested on Dominic's arm as he held her.

"You'll be alright now, Calida. I promise to never leave your side again."

He left her side before, and they kidnapped her.

She shook her head mentally. He was not at fault for her kidnapping, but expecting him to see it was foolhardy.

They spent hours in silence, just holding each other and reminding themselves Calida was safe once more.

Dominic and Calida couldn't find it in themselves to fill the silence with chatter. The memories of the event couldn't be described, and it was something she couldn't bring herself to share with him. He cared about her, and the hurt and pain she went through would cause him the same pain.

No matter what, she couldn't do that to the man she loved.

The man she loved.

Yes, she loved him. Calida could remember Dominic when they first met. He had been so chaotic and full of life. She had been expecting a lunatic, but he was nothing like she thought. Dominic was among the smartest people she knew. The presence he exhibited in a room was astounding. Without a single word, he could command the attention of everyone just by moving in a certain manner.

Over the last while of getting to know him, Calida realized

she admired that about him. Before, it had irritated her that he could gain someone's attention so easily. Growing up with her mother, it accustomed her to feeling invisible and alone. So, seeing him gain attention by only lifting a finger had her wanting to bite an ear off.

His looks had attracted her from the start, but Calida pushed herself to ignore them. Now that she was being free with her thoughts, all she could think about was how he would look in alluring shirts or shirtless. Better yet, in a bed. He wore a nobleman's outfit well, arms fit snug, and Dominic's shoulders were broad enough to carry the burdens of the world.

Calida had always envisioned herself marrying someone with darker hair, but when she saw Dominic, any ideas of a dark-haired man flew through the window. Something as trivial as hair colour could not override attractive personality traits. He could look her straight in the eyes and cause her to melt into a puddle on the ground.

She could remember holding hands gently on their date together. The flowers in the meadow as they felt the surrounding breeze. The tranquillity even as she met his wolf companion.

There were some secrets he still hadn't told her, but she expected to hear more about them at some point. Their betrothal had been fast-tracked and sharing information hadn't been a top priority.

Calida looked up at Dominic, also lost in thought.

She gathered her courage. This was the moment to tell him. Any other moment would be filled with distraction, but right now they were alone.

"Dominic...." He didn't respond, too wrapped up in his thoughts.

Calida put her hand on his chest and shook him gently.

"Dominic," she said.

He looked at her in confusion. She breathed in slowly.

"There is something I need to tell you."

He stilled and waited for her to continue. Without breaking eye contact, she summoned her courage and inhaled sharply. Regardless of whether he rejected her, at least she said something.

"I love you, Dominic." She held her breath as she waited. And waited.

He stared at her in silence, his face and body still. No reaction at all.

Calida withered inside. As she stared further into his eyes, hoping for even a small sign he cared, she saw them grow wet. But then he closed his eyes and turned away. Still holding her, Dominic acted as if she had said nothing.

The moment she had been summoning up the courage for was now another experience she would rather forget. In the frustration and sadness, Calida lay in his arms as she fell asleep.

Her last thought was of the sting of his rejection.

Thirty-Two

Her eyes snapped open in sudden awareness.

Calida had fallen asleep with Dominic, but now she couldn't see him.

So much for not letting her out of his sight.

In a huff, she jumped off the bed and stormed for the door. If he thought he could evade her, Dominic had a rude awakening coming. She knew now he cared about her. The reasoning had not quite caught up with her, but her instincts told her he did. And the "new" Calida was not going to let that slide.

She ripped open the door, and Jetta and Braxton were standing guard as if they had never left their post last night. Normally she would feel guilty for not letting them sleep even a little, but any empathy had flown out the window with Dominic's rejection.

"Where is he?" Calida hissed through gritted teeth, her hair sparking as her temper rose.

Jetta glanced at her, then stared in wild fascination when she recognized the temper in her friend. Her mouth opened to warn Braxton against saying something rude, but Braxton's response was a grunt.

He was obviously in a foul mood. Calida was in an even fouler mood. The man she loved had said nothing to her confession and normally she would say something was wrong with her. After this experience, the self-pity would kick in to make her feel pathetic and whiny. However, she was on a roll, and she wasn't about to stop.

If she wanted him, Calida was going to capture him.

She stepped forward and got up in Braxton's face.

"Excuse me? Was that your response to my question?" Calida growled. Enunciating the words as verbal punches caught Braxton's attention. He lifted an eyebrow at her but responded clearly this time.

"He is in the dining hall, milady. May I ask why you want to know?"

Her hair burst into flame at the reminder of Dominic's failure to respond and then waking up without him there. She wouldn't let him go that easily.

Braxton looked up at her hair, seemingly unstartled by it any longer, but merely curious.

She forced a graveyard smile..

"Dominic left before we finished talking. Isn't that just quite rude, soldier?" Her grin completely gave away the boiling anger she was feeling.

Braxton went a shade of pale and looked over at Jetta for help.

Jetta glanced at him with a look saying, *You're on your own.*

He gulped. "Yes, Countess Goldwyn. It is rude."

Dropping the smile, Calida turned around and marched toward where she assumed the dining hall was.

"Milady, the dining hall is in the other direction." Jetta held her breath and then let it out when Calida grunted and marched in the right direction of the dining hall.

C alida stood outside the dining hall. Her walk had burned off her anger, mostly. She wasn't necessarily angry with Dominic. Okay, that was a lie. She was definitely angry with him, but because of his non-response. Never had she seen him shy away from the unknown. Before they kidnapped her, it was different. Dominic was sure of himself. He addressed their relationship with steady feet and guided her with loving hands.

Now, he had almost closed off. Dominic's presence wasn't the same. If their relationship was to work, they needed to be on the same page.

She took a deep breath and a moment to collect her thoughts. Then she entered the dining hall.

Guards pushed open the doors as she walked forward. Her angry thoughts stalled in the presence of the vision in front of her.

Dominic sat among other nobles and the queen.

There in her regal crown and seated at the head of the table was the woman she met at the palace ball. The queen had comforted her when she was feeling insecure, and it was something she hadn't experienced before.

The queen was as beautiful as before. Her long raven hair was pinned up elegantly and brilliantly clashed with but complimented her ivory complexion. She was the perfect example of radiance. It was one of many reasons she admired the queen.

Dominic stopped mid-sentence to watch her entrance as everyone else stared.

Insecurity prickled on her neck, and Calida blushed in embarrassment. She was now regretting her insistence on confronting Dominic.

The other nobles who sat at the table were all very important. Seated on either side of the queen were the dukes. The one she knew by name was Lord Charles Goldwyn, Dominic's father. However, the seat beside the other duke was empty and she could only think it was because of Lord Sullivan's actions.

There were several nobles there she didn't know, but assumed they were there for Dominic's duties as the Earl of Eleari.

Looking down, Calida realized they were staring at her clothing. She had only a moment to adjust her dress since her carriage ride back from the mansion. Luckily, Calida had changed at the healers, but the clothing she wore wasn't any better. The dress had a low neckline and squeezed her stomach in tight. The skirt was also just below her knees at mid leg, and the corset underneath was visible through the thin fabric. It was the definition of scantily dressed.

With a fiery blush on her cheeks, Calida walked to the end of the table as the doors behind her shut with a definitive thump. It was obvious she was interrupting, but now that she was in the room, she didn't know how to interact without making a fool of herself.

"Ah, what perfect timing, dove! You have arrived at the right moment for my announcement," the queen chirped. Her smile beamed at Calida. Her comment had the nobles looking the queen's way now, allowing Calida to breathe, but she still didn't know what to do. Did she sit beside Dominic or was that presumptuous?

The queen extended a hand to her and spoke once more.

"Dove, please come sit beside me here." She gestured to the daughter's seat beside her. Calida's eyes widened. It was a specially reserved seat for queen apprentices or her own biological daughter. But if the queen summoned you, it was rude to hesitate.

Slowly, Calida walked toward the queen. Dominic had a look of concern and curiosity on his face. She paced past him and stood nervously in front of the daughter's seat. She glanced at the queen, who nodded with a smile, and then Calida sat.

She didn't know what the queen had in mind, but she hoped it couldn't be anymore humiliating than she already felt.

"Before we continue, gentlemen, I would like to announce a decision."

Everyone turned their attention to her.

"Between now and the end of the Ordellius festival, I will introduce an apprentice."

Calida gasped, but quickly covered her mouth to quiet herself. The queen hadn't selected an apprentice since before she was born. The story behind that last apprentice was quite the tale as well. The murmuring of the nobles at the table filled the silence.

After Calida and the others breakfast finished eating breakfast, everyone stood from the table and paid respects to the queen as she passed. She also went to bow when the queen ushered her to her side.

"No need for such formality, Calida." The queen waved her off dismissively.

Calida stared at the queen. "Your Majesty, you know my name?"

The queen hid her giggle with her hand and continued, leaving Calida in her wake, desperately attempting to keep up.

The nobles gathered around the table in the palace war room, with Dominic standing at the head of the table, a box positioned in front of him. For once, the queen sat off to the side instead of being in the decisive position, which was disconcerting.

"Gentlemen, today we will discuss the taxes collected in Eleari and delinquent fines. Remember, we will also go over issues that need to be dealt with accordingly. If there are no questions, I will get started with my report." Dominic looked at his father, the duke. "To start off, I send my gratitude to Lord Charles Goldwyn for his attendance at the side of the queen today." He bowed swiftly before continuing.

As the Earl, he was the delegated over the region of Weommadran in Eleari. Because it was located close to the palace, that's where they discussed the proceedings. Calida figured it was common for the queen to sit in the meeting too with how relaxed everyone seemed by her presence.

Calida sat beside the queen quietly as she watched Dominic transform from the man she knew into an earl who knew exactly what to do and where everyone should be. His arms pointed and guided the men in what they had to adjust as she watched from beside the queen.

Calida sat silently, not thinking to fill it with conversation. She would rarely fill a room with chatter. In the past, it would've led to saying or doing the wrong thing, thus getting into trouble with her mother.

As she stared blindly at Dominic, she realized it had been some time since she had thought about her mother or her past. Maybe his effect on her was stronger than she had given it credit for.

"I can see Dominic fascinates you," the queen said.

Calida whipped her head around to peer at her.

If it had been weeks ago, she would have quickly denied it, insisting that she couldn't possibly be in love with him or he with her. That they weren't a good match. With the new revelation, Calida's face softened as she fondly stared.

"Yes, I love him."

All the while, she observed Dominic. Admiring how he got right down to business and the diplomacy he showed with his fellow noblemen. Soon enough, she closed her eyes to rest as the meeting was taking a long time. His voice turned into a soothing lullaby, one sending her into a blissful state between sleep and conscious.

The queen chuckled, startling her awake. Her head jolted off the queen's shoulder.

"Yes, I can see a promising future for you two."

Calida shook the sleep out of her mind to focus on her conversation with the queen.

"My apologies, Your Majesty, for falling asleep momentarily on your shoulder."

The queen's arm reached over and grasped Calida's hand.

"Nonsense, dove. You're finally feeling safe. Tis a good thing. Sleep some more if you can."

Calida's eyes drifted shut once more, as if a sack of flour sat on each of them. Her breath evened out as the darkness comforted her into slumber.

How will I survive with the skills of a commoner, though?

Her breath hitched. All the sleep fell away, and a sense of awareness flooded her body.

Calida had tried to accomplish the same as a born noblewoman, but she didn't have someone to show her the way. Her tutor was the type to give her a list of books and a swat on the hand for discipline and nothing more. It wasn't like elder noblewomen jumped at the chance to teach her, either. In fact, it seemed to be the other way around. Almost like the women were trying their hardest to keep her on the outside, as if she would just disappear if they ignore her.

"I fear how much blowback Dominic will receive, though." Calida looked down at her hands. "I still have the skill sets of a commoner. I don't know the difference between curtseying to a queen and curtseying to a nobleman. Nor the proper way to address a snobby noblewoman."

Calida didn't know many things about how to be a noblewoman, but she wanted to learn. If it meant staying at Dominic's side, then she would do it.

"Soon enough, such things will be of little concern to you." The queen glanced at her with a secret smile. Calida squinted with a curious, reluctant smile.

S oon enough Dominic finished the meeting and everyone arose as the queen exited with a wave of goodbye.

As the men slowly filtered through the door, Calida took a deep breath.

She took a moment to gather her thoughts. There would only be one moment. Now. She and Dominic were alone. It could be a long time before they were without distraction.

Just jump right in, Calida.

She shook her head to clear it before slowly making her way over.

"Dominic?"

He hummed in question, not fully paying attention to her.

"We need to talk about my confession at some point."

"Not right now." He stared at the parchment in front of him. His voice was firm. Clearly, this was not a subject he wanted to broach.

See, he doesn't want to talk. You won't get anywhere.

Taking a deep breath, she shook off the anxiety. He wouldn't deter Calida now. Her love was not fragile. Relaxing her shoulders and summoning more courage, she turned to Dominic.

Leaning forward, Calida laid a hand on Dominic's.

"Please, Dominic. Just listen to what I have to say." Her

voice was steady. Mentally, she clapped herself on the back for the level tone.

Dominic looked up at her briefly. Then returned to the papers in front of him, neither reading nor focusing up on her.

Inhaling, Calida readied herself because whether or not he looked, she was going to say her piece.

"There are several moments that I keep precious to me. Moments with you. The meadow, walking in the gardens, the dance at the palace ball with you, your compliments even when I failed. You comforting me when my father died and getting angry on my behalf."

Taking a moment, Calida gently caressed his cheek. Guiding him to look at her.

"I love you, Dominic."

His eyes were still firm. Unmoveable from what he believed. But there was a spark. His eyebrows unfurled slowly, his face showing some clarity coming to his mind. It still wasn't enough. Calida needed to tell him more.

She needed to tell him about the incident.

Closing her eyes, she allowed herself the moment to be vulnerable. Readying herself for accepting rejection. Inhaling, she opened her eyes when she was ready to face her past head on.

"There is one thing I didn't tell you about."

Dominic's gaze changed into confusion. It was at least something.

"I was a small child when this happened…"

Dominic turned around, his face calm.

Calida's eyes blurred as a throb stung through her head.

Suddenly, she's on the stoop of her house.

A gasp escaped her as the image in front of her almost caused her to stumble back in shock.

While she was used to animal blood, it was scary to see so much blood from a person. The idea of it all being her mother's left her feeling sick.

The once warm, welcoming home with delicious smells and comforting hugs was now dark and scary. Cold sweat filled the air. Melted candles adhered to the walls, curtains ripped open, and bedding stained crimson.

Fear tingled up her spine as she looked around. It didn't feel like they had been gone that long, but as she hesitated to walk further in, the light from the setting sun peeked through a window on the other side of the house.

"Calida, I told you to stay back!" She jumped as her father's voice boomed through the house. Her gaze filled with fear stared at Rayner, who blocked the entryway to his bedroom.

Papa had never talked to her like that before.

She searched his eyes, hoping he would explain. But his mouth set into a grim line. Tears prickled his eyes.

"Where is M-Mama?"

His jaw clenched and he looked away from his daughter before he strode into his room.

Calida searched the vacant living room. She trembled as she stared at the slashes in blankets strewn on the ground like giant claws. Almost like those monsters from the stories told to the children in town. That clan of villains who weren't afraid of hurting mothers and babies. Chairs were upturned and the fireplace, which was once spotless, was now covered in ash.

Calida followed close behind her father until he blocked her with an arm. He stiffened at the sight in front of him, then shuffled forward. With his arm removed, she could clearly see the figure on the bed. Calida watched for a moment before stepping inside. Each step settled a stone of doom in her stomach. The bloodied, torn up blanket covering her mother hung off her frame. A hand peeked out and limply dangled off the edge of the bed.

The seven-year-old couldn't tell if her mother was dead until the faint sign of breath escaped.

Rayner's frame shook as he collapsed to the floor.

She drifted further into the room as her father reached out to peel the blanket off Cressida. Her hand shot up as a whimper almost escaped Calida. The flesh of her mother's thigh peeked out from the slashed skirt that barely covered her body as it curled up to her. Calida's head swirled as she became over-whelmed with possible reasons. Maybe the beasts from the tales had come for her. The ones so vile they would try to take away the queen.

Cressida's blonde locks were tangled and matted, some braids still left in, hanging in her mother's face and covering her eyes.

Her mother's ragged breathing filled the room as she lay there with her favourite dress torn. Blood drenched the fabric and hung from her frame. Her knees were drawn up close. Not a word from her. Tears wetted her stained face and purple marks littered her arms and legs.

Calida held her breath as her father reached forward.

Rayner laid a hand on Cressida's arm, causing her to flinch suddenly.

Thrown off balance, Calida jumped back and stumbled over strewn objects, landing on the ground with a loud crash. Cressida started from the bed.

Her mouth opened but nothing came out.

The memory of her mother before was destroyed by the woman in front of her. Cressida Rhodes was no longer the warm, kind woman Calida had always recognized. The skin that had once been warm, soft, and glowed like apple blossoms was grey and coarse, blotched with red stains resembling a rash. The matted hair, which looked like a rat's nest, replaced the hair Calida had once wished to have. Her mother's once white apron that had always been on her was attached to her wrist instead of around her waist, was now stained a dirty gray and pink.

As Calida stared into the eyes of her mother, a chill spread down her spine. Cressida swayed on the bed as she gazed blankly. The utter abandonment of life in her eyes scared Calida. She looked like a deer after it had gone to see Eesa.

The woman in front of her was a cold stranger. Numbness pinched at Calida's fingers while her chest ached in pain.

Her father cradled her mother as he wept for her.

On the inside, a piece of Calida fell through, and heat simmered from the depths of her being. An unknown power flooded her nerves.

Calida stood frozen as Rayner's body shuddered. "M-my Cressida... I was back so late. How could you ever forgive me?"

Her mother's lips parted, but the sound that greeted Calida's ears was not human. The breath that escaped Cressida in an eerie gasp resembled the air hissing from a snake.

Her mother rocked on the bed, lost to the world without noticing the ones around her.

A chair clattered in the living room. Followed by the hurried escape of someone out the door. She jumped again, her nerves on edge. Fear prickled at her with the thought of someone else being in their home at that moment.

Why would someone be here right now?

Rayner's gaze jumped to Calida, then he raced through the door after the intruder.

"Stop where you stand, you sadistic bastard!" Her father's voice echoed through the house and out the door. Shivering and unsure what to do, she looked up at her mother.

As their eyes met, Cressida's gaze changed to a glare.

"This is all on you. You are to blame." A harsh whisper escaped her throat.

Then with a grimace, she turned away from her daughter, effectively shutting Calida out.

Tears overflowed from her eyes as Calida took off for the door in hopes of escaping to the one place she longed for, her own room. Acute rejection and pain licked at her with a hot, burning sting. Her mother's stony glare was all she could think about.

As she passed the doorway, she froze at the noise of grunts and hisses between her father and the intruder.

The words of the man pinned down stabbed through her dizzying dream.

"May you be prosperous in death! Her days are numbered. He will claim her as his own soon. The bitch will come to heel at her master's feet!" A cackle wheezed from him.

Then his mouth was no longer moving and his arms were limp. A gouge through the middle of his forehead filled Calida's vision. The blood was all she could see. So much blood. A stain poured from his head in a puddle that gradually grew bigger.

Calida rushed across the destroyed living area for her room, the one place she prayed that went untouched.

Shakily, she slammed her door shut and huddled in the furthest corner from the door. Her eyes locked on it like it would burst open and the man would be alive. She had never seen her father kill a man. The sight of the blood and the smell overwhelmed her.

Her papa had killed someone.

Her eyes never moved from the door as her mind whirled. Maybe she was confused. It was all so confusing, but she knew her room. Her cozy room that was a beacon in her hardest moments.

A place that held her charcoal drawings.

Drawings of flowers and plants and... Mother.

"I spent the time with him, but I also kept him from being with my mother. I had selfishly hogged him," Calida said.

Dominic gripped her shoulder firmly and looked her in the face. "You know that's not true."

Calida shook her head as she held his hands. "It was what I

believed for so long. During that time, unbeknownst to my father and I, my mother was being assaulted by the town drunkards."

She clenched her teeth at the memory.

"We headed home and my father noticed blood on the ground just outside our house. He insisted I stay outside, but I couldn't stop my childish curiosity."

Dominic gripped her hands, encouraging her but also letting her know she didn't need to keep going.

"I followed him in and found my mother on their bed. Her clothing was ripped nearly to shreds, and they sprayed her blood all over her."

Calida shivered at the memory.

"My point is, I have believed I was the one in the wrong and I was responsible. It was part of the reason for my acceptance of our engagement the first time. Now, I know I'm not to blame. You have proved to me I am deserving of love." Tears welled in her eyes as her voice cracked. "I love you. Truly."

Calida exhaled deeply. It was up to Dominic now. She shared it all with him and put her heart on the line.

A moment passed. When she was preparing to close the conversations and lick her wounds, Dominic pulled her down onto his lap as he sat on the seat at the head of the table.

His arms wrapped around her, comforting her once more. Their eyes locked as his expression changed to a loving stare, and then playful. His lip quirked as they each refused to blink first.

"So you love me, my dear one." His eyes returned to the bright blue she was familiar with as his hands skirted up her arms.

Dominic's eyes pinned her in place, silently promising things that could only happen on their wedding night. A hot, fiery blush scorched her cheeks as she fantasized about those activities .

"Y-yes. I do."

Calida nibbled on her bottom lip as she squirmed in his lap. It was becoming harder and harder to keep eye contact with him. He grinned at her discomfort, and suddenly, she found herself with an uncomfortably tense belly and the need to relieve herself.

His eyes zeroed on her lips as she nibbled.

"It would seem like you are having an issue there, Calida." His voice slurred her name slowly. Each syllable of her name from his lips created a warmth from within she didn't know how to quench.

She looked away and coughed.

His hand reached out and tipped her head up to look him in the eye once more.

"I want to kiss you."

Calida's breath quickened. She wanted him to kiss her. More than anything. The intensity of the moment had her chest fluttering like a bird. The pressure in her belly intensified until it seemed like she needed to do something, anything, to fix what was missing. It was a delicious combination of pleasure and ache. Then his lips pressed against hers. Everything froze around her. Her breath, the room, even the air, was still.

Then Braxton slammed open the door.

Calida startled. She moved to get off Dominic's lap quickly, but his immovable arm around her sent her flying back onto him, her back splayed against his chest. Dominic showed no signs of being embarrassed at his friend catching them in an intimate position.

"We have confined the kidnappers to the palace dungeon. They are waiting for you," Braxton said. He strode into the room, glancing between them. A swift smirk lit up his face before it faded just as quickly into a look of indifference. With a quick heel turn, Braxton exited the room and awaited them outside the room.

Dominic turned her in his lap.

"Calida Rhodes, are you willing to accept the position of my wife, of Countess Goldwyn?" Her breath caught. Did he mean it? She was willing to accept it, but what if she hadn't convinced him?

No. He wouldn't have hidden that. Dominic was more straightforward than that.

An enormous smile lit up her face as tears stung the corner of her eyes.

"I accept the position, Lord Goldwyn." If only she had the composure to attack his face with kisses as a brilliant smile broke out . Then he leaned forward and kissed her once more, leaving her floating in a delirious fog of heat and happiness.

The two arose from the seat in the war room and walked out together, hand in hand.

Map2

Calida stood beside Dominic as they travelled down a damp, dark passage in the palace's basement. Braxton, Dominic, and Calida met up with Jetta. They stopped outside the cell holding her kidnappers. Sullivan and Stalson were strapped to their seats.

Sullivan was sweating so much that his stained shirt was almost transparent. His bulging belly jiggled as he pulled desperately to get out. Hearing footsteps, the prisoners looked up, and Sullivan growled at Calida.

"Come back for more, wench? Why not come closer so you can warm me up!"

Calida stepped back, a chill running down her spine as she remembered his slimy hands on her.

Jetta pushed past Calida and walloped Sullivan across the head, leaving his head swinging in a dizzying motion. She stood up straight and intimidating, then she leaned forward and hissed something unintelligible. His face grew pale and his mouth was no longer running itself into the grave.

Whatever she had said to him had shut him up.

Jetta grabbed his hair and held his head in a firm grip so he could do nothing but look up as Braxton entered the room holding a tool she had never seen before. It had two handles, and they both narrowed down and met together. She could only imagine how painful it would be.

Braxton stood tall as he stopped in front of their captives. The hand holding the tool opened and closed it, acting like a small clamp.

Sullivan peered up and straightened at the instrument. Stalson didn't react.

"Under Her Majesty the Queen's word, she ordered us to uncover information about what happened after leaving the Baekkioron Ball with Calida," Braxton said.

Stalson's and Sullivan's faces were a significant contrast in reaction. One was in a pure state of fear and the other had the face of indifference.

Braxton walked to Sullivan first and spoke directly to him in a menacing tone. "Normally, you would be referred to by your title, but I have an official scroll from the queen."

From his words, Calida could feel the sharp, predatory grin on his face.

He reached into the recesses of his tunic and pulled out a scroll with an official sleeve and seal. Peeling it back, Braxton recited word for word.

"On the Authority of Queen Bedelia, we have stripped you of your title and land. We will leave you for the dogs and birds to eat. No mercy will be shown to the creature who would dare not only harm a child but kidnap a nobleman's wife. You have been condemned to death by Her Majesty. May you wish for your death swiftly. Signed, *Queen Bedelia Ida Milena Eleonora Severina*, Ruler of Eonifond."

Calida had watched Sullivan's face as Braxton read the letter. By the end, he looked as if the consequences of his actions had finally come home to roost. He was pale and panting shallowly.

Jetta pulled his hair until his head was looking up at her.

"You hear that, you sniveling little toad? We get to give you what you deserve!"

Her eyes glowed in contrast with the dim lighting in the dungeon. The colour of metal shone in her eyes, a molten orb of mercury. It was something Calida had never seen before. Jetta's eyes had always been a dark brown.

Braxton and Jetta circled Sullivan. They had moved Stalson to the side and were focusing all their attention on the former duke.

Jetta pulled out a small hammer from her pocket.

"Feeling cold?" She inspected the hammer in her hand as she slowly circled him.

"Ye-yes..." Sullivan's eyes never left Braxton and Jetta. Sweat beaded his forehead as he tried to contain his fear. He had already pissed himself, leaving a sour smell.

Jetta's grin sharpened as she realized just how nervous he was. She slammed the hammer down on Sullivan's thigh. A howl of pain rang from him.

"Not so cold now, huh?" Her teeth bared as she growled.

Braxton walked around the other side of him, his stance intimidating. His sharp gaze pointed at Sullivan as he tried to adjust to the injury.

"Hmm, I don't think he's warm enough."

The clamp that had been in Braxton's hand was now attached to Sullivan's earlobe. A whimper escaped Sullivan's mouth as he eyed the device.

It wasn't until Braxton started pulling and the tendons and skin of his ear separated from his body that his scream left him. Blood trickled in a steady stream from it. His earlobe swayed from the place it where was a moment ago.

"How are you feeling now? Comfortable?" Jetta crouched to meet him in the eye, a look of false concern on her face.

Tears streamed down Sullivan's face. Jetta clucked her tongue in disappointment when he didn't answer her.

"This one is so unmannerly." She stood up and walked to a table in the corner filled with tools. All of them were clean and newly inspected to make sure they were functioning.

Braxton joined Jetta.

"This one might be more difficult than we gave him credit for. Are you sure you want to continue?" he whispered.

Her hand picked up the first tool she had been looking at, flustered. "I'm not about to collapse from exhaustion or something."

Braxton grabbed her arm to pull her back, but Jetta strode forward with a pair of forceps in her hand, heading for the tied-up victim at her mercy.

Striding up behind her, Braxton took the tool from her hand. She turned around.

"You almost forgot these, immortal beloved." He handed her a curved blade.

Jetta's face scrunched but she chose not to comment. She muttered a thank you and continued back to Sullivan. Standing in front of him, she glared.

"Seeing how we still have to get to your friend over there" —she gestured to Stalson—"we should hurry this along. "

Jetta stabbed the curved blade into his midsection and dug it upward. Sullivan squirmed as a wheezing scream escaped him.

"What did you want Calida for?"

Sullivan panted, without a sign of responding. Jetta dug in the blade further. He grunted in pain.

"I wanted another slave for my harem."

Jetta's face contracted in disgust. Braxton's hands gripped

into fists to control his anger. His face was thunderous and was promising Sullivan's demise.

◊

After a bit of fruitless effort, Sullivan had no more to offer.

Calida watched from the other side of the cell as they ruthlessly interrogated Stalson after beating Sullivan to a pulp. It had upset her, and she would have found it somewhat frightening if it hadn't been for the reminder of who the torture was happening to. Sullivan had everything coming his way.

Jetta and Braxton were getting nowhere with Stalson.

The most they seemed to have gleaned from him was a noble had hired him to torture Calida for information and then kill her. Which caused Sullivan to whimper in protest. Someone feared what Calida knew and what she could reveal.

Just when they were about to get him to reveal more, a loud boom sounded down the corridor.

A swarm of guards appeared around Calida and Dominic and ushered them out of the dungeon while the others frantically searched for the cause of the distraction.

Calida glimpsed over the guards as she was rushed out.

In the middle of the mayhem, Stalson bit a bracelet that had been on his wrist. He swallowed a bead and immediately foamed at the mouth. With his dying words, he said only one phrase. "From where those capped perception stands, their perseverance salutes."

Jetta thumped the ground in frustration as he died.

Suddenly, she feels a sharp white hot pain course through her midsection. Jetta froze, clutching a blade sticking out of her abdomen. Sullivan limped away from her and escaped down the corridor. Braxton, who had been looking over the tool table, whipped around at the noise and rushed to Jetta's side.

He knelt beside her. Jetta grunted in pain and shooed him away.

"Go get him, don't worry about me."

He shook his head. "No, immortal beloved. I am not leaving your side."

"Don't call me that," Jetta growled in frustration.

Braxton held her to him and slowly helped her stand up. He examined the wound and assisted Jetta with straightening herself up.

"I shall call you what you are, Jetta. Regardless of whether you agree, you are and will always be my immortal beloved."

She rolled her eyes and pushed him away so she could walk down the corridor. Jetta clutched her side as she limped slowly to the exit.

The guard's footsteps stomped around Calida and Dominic as they rushed them to a small court in the palace.

Dominic's arm stayed around her as they moved. She had tried several times to look behind her at what had happened, but the guards were constantly standing in the direct pathway. It was frustrating and Calida had asked them to move so she could see, but they hadn't responded.

She looked over at Dominic.

"Is there no way you can find out what happened? We cannot just lose one of my kidnappers! I won't ever be able to rest well knowing they are still on the loose!" Her voice was pitched anxiously high.

Dominic stopped walking. Turning around, he hugged her close.

"My dear one, I know I have failed you once, but I vow to never let you be in harm's way again."

Calida snuggled in close, his voice and the strength behind his words comforting her.

Her mind still filled with endless possibilities, she whispered. "I don't want to leave your side like that again."

The guards nudged at Dominic to keep walking. Calida wanted to stay exactly where she was, but Dominic listened to the guards. However, instead of walking with her, Dominic swooped down and picked up Calida under her legs.

She scrambled to find her footing until her arms rested around his neck. Dominic continued walking under the guidance of the guards.

In the small courtyard, Dominic sat down with Calida in his lap. She tried squirming to move onto the bench beside him, but his arms were firm and held her close.

"Dominic, I really am worried."

He looked her in the eye, seeing her anxiety and fear. "Jetta and Braxton are the most qualified at their job, Calida. Being worried about their responsibilities is like saying you do not have faith in their abilities."

Calida shook her head. "I believe in their abilities—"

"Worrying before anything has happened will not help them succeed."

Her hair was growing warmer from the degree of her anger and frustration. She felt like her point was not getting across and Dominic was saying things that made little sense.

Her worrying wouldn't affect her friend. Right?

"Listen to me, Dominic!" Her voice grew louder.

His eyes were still boring into hers, so it was impossible for him to not see her building emotions. Tears pricked her eyes, and her mood took a swan dive into sadness.

"What if Jetta gets hurt in the process?"

With nothing to say, Dominic held her as close as possible.

Suddenly, a crash came from the hallway. A shout and a flurry of footsteps rushed their way. The guards surrounding Dominic and Calida tensed and took their position to shut off access to the noble couple.

It was not the kidnappers who straggled through the archway. Jetta leaned against the frame of the archway as she took a breath. Braxton stood right behind her, his hands outstretched and ready in case she fell.

Though Calida saw Jetta was tired, it wasn't until her friend moved her hand to wipe it on her tunic that she noticed the ever-growing stain of blood on her mid-section.

With a cry, Calida leaped up and pushed past the guards. Their stance had relaxed after noticing it was Jetta.

Jetta looked up into Calida's eyes as she delivered her a message. "Your kidnapper is dead." With a gasp for air, she continued, "But Sullivan is free. I take full responsibility, milady. It's my fault for what happened."

Calida could hardly focus on the devastating news. Her friend stood bleeding out in front of her.

Jetta gulped, and then panted heavily before speaking once more. "The kidnapper gave up a phrase. But I do not have an inkling of what it means." Taking a moment, she said, "'From where those capped perceptions stand, their perseverance salutes.'"

In a panic, Calida shouted for a guard to take Jetta to the healer at once. Jetta protested weakly, but Braxton silenced her with a caress of the forehead.

Braxton looked over at Calida. "We will find him again, milady. I vow to you, upon the queen's name, that I will find out what happened and will give Sullivan his due consequences."

Before she could say anything, Braxton hurried Jetta down the hallway to find a healer.

Calida froze for a moment, not knowing what to do or what to feel first. There was too much to cover, and everything overwhelmed her.

She clutched her head as she crouched on the ground. Calida's head was swimming, and the shore was not in sight.

Dominic's hand rested on her shoulder, startling her from the tidal wave of emotions that had taken her mind prisoner.

"My dear one, the palace healer is the best there is. You need not worry about Jetta. She will recover." He knelt behind her, gently pushing her head to rest on him.

Her heavy breathing slowed and the swarm inside her mind calmed, but the most worrying thought stood tall.

Sullivan was free, and she was still his desired prize.

"Dominic... Jetta had a message. That's why she stopped here, instead of going straight to the healer."

He murmured for her to continue. "Sullivan is free, and the kidnapper parted with a phrase on his tongue."

His arms held her closer, the frustration he felt relayed through his tension.

Calida's eyes squeezed shut and adjusted her position until it looked like Dominic had completely hidden her from sight. Resting her head, she clutched his tunic .

"From where those capped perceptions stand, their perseverance salutes."

The two crouched in silence as they contemplated what would need to be done to understand the meaning of the phrase.

Dominic leaned in close, his lips just a hair away from hers. "Calida, this past month has been chaotic, but there is no one else I would have rather spent it with than you."

Her gaze locked on his, hoping he would take the initiative. That he would kiss her.

<h1 style="text-align:center">Thirty-Four</h1>

It had been an hour since Jetta left for the healer. As quickly as she was swept off to see the healer about her wound, the same door she had gone through opened again to a woman robed in a healer's tunic and pants. She had the royal crest on her tunic.

The woman walked up to Calida and folded her hands in front of her before gazing straight ahead at the couple standing in the courtyard.

"The body has been prepared and robed for identification. Please come this way, Countess Goldwyn." The healer gestured toward the door she came from and walked that way again without confirmation Calida and Dominic were following.

They glanced at each other in bewilderment.

What body? Did someone die in the explosion?

Dominic caressed her back and guided her along the path.

Their footsteps echoed in the silence as the couple and the woman travelled through the corridors. The only light shed was from the lanterns scattered on the walls. Each step closer on the stone floor felt familiar to Calida. There was much of the palace she still had not explored, but this looked and felt like she had walked it before.

Then the woman stopped at a door. It was the entrance to the dungeon.

She had been in such a rush and surrounded by the guards, Calida had not realized this was where she exited.

"Why are we going back down here? Has Lo-Mr. Sullivan been captured again?" Calida asked.

"No. This is where the body is."

"What body are you speaking about exactly?" Dominic asked.

At first, Calida thought maybe someone died and there was something strange or pertaining to the current circumstances they should see, but then she remembered the other body in the palace. The one she hadn't seen since her argument about her betrothal to Dominic.

Her father, Sir Rayner Rhodes.

"It's my father, isn't it?" A twinge of pain spread from her chest and tears burned in the back of her eyes.

The healer gazed over her shoulder at Calida with pity in her eyes for a daughter who had to identify her dead parent.

Something I won't recover from.

Dominic caressed her back in a soothing circle while the healer turned around and opened the door. They descended into the dungeon for the second time that day.

The dark steps into the musky dampness left a foul taste in her mouth. She was with others, there was no reason to be scared of the dark abyss.

As the threesome journeyed through the dungeon, the squeaking of mice skittering about and drip-drops of water descended from the barred windows filled the silence. They turned a corner at the end of the dark corridor, and dim light shone from a door near the end of the hallway.

"Please be warned that he may not look like himself, so

take a few moments to adjust before deciding whether you are sure it's him," the woman said.

Calida nodded and walked forward with Dominic. The healer followed them until she reached the entrance. Calida stepped in with a deep breath.

There is no going back now.

She could say it was too soon. That the image of her father was too much to bear. However, she also knew this step was important to move forward.

Calida gazed into a small room with a single body in it. The healer from before was at the foot of the table. Candles shone from every corner of the room, casting an orange tint to the death garb and sheet. The vibrant warm tones sewn into the fabric clashed against the greyed sheet and her father's familiar armor. Never once had she seen his chest plate shine so brilliantly. It was like the reflection from calm water.

She walked closer until she could touch the body in front of her. The dead body of Sir Rayner Rhodes. The man who had been her hero. Who had made her laugh and smile. The same one who had taught her so much about nature and the world.

Her vision clouded with tears. She reached out blindly and clumsily touched her father's arm and then his chest. Her fingers found their way to the embroidered runes on the fabric covering him. The same ones that would protect him from the worst outcome for a dead body. Reanimation.

This is it. The last time I will see my father.

Calida sniffled and then wiped the tears from her eyes. After blinking a few times to make sure her vision was clear, she nodded to the healer who had walked to the head of the body.

"I am alright now. Let's commence the identification."

The healer took one last glance at Calida before she pulled

back the embroidered garb from his face, then took a step back.

Calida gazed down at the face of the man who had raised her. She hadn't realized just how many wrinkles and greying hairs her father had. It had been like those traits came naturally over time and were completely overlooked due to time spent with him.

In the time apart, his face resembled his features from when she had been a child. This man was different, yet still familiar. The corners of his mouth still quirked upward, and the eyes sat peacefully, but she knew behind the lids were the brightest eyes she had seen, until she had met Dominic.

His skin lacked its usual warmth and the runic spell in red on his forehead stood out, but it still looked like him. It looked like the times he had come home sick, vomiting from spoiled food he had eaten. They had been lucky he didn't die and he could be taken to a healer. Calida couldn't have thought of what she and her mother would've done without him.

The same thing I will have to do now.

With a sharp breath, Calida steadily stared at the healer who had fixed her arm in Baekkioron.

"This is him."

"I need you to confirm by saying his name." The healer stared back.

Calida's emotions bubbled up, but she cleared her throat and refused to take out her overwhelming emotions yet.

"This is Sir Rayner Rhodes. M-my father." Her throat stung as the pain streaked from her eyes.

Calida gripped the table holding him. Her knees shook until she collapsed onto the ground.

A wail escaped as she panted to control her breath. A hand still gripped the table as she forgot her surroundings. Calida's memories of her father played through her head like it was happening in front of her.

His warm hands picking her up and swinging her around as she squealed with giggling joy. Her father's hugs that gave her comfort in her darkest nights. The warmth slowly faded until she couldn't feel anything but the coldness that came with isolation.

Her mind dropped into a vision of an island surrounded by black. The visceral sting cut through until she remembered where she was.

Calida gazed up at the hand resting near her own. It was his hand, but it was different. It wasn't going to hold her ever again.

Slowly, she stood, a hand on his chest. His armor would be by his side when they buried him. *He would have to be buried.* Calida inhaled as a needle of pain shot into her heart.

With a hand on the garb, she put it over his face and said her final goodbyes.

I will find out who is responsible. For his sake.

About the Author

S.P. Stavros is one of the few bookworms in her family who consumes romance and fantasy content.

Writing has always been a part of her life. After years of researching and diving into the industry, she's releasing her debut novel. She decided to self-publish crafted in her unique voice and style.

When she isn't writing, she is glued to Viki, Crunchyroll and YouTube podcasts about true crime, or immersing herself in a good MMORPG game.

Word of warning before deciding to read S.P.'s books:
Intriguing mysteries. Lovable characters. Dynamic plots.

She is available on Tiktok, Instagram, Facebook and X (formerly Twitter).
Check out her website for behind-the-scenes facts and clips.

Acknowledgments

Alex T. – Reedsy

Thank you for the constructive criticism of Phoenix Child in 2022.

Nick O'Brien

Thank you for all the help you provided over the years.

Emily Michel

Thank you for all the hours you put into my book and the learning experience you provided along the way.

Joseph Harkreader

Thank you for designing the final step before publishing. You have been so helpful and an amazing person to talk to.